RACHEL & JONAS

BOOK 1

The
GOLDEN
BOYS

RACHEL & NIKKI
JONAS   THORNE

Kings of CYPRESS PREP

CONTENTS

Copyrights	1
Written by Rachel Jonas	3
Prologue	8
Chapter 1	9
Chapter 2	22
Chapter 3	29
Chapter 4	37
Chapter 5	47
Chapter 6	58
Chapter 7	65
Chapter 8	75
Chapter 9	86
Chapter 10	94
Chapter 11	100
Chapter 12	106
Chapter 13	117
Chapter 14	120
Chapter 15	125
Chapter 16	134
Chapter 17	144
Chapter 18	153
Chapter 19	159
Chapter 20	167
Chapter 21	175
Chapter 22	184
Chapter 23	191
Chapter 24	200
Chapter 25	207
Chapter 26	212
Chapter 27	216
Chapter 28	227
Chapter 29	235
Chapter 30	245
Chapter 31	253

Chapter 32	264
Chapter 33	275
Chapter 34	281
Chapter 35	291
Chapter 36	298
Chapter 37	311
Chapter 38	316
Chapter 39	330
A note from the Authors	336
Join the Shifter Lounge	337
Soundtrack	338

COPYRIGHTS

This is a work of fiction. All names, characters, locations, and incidents are products of the author's imagination, or have been used fictitiously. Any resemblance to actual persons living or dead, locales, or events is entirely coincidental.

No part of this e-book may be reproduced or shared by any electronic or mechanical means, including, but not limited to printing, file sharing, and email, without prior written permission from Rachel Jonas & Nikki Thorne.

Copyright © 2020 Nikki Thorne & Rachel Jonas
All rights reserved.
ISBN: 979-8692081797

Edited by Rachel Jonas.
Cover Design by Rachel Jonas. All Rights Reserved.
Interior Design and Formatting by Stephany Wallace at @S.W. Creative Publishing co. All Rights Reserved.

This e-book is licensed for personal enjoyment only. This e-book may not be re-sold or given away to other people. If you would like to share this book with another person, please purchase an additional copy for each person you share it with.

If you are reading this book and did not purchase it, or it was not purchased for your use only, then you should purchase your own copy. Thank you for respecting the author's work.

Published October 16th, 2020

WRITTEN AS RACHEL JONAS

THE LOST ROYALS SAGA
The Genesis of Evangeline
Dark Side of the Moon
Heart of the Dragon
Season of the Wolf
Fate of the Fallen

DRAGON FIRE ACADEMY
First Term
Second Term
Third Term

THE VAMPIRE'S MARK
Dark Reign
Hell Storm
Cold Heir
Crimson Mist

Written by Rachel Jonas

WRITTEN AS RACHEL JONAS & NIKKI THORNE

KINGS OF CYPRESS PREP
The Golden Boys

DESCRIPTION

West Golden—so easy to hate, yet so hard to resist.

Don't let that pretty face of his fool you. He isn't the boy next door, or the kind you trust with your heart. He's the devil in designer jeans, with all the charm of a bona fide psycho.

Trust me.

He swears I did something to cross him before I even stepped foot inside Cypress Prep, but it's a lie. No one knows better than me that I'm all out of chances. One more misstep and I can kiss my future goodbye, which means I can't possibly be guilty of whatever he thinks I've done.

West marks me with a target anyway, and as this town's football star, no one dares to go against him. His money, status, and the loyalty of his equally entitled brothers makes him seem untouchable. Only, I know better than that.

This false god isn't infallible like he wants the world to believe. Whenever I stare into those devilish green eyes, I see it plain as day. The chink in his armor. His one and only weakness. Me.

The king of Cypress Prep has finally met his match and taking him down just became an inside job.

To my Blue-Jay:

You looked so peaceful I didn't have the heart to wake you. If I'm being completely honest, writing was the only way I stood a chance of getting through this without crying. Wish we could all be tough girls like you... Since I know how much you hate when I get all worked up, I'll make this quick.

I'm taking off for a bit, sweetheart. You, Scarlett, and Hunter are my world, so I won't be gone long. Two weeks tops. You'll barely have time to miss me. Promise.

Before you even think it, this has absolutely nothing to do with you guys. Me and your dad's mess is just that.

Our mess.

Thin walls make it hard to keep secrets, so I'm sure you noticed the screaming matches have gotten worse. I think the only way to fix what's broken between him and me is to give each other space. We'll never learn to make it work if the only way we communicate is through an argument. Hopefully, some peace and quiet will help me sort through it all. Maybe he'll put the bottle down and do the same while I'm gone.

Not a day will go by that I won't be thinking about you three. Hunter's working on something that might bring some cash into the house, so he might be hard to reach for a while. That's why I'm counting on you to take care of Scar, but I'm not the least bit worried she won't be looked after. You're so good with her. Sometimes, I think you're a better mother to her than I ever was. God doesn't make big sisters like you very often, so she looks up to you for good reason.

I'm getting out of here before your father wakes up and raises hell when he realizes my bags are packed. He drank himself to sleep last night, which means he'll be a bear when he stumbles out of bed in a little while. It's probably not a bad idea for you girls to stay out of his way if you can.

To keep my head clear, I turned off my phone. Just leave a message and I'll call when I can.

There's a twenty on the kitchen table to put a few groceries in the fridge until Hunter comes back with whatever he gets his hands on. No junk food, Blue! I mean it! It'll come back to haunt you during basketball season.

Miss you kids already. Kiss Scarlett for me. Be home when the dust settles.

—Mom

Chapter 1

—June, Four Months Later—

BLUE

Crumpling her written words lifts a weight.

It's something I should've done the morning I found this very sheet of coffee-stained paper taped to my door. Instead, I'd folded it neatly and placed it inside my wallet, like a tiny shrine I carry with me wherever I go.

I've always pined over the scraps of love she leaves behind, littered throughout my life. Then, at the worst possible times, I stumble across them again. Like now, while an epic party rages all around me and I forego a perfectly good opportunity to just be young and free. Why? Because rummaging through my clutch for a stick of gum led me to this note and I'm suddenly stuck, contemplating Mom's twisted version of love. I should be chatting up some cute guy, or dancing like the world is ending tomorrow, but nope.

"Found you! Looks like my hoe-bag radar is still spot on," Jules slurs.

A smile replaces my true expression so quickly it's scary.

"You say such sweet things," I tease back, smoothing both palms down the white, linen shorts she insisted I borrow. They were part of a package deal—black tank, black heels and silver hoops included. The only visible article that actually *does* belong to me is my clutch.

More playful than usual, Jules gently tugs the blonde, fishtail braid on my shoulder. She'd styled it for me while we waited for our ride a few hours ago. Could've done it myself, but this stupid splint on my finger makes the simple things practically impossible.

For future reference, the downside of punching someone in the face is the fractured knuckle that comes along with it. But I gotta be honest; it was *so* worth it. Even if it did result in an end-of-year expulsion and nearly cost me my impending shot at Cypress Prep.

It isn't something I'd do again, but also isn't something I regret.

Taking note of Jules' glassy eyes, her intoxication means I've failed. It was on me to make sure she didn't get out of hand tonight, but finding the letter served as the perfect distraction.

"Whoa! Where'd *you* come from?" she hiccups, speaking directly to the brick wall she's clumsily stumbled into.

My hand shoots out to steady the klutzy red-head now leaning beside me. She's lucky I have quick reflexes.

"Enjoying yourself yet?" she asks reluctantly. "I know you'd rather be at the court or something, instead of hanging on the north side, but I think tonight's important."

"So you keep telling me," I murmur.

Her eyes dart to the back of her head when she rolls them. "Because Jules knows best," she so readily reminds me.

This—the party scene, these clothes, the lashes and makeup—it's all *her* thing, not mine. Especially in this part of town.

As if cued by the universe, sharp screams pierce the air. I look left, toward a trio of girls cannonballing into a well-lit, turquoise-colored pool.

North Cypress is home to the wealthy, the elite. Southsiders like Jules and me stick out like a couple sore thumbs. I can feel it. Standing here—on the lawn of some privileged, rich dick's sprawling estate—I'm more than aware that we're out of our element. Yet, I kept my word and came.

Sure, the lure of free drinks and an overabundance of eye candy played a part in Jules insisting I be dragged here against my will, but it's more than that. This is her way of helping me get acclimated to this world, before I'm shoved into it without a harness at the start of the coming school year.

Starting early September, I'd be at their mercy Monday through Friday. Only to make the trek back to reality at the end of the day, back to my side of town where every night ends the same. With me being serenaded to sleep by the only tune South Cypress has ever known—police sirens and barking dogs.

Home sweet home.

"Do you even know anyone here?" As soon as I ask, my eyes follow a couple who pass by without even noticing us. Mostly because they're tearing at one another's clothes like animals, before slipping into the guesthouse through the side door.

"Nope," Jules answers. "Pandora mentioned the party would be wild, dropped the address here in Bellvue Hills, and I decided we had to crash. Don't even know whose pad this is."

I love that she decided my fate before I was even made aware.

"Pandora?

Jules nods. "Mystery girl who tells everyone's business on all her social accounts."

"Is—" Before I can ask for clarification about this Pandora chick, I'm cut off abruptly.

"There have to be at least a few hundred people here, don't you think?" Jules' words are muffled because she's speaking them down the neck of a bottle.

She finishes the sip and her head hits my shoulder as I shrug. "Somewhere in the ballpark."

"Took me forever to find you. I was starting to think you were hiding from me." There's an added layer of emotion beneath the statement because she's more drunk than I realized.

"Never from you, beautiful," I tease. "I always stand near vomit-filled trashcans at parties. It's kind of my thing."

A man-sized burp slips from between her lips and she hardly notices.

"I know you're being sarcastic," she observes, "and if I remember in the morning, I'm sure I'll be offended. So, be ready for an earful."

Even drunk, she can draw a laugh out of me.

The sound of my ringtone has Jules' attention before mine. She's surprisingly alert, considering the state she's in. Or just plain nosey.

"Him again?"

"Yep." I barely glance at the screen before pressing *'ignore'*.

"You know you can't dodge his calls forever, right?"

When I shrug again, her head lifts with the movement. "It's been working out great so far."

"Keyword: so far." The booze-infused breath that wafts past my nose with the comment has me turning my head in the other direction before she continues. "He's pigheaded. You know that better than anyone."

Unfortunately, I *do* know that better than anyone.

"Maybe you should call back? Maybe he's heard from Hunter and—"

"And, truth be told, I'm good either way," I cut her off. "Hunter did what he did, and now he's right where he belongs. End of story."

Her glassy stare doesn't let up. I feel it.

"Fine," she concedes, "I'll drop it."

"Thank you."

Wild, red curls bob when she lifts her head to nod, but she's suddenly focused on my hand. Or, rather, what I'm holding.

"What's this?"

I miss the chance to withdraw the letter I'm clutching and it's hers now. She's managed to uncrumple it some before I snatch it back, but not without tearing the small corner she gripped.

"It's nothing important."

Which is true. My mother's words *aren't* important. Lies never are.

"Geez! Could've fooled me," Jules scoffs, speaking to my back now because I've started toward the bonfire.

People dance around the flames, screaming the lyrics to Ice Cube's *'Today Was a Good Day'*, and it looks like they're taking part in some kind of new-age mating ritual. Hell, that might be a pretty accurate conclusion.

Before I can talk myself out of it, I straighten the letter and hold it to the flames, letting it catch. I wait until the last possible second to finally release it, nearly burning my fingertips when I stall. This seems fitting, though. That's me in a nutshell; never quite sure when I've had enough.

A family curse, in fact.

A beer is slipped into my hand half a second before Jules steps into my peripheral. Momentarily, I'm fixated on the fire through the tinted brown glass of the bottle when I bring it to my lips for a drink.

There's a strange tug in my heart as the last visible fragment of paper disintegrates into nothing. Unlike most girls, I don't own trinkets or mementos passed down from my mother. The only gift either of my parents ever gave me was a list of vices longer than my arm.

"You good? We can take off if you want."

Jules' hand settles on my shoulder, and I don't miss that she's trying to be thoughtful. However, I know this girl like the back of my hand, and her heart is nowhere in the offer.

"I'm fine. We can hang out a couple more hours if you want."

I barely have the words out before she floats off again, finding some rando to grind all over. It's cool, though. There's a brick wall near a vomit-filled trashcan with my name on it.

I glance toward the flames one last time, knowing what they've just burned out of my life. However, the aching grip of sentiment fades quickly. All because my attention is drawn above the blaze, lured higher by an invisible force to meet three matching stares already fixed on me. Beneath half-mast lids, their brooding eyes— close-set like a pack of marauding predators—have me feeling soul-obsessed and I can't turn away. Their physical features are too similar, which is why I draw the conclusion that they must be brothers.

These raven-haired deities have definitely noticed me, and now I even think they might be talking about me. Two lean in to speak closely to the one in the middle. Like some beautiful huddle of hotness.

Seriously? A 'huddle of hotness'? That's the best you can come up with, Blue?

Clearly, my brain is fried. Only becoming more frazzled by the second.

There they sit, perched on chairs identical to the others scattered across the yard. Only, beneath *them*, I'm convinced they're thrones. It's their presence that makes the difference, sets them apart from all the other guys I noticed tonight.

They're large, broad in all the right places—across the shoulders and their chests. The effects of this are emphasized by the tapering of tight, athletically lean torsos. I've met people who command a room, but never anyone so formidable in the wide-open space, as these three are.

Where have they been hiding all night?

Even when the two at either side become distracted by the pair of wet, bikini-clad robots who bounce over to vie for their attention, the one in the middle stays focused. Firelight burns in his eyes like hellfire, this creature I swear emits sex like trees give oxygen. Completely gone on him, I swear his soul moves right across this yard, steps through the flames, and breathes the heat of a million suns over my skin. He's all I see, and I'm not sure how I feel about that. Simply because I'm not sure he's deserving of that.

Don't overthink it, stupid.

Black images slink upward, wrapping around the length of his arm. From the diamond-studded watch that gleams in the light, until they disappear beneath the sleeve of the white-tee squeezing his dense biceps. He sits there, like a god watching over his people, frozen in time while the world moves around him. Actually, it isn't hard to imagine he plays that role well.

The steady surge of bass pulsating from tall speakers ends and a new song starts—something deep and evocative, fitting the ambiance perfectly. Suddenly, I have Jules back, marginally more sober than when she'd run off to dance. I'm aware of her huffing breathlessly at my side, and I totally mean to pay her the attention she deserves, but I can't. Because the Greek statue cloaked in flesh has risen from his throne and, if I'm not completely insane ... I think he's coming my way.

Ho-ly crap.

His height is as staggering as I imagined, and I'm transfixed as the crowd parts in anticipation of his every step. The sharp angles of his jaw and cheekbones would make any model lose all hope of ever reaching this new bar he's set for perfection. Not a single feature is average. Not a single one possibly measured on anyone's scale of beauty.

Broad shoulders roll and dip beneath his t-shirt with the slow, intentional gait that practically has me melting in my heels. I more than appreciate how the fabric hugs his frame to his waist, where only the front of the shirt disappears behind the designer belt looped through his dark jeans.

His stare is set on me and I swallow hard, only remembering I'm not alone when Jules speaks.

"Oh, my gosh, girl... Do you have any clue who that is?"

I don't turn, but know Jules must have followed my gaze. The only response I give is an embarrassingly distracted shake of my head.

"King Midas himself."

She says that as if I know what it means. However, I'm not coherent enough to seek clarity.

"This must be their place," she adds. "Well, *one* of their places, anyway. Their family's main spot is downtown, the penthouse in one of their dad's hotels or some shit. I think the boys actually have their own floor, but that could be a rumor. All jokes aside, though, I'd trample my own grandmother to tap that. Hell, I'd do it just for a lick," she adds cheekily. "Not even kidding."

There was a moment of silence where I didn't speak, and neither did she.

Then, suddenly, "Is he coming over here?" she screeches.

Right away, she moves to fix her hair in my peripheral. I'm not offended by her assumption that *she's* the one he noticed. It has nothing to do with her vanity, or her seeing me as some kind of ugly duckling. This is just kind of the order of things in our friendship. I'm the tomboy who cursed the day she got boobs. Meanwhile, Jules had been stuffing since fifth grade, because she lacked the patience to wait for Mother Nature to give her a rack of her own.

Flirting and dating, her thing. Work and ball, mine. It's only due to a grueling weekend of practice freshman year that I know how to walk in these shoes. Jules wouldn't stand by while I rolled into the ninth-grade Homecoming dance wearing high-tops.

I, on the other hand, saw no problem with that at all.

"Please let me get lucky tonight," I think she means to whisper to herself, but instead repeats it three times like a chant.

He's closer now, just on the other side of the bonfire. But before he can even round the flames...

Intercepted.

Hardcore.

By a busty cheerleader-type, no less, with brown hair stretching to her waist. I stare as she bounces into the picture, blocking my view. At first, she's not much of a threat, because there are only whispers exchanged between them, but my heart sinks when she slides her tiny, manicured fingers down his stomach. They don't stop until they reach the front of his jeans. And I'm not just talking some casual caress, either. I mean, this chick grabs a whole *handful* of him. Like there's no one else around.

It's then that his gaze leaves me, slowly tearing his eyes from mine down to hers. She whispers something else and it brings a telling smile to his fleshy lips. At this point, I realize there's no chance of stealing his attention back from her. No guy would ever pass up a sure thing for a maybe.

He doesn't resist when *Do-Me-Barbie* takes his hand to lead him off toward the main house, and likely toward a bedroom.

I realize my stare still lingers in the direction where they've just disappeared, and I probably look like a helpless puppy. But that's what I feel like. A puppy who's just been shoved backwards off the porch, into the freezing snow.

"Oof," Jules sighs. "Well, *that* sucks a little. Talk about anticlimactic."

Despite disappointment twisting in my chest like a knife, I laugh. "Story of my life."

She turns abruptly when my comment seems to register.

"Wait a freakin' minute!" she says, drawing the syllables out for dramatic effect. "*You* ... the ice queen herself ... were interested in him?"

A sigh rushes from my lips. "Don't get too excited. The moment didn't exactly end with a bang."

"Maybe not, but this breakthrough *still* deserves a moment of recognition. Has there even been anyone since—"

"*Don't* ... say his name," I warn sharply, which has her hands shooting toward the sky in surrender.

"Okay, okay," she concedes. "Well, as fun as this is, I think I'm over this little soiree," she announces. I'm surprised, but too happy at the prospect of leaving to question what changed her mind.

"I should get home to check on Scar anyway. She's always trying to sneak Shane in when I leave my post."

Clutching my arm as we cross the lawn, Jules laughs. "Lighten up, BJ! They're just friends. Despite being brothers, Shane's nothing like—"

"Don't ... say his name!" I interject again. "If you say his name, you'll summon him like some kind of ... I don't know ... wickedly persistent demon."

"Wickedly *hot* demon," she mumbles, which prompts me to nudge her ribs.

She rolls her eyes with a smile. "Fine. Whatever you say. I won't say his name."

My heart relaxes a bit as we stumble through the grass arm-in-arm. "Thank you."

She's eyeing me, and it's when she bites the side of her lip that I know what she's about to do. I'm too late to stop her.

"Ricky Ruiz!" She blurts it out to the universe and there's no taking it back. Not even when she clamps a hand over her own lips. The big, dumb grin she's hiding behind it makes me want to arrange a meeting between my fist and her nose.

"See?" she beams. "I said it, and nothing happened."

I hear her loud and clear, but she knows why I keep distance between Ricky and me. Because rules equal order—no unsolicited visits, no casual phone calls.

Not that he's respected either boundary in recent months.

I'm hit with a barrage of memories, reminders of how he morphed from being my big brother's best friend, into... it honestly doesn't even matter.

Water under the bridge.

"The sky didn't fall," Jules' continues, trying to push her agenda. "The Earth didn't open up and swallow us whole. You were worried for absolutely—"

The phone sounds off and I'm speechless for a few seconds, in shock by how accurately I called it.

"Looook what you've done, Jules!" I scream toward the sky, unable to hold in a smile when she belts out a laugh.

"But wait, you seriously have this dude saved in your contacts as 'The Mistake'?" She'd seen that before I hit *'ignore'*.

I decide not to answer her *or* him. Meanwhile, her red mane quivers with a head shake.

"A little harsh, don't you think, BJ?"

"About as harsh as you continuing to call me that, after I've asked you not to on countless occasions." I conveniently ignore the rest of her comment.

"Yes, we've discussed it, but after over a decade of friendship, I think I've earned the right to discreetly call you 'Blow Job' for a cheap laugh," she argues. "Now, stop trying to change the subject."

Busted.

"You know from the bazillion texts he's sent he's not calling about a you-and-him thing, so why not pick up? Put him out of his misery, maybe?"

In theory, Jules is one-hundred percent right, but she's forgetting something. I have no interest in speaking to or about Hunter. He's made his bed, now he'll lie in it.

Alone.

"How far is the Uber?" I ask, instead of continuing this conversation.

Jules clearly doesn't want to drop it, but she knows I'm stubborn, hard to push once I plant my feet.

"Five minutes away."

Cool. Pretty sure I can avoid a resurgence of that conversation for five measly minutes.

We stand at the edge of the road in silence, which is unlike us. Her stare is burning a hole through the side of my face, now that she's frustrated I've shut down.

"Fine, we'll talk about something else," she concedes, and then releases my arm to cross both hers over her chest. "Tell me what you thought of tonight."

I'm not quite sure what she's getting at, so I shrug. "It was fine, I guess. Bunch of spoiled rich kids smoking weed and drinking. Just like the south side, there's just bigger houses and money."

She rolls her eyes, which means that isn't the answer she was looking for.

"Do you think you'll, you know, be okay?" I don't miss the genuine concern in her tone when asking. "Most of these people will be your classmates at Cypress Prep. Guess I just need to know you're cool with the change."

"CP is a means to an end," I answer with a sigh. "It's an opportunity, and I don't get many of those, so ... carpe diem and whatnot."

I fall silent when my thoughts shift to *how* I lucked up on said opportunity. As much as I don't want to think about my brother right now, I have Hunter to thank.

"You're always so evasive," Jules accuses, which isn't a lie.

"And you love me just as I am."

"Mmm ... more like I *tolerate* you just as you are. Big difference, BJ."

The set of headlights heading our way brings a sigh of relief to my lips. It's the first step to there being an end to this night. I've had my fill of pretending I fit in here, had my fill of pretending my life hadn't been turned upside down this year.

In so many ways.

All I want is to go home, enjoy summer break, and revel in the last stretch of normalcy I'll have for a while.

With the clock winding down, I better enjoy it while I can.

The Golden Boys

Chapter 2

—July, one month later—

WEST

Sterling sticks his head into the study from the hallway. He's on lookout, and also scared shitless, which isn't exactly helpful.

"Hurry the hell up!" he warns. "Dane just texted. They're pulling in."

I hear him, flip him off, then keep searching. They'd spend a couple minutes inside the parking structure, then a minute and a half riding the elevator up twenty-six floors. If I'm not done by then, we're screwed.

"Where the hell is it?" I whisper the question to myself, wishing Dane had stayed to help me cover more ground, but having him keep watch in the lobby is better. It's the reason we now have an ETA on our parents. Still, we might've planned better if the whole *'heist idea'* hadn't been drafted up about ten minutes ago.

It started with the phone call—turned screaming match—between my father and me. A neighbor at the Bellvue Hills house decided tonight was a good night to snitch, telling that we'd had parties there nearly every weekend since the start of summer. So, as he sped through the streets of downtown Cypress with Mom listening in the background, he informed my brothers and me that access to all our bank accounts had been blocked until the start of the school year.

He's pissed, but it has nothing to do with the house. He hasn't even been by there in nearly a year. This is about control. The almighty Vin Golden hates the idea of something like that going on under his nose without his permission.

So, instead of losing out on the deal I struck with the owner of a 1970 Chevelle, I'll let good old Vin pick up the tab.

My phone notifications are going off like crazy, and on the other side of the threshold, Sterling's resorted to cussing me out under his breath. The combination of both sounds only makes my nerves worse. He's losing his shit, which makes me start losing *my* shit.

"Pandora's starting with her updates," Sterling pops in to say. "One of her minions reported in on Vin, said they saw him blow through a few red lights to get here."

Which means he'll be rushing up here double-time if he's *that* pissed. My window of escape just closed in a little more.

I move down a drawer on the desk, still holding on to hope that I'll stumble across a very specific credit card. The black one with no limit. The one my father only brings out when he's *really* fucked up, so bad the only remedy is to buy Mom something expensive enough to stop the tears.

Sad thing is, that's usually no fewer than three or four times a year. Perks of being an asshole.

I won't be using it to purchase diamonds or some exotic vacation. My splurge has a LS6 454 engine under the hood.

"Junk. Trash. Bullshit."

Stacks and stacks of unopened envelopes only slow me down as I rifle through. I push them aside and still find nothing.

"Forget it. I'll have to come back once they're in bed."

"About fuckin' time." Sterling barely has the words out before I hear his feet shuffling across the marble, ready to hightail it out of there. Pretty sure he's already made it to the elevator, waiting to take it down a floor to our own place.

"When the hell did you become such a pussy?" I call out, knowing he's probably too far away to even hear me by this point.

It's been a while since I've seen him so on edge. The whole team swears off weed from July through the end of our football season every year. It just hits Sterling a little differently than the rest of us. Whereas we *enjoy* that shit, he damn-near needs it just to function. Dude's wound tighter than a drum and the only thing that offsets it is getting laid more often.

Lucky for him, ass is never hard to come by.

I'm almost to the door and in the clear, but the soles of my sneakers squeak across the tile when I halt. Doubling back is about the dumbest thing I can possibly do, but … I have an idea where the card might be.

"Shit."

I glance over to the far wall. The obnoxious, gold-framed oil painting hanging just above the fireplace is more than art. It conceals a safe. My dad has no clue I've known the code since I was ten, but it's one of his many secrets I've kept over the years.

Only, this one might actually help me, which is new.

I glance in the direction of freedom, and then back toward the art.

"Shit," I mumble again.

Moving at lightspeed across the room, I flip the painting at its hidden hinges. An array of glowing, green numbers glare back at me from underneath it. I punch in the six digits permanently etched in my memory. The buttons beep with every touch, and fucking Sterling's anxiety has taken ahold of me now, too.

I press the last digit and … success. For a hot second, I swear I'm 007 in this bitch, before remembering the ticking clock. I peer inside the small space and take inventory.

A silver USB.

One of several pistols he owns.

A box of ammo.

The card I came for, and … a cell phone.

I fully intend to ignore everything except what I've been in search of, but I lose focus anyway, zeroing in on the dark screen resting at the back of the safe.

There could be a perfectly reasonable, innocent explanation for why my father—a respected real estate developer here in Cypress Pointe and beyond—has this in his possession. However, in order to believe that, I'd have to pretend not to know the man behind the mask.

He's cold, manipulative, a shit father and husband—the dickhead trifecta.

Temptation is too great. The phone is in my hands before I can talk myself out of it. Glancing over my shoulder quickly, I power it on. The fifteen or twenty seconds it takes for the thing to get going feel like hours. When it finally does come to life, I'm prompted to type in an access code. It could have been anything, but I didn't have to try more than once. It was the same six numbers as the safe, the same as the passcode he chose for the elevator that grants access to their penthouse and ours.

My mother's birthday.

A guilty habit, no doubt.

There aren't many icons for apps, which means it's not likely he uses it all that often. I start by scrolling through what seems to be a dummy email account set up for linking it to the phone. Nothing sent, nothing received. I move on. The next logical place to snoop is in the text messages and call log. Whatever may have been there at one point is gone now. So, I move on to the gallery and, immediately, I'm confused as hell.

In a different reality, I would've been shocked to find pics of some half-naked chick in my father's possession, but I'm beyond thinking he's infallible. Women are his weakness. It's not even a secret at this point. But something *does* knock the wind out of me when I zoom in and have a clear view of her face.

Because I know the girl in the image.

Well, we haven't met officially, but ... I hadn't forgotten her face.

I'd first laid eyes on her when she stood framed in flames at the bonfire, little over a month ago. She stood there, doe-eyed, innocent. Shit, you'd never guess that now, seeing what I'm seeing.

She's posed on a white sheet, full lips smiling up at the camera for a selfie, tits exposed and pointing skyward. At the bonfire, I remember wondering what she'd look like naked, sprawled out in my bed just like this. In fact, if Parker hadn't distracted me with her promise of *'the best head I ever had'*, I might've found out for myself.

P.S. Parker lied. Her head game is weak as hell, but I digress.

The girl in this picture couldn't be any older than my brothers and me—eighteen, maybe not quite even. In other words, she's way too young for my father.

I let my eyes drift lower, down the plane of smooth, tan skin, all the way to her navel ring. I find myself wondering if the frame hadn't ended there, would I find her completely naked?

Realizing I'm actually lusting after this girl, I shake my head to clear it. When I refocus, my new goal is to connect the dots, determine what might've led up to the moment. The context is hard to gauge, though.

Had he been there when she captured the moment?
Was this her answer to a special request he made?
Had she just sent it simply to remind him what he was missing?

My stomach turns and I swear my blood becomes venom, burning me up inside as it passes through my veins. Bitches like this only see one thing when they look at my father.

They see money.

What they miss is that there's a woman standing beside him. A woman who's been there through everything—the good, the bad, and the ugly. My mother's a hopeless romantic when it comes to his sorry ass. Emphasis on the *'hopeless'* part. Problem is, he knows she'll never leave. So, in turn, he never changes.

Now, here comes this new distraction, primed to suck up the tiny fragments of time he doesn't spend at the office. Another reason for him to stay gone for days on end. Another gold digger to leech off his bank account.

Perfect.

Instead of taking the phone and hoping my father doesn't notice, I pull out my own and snap a pic of the image.

Whoever she is, whatever she thinks she's going to take from this family that other women before her haven't already stolen, she has another thing coming.

When I find her—and I *will* find her—I swear I won't stop until I tear her whole fuckin' world to shreds.

Eye for an eye, bitch.

Chapter 3

—Late August, seven weeks later—

BLUE

Mike's door will be nothing but rubble when I'm finished with it. He's got this long-standing rule about not being disturbed before noon, but screw that, and screw him. Screw the slurred lecture I'll have to sit through once he's finally conscious again, too.

Just thinking about it, I can practically smell the day-old whiskey on his breath, feel the moist heat hitting my skin when he gets in my face. A sign he's *really* angry.

He's always angry.

Still, even knowing what's to come, all that matters is the shut-off notice crumpled in my fist. If I hadn't been digging through the junk drawer for a pen to forge his signature on papers for Scarlett, I never would've found it.

The sound of my palm slamming his door fills the house again.

"One Week, Mike! That's when the electricity will be turned off. Thank you *so much* for the heads up!"

Who am I kidding? This is pointless, and as I sink to the floor, I'm reminded that the only thing the man has ever loved besides Mom—

dysfunctional as they are—is his booze. And with her gone, he seems to care about everything else even less than before.

Including us, his kids. Father of the year he is not.

The rustling inside his bedroom has me pressing my ear to the door, but then a loud thud and a groan are the last thing I hear before he goes quiet again. Reality sets in and there's no doubt it's on *me* to fix this.

Like always.

Furious tears flood my eyes and I only quench them at the sight of a wobbly, messy-haired girl Frankensteining her way down the hall. Feeling a bit guilty for waking her with my tirade, I force a smile. It's the best I can do to shield her from the truth of our life here under Mike's roof.

Mom used to say Scarlett was as much *my* kid as she was hers. It's true, even if I *do* want to throat-punch the girl right out of her flip-flops sometimes. Sure, she's grown to match my height now, but she'll always be my little sister.

Always.

"Geez! What's all the noise?" She slides down the wall until she's seated beside me, her hip pressed against mine.

Quickly tucking the shut-off notice into the pocket of my pajama pants, I smile again to mask that I'm so *incredibly* pissed.

"Nothing you need to worry about," is the best answer I can come up with without lying. Although, I suppose it's still a lie. We *all* needed to worry about sitting in the dark. However, it's not her burden.

It's mine.

My only hope of not being questioned to death is to change the subject, so that's what I do.

"I signed your form. Should be all set for Monday."

One corner of her mouth tugs up as she leans to rest on my shoulder. "Thanks, Sis."

I nod to let her know she's welcome. "So, a few more days and you're officially a high schooler. How's it feel?" When I nudge her knee with my own, she shrugs.

"Fine, I guess. Would've been cool to have you around, though."

Guilt follows those words, even though I wasn't the one who secretly applied for my Cypress Prep scholarship. Hunter was to blame for that. Apparently, he saw something in me he didn't trust our parents ever would. So, submitting the application in secret was his way of showing me I was more than I realized.

And then, he went away.

His efforts got me waitlisted a year ago, and then the admission letter finally came for me to attend this coming semester, the start of senior year. You know, when *all* teens love being shoved into a new school where they don't know a soul.

Insert sarcasm here.

I felt obligated to say "yes" when the letter arrived, but giving that answer comes with a high price. It means leaving Scarlett to face the harsh landscape of South Cypress High—the worst of the city's iffy schools—on her own. Sure, Jules will look after her, but I'm not convinced anyone can do that job as well as I can.

I keep telling myself she'll be fine, because she and I are resilient like that, but I worry. We can't afford to let emotion rule our decisions right now, though. I have to do this, for *both* of us.

"I'm not the one who should be nervous, Preppy," she teases. "How will you adjust being under Pandora's watchful eye?"

I frown. "Who is this Pandora person? I've heard Jules mention her."

Apparently, my ignorance annoys my sister, because I get a big eye roll in response.

"You live under a rock. I swear," she scoffs. "She—or he, no one really knows— is a social media influencer. She posts whatever she or her minions see. I mean, like, on her app and *all* her social accounts. If it goes down at C.P.A., and it's newsworthy, you best believe Pandora knows about it and she *will* tell. It's usually only stuff about northsiders, but *everyone* follows," she adds. "So, consider yourself warned."

I can't help but to laugh. Scarlett means well, but she's always been a bit dramatic.

"Well, I'm pretty sure I'm going to start my year invisible and end it the same way. So, no need to worry I'll sully our good family name," I tease, knowing our name means crap around here.

On cue, as if to punctuate the thought I've just had, Mike—still drunk and passed out—lets a huge fart rip on the other side of the door.

Scarlett's mouth gapes open while struggling not to laugh, and then we both lose it at the same time. That's us, cut from the finest cloth. A real class-act.

My eyes shift to the clock on the wall, just over the long, catch-all table that holds the clutter and junk we've been too lazy to put away over the past week.

"Shoot!" I bolt up from the ground. "Gotta go. Senior orientation starts soon."

"You're always running off somewhere," she says casually, but it gets me right in the heart anyway. I pulled a lot of hours at the diner this summer, with hopes of having enough left to get us both a few new things for school. But after the bills were paid, and now with the shutoff notice, I'm not so sure that'll happen.

"I know," I sigh. "Seems never ending."

"Well, do yourself a favor," Scarlett calls out.

I slam my bedroom door and wriggle into a pair of jean shorts. "What's that?"

"I'm shooting you a text with the link to download the gossip app," she says from the hallway. "If you intend to survive the drama, I suggest you stay ahead of it."

Again, with the dramatics.

Pulling my hair into a ponytail, I ask, "Why are *you* so interested in all this anyway? I mean, you don't even know these people. Isn't it just a bunch of dirt on northsiders? A bunch of snobs bragging that they've returned from their latest European tour, or how they just turned down an invite to some movie premier?"

I'm trying my best not to sound bitter and frustrated, but the pink paper that just ruined my morning makes that difficult.

"You couldn't *possibly* want to be a part of that world," I say to her, but when there's silence from the hallway, I tuck in only the front of my tank top and snatch the door open to ask again. "You couldn't possibly want to be a part of that world, right, Scarlett?"

She shrugs but doesn't give a straight answer.

"I mean, don't we *all* kinda want that? To have the world in the palm of our hand?"

I bite my tongue to keep from saying what's come to mind. That dreaming about those things has led a lot of girls to do some incredibly stupid and reckless things.

"Careful, kid. You've got stars in your eyes," I warn, but can't say for sure I'm being heard.

She sticks her tongue out and, as I pass her in the hallway, I mess up her pink-tinted hair more than it already is. Reaching the kitchen table, I bend to grab the pair of Mom's sneakers I borrowed from underneath it.

"Download the app," Scar repeats. I roll my eyes while she isn't looking.

"Fine, but only if you do the dishes while I'm gone. They've been sitting here for three days and the house is starting to smell worse than your socks."

My statement barely gets a response because, like always, her eyes are glued to the brightly glowing screen in her hand.

I hate what I'm about to do, but storm toward her anyway.

A loudly spoken, "Hey!" hits my ears, and I fully expect the look that darts my way after snatching her phone.

"I asked you to get them done days ago, Scar. So, I'll keep your phone until you follow through," I declare, which makes her mouth fall open.

"What the …?

"If there's an emergency while I'm out, Ms. Levinson won't mind you using her landline."

"But what if Shane tries to text?"

I envision her too-cute-to-be-trusted bestie and shrug. "I'll text him back to let him know you're grounded. Meanwhile, if he stops by, you're allowed to sit on the porch and talk. Provided the dishes are done," I add. "But I mean it, he is *not* to come inside the house while I'm gone. Understood?"

A defiant huff hits the air. "Seriously? I'm not allowed to have friends inside now?"

"Not ones with dicks," I say quietly to myself.

"We've known the Ruiz's our whole lives, Blue. Be reasonable."

She has no idea that reminding me of Shane's relation to Ricky is only hurting her argument.

"He's helping me plan for the bake sale," she adds.

I do a double-take. "Bake sale?"

She rolls her eyes, which means she's about to give a recap of something we've already discussed. Something I should already remember.

"I'm selling cookies and brownies again at the block party next weekend. Figure whatever I sell can help toward groceries or something."

Heart. Broken.

She's fourteen. Where our next meal is coming from should be the least of her worries. But … alas.

My only hope of not getting emotional is to stick to my guns. So, I pretend to ignore the fact that she's starting to feel the burden of the household bills like I have for years.

"He's not to come within six feet of this house, Scar," I reiterate. "Understood?"

She rolls her eyes again. "Yes, rat. I understand."

"Good." When I flash a big, toothy grin just to annoy her, she grabs the closest thing she can find from the hallway floor—a thin notebook—and throws it my way.

She misses and I rush to the back door, purse and keys in hand. The paperwork I'll need for this morning is already filled out and waiting on the passenger seat.

"Bye, kiddo," I tease. "Dishes."

"You're a dictator!" she yells. "Emphasis on the *'dick'* part."

"Keep talking and the phone's mine 'til Monday."

"Okay, okay, okay! Stop being so serious all the time!" she

concedes, knowing my threat is anything but empty. "Just ... download the app. Please."

She does that stupid puppy dog thing with her eyes that shouldn't work on a big sister, but like I said, she's more like my kid than anything.

"Fine ...," I cave, sighing as I close and lock the door behind me.

As soon as I buckle into the Cutlass, I find the app and make good on my promise. A pink and black, tiger-striped icon pops up on my screen, and I'm officially connected to this online world my sister insists I ought to be a part of.

Curious, I nearly open it, but come to my senses and toss the phone to the passenger seat instead. Scarlett will *not* goad me into following her down this rabbit hole, digging through the digital laundry hampers of the rich, the elite.

Their filth is none of my business.

With that, I resist the urge to pry and start my engine instead, pumping the pedal until she purrs. The day I do more than simply allow this app to exist on my phone to quiet my sister, will be the day hell freezes over.

Chapter 4

WEST

Summer basically ended for the team two weeks ago, the moment mandatory two-a-day practices commenced. Since then, it's been all day in the sun, very few breaks, and zero sympathy. When we aren't on the field, we're in the weight room.

With varsity mostly being seniors, we were given a rare pass today for orientation. Then, it's back to the grind at eight a.m. tomorrow morning for a Saturday make-up practice.

Sometimes I wonder why I put myself through this every year, but then remember the rush only football has ever given me.

I use the ten minutes we have before this thing starts to wipe the water droplets beading down from the mirrors after a quick run through the car wash. If the stars align, I'll have the Chevelle road-ready soon, too. Possibly in time for Homecoming if I'm lucky.

I glance up every now and then, usually when a short skirt passes by. The girls wearing them wave once they have my attention and, already, I know it's about to be a good year.

Dane's in the passenger seat posing. With one foot down on the pavement, he leans until half his face is in the sunlight for a selfie. His vain ass thinks his followers are obsessed with his green eyes. Then again, with how they eat that shit up, I guess he's right.

"I hear South Cypress High might be a problem this year," Sterling sighs, resting against my hood.

I peer up. "How so?"

"Apparently, they just had a kid transfer in from Ohio. He's supposed to be some kind of football phenom."

"Position?" Dane pauses from his photoshoot to ask.

"Quarterback," Sterling answers.

"Stats?" I'm curious, but not worried.

"Throws a seventy-yard pass in the air. He's got a good eye, too. Reads the field like a pro."

"Big deal. *I* throw a seventy," I counter.

"Yeah, but ... not coming out of freshman year, you didn't."

Now I'm intrigued. They can probably tell because I've stopped working on the car.

"I hear they're getting cocky, too," Sterling adds. "Whole team's talking shit about how they have district and maybe even regionals on lock."

No fucking way. If I ended this season without a championship under my belt, it wouldn't be because some punk-ass sophomore walked away with it.

While winning is our entire *team's* goal, I need this for other reasons. As a safety net of sorts. A reason for the coach at NCU to consider giving me the spot I deserve despite anything else he might hear about me.

Guess you could say I haven't exactly been an angel.

"We got somebody to go check him out?" I hide that I'm frustrated, but feel the tension across my shoulders.

"Not yet, but I agree we should get on that sooner rather than later. I'll check with Trip," Sterling offers.

I nod and toss the used rag into the trunk before slamming it closed. Then, before I can say more, Dane interrupts with a drawn out, "Damnnn..."

Sterling and I follow his gaze until we spot who he's gawking at.

The one who has him rising from his seat and setting his phone aside, despite the thirsty fans he leaves hanging.

This, alone, is no small miracle.

Not sure who I expect to find has stolen his attention, but I definitely don't expect it to be Joss. Yet, she's the only girl bounding toward my car at full speed, screeching with a huge grin, arms already stretched this way despite still being halfway across the lot.

It's understandable why Dane's caught up, though. A summer spent visiting both halves of her family—first in Haiti, then Cuba—has certainly done that body good. She was smokin' hot even *before* she left, but '*damn*' was the perfect reaction.

A short dress that ties around the waist leaves her golden-brown legs exposed underneath it. Sunlight shimmers over her skin with every step she takes. It does the same with the gold highlights twisted into the braids piled on top of her head.

I can practically hear my brother's heart beating, and it's pretty damn pathetic. No Shade to Joss. It's only pathetic because Dane's loved the girl since we first met her at age twelve and dude still hasn't grown the balls to do anything about it.

With only seconds to spare before she reaches us, I lean in toward Dane with a huge grin on my face. I can't let this moment pass without giving him shit, so I do my best Valley Girl impression to further annoy him.

"Like, imagine your best friend, like, being super hot. *Then* imagine, like, *not* ... being able to tap that."

Sterling laughs behind his fist, but Dane isn't amused. His only reaction is the elbow I take to the ribs. Then, Joss is right in front of us, colliding with Dane so forcefully she practically knocks the wind out of him. His back slams against the broadside of my car and both arms lock tight around her waist. It's just a hug, yeah, but not the kind you expect between '*best friends*'.

They're both full of shit. They just haven't realized it yet. One of these days, they're gonna get tired of beating around the bush, and someone will make a move.

My money's on Dane, but Sterling swears it'll be Joss.

We'll see how it plays out, but for now, both try extra hard to convince themselves and each other they'll never be a thing.

"When'd you get back?" Dane asks. "Didn't expect to see you until Monday morning."

His eyes are all over her when they finally put some space between them. She either doesn't mind, or she's so used to him eye-banging her she doesn't even notice anymore. Probably the latter.

"We got in early so I wouldn't miss orientation. Plus, I wanted to get back for Casey's B-Day party tonight."

As soon as she mentions that name, I see regret in her eyes as they flit toward me. But if she's expecting me to lose my shit, it won't happen. There's so much to unpack with what has now been dubbed *'The Casey Situation'* I don't even have the energy.

"Her nineteenth, right?" I ask casually, pretending the whole thing doesn't still fuck with my head when I let it.

Joss nods. "Yeah, she invited a bunch of girls from *our* dance squad and most from Everly Prep to celebrate. She's only home for the weekend, then she's headed back to school tomorrow night. I'll tell her you asked about her," Joss offers.

"I'd rather you didn't."

The words leave my mouth quickly, which doesn't seem to go over her head. She knows the history, so there's no need to explain my reaction. My brothers expressions are blank and an awkward silence takes over what could've been a pleasant conversation. However, Joss manages to rebound after a moment.

"Well, did you miss me?" she bites her glossed lip after asking Dane the question, slowly peering up at him with a ghosting smile.

"I ... well ..."

I feel him about to say something stupid, so I intervene. As much as I enjoy giving him a hard time, I won't let him embarrass himself.

Not in front of other people, anyway.

"We *all* missed you," I tease. "The north side hasn't been the same since you left."

The mood lightens when she laughs and rolls her eyes. "Yeah, I'm sure. You guys probably didn't even notice I was gone. Hard to keep track of who's where when you're always either drunk or high."

She shoots Dane a look and he pushes a hand behind his neck, letting out a nervous laugh. "I take it you kept up with my posts."

"Sure did, and I'll bet the admissions committee at NCU is keeping up with them, too," she warns.

It's then that I remember why there's a gulf between these two, keeping both in the other's friend zone. Joss is all books, grades, and Advance Placement classes. Meanwhile, Dane never passes up a good time. They're polar opposites, which works for some, but not so much for them.

"Did you even research the internship programs I emailed you?" she asks. "They're perfect for the digital marketing field."

Dane's stare lingers on her a moment and I know for a fact that he loves her fire, how she scolds him with her eyes, puts him in his place every chance she gets.

"I did. Even made a spreadsheet of each one's requirements," he answers after another round of eye-banging.

Joss nearly succeeds at holding back a smile. "Good. Because the thing with my uncle isn't guaranteed. You need a backup plan just in case."

"Yes, ma'am," Dane says, cocking his head with the words.

Joss holds his gaze as long as she can, muttering a faint, "Smart-ass," when she grins. Then, she draws in a breath and her eyes shift across the parking lot.

"So, other than wishing you were here to kill my buzz, how was your trip?" Dane asks.

That smile Joss tried holding back widens now.

"Great, I guess. If you overlook the fact that my dad didn't let me do anything without hawking my every move," she sighs. "I did manage to get out and have *some* fun, though."

Dane's brow twitches, and so does the corner of his mouth, but he hides it well with a smile. "I'll bet. Does *'some fun'* have a name? Or ... names?"

Joss is biting the side of her lip again, but lowers her gaze to the ground instead of answering.

"Well, on that note, I think I'll head inside," she announces, passing a lingering glance toward Dane right after. "Call me later. We have a lot to catch up on."

His eyes don't leave her when she walks away. With the energy between them, I'm starting to think Sterling and I might have the bet resolved before graduation.

It's just us three again, heading toward the building with the rest of the crowd. We get stopped a few times along the way, but most know not to even try it. It's public knowledge that 'friendly' isn't something we do casually. Our circle is small and we intend to keep it that way.

The lines at the staff-run stations are already insane. One to get updated student I.D.'s. One for schedules and locker assignments. Another for anyone claiming a parking space in the student lot.

I have to be here, but I'm definitely not interested. Bored while I wait in line, I scan the atrium, not looking for anything in particular. But then, I spot someone who has me alert again.

Completely alert.

"...The fuck?"

Sterling follows my gaze, straight to the one it seems fate delivered right here, to the very place I rule, the place where my word is law.

"You know her or something?"

"Yeah. Something like that." I'm intentionally careful with my words.

He doesn't recognize her, which comes as no surprise. Of the three of us, I was the jackass who couldn't stop watching her at the bonfire. I'm also the one with a compromising photo of her hidden on my phone.

My brothers know nothing of what I found in our dad's safe, and I'll likely keep it to myself, unless I have good reason to reveal what I know.

A few seconds behind, Dane freezes with his mouth half-open

when he finally spots her. Then, his brow jumps and he's taking it all in, the details I refuse to find appealing about her—tight little waist, sun-kissed skin, legs for days, nice size rack, pretty face. Not the typical, magazine-class pretty face, either. It's unique and ethereal, makes you want to stare. Makes you want to get closer.

She's the human equivalent of oleander.

Beautiful.

Delicate.

Dangerous.

My feelings are all twisted, edging on two different extremes. The man in me knows she's on fire, hot as they come. But there's more to her than that, and it's that hidden truth that fuels my rage.

If that picture proves anything, it's that there's a strong possibility she's been in a myriad of compromising positions with my father. She looks like the type to do whatever freaky-ass shit he wants. Anything to make sure he doesn't snap his wallet shut with her greedy little fingers in it.

She isn't the first. My dad has an M.O. when it comes to these things and it's predictable as hell. He likes his sidepieces young, usually blonde, easy to manipulate, easy to blind with diamonds and fancy vacations he tells my mom are *'business trips'*.

I eye her, positive she doesn't even know that dick's real name. He's become somewhat of a ghost, the reason for the blacked-out windows on his truck, the reason he's turned down television interviews with every local news outlet. To some, Vin Golden is the phantom who manipulates this town like a puppet. To me, he's just an asshole with money.

Whatever the case, there's only one fact about this situation that matters. This girl's decided to be my dad's plaything until he tires of her, which officially makes her my enemy.

I lean in so my words don't go beyond my brothers' ears. "I guarantee what I'm about to say won't make any sense, but I need you both to hear me out."

The statement is met with two questioning stares.

"What's up?" Sterling faces me, looking stern before crossing both arms over his chest.

I second-guess myself for a moment, but I know I can't pull off what I have in mind without their full cooperation.

"That girl is nowhere near as innocent as she looks," I explain.

Dane laughs and passes another glance her way. "Good. Innocence has always been overrated in my book."

I'm shaking my head before he even finishes. "No, trust me. You don't want anything to do with this one."

I feel my expression morph into an angry scowl when I peer up at her again. I'm over beating around the bush and just tell them straight up.

"We have to take her down. And not just '*make her cry and write about us in her diary*' type shit. I mean, I want this bitch *broken,* ground into dust."

I have their full attention and see the questions brimming in their eyes.

"You know we've got your back, but—"

"No questions," I say more harshly than I mean to, but seeing her again has me feeling like I'll lose it.

I've never had this chance before, to deal with one of Dad's sluts as I see fit. In the past, I was either too young to step up, or he'd covered his tracks too well. This time, he hadn't been so careful.

Telling Mom about the late-night phone calls I overheard, or the many other glaring clues I've found over the years was never an option. Having his infidelity shoved in her face would shatter her world. Completely. It's the reason she willingly ignores all the signs, sticks her head in the sand and keeps cleaning and baking like her husband *hasn't* fucked half the town.

Dane's watching her again, my new target. She steps up with a nervous smile to hand one of Headmaster Harrison's administrators a packet of paperwork.

"All you need to know is she deserves everything that's coming to her," I assure them.

There's a staggering silence between us that lasts an uncomfortably long time, but I assume they need to process. We're not the friendliest pricks on the planet, but we don't usually turn up the heat on people just for shits and giggles. I know it's a lot—asking them to unleash hell on someone without explanation—but I hope they know I wouldn't go to such extremes without good reason.

"All right," Sterling agrees first, then Dane nods wearily.

"I'm in."

We're all turned in her direction, focused solely on our unsuspecting mark. I circle back to the belief that fate brought her here. I have no clue what other messed up shit she's done in her lifetime, but something becomes crystal clear to me.

The universe wants her to suffer. It must. If that wasn't the case, it wouldn't have dropped her in my path again.

This girl's entire world is about to go dark, and I'm gonna love every second of it.

Chapter 5

BLUE

I should've brought Jules. At least I'd have someone to talk to while I wait.

The lines were brutal, but I made it through quickly enough. Now, I'm forced to wait in the auditorium with everyone else, where we've been herded for an assembly.

The entire row beside me is empty, but it's probably got something to do with sitting in nearly the farthest section from the stage. Still, it shoves the loneliness of being so far out of my element right in my face. An entire year of this, that's what I have to look forward to. It'll be pure hell, but I know why I'm doing it.

For Scar.

For me.

For change.

'*Still alive, Preppy?*'

I smile at the text from Jules, feeling a little less invisible.

'*Barely. Have to sit through some lame assembly, then home. Thank God.*'

The lights dim a little and a middle-aged woman wearing an unseasonably warm plaid blazer over a cream blouse starts across the stage. When she takes the mic, I shoot Jules a quick, *'Gotta go,'* text and drop the phone down in my purse.

The lady goes over standard issue stuff—a short spiel about how she hopes we all had an enriching summer, something about why they decided to forego uniforms this year, and then a rundown about what clothing articles will and won't be allowed on campus.

Then, right after that, I blank out.

It's not that I've suddenly gone deaf and blind. It's because of who I see sliding into my row from the opposite end, like he's *not* the most delicious thing any girl has ever laid eyes on.

A backwards baseball cap hides the dark, tousled hair I remember wanting to run my fingers through, but ... it's definitely him. His tatted arms are bare today, from the shoulders down. The wifebeater he wears is most certainly against the dress code the woman just dutifully recited from stage, but I don't imagine this one fears much of anything or anyone.

A blatantly cocky stride tells me I'm right.

The white, ribbed fabric clings to his pecs, as well as the discernable ridges of solid abs that have me biting my lip. Then, I'm done in by the rest of his godlike features, the towering height, the half-smile revealing perfect, white teeth set behind fleshy lips.

But he's not smiling at *me*. I'm not even sure he's seen me yet. He's smiling at *them,* the two he's conversing with. The two I know must be his brothers, or they're possibly even triplets, considering they're all here together at orientation. They're not identical, but nearly. Each one obviously aware he could have any girl in this world, but somehow giving off a vibe that they don't care.

Oh, they care.

I'm a fidgeter around boys. Always have been. So, to keep my hands busy when I realize they don't intend to sit at the other end of the row, but instead close to *me,* I shove the abundance of paperwork I've gathered today inside my purse.

Then, he looks up, and that *have-my-babies* smile of his casts it's spell.

For a second, I wonder if he recognizes me from the bonfire, but he can't. He's probably had twenty or thirty girls on their backs and/or knees since then.

I'm smiling, but it feels weird, like I'm thinking too much about what my face is doing. He's still coming this way and I'm starting to think he spotted me before I realized. Actually, I wonder if he spotted me and then decided to approach.

Don't say anything stupid, Blue. They're just boys. Yeah, they're really, really cute boys, but boys, nonetheless.

I tell myself not to look up when he stops and hovers over me, but that would be even more awkward than acknowledging him. So, I take a chance, only to realize I wasn't anywhere near ready.

He wets his lips and I hold my breath when he speaks.

"Anyone sitting here?" His glance shifts to the seat beside me when he asks, and I try to recover from the shockingly deep voice that left him. It's smooth and melodic. Perfect for talking girls out of their panties, I imagine.

My throat is so, so dry. "Uh, n—no! It's just me."

I sound super eager, which I hate. For that reason, I tone down the smile I offer.

"Cool. Mind if we sit?"

I blink up at him, and then shake my head. "Sure. That's fine."

I turn away as all three drop down in the seats beside me. When I do, I'm suddenly aware of all the eyes on us. Even with the lights dim, everyone seems to have taken notice that these three have sought me out.

Great.

Not exactly helping me fly under the radar.

When I turn, I sense the one Jules identified as King Midas staring, and I'm right. He is. His gaze makes its slow trek upward, from where my shoes are propped against the back of the seat in front of me, to where my knees and thighs press toward my chest. Aware of having his attention, I lower both feet to the floor. The sudden movement brings his eyes to mine with a snap—the perfect shade of what Mom calls 'heartbreaker green'. She coined the term before I was even thought of, but she's used it often. So often I know it describes irises such a deep green they look like true emeralds.

"I'm West. These are my brothers—Dane and Sterling," he adds.

"Hey."

"What's up?"

I wave after both brothers offer their short greeting, then decide to ask a question I believe I already know the answer to. "So … you're triplets, right?"

West nods and my stomach fills with knots when he smiles. "That obvious?"

"Kind of," I manage to say through a super cheesy grin. "I mean, there's obviously some sort of relation, but seeing as how you're all here for orientation, I kind of put the pieces together."

He's nodding again and I realize I still haven't given my name.

"Oh, I'm Blue. Blue Riley," I share. He gives me the same look everyone does when I tell them.

"Is that short for something? Or a nickname?"

My cheeks feel hot and I'm grateful it's dark, because my entire face is probably red.

"Uh, no," I admit. "My mom thought it'd be cool to name my siblings and I after colors. She's … a little eccentric, I guess you might say. So, she named us Blue, Scarlett, and Hunter."

When he nods and his smile grows, I'm not really sure how to take it. He's either trying to hold in a laugh or he's thinking my mom must be a little unhinged.

Which wouldn't be far from the truth.

"I hated it most of my life, but it's grown on me," I share.

He's thoughtful for a second, and it's in this moment I become even more aware of his intense energy. He's confident, which is why he hasn't broken his gaze. Meanwhile, I'm fighting the urge to fidget again.

"Blue." It seems he's deep in thought when my name rolls off his lips. Then, my gaze lowers to his mouth when he adds, "I like it."

"Thanks." The burning in my cheeks grows warmer.

Those heartbreaker-greens stay trained on me a few seconds

longer, then they flicker back toward the stage to listen. We're silent through the rest of the assembly, but it's an *uncomfortable* silence. One where I'm overwhelmed with the urge to turn in West's direction just to see if this is real.

The lights brighten and I reach for my purse where it rests on the floor between us. Pulling out the forms I was given earlier, I stand. When I do, West and I are eye-to-eye. Well, sort of, considering he's so much taller.

Feeling the need to put at least a little space between us, I step out into the aisleway and the boys follow. More of the fiery stares from strangers fly my way, and I gather there are a number of these girls who'd like to be me right now, but I don't let it go to my head.

They're just boys, Blue.

A paper slips from the folder I'm holding and, before I can bend to grab it myself, West crouches and has it in hand. He rises to stand, reading the header out loud when he does.

"Sports Physical. What do you play?" He hands it back after asking.

"Basketball. I played all three years at South Cypress."

His brow twitches and he doesn't respond right away, but when he does there's a tone I notice. "You're from the south side?"

I'm unsure if that's judgement I hear, or just surprise.

"Uh, yep. Born and raised," I say chipperly, refusing to feel ashamed. I am who I am, whether he accepts that or not.

"You still live there?"

I nod. "Same house since I was born, actually."

All three of their faces are hard to read now.

"So, you're a scholarship kid."

I feel my brow twitch at Dane's wording. *'Scholarship kid'* feels like a label. Like one of those petty insults the rich kids toss around while wearing those smug-ass grins.

"Not exactly," I lie. "My tuition is already covered."

West's stare turns inquisitive and I have never wished I could read someone's mind more than I do right now. Maybe he knows I'm not telling the truth, but it's no one's business that I am, in fact, a scholarship recipient. Only a few are given out each year, as the board's version of a community outreach program. Even still, they only let in students with considerably high GPAs, and there are some pretty serious caveats attached. For example, their already strict zero-tolerance policy for BS is even stricter for those of us from the outside.

Which is why I thanked my lucky stars I was still admitted, considering the scuffle I got into at the end of last school year.

Long story short, I'll be walking a very thin line here, and my counselor, Dr. Pryor, will make sure of it.

West is quiet for a sec, then he nods toward the auditorium doors. "Since you're new, why don't I show you around?"

I draw in a nervous breath before nodding. "Yeah, okay. I could probably use some help finding my locker, anyway. Thanks."

An easy smile curves the corner of his mouth. "No problem."

Mostly everyone makes a beeline for the exit now that the assembly has let out, leaving only a few students lingering. The four of us take to the hallway as a group—West to my right, Dane and Sterling to my left. I feel small sandwiched between them, but it isn't a bad feeling. The looks of admiration from the guys we pass, and downright fangirling from the female population, is overwhelming.

It's more than clear that my assessment of these three ruling this school is one-hundred percent accurate.

A few twists and turns and we're here. I'd given West my locker number, so he knew exactly where to go. According to my schedule, and the little map printed at the top, it isn't far from my first hour, which is nice.

"We get five minutes between classes, so it's probably not a bad idea to fit as much as you can in your bag," Sterling offers. "Teachers here probably aren't as lenient as where you're from. One tardy and you can expect a detention."

On the surface, what he says seems kind enough, but it's the *'where I'm from'* part that's rubbed me the wrong way.

What the hell does he know about what standards were upheld at my old school? I'm guessing they think anyone from the other side of the tracks must be some kind of thug or criminal. Typical. It would probably blow his mind to know that *several* kids in my class have full scholarships to some very desirable universities.

In short, I feel judged.

I force a smile, but don't say anything.

"We should head toward the cafeteria," West suggests, leading us down a hallway lined with windows on either side.

We hang a sharp left and I see the lunchroom at the end of the hall. Through the double-doors, we're able to peek inside. It's pretty standard from what I can see.

"When weather permits, most of us eat in the courtyard," West shares.

I'm not sure if that's an invitation to join them, but when he doesn't spell it out, I'm even more confused. We move on again and I'm not given a clue where we're headed next, but my companions have suddenly gone quiet on me, which is unnerving to say the least.

We turn down yet another passage, but this one is a dead end, only a few dormant classrooms on either side. Confused, I peer down at my schedule to see if any of the room numbers match, but nope. No idea why we had come this way.

"So, what are the teachers like here?" I ask. Someone had to say *something*.

Dane glances toward me briefly, but his eyes dart ahead quickly after. "Like everywhere else, I guess. Pains in the ass."

A nervous laugh slips out, but the others are all quiet. This sudden change in mood can't be my imagination, and I'm sure of it when we come to a stop in the middle of this dead zone. West faces me and I'm overwhelmed by the sheer size of him when he steps closer, peering down on me with a look that's grown increasingly dark. Whatever hope I held on to that this moment would rebound has mostly faded now. I realize I hadn't imagined being given the cold shoulder, but it's possible I imagined the kindness these three had shown only a moment ago.

Something's very, very off about this whole thing. This point is only driven home when harshly spoken words fly from West's mouth the next second.

"I'm just gonna come right out and ask." A soft, yet wicked, laugh slips from between his lips. And when his shoulders square, I feel every bit as intimidated as he wants me to feel. "How exactly can you afford all this? Your parents must've sold a shit-ton of meth, because Cypress Prep ain't cheap."

Shots fired.

I feel his words hit me right in the chest and there's no question about it. I misread this entire interaction. Completely. And, of course, it stung so much more coming from him, because I'm the idiot who thought we had chemistry.

"Who the hell are you talking to? I don't have to listen to this." The words leave my mouth shakily. Then, the first step I try to take away from them is halted when West takes my arm. His grip is firm, but not painful. Still, I'm keenly aware of his strength.

Dane and Sterling flank him while staring me down, but neither speaks. My gaze flickers from them to West when I'm backed against the brick wall, and then boxed in by his large arms at either side of my head. He's formidable in stature, but also in presence, which I can't forget as he lingers deep in my personal space.

They have me thoroughly cornered, and I hate it.

"Come on now, Southside," he calls me coarsely, as if it's my name. "Can't blame me for being curious how someone from the ass crack of Cypress Pointe can afford this school. So, if your parents didn't rob a bank, then you must've come up with the cash yourself." He steps closer and every breath I take presses my chest to his. "Who'd you suck off to get that kind of money?"

I'm wounded emotionally by the cruel words, and because it's still so surreal that he's turned on me, I'm not sure how to process it. I didn't expect this. Not at all.

Rage in its purest form seeps into my veins, but I quench it when I remember being narrowly allowed through the wrought iron gates out front. Being on probation means I can't stray outside the lines, means I can't give this bastard what he deserves. I'm trapped literally and figuratively, and it sucks.

"All you need to know is I'm not here on *your* dime, dipshit."

"Sure about that?" He's so close the heat of his breath moves over my lips.

My heart races. Only, this time, it's not because of the misguided infatuation that got me into this mess—those feelings are so long gone I swear I never had them at all. Now, it's throbbing inside my chest because my blood's suddenly boiling out of control.

"What the hell is that supposed to mean?"

"It means there are a lot of blind spots just like this in a school this big," he warns. "Lots of places for someone who doesn't belong here to get into trouble."

This anger of his, where is it coming from?

My entire body shakes, from head to toe. I hadn't done anything to them or *anyone*. Was having me here such an insult? Did having someone around who hadn't been born with a silver spoon in their mouth offend them that much?

Both fists tighten at my sides and I'm so tempted to use them, but then I think of Scarlett. Like, how I'd dropped the ball last year because things were so screwed up, and now I can't waste this chance. I need to make this work. I need to make sure I do everything I can to give my sister the life she deserves. The life our crappy parents have robbed us of having thus far.

So, I loosen my hands and let them fall limp.

West sees the fight leave my body and I know he's taken it as a sign of weakness when he smiles. I force myself to press tighter to the wall, preferring to have the rough stones scrape the backs of my thighs, versus being any closer to him.

"I've heard all kinds of freaky shit about girls from your hood. Rumor has it, you'll do practically anything if the money's right. That true, Southside? Cause I have a few dollars in my pocket if you're game."

His stare is wicked, smoldering with misguided hatred. But now, I'm filled with hatred of my own.

"Tell you what," I seethe, feeling my teeth grit as I speak. "If you can somehow find that short dick of yours, we'll see where things go from there, asshole."

He's practically panting in my face, fury burning in his eyes.

"You'd love that wouldn't you?" he bites back, leaning in even more, until his lips graze the rim of my ear. "But fair warning: the only thing short about me is my fuse. Test me if you want to."

My breath quivers and I know he feels it, which I hate. I'm not afraid of *him*, but I'm afraid *for* me. The semester has yet to begin and I cannot start the year proving them all right, proving that where I come from automatically means I'm trouble.

I'd seen the pull West has here, the reverence everyone who passed us held for him. What if that power extends further than just the students, to the staff?

I've seen enough of the world to know how these things work. These kids' family's checks are the foundation on which these schools are built. The rich, the powerful, they defend their own. It'd be his word against mine and I couldn't take that risk.

"Thaaaat's right. Settle down like a good little bitch," he growls against my neck. His deep timbre is low and even, calm, because he knows he has me right where he wants me.

"I'm not breaking for you," I choke out. "I'll *never* break for you. You have my word on that."

This brings a dark laugh out of him and his weight presses into me more completely now, until I feel all of him.

"Never say never. We've got a whole year ahead of us. Anything could happen."

He's right and I know I'm outnumbered here, but it's not in me to give in. My pride is the last thing I have left that's worth anything.

I feel his long, hot fingers slink around my throat. Then, just as they tighten over my racing pulse, he lets go.

"See you around, Southside." A deceivingly sweet smile tugs at his lips as he backs away, adding a sinisterly spoken, "...Welcome to Cypress Prep."

Chapter 6

BLUE

Turning the radio up does nothing to clear my head, and I'm certain Ms. Levinson would agree. She's been watching me shoot around from her patio, and while I don't look to confirm she's scowling about the loud music, I don't need to. She is.

Normally, I'd be a bit more considerate, but I'm still fuming. Just as much as when I stood face-to-face with that bastard. All three of those bastards, actually.

It's unbelievable that people like that exist in the world.

The ball rolls off my fingertips and ricochets off the rim. West has even messed with my shot.

Another reason to hate that dick.

"Damn, Blue. Your finger still busted or something? That was ugly."

Without turning, I know that voice. When I sigh, it draws a laugh out of him.

"What ... do you want, Ruiz?"

"You only call me that when you're mad, but that's not possible. I haven't had the chance to piss you off, seeing as how you've been dodging me for months."

I shoot again and ... miss again, mumbling a few choice words under my breath.

"You clearly didn't get the hint," I say aloud, dribbling the ball between my legs. The weeds sprouting through the cracks in the cement make this more challenging than it has to be, but I've got a good grip. Hopefully, I'll find my rhythm soon.

"Well, what if I told you I come bearing gifts? Would that change your mind?"

Curious, I almost turn. "Depends on what it is."

I should've just told him to kick rocks, but I'm not myself today for obvious reasons.

"Told my aunt I was stopping by today to talk, and that I needed to soften you up first. So, she made you these."

Ugh ... he knows his aunt Carla's food is my weakness. Back when we were kids, she used to make all my birthday cakes, because Ricky never forgot when it rolled around.

Deciding to grant his request, I turn to face him, immediately regretting it. One look and I'm reminded why I've kept him away.

Out of sight, out of mind.

I'm also reminded why I let him into the house that night a little over a year ago. He'd stopped by to see Hunter, but I was the only one home. It wasn't unheard of for him to stick around to keep me company, so I still let him in. However, at some point in our otherwise innocent friendship, things between us got ... weird.

The brief sibling-like hugs we shared on occasion since elementary school started lasting a little longer. Then there was the *'accidental'* kiss when I was fourteen and he was sixteen. Then, the *other* accidental kiss two years later. The next thing I knew, my v-card was in Ricky's pocket, and after the *first* time, it happened with him a *lot* of times.

Like ... a *lot* of times.

Yep, definitely shouldn't have turned around.

He's every bit as attractive as when I first started avoiding him. The shadow of his dark, buzzed hair is freshly lined up, and he's rocking a low goatee now. It suits him, which makes me uncomfortable to acknowledge.

A fitted tee and dark jeans look as new as the crisp-white sneakers on his feet. That's not unusual for him, though. He has more than enough cash coming in to afford it. At the thought, the diamond stud in his ear catches the sunlight and the glint snaps me out of the daze.

"Brownies," he says casually.

I blink a few times before speaking. "Can't ha—"

"I reminded her about the nut allergy," he interjects, playfully rolling his eyes. "I don't forget shit like that." He expectantly holds a plastic container out for me to take it. I swear he has the memory of an elephant.

"Thank you."

I don't hesitate to pop the lid and bite into one, which draws a laugh from him. Next thing I know, my arm drops as the ball once tucked beneath it is stolen and there's nothing I can do about it, because … brownies.

Links of the chain connecting the wallet in his pocket to his belt loop make a clanking sound when he shoots. Of course, the ball swooshes into the basket on his first try. Freakin' show off.

"Not *'working'* today?" The question leaves my mouth snidely, and he doesn't miss it.

Another shot sinks into the basket, then he passes a look over his shoulder with a knowing smile. His idea of *'working'* and mine are oceans apart. In fact, it's the same ocean that caused our breakup, and it will be the same ocean that ensures we'll never revisit what we had.

"Nah, I'm off today. Pays to know the boss," he teases, referencing his uncle, Paul.

Ricky's been *'running errands'* for the guy since he was about thirteen. This is right around the time Uncle Paul took Hunter under his wing, once our father proved to be useless. Unfortunately, though, Paul isn't exactly a stand-up citizen. Some actually argue that he's at the heart of everything wrong with South Cypress. Well, him and his connections across the city.

Another ball goes in and I snatch it back while swallowing the last of the brownie I wolfed down.

"Good for you," I say with a disinterested sigh. "You should probably take off then. You know, enjoy having the day to yourself. Guess I'll see you when I see you."

Before Ricky can even get a sentence out, I climb a few of the porch steps, heading toward the back door. Only, the light hold on my wrist halts me. The touch is gentle, but acts as a reminder of being grabbed by West earlier. I snatch away and my eyes dart toward Ricky and I'm fully aware that I'm projecting anger meant for West toward the wrong guy. However, I'm too proud to apologize.

His head cocks and I know what he's about to say. "You good? I wasn't trying to upset you. I just need you to hold up for a sec."

An exhausted sigh escapes and I force my frustration to subside. At least momentarily. "It's just been a long day," is the only explanation I give, which is an understatement if I've ever heard one.

Staring out at the rusted garage door where my rim hangs, I prop myself against the rail. Ricky's staring, but I refuse to meet his gaze. Instead, I focus on the black web of telephone and electrical wires that zigzag back and forth from the roof of the house, to the wooden posts that tower in the alley.

"I think—"

"Not in the mood to hear what you think," I cut in, still refusing to meet his gaze.

"You don't even know what I was gonna say," he counters with a laugh.

It's so hard to rattle him, which I used to love *and* hate. But when he's pushed, there's a ruthless side no one, including me, wants to see.

When I don't take the bait, he takes a different approach. One I didn't see coming by a mile.

"Wouldn't expect a girl who's about to lockdown the king of the north to be in such a shitty mood." There's an undertone of amusement in his voice that annoys the hell out of me. He's grinning when I finally level a look down on him from the steps.

"What's *that* supposed to mean?" The words fly from my mouth like fiery darts, filled with suspicion.

Before answering, he pulls the phone from his pocket and scrolls. When the screen is turned toward me, my stomach sinks at the sight of that pink and black, tiger-striped icon.

"Folks seem to think there's a hookup in your future," Ricky adds.

So many thoughts flash in my head, most of which would end in an angry rant about what I just went through after orientation, but these aren't the kinds of things I share with Ricky. We aren't friends. We aren't *anything* but exes, so I hold it all in.

Jules, on the other hand, will certainly be getting an earful the second I make it inside the house and dial her number.

"Following gossip apps now, Ruiz? Seems a little beneath you."

He laughs, but it's a bit more subdued than before. Like, maybe his ego is slightly wounded with whatever he thinks he knows about this whole West situation. I've been super cold toward Ricky these past few months, so there's some guilt lurking beneath the surface, prompting me to ease up a little.

"It's not like … whatever they're trying to portray. Trust me," is all I say, but I leave out the part about those bastards separating me from the herd to threaten me.

I don't need Ricky's pity or whatever reaction he might have. My problems are not his problems, despite what he thinks.

"If you say so," he replies with a slick grin, like he thinks there's more to this story. I suppose there is, but it's nothing like what he's imagining.

"I'm not talking to you about this," I say, shutting down that portion of the conversation.

There's a brief standoff where I feel him wanting to press, but he refrains, which is lucky for me. Instead, he changes the subject, but of course he brings up the one *other* thing I refuse to discuss with him.

"Your brother's still asking for you. Every time we talk, actually," he adds. "He says it's important, but he refuses to talk about it over the phone or in letters. Says it has to be face-to-face."

Sighing, I lift my gaze to the sky. "And like I keep telling you, Hunter made his own bed, and he will lie in it alone. It's bad enough he left me to deal with everything on my own. I've got Scar to look after, plus work, and school in a few days," I ramble. "He should be here. He knows how our parents are, so he should've thought enough of me and Scar to be better."

"Don't say that," Ricky cuts in. "You know he was *always* thinking about you."

My stare turns cold. He's always sticking up for Hunter, good or bad, right or wrong. There's such a thing as being loyal, and such a thing as being an enabler. Sometimes, I struggle to decide which role Ricky fills in Hunter's life most often.

"If he cared, if he really wanted what's best for us, he'd be here," I conclude. "Period."

I can't admit this out loud, but I'm also one-hundred percent sure I couldn't stand seeing my brother like that—locked in that place, knowing he'll be there for decades without any chance of release. I prefer the memories I've managed to hold on to.

My heart lurches inside my chest, but I hide how bad it hurts.

"I won't see him like that, Ricky. I don't care what he has to say, I need to move on from this."

A warm hand covers mine where it rests on the rail, and I don't move despite knowing I should.

"I know you're angry, but it doesn't change the fact that he's your family. Whether out here or in there, he's blood."

One tear streaks down my cheek, but I don't rush to wipe it.

"My mind is made up, Ricky. There's nothing else to talk about."

I feel his stare looming over me, but I stand my ground.

"If that's what you want, I can't force you." His hands slips off mine and he shoves both his in the pockets of his jeans.

A rumble of bass from a passerby's speakers fills the silence between us. But just as I decide to meet his gaze again, I lose it because he's pointing behind me.

"What's that?"

My heart sinks when I turn, rushing to snatch the pink shut-off notice from where it's been placed on the screen door. It doesn't matter, though, because he's already seen it.

"How much do you need?"

I ignore his question and focus on the two kids pedaling through the alley on bikes instead.

"So, I'm such a terrible person that I'm not even good enough to help you?" he asks, only now showing signs of frustration.

"Don't do that," I shoot back.

"Do what? Point out the truth? Why don't you just admit what we both know? You think you're better than me."

It's been a terrible day already and I don't need this. Not on top of everything else.

Stretching my arms toward my house, and then toward my piece-of-crap car, a humorless laugh slips out. "Yes, living in this palace has *certainly* gone to my head, Ruiz. Thank you for putting me in my place."

"You know what I mean."

"I don't want your money because I know how you get it," I shout, correcting his bullshit logic, while also earning Ms. Levinson's attention. "What makes you think I'd accept dirty cash from *you* if I wouldn't take it from my own brother? The problem has never been that I'm too good for you. The problem is that you're too good to blindly let yourself turn into your Uncle Paul, and we both know it."

"Whatever," he sighs, waving me off as his nostrils flare—a sure sign I've pissed him off. "I have your address. The electric company won't need more than that. It'll be taken care of by morning," he declares.

"Mind your business, Ricky." My words are pointless, because he's already disappeared into the alley, hidden from view by Ms. Levinson's garage.

I swear, every guy I've encountered today needs a swift kick in the dick.

Every. Single. One.

Chapter 7

BLUE

Chin up, eyes trained on the building.

Tucking my keys into my pocket, I pop both earbuds in and tune out everything else.

Today doesn't have to suck, Blue. There's no guarantee you'll even see *those knuckle-draggers. Think positive. Think ... positive.*

The lot is packed. Nearly every space holds some expensive car or oversized SUV—more room than any teenager would ever actually need. Dressed to kill while leaning against these beasts on wheels, are my new classmates. The music in my ears drowns out their conversations and laughter, but not my own envy. They have a lot that I don't, but what I covet most is their peace of mind.

They fit in here, they've formed alliances that help them navigate the day-to-day. Even those who aren't with the in-crowd have likely found their place, formed small cliques that serve as buffers against the sometimes-harsh landscape of high school. Most have probably attended school together all their lives. Then, there's me—NewGirl, as Pandora has apparently marked me.

I'm ashamed to admit that I finally took the plunge and got swept away by Pandora and all her musings. The conversation with Ricky left me no choice. After what he mentioned about her getting things between West and me *way* wrong, I couldn't help myself.

So, after talking to Jules, and realizing I didn't have it in me to tell her the hell West, Dane, and Sterling put me through, I ended the call and scrolled.

For hours.

These peoples' lives are messier than any soap opera I've ever seen, and now I know a handful of their secrets. Too bad I don't know the real names behind all the monikers, the missing pieces that would have made what I read just a little bit juicier.

However, what I *do* know, is that *KingMidas*—leader of the pack—is undoubtedly West; Sterling—the voice of reason—is *MrSilver*; and Dane—the vain one with a penchant for selfies—is *PrettyBoyD*. Collectively, these three are *TheGoldenBoys*.

Also, these three are major assholes.

Just saying.

Cranking up the music, I glance down at my tattered jeans. Lucky for me, the hole in the knee *looks* stylish. What no one will ever know is I *got* that hole running for my life when the Huong family's dog decided to hop their fence and chase me. An adventure that ended with me skidding down the sidewalk.

Then there's my gray tee. Or rather, the gray tee I stole from Scar. It barely comes down over my belly ring. Hopefully, the self-appointed dress code police won't notice.

A group of girls pass, and we lock eyes. One tosses her head back, cackling while the other two whisper to one another. I'm probably just being paranoid, but I'd swear they're laughing at me.

The feeling snowballs when I glance back over my shoulder, and all three are staring right back at me, smiling like they know something I don't.

Whatever, skanks.

Holding the straps of my backpack, I jog quickly up the cement steps, slipping inside the open door after another kid passed through. The volume has picked up considerably, so the ambient noise can be heard over the song blaring in my ears.

And then, reality sinks in.

Everything looks so different from South Cypress. Dark, rich wood has replaced the large, tan tiles that lined the hallways of my old school. The unflattering fluorescent lights are nowhere to be found either. Instead, modest chandeliers are spaced out in a row down the long stretch of ceiling. Paired with the yellow stained-glass windows in the atrium, it feels more like passing through a church sanctuary than a school, but the hallways with classrooms aren't nearly as formal, although the mahogany carries throughout.

I pass a pair of giggling freshmen this time—or at least they're small enough to be freshman—but I know I'm not going crazy. There's a sheet of paper in their hands, and when they peer up and see me, their eyes widen like they've seen a ghost.

Don't freak out. It's probably nothing. Just go to your locker, then go to class. You've got this.

I intend to stick to this plan, keeping my head down to avoid trouble, but I suddenly realize trouble has found *me*.

A group of boys at the end of the hallway stand out like giants, their shoulders rising above the heads of nearly everyone they pass. But it isn't only the Golden boys. There are others, an entire squad moving through the halls as a unit, with West front and center.

It isn't a surprise that he's already spotted me. Those piercingly green eyes can be seen even from this distance, and so can the fury within them. Passing one another is unavoidable, but I refuse to let him think I'm intimidated, because I'm not.

He hikes the single strap of his backpack higher on his shoulder and his bicep flexes with the movement. We're nearly at one another's feet now, but I step aside at the last second, narrowly avoiding a full-on collision since it's clear he's perfectly content bulldozing over me. My shoulder brushes his arm and he stares down on me with that devilish half-smile.

"Welcome back, Southside," he grumbles low and menacing, getting the words out as we pass.

I say nothing in return.

The whole thing is over quickly and I'm grateful for it. But the second I turn down the hallway to access my locker, my heart sinks.

Almost every single pair of eyes is locked on me. Those that aren't, are focused on the sheets of paper in their hands. The same sheets of paper plastered all over the lockers like wallpaper. Only, instead of a printed floral array or some stupid duck pattern, it's an article. Copy upon copy of the *same* article, actually.

Whatever didn't get posted on the wall looks like it's just been tossed into the air and has landed on the floor. I stoop to take one, and instantly feel the wind get knocked right out of me.

The copies are the newspaper's full account of Hunter's crime, every gory detail that paints him as the monster he was discovered to be. Then, below the text, the responsible party took it upon themselves to add my school pic from last year, just to make sure no one misses the connection.

To make sure no one misses that I'm the sister of a murderer.

"Oh my gosh! Is it really her?"

"I bet she knew and helped him cover it up."

"Psycho probably runs in the family."

The ugly whispers hit me from all directions, but I don't bother trying to pinpoint who said what. It doesn't really matter. Everyone's thinking the same thing. I can feel it.

My eyes sting with tears, but they're not steeped in sadness. These are *angry* tears.

Practically panting, I pull down the pages I can reach, but there are so, so many. Hundreds, maybe a thousand or more. There's no doubt in my mind who's behind this, and I can't help but to think of all the trouble he'd gone through just to humiliate me.

The research to discover who my brother is and what he'd done, the work of spreading the info he found to the masses.

When the onlooker's gazes suddenly shift toward the end of the corridor, my head whips that way, too, finding the Golden boys standing there, so satisfied with what they've done. They've doubled back just to witness this moment. I mean, of course they'd want to see the fruits of their labor, right?

Before I can think about what I'll do when I get to them, I'm already storming in their direction. West doesn't flinch, just smiles at me like he's proud of this. Proud he's just let the entire school in on my deepest, darkest secret.

This blight had been the fuel that lit the fire, which eventually led to the fight that nearly cost me my chance of admission here. The wrong girl said the wrong thing about this situation, and I lost it.

Completely.

My consolation prize for beating her bloody was a fractured knuckle and a late-term expulsion.

No one knows better than me that my family is screwed up, but that doesn't give people the right to point that shit out.

Or … create an entire exposé, for the express purpose of humiliating me today.

I'm nearly to him now, and I have every intention to wipe that smug grin clean off him, but a familiar face pokes her head out of the counselling office, creating a barrier between West and me.

"Ms. Riley? My office, please." Her timing is impeccable, but then I wonder if that isn't the point. Perhaps Dr. Pryor is trying to save me from myself.

I halt, taking longer to do as she's asked, but I remind myself why I'm here, why I'm letting this pissant get away with this crap.

If doing it for yourself isn't enough, do it for Scar.

"Ms. Riley?" Dr. Pryor steps out of the doorframe completely, volleying a look between me and the guys, then stares me down as she crosses both arms over her chest. The glare she shoots me next is stern, and I know she isn't playing.

Casting West a look that could kill, I brush by Dr. Pryor rougher than I mean to, and pass through the small waiting area before dropping down in the seat across from her desk. She rounds the corner of it, still giving me a look, and then takes her seat, too.

She pushes the length of dark dreadlocks over the shoulder of her gray blazer. She's always super stern, but has also made more than one exception for me, so I like her well enough.

Rage burns through my veins at warp speed, which is precisely the reason my knee is bouncing like crazy. More than anything, I want to tear West's eyes right out of the sockets. That's about the only thing that will settle me.

"Mind telling me what this is all about?"

"Short version?" I snap. "That prick, W—"

I can't get his name out. Not because I care about protecting him, but because of what I suspect about the way things run around here. If West or his family have enough pull, whatever I say will only make things worse.

Dr. Pryor's brow quirks. "It looked like you were ready to pounce on West Golden a moment ago. Do I need to have him step in here to get some answers?"

Despite wanting to snitch on that tool more than I want my next breath, I suppress it all.

"No, ma'am," I mumble under my breath.

The way Dr. Pryor purses her lips tightly suggests she's unamused, but I'm not forced to say more than that.

"I've reviewed the surveillance content from earlier this morning. Looks like a group of ten slipped in wearing dark hoodies and plastered their paraphernalia all over the place. They were a little on the small side, so my guess is that the culprits are either a group of girls, or perhaps just underclassmen."

That bastard is smart. He and his boys are larger than life, which means anyone who saw the footage would immediately know who was behind this. So, he used his status here to his advantage, coaxing *others* into doing his dirty work.

"A small crew from the custodial team are on their way to clean up the ... *artwork* in the hallway. And since you seem determined not to share what you know, now seems like as good a time as any to discuss another pressing issue."

When she folds her hands on her desk, my heart sinks. No good conversation ever starts that way.

"With the incident that took place before you left South Cypress, it's made the job of helping you secure your future a bit more difficult, but it's not a lost cause."

I flex my once-fractured knuckle with the reminder, then stare as Dr. Pryor reaches for a file with my first and last name printed on the tab. She begins to pour through the stack of documents inside, while I sit wondering what this is about.

"I know this must have come up before now, but I don't have anything on file regarding your plans to pay for college. You were accepted to Cypress Valley University, which is a great school, but I see nothing about covering expenses beyond what you'll be able to acquire with financial aid. Am I missing something?"

Her question deserves an answer; I simply don't have one.

When the stretch of silence between us grows, Dr. Pryor sighs and eventually closes the folder.

"Listen, Ms. Riley. I'm aware you've had a rough go at life, but I know a little more about that than you might think," she shares. "Branch Street, born and raised."

My eyes flash toward hers curiously. "That's only a few blocks from my house. You lived there?"

She nods, and that stern look softens a little. "I was the first in my family to attend college, and I swore that once I finished I'd find some way to make a difference in that community, give kids from the south side a chance no one else is willing to offer. It's the whole reason I started this program."

Before this, I knew she was invested, but had no clue she was the founder of the program itself.

"So, while you might feel a little like a fish out of water here, know you're not in this alone. I'm doing everything in my power to help you, but you have to meet me halfway."

Another dim smile brightens her face, and it's then that I realize she's actually beautiful. Not at all the wicked witch I assumed she'd be, based solely on the fact that I naturally conclude such things about authority figures.

"I see here you played basketball all three previous years."

Nodding, I agree. "That's right."

"I'm guessing you'll be trying out while attending Cypress Prep as well?"

My lips part, but I choke on my words. In truth, I don't want to spend the extra time out of the house, away from Scar. Last season, Mom and Hunter were still around, so that made a *slight* difference. However, now that they're gone and I work whenever possible, joining the team will mean my schedule becomes even fuller.

"Actually, I thought I'd sit it out this year," I begin, but I never get to finish.

"That won't work. You need to try out," she asserts. "You've got to get involved in as much as you can to pad your transcript. I've got a few leads on scholarships you might qualify for, but the requirements are strict. Which means we've got our work cut out," she shares. "They're not huge amounts, but possibly enough to cover your first year's overages for tuition and textbooks. So, aside from not getting into any more trouble, I need you to get involved in at least two auxiliaries. Basketball will cover one, but you'll need another."

Another thing to add to my plate.

Perfect.

"...Like what?" I ask, trying not to let my frustration show.

She reaches into her drawer and pulls out a flyer. "The school newspaper is short on help this year. I already told Mr. Dansk to expect you to drop in after school to introduce yourself."

I could practically *smell* my future boredom. "Isn't there something else? Something less time consuming? Something less ... lame?"

Her brow quirks. "The Mathletes have room. Is trigonometry on weekends any less lame?"

And now I know she's heavy on the sarcasm when provoked. Duly noted.

"School newspaper it is," I concede.

The flyer is shoved across her desk for me to take. "Remember, Mr. Dansk after school. Then, basketball tryouts in November. Do you need a form for your physical?"

I shake my head. "Got one during orientation. Out of habit, I guess."

She nods and then goes back to the mountain of paperwork on her desk. Halfway to the door, I glance back.

"You don't have to go through all this trouble for me," I admit. "So … thank you."

A faint smile curves the corners of her mouth. "Close my door on your way out."

Chapter 8

BLUE

"So, YOU'RE the one Pandora's been going on about? The one KingMidas is into? OMG, Blue, you're basically famous!"

Rolling my eyes at Scar's text, I shove the phone down in my pocket. She likely hadn't made the connection until this morning's post referencing Hunter. Leave it to my sister to see the silver lining in this fiasco.

Leave it to my sister to think West Golden is a god.

Demon is more like it.

It's true what they say. Speak of the devil and he shall appear. Or, in this case, *think* of the devil and he shall appear.

I spot him across the courtyard. There's no denying how good it would feel to rush across the lawn, march right up to their table, and dump that entire can of soda on his head. Instead, with Ms. Pryor's words from a few hours ago still fresh in my brain, I just stare as he chugs it down. This guy doesn't have a care in the world.

When he lowers the can from his lips with a smirk, nodding once in my direction, it's like he's taunting me. King Midas knows he's untouchable, knows I'm alone here.

Clutching the edges of my lunch tray so tight I could snap it in half, I double back toward the cafeteria, deciding I'll eat inside. Beats having to stare at *his* hateful mug while I eat.

I only grip the handle when my name is called. Well … a *version* of my name, anyway.

"New Girl."

Peering up, there's only one person close enough for me to have heard her voice. A girl propped against a tree, not making eye contact as she discreetly puffs smoke from the side of her mouth.

"Are you … talking to me?" I ask. Maybe I was mistaken, because I have no clue who she is.

"You're the one Pandora calls New Girl, right? The one from the posters?"

Great. Just how I want to be identified. "Yeah, unfortunately."

She flicks ashes from the end of the cigarette hidden behind her thigh, out of sight from the teachers and monitors hanging around. Dark, inquisitive eyes look me over as a breeze incites an explosion of long, black curls that frame her face.

"Who'd you manage to piss off so early in the game?" I don't miss the smile that accompanies the question. It isn't menacing.

Taking slow steps toward her, still holding my tray, I sigh. "Eh, you know. A little bit of everyone, apparently." That's all I'm willing to say, hoping to avoid widening the target on my back even more.

An easy laugh puffs from her mouth before dropping the butt of a cigarette in the grass. The sole of her heavy boot comes down to snuff it out. Then, she eyes me again, with the same scrutiny as before.

"You got a real name?"

"I do," is the only answer I give, and my response seems to amuse her.

"Just what the world needs. Another smart-ass," she points out. "Fine. Name's Lexi Rodriguez. You are?"

Her feigned politeness draws a laugh from me, too. "Wait. Did you not read the posters? Someone made sure *everyone* knows who I am."

Her shoulders lift with an indifferent shrug. "I skimmed but stopped when I realized it was just more of the usual toxic bullshit that circulates around here. These robots thrive on grinding each other's self-esteem to dust."

Lexi's perfect description of West has me glancing at him again and, sure enough, he's watching.

"I'm Blue," I finally answer. "And, before you ask, that's not short for anything. It's just Blue."

"Wasn't gonna ask," she replies.

With how everyone *else* here seems hyper obsessed with others' business, her statement comes as a surprise. Then again, there's a laidback vibe about her that seems genuine.

My guard lowers just a little, and I drop down to sit in the shadow beneath the thick canopy of branches and leaves. I'm starving, so I immediately start in on the apple and yogurt I grabbed from the lunch line. Being careful, of course, to avoid foods that set off my allergy.

Peering up, I watch as Lexi slides down the tree trunk to sit, too. Seeing she's currently snacking on nothing but a bag of peanut M&M's, I hold out the bag of chips I hadn't touched yet.

"I'm not gonna eat these. You should take them," I suggest.

Pretty sure she's not light on lunch because she can't afford more, but knowing what it's like to go hungry, I'm still inclined to offer.

That wild, beautiful hair of hers quivers when she shakes her head. "I'm cool," she answers, but then holds her bag of candy out to me. "Want some?"

"Would, but things go bad for me when nuts are involved."

When she smiles, I know she's about to say something crass. Jules always does when I'm not careful of my wording.

"Things *always* go bad when nuts are involved. Pretty sure it has something to do with the dudes they're attached to, though."

My smile widens. "Facts."

She's quiet for a second, but then scoffs suddenly. Like there's a bad taste in her mouth or something. However, when I look up and follow her gaze, she's eyeing West's table and I get it.

There, he and his brothers sit front and center, like royalty. Surrounded by their crowd of underlings, each one vying for just a morsel of the trio's attention. It's disgusting the way they fall over themselves, just for a chance of being accepted into their world.

Pathetic.

"They're all just so … fake," Lexi declares, and I don't disagree.

"Those are the future leaders of Cypress Pointe," I say back, adding a lackluster, "Lucky us."

"Thing is, some of them weren't always so pretentious. Seems like the moment we got to high school, the girls turned into blithering idiots who only make moves that earn the attention of some guy. Meanwhile, the dudes became pussy-crazed nymphos who think the sun rises and sets on their asses."

"I think that epidemic is widespread, even beyond Cypress Prep. Unfortunately," I add. "Boys, in general, suck."

Nodding, she doesn't object to the point I've just made. "Do you know who everyone is yet?"

I shake my head instead of speaking with my mouth full.

She points and I cast my gaze on West and crew once again.

"Tall Brunette is Parker Holiday—head of the dance squad, head groupie of the Golden boys. West, in particular," Lexi adds. "Daddy owns a few luxury car dealerships across the state."

The designer handbag perched on the table in front of Parker suddenly seems fitting, considering the fortune I imagine her father has amassed.

"The two blondes beside her are Ariana and Heidi. Both rich. Both on the dance squad," Lexi continues. "The other brunette and the red head are *also* on the squad, but I can't remember their names, which goes to show how important they are."

Laughing, I lean back to rest on my palms, balancing the tray on my lap.

"The three seated directly across from the triplets are Austin, Trip, and Ryder—more football Neanderthals. And the chick who's almost too pretty to look at, the one with the braids sitting next to Dane, is Joss Francois," she explains.

"Another groupie?"

I expect Lexi to confirm my suspicion, but she doesn't.

"Far from it. Peep that disinterested, *I'd rather be at the beach* look on her perfectly made-up face," Lexi answers. "I'm actually willing to bet she's the only chick at that table who was *invited* to sit there."

Admittedly, I'm intrigued. "What's her story?"

"Well, she's super smart. As in, our most likely candidate for valedictorian," Lexi shares. "Daddy's in politics and Mom's Chief of Staff at Cypress Pointe Memorial Hospital. She also has this super loaded uncle who's top dog at a major marketing firm. As if they don't already have enough money, her parents are shareholders in a few startups that took off. To summarize, Joss is what I like to call *rich, rich*," Lexi jokes.

"Sounds accurate," I say, eyeing the lineup at that table. Their carefree demeanors, their outward perfection.

"She and her parents spent the entire summer visiting extended family in Haiti and Cuba," Lexi continues. "And who can forget her sweet-sixteen on their yacht a couple years ago? I wasn't invited, but Pandora posted all the pics. I've even heard rumors that she's got a solid gold bust of herself showcased in her bedroom, but that's probably not entirely true," she mumbles. "But, yeah, she *is* one of the dancers. However, she's not like the other girls. At least not in the Golden boys' eyes. They respect her; therefore, the entire football team respects her, which means so does everyone else because we're, apparently, all mindless drones when all is said and done."

Well, at least I have *one* of my questions answered. I knew the guys were athletes, but it's now been revealed that football is their sport. Still, I don't quite understand what it is about Joss that's earned her such high esteem. I study her during a quiet moment. She's remarkably gorgeous, yes, but so are all the other girls. Besides, I know for a fact that a girl's good looks don't make her an automatic shoo in for respect.

"So, what's the deal? She dating one of them or something?"

Lexi's brow arches upward. "Nope, but she and Dane are besties, which is almost the same, I guess. They've been tight since, like, early middle school. Everybody knows he'd get on that if the opportunity arose, but it'll never happen. They're complete opposites."

After taking a sip, I lower the water bottle from my lips before speaking. "How so?"

"Well, for one, he's had more girls on their backs than all the gynos in the county combined. Meanwhile, Joss is a known virgin. The wicked playboy and the angel don't exactly scream *'match made in heaven',*" she points out.

A laugh slips when I realize how ridiculous that sounds. "I'm sorry but *'known virgin'*? What does that even mean? How could anyone possibly know something like that for certain about a person?"

Lexi chuckles while explaining. "I mean she's, literally, taken a vow to save herself for marriage. Granted, I think it's something her parents put her up to, but she wears this symbolic ring and everything. Takes it pretty seriously from what I hear."

The dynamics of their group are interesting enough, but I still see them all as a bunch of arrogant tools who'd plaster an entire hallway with one, unsuspecting girl's dark secret.

"But enough about Cypress Prep's royal court," Lexi says with a sigh. "How are you liking your classes so far?"

My shoulders lift with a shrug and I sink my teeth into the apple again. "Fine, I guess. Same shit, different side of town."

Although, my day had gotten off to a particularly ugly start.

"I actually got some pretty good teachers this year," she comments. "At least, most of them *seem* chill."

I nod, thinking to myself that I'd settle just for not having any classes with the triplets. So far, I'd gotten lucky, but there were still three class periods for all that to change.

"What's your elective?" she asks.

"Mm ... I got placed in Gym this semester, but not by choice. Pretty sure they gave me whatever scraps were left."

I assume that's how it goes for *'scholarship kids'* like me.

"What hour?"

It takes a sec to remember, since I don't yet know my schedule by heart. "Sixth, I think."

"Sweet. Looks like we'll be suffering through that one together," she replies.

"Cool! Should make things more bearable."

She nods casually before checking her phone. "Shoot. I gotta run and catch my weed guy. He bails from his post about five minutes before the bell rings." I watch as she quickly gets to her feet. "In the meantime … don't let this place steal your soul," she warns. "Happens easier than you think."

After that, she walks off, disappearing inside the building in search of her *'weed guy'* or whatever. It's just me again, although I feel someone watching. Even before I search for his heartbreaker-greens across the courtyard, I know it's freakin' West. Unable to fight it, I let my eyes wander until locking with his.

Only, he's closer than expected, because he's coming right this way. Like the stalker he is.

Suddenly feeling a loss of appetite and wanting to avoid whatever his evil ass has in mind, I toss what's left of my food into the trash bin. My hope when I hightail it toward the door right after is that I'll make it inside before he reaches me. However, just as I snatch the door open, it's slammed shut and a large hand catches me across my torso.

Hot, lengthy fingers splay across my bare skin when his palm lands just beneath the hem of my cropped t-shirt. I'm spun quickly to face him, then those inked arms cage me between his impressively massive body and the glass. Having flashbacks of being cornered just like this a few days ago, one fist tightens at my side while I'm contemplating smacking him with the tray I have in the other.

"I see you've made a friend," he teases, grinning like the villain he is. "Makes sense the two of you would link up."

I fight the urge to ask what that means, knowing he won't explain. "What do you want, West?"

With my question, the small space that exists between us suddenly disappears.

"Just making sure you enjoyed that little surprise I arranged for you this morning," he growls against my ear, moving strands of my hair with his breath. "*I* sure did."

I'm, legit, quivering as my eyes dart around, wondering why none of the monitors have stepped in. But I suppose, from a distance, it might be difficult to tell what's going on exactly. West isn't using much force, and with the sick smile he's wearing, this could look like something else. Like something startlingly less awful than the truth.

I'm sure Pandora will have a field day, likely labeling it foreplay.

"Get away from me!" My voice isn't loud, but it's forceful, leaving no room for him to misunderstand the seriousness of it.

"Get away from you?" he asks incredulously, leaning away as he pops a brow. "But I'm just getting started."

There's a promise embedded in those words and they fill my very soul with dread. Because, beyond the shadow of a doubt, I know he means them.

"You'd be wise to watch your back," he warns in a low, gravelly whisper. "I've sicced the dogs on you now, so I'm not the only one you need to look out for. I've only brought the *girls* up to speed for now, but they definitely won't be playing nice."

The sense of dread deepens with what I imagine that means, and I'm sure he notices. The stare-down between us intensifies and I want to knee him in his balls. Especially when that dark gaze of his unhurriedly slides from my lips, down my neck where I feel my pulse throbbing, to my breasts.

His expression shifts then, but his eyes stay glued to me. Within his gaze, there's a strange mix of raw lust and hatred and, apparently, it's contagious.

Because now, I feel it, too.

His heartbreaker-greens flash up to me again and the evidence of his need quickly burns away, like it never existed. It leaves behind only the fury I'm used to seeing there. Maybe even more than usual, and I'm not sure I realized that was possible.

"You should've stayed in the gutter you crawled out of," he growls, "but since you're here, guess that just means I get to enjoy destroying you," he promises.

I'm sick of his arrogant ass, his bullshit threats, all of it. So much so, I'm nearly frothing at the mouth with rage, like a rabid dog waiting to attack.

Feeling a bit bolder than usual, I crane my mouth toward *his* ear this time, making sure he hears me clearly.

"There are lines you do *not* want to cross," I warn. "I'm sure no one's ever called you on your shit, but I'm not like the rest of them. I'm not here to be lorded over like one of your peasants."

A quiet laugh escapes his lips when he lowers his head. The sick bastard actually *likes* it, being challenged, talked to like this. I can see it when his dark stare returns to mine and that thick vein in the side of his neck throbs.

"That's what I like to hear, Southside. Keep it interesting for me," he croons.

Those are his parting words, as the space between us widens again. The moment I realize he's leaving, my breaths deepen with relief. I'm still the only thing he's focused on as he backs away, until he turns and trudges back toward his table with that cocky *'the world is mine'* stride that used to be such a turn-on.

Before I saw the real him, anyway.

It takes everything in me to suppress a growl. Initially, I believed this feud between us was all about status, his belief that I don't belong here at his school. But with the stunt he pulled this morning, and the way he came at me just now, it feels more personal than that.

Deeper than that.

It's as though I've somehow wounded him without realizing it and he needs me to feel his pain.

All of it.

His obsession with ruining me runs deeper than I thought, which drives my need to understand why. At least then, I'll know what I'm up against, giving me a chance of defending myself.

Or ... maybe I'm looking at this from the wrong angle. Maybe I should be doing my bit to get dirt on *him*. As in, fight fire *with* fire.

The tricky part will be discovering a way to level the playing field without ruining my chances of succeeding here at Cypress Prep.

It's a very tall order to fill, but I have to try.

With his latest threat, everything important to me could be riding on this. I will not let West Golden win.

At least, not without a fight.

Chapter 9

BLUE

Two uneventful hours come and go. They lull me into a false sense of security, and then BAM! Sixth hour rolls around, my guard is down, now here I sit at the center of the gold and black logo on the gym bleachers, pretending *they* aren't sitting two rows behind me.

All of them—West, Sterling, and Dane. Along with Parker and her girls, who Lexi pointed out during lunch. Speaking of, *she's* missing in action, which means I'm on my own.

Glancing down at myself, I can't help but wish I'd chosen cuter gym clothes. But since I remembered to grab them at the last minute, I took what I could find—a faded pink tee and black basketball shorts I *thought* were the ones from last season. However, turns out I took the pair from freshman year that should've gotten tossed out eons ago. I'd grown four or five inches since then and filled out a bit. So, yeah, they're ridiculously tight and weird-fitting.

Fun.

A sudden outburst of high-pitched giggling from behind may have nothing to do with me, but I'm willing to bet money it does. One of those douchebags probably took a shot at me. The thought of them sitting there, getting off on making fun of me raises my temp.

Doesn't help that I can still feel West pressed against me, locking me against the glass. He likes that position, asserting power over me. I, on the other hand, hate it. To the core.

Anxiously tapping my foot, my gaze shifts to the clock mounted above the double doors, praying Lexi comes through them at any second, but we're already six minutes into class. I can't help but wonder if her absence has something to do with Pandora's latest reveal. With mention of our siblings both being incarcerated, I suppose I now know what West meant about it *'making sense'* that she and I would link up. It was bad enough *I'd* been outed for my family drama, but it seemed Lexi was now a target, too.

All because she dared to hold one conversation with me.

If she's smart, she'll take this as a sign and never speak to me again, for fear of getting dragged into the muck. However, the selfish side of me hopes she'll stick around despite the risk.

Even if I'm not so sure I would do the same.

A woman has been sitting at a desk behind a floor-to-ceiling window since we walked in, but she's standing now. A few seconds later, there's an energetic spring in her steps when she pushes through the door separating her office from the actual gym. She crosses the court, grinning at all twenty-something of us like there's no place she'd rather be than right here, looking after a bunch of hormonal teens for the hour.

"Afternoon, kiddos! I'm Mrs. C, your drill sergeant for this quarter," she teases. "Looks like you've made it to the end of the day in one piece. Hopefully, everyone had a refreshing summer and you're ready to hit the ground running. Literally," she adds with a laugh. "For the rest of the week, we'll be up on the track."

I follow her finger when she points above, to the second-floor track that overlooks the court.

"Then, Monday, we'll get started on our first unit. Swimming," she adds cheerfully, pushing her cropped hair behind both ears.

A number of gripes and groans hit the air, likely because my classmates are dreading having to mess up their hair and makeup every day, but *my* dread stems from something else.

Like, the fact that I can't freakin' swim.

More than a decade ago, on an impromptu trip after he and Mom got into a bad fight, my dad whisked me and Hunter away to a friend's lake house for the weekend. As usual, he was passed out drunk on the couch by eight P.M., letting the TV watch *him*. Hunter and me, left to our own devices and very little to do, decided to take the small rowboat tied to the dock out on the water.

At ages six and nine.

Long story short, tipping out of a boat in the dead of night when you can't even tread water is enough to leave a kid scarred. Thankfully, Hunter managed to pull me out and get me back to the dock, but the damage was done. To this day, I don't even entertain the idea of getting into water deeper than my waist.

Until now, I guess.

"Head upstairs and get a few laps in. No goal other than to keep running," Mrs. C. concludes before grabbing a clipboard from the front row.

I stand, unable to help glancing at the door one last time, looking for Lexi.

Guess I'm on my own for real now.

One step into my descent and a bony shoulder slams mine. I peer up to find none other than Parker glaring back as she trudges down the steps. There's fire in her eyes when I open my mouth to scream at her.

"What the hell?"

"Better watch your step, Little Manson," she warns in the bitchiest of toxic tones.

I barely have a chance to recover from the *first* shock when another heavy blow hits my back. This time, it's more than just a shoulder check. The chick full-on shoves me. So hard I nearly lose my footing and do a nosedive down ten rows of seating.

"Whoops. Clumsy me," she says with a grin—Ariana, one of Parker's minions. She had likely acted on Queen Bitch's command.

At first, my focus is on the two who just assaulted me, but then it shifts to the one who's *really* to blame—West.

Surprise, surprise ... he's watching with both brothers, getting yet another laugh at my expense today. He spots me and barely even acknowledges my existence, storming down the bleachers two at a time. I'm seething under the suddenly watchful gaze of Mrs. C., so I keep my cool, staring as their crew heads up to the track together, still laughing at my near-death experience.

I take my time going up, but when I finally reach the second level, I quickly blend into the crowd. Weaving my way through the moving ocean of bodies, I focus on the ones who've targeted me for no other reason than because they can. In their eyes I'm weak, which gives them a pass to push me around without consequence.

Only, I refuse to let it go down like that.

I weed out Parker with her prissy little run, and then I pick up speed. They don't even realize I've gained on them, and they won't until it's too late.

Timing the maneuver perfectly, I stick my foot forward and hook it over the top of Parker's. She struggles to steady herself, stumbling awkwardly while I watch the scene unfold. I can't fight a smile, especially when she finally goes down.

Hard.

A blood-curdling scream rings out into the open space and I back into the crowd. Parker clutches her tiny ankle, and that perfectly tanned face of hers is suddenly red as a beet.

"Step aside," Mrs. C. calls out, pushing through the tight circle that's formed on the track. She's barely even stepped inside it when Parker snitches.

"*She* did it!" Parker points. "She tripped me on purpose!"

I put on my best '*Who me?*' face, and even look around as if to imply that she *must* be talking about someone else.

"Why would I do something like that?" The words leave my mouth sounding so believable, proving that my acting chops are much better than I realized.

"Don't even try it, bitch," Parker hisses, beginning to sweat a bit.

I'm guessing the pain is starting to get to her. While Mrs. C's back is turned, I don't hide my smirk. I *want* them to see, *want* them to know I'm not afraid to strike back. Their whole crew.

My gaze flickers up toward West as he stares me down, both arms locked across his chest like he wishes he could hurt me.

Sorry, dick. Ain't happening.

"I'm head of the dance squad! Do you have any idea what you've done?" Parker cries out. I mean, legit, cries out.

So dramatic.

"Relax," Mrs. C. interjects. "We'll get you down to the nurses office so they can take a look at you. I'm sure it's not as serious as you think."

Mrs. C's gaze shifts to me, but I've long-since replaced my snarky expression with one of concern.

"In the meantime, you and I are gonna have a little chat," she concludes. "In my office. Now."

The crowd quickly disperses when it's clear there won't be much drama to come of this. Well, none they're aware of, anyway. In fact, they completely miss that West hasn't moved a muscle since I injured his little girlfriend. It isn't until Sterling helps Parker to her feet and she loops one arm around his neck and the other around West's that he even blinks.

It's impossible to fight the smile on my face now. Told his ass not to mess with me.

"You're here on scholarship, is that correct?" Mrs. C. rocks back in her seat when asking. I can't help but wonder what that has to do with anything.

"Yes, ma'am," I answer, knowing I'm expected to be on my best behavior. My stupid temper got me into this, now I need to turn up the charm to get me out of it.

"Well, Ms. Riley, are you aware of the behavioral guidelines associated with your continued enrollment here at Cypress Prep?"

I'm nodding before she even finishes.

"Yes, ma'am," I repeat. "But I swear to you, I didn't do anything to Parker. Or, if I did, I assure you it wasn't on purpose. Maybe I got too close?" I suggest, trying to get at least somewhere in the *ballpark* of the truth, just in case someone did witness the act and decides to speak up later.

Her stern gaze is locked on me. "I heard about that little prank in the main hall this morning. Did Parker and her friends have anything to do with that? Is that what this is about?"

Yes! They're all guilty.

I want to scream those words, but know it'll only give me a motive, which would make pinning this on me that much easier. So, I lie.

"Honestly, I'm not sure who was behind it, but I don't have any reason to believe Parker was involved."

Speaking these words makes my chest throb.

She keeps her eyes on me a moment longer, before jotting something down on her clipboard.

"Consider this a warning, Riley," she states dryly. "If I hear of anything else brewing between you and Parker, I won't hesitate to take action."

"Of course. I understand."

She keeps eyes on me as I rise from my seat and head back out into the gym. The moment I reach the stairs, preparing to make my way back up, the main door opens suddenly. I half expect it to be West and Sterling returning after escorting Parker, but I'm wrong.

Thank God.

"I was starting to think you wouldn't show."

Lexi gives an easy smile, and then makes sure Mrs. C. hasn't noticed her slipping in.

"Just went to the bathroom to make a call first," she shares. "Pandora's post has my mother up in arms. So, naturally, I needed to put out that fire before I went home. Or, better yet, so I could decide if I even *wanted* to go home."

My heart lurches a bit. "Yeah … about that. I guess I should've mentioned I'm patient zero around here. Apparently, even being seen *talking* to me is social suicide."

Lexi waved me off before I could even finish. "Don't worry about it. My rep is shot to hell already. Mom's just sensitive about my sister's name being dragged further into the mud," she explains. "Although, getting her third DUI and hitting a family of four head-on did most of that damage, so…"

I don't know what to say to that.

"It's been years, but Pandora doesn't forget the past. Keep that in mind," she warns. "She sees to it that none of us can outrun even the slightest mistakes we make."

I nod, thinking about what she said. "Your mom's okay, though?"

"She'll be fine. Just wanted to make sure I wasn't hanging out with the wrong crowd," Lexi says with a laugh. "Obviously, she doesn't know her own kid very well," she jokes. "I *am* the wrong crowd."

I manage to smile despite still feeling bad for having caused a disturbance in her home.

"Don't sweat it," she assures me. "It'll take more than some stupid post to scare me off, New Girl."

She's tough, and those are the kinds of friends needed to weather a storm. We might, literally, be from different sides of the track, but it seems we're still cut from the same cloth. West may have gone out of his way to make me feel like an outsider, but I told him he wouldn't win.

And I meant it.

Chapter 10

WEST

We're all at our best this year, well-conditioned and completely focused. Every practice, we're showing improvement. In the very least, we've got State semifinals on lock, which will *definitely* up the ante for college next fall.

With NCU's star quarterback set to graduate next spring, this is guaranteed to put me in the running for their QB-1 slot. With any luck, my soon-to-be coach, Coach Wells, will allow it.

"So, Pandora got it right, huh?"

The question jars me from my thoughts, and as I glance over my shoulder, I catch Austin's nosey ass waiting for a reply.

"What are you talking about?" There's a clear lack of interest in my tone, as I toss my helmet into the locker with the rest of my gear. Somehow, he misses it. Slipping off my jersey, I'm down to just pants and ready to shower.

"She says you and that new chick are into each other," Austin clarifies, filling me in on what the queen of gossip has had to say about my run-ins with Southside.

"What's her name again?" Trip asks. "Blue or something?"

"It's weird, but she's hot enough that I don't really care." Now

Ryder's getting in on this, too, and things are quickly headed in the wrong direction.

Up to this point, only my brothers and Parker and her girls know Southside has a target on her back, but now I'm thinking I should've cast a wider net. Should've known my boys couldn't look past a set of nice tits and an ass any one of us would happily eat a meal off of.

But that's beside the point.

"So, you hitting that or what, West?" Austin finally gets to the point he's been trying to make all along.

This conversation might take a while, so I get comfortable, lowering to straddle the bench.

"Depends," I say calmly. "There a reason you're asking so many questions?"

When I peer up at him, it looks like he regrets bringing it up. Only, now, there's nothing left to do but follow through at this point.

"Just saying, it'd make sense that she knocked Parker on her ass today in gym. You know, if you two have a thing," he explains.

The fact that he wasn't even there, and yet already has the play-by-play isn't a surprise. Not at this school. Not in this city.

A frustrated sigh leaves my mouth. I'm tired, drenched in sweat, and *this* idiot wants to gossip like a couple grannies sipping tea on the porch.

"I mean, cause let's just put it out there," Trip jumps in again, "chick's sexy as *hell*. There's all kinds of fun I could have with a body like that," he adds. "You know, if you're not already hooking up with her, that is."

That's his attempt at showing respect if, in fact, I do confirm that Blue and I are a thing.

There are muffled laughs floating from every direction when he finishes and then zones out, imagining some of those 'fun' things he'd like to do to Southside, I'm guessing.

I hadn't taken this into account, that some of the guys might see Blue and think she's an option. But there's no way in hell I'm letting them get near her. The last thing I need is her getting inside *any* of my boys' heads, thinking my people are candidates for becoming her allies. As it stands, the only reason I haven't shut down the whole Lexi Rodriguez thing is because the girl's damaged goods. That train wreck self-destructed a long time ago.

"She's off limits," I grumble, not bothering to meet anyone's gazes.

Without even turning, I feel Dane and Sterling's stares, wondering what the hell is up with me. They wouldn't understand, though. Not without revealing things about our father I've kept to myself since I was a kid. Things I confirmed hadn't changed when I found that pic in the safe.

That I can't control. But nothing goes down at Cypress Prep without me allowing it. To start, Southside needs to know a line's been drawn in the sand. Added to that, *my* people can never become *her* people. She needs to know where their loyalty lies.

With me.

There's a noticeable silence among my teammates as my declaration lingers in the locker room.

"So, does that mean the answer's yes? You fucked her?" Austin presses.

I peer up to glare at him again and want to smack that smug grin right off his face.

"It means you need to mind your damn business," is my only reply.

I'm sure he still doesn't know what to make of the situation, but he retreats and I'm good with that. The guys disperse and, unfazed, the topic of conversation changes quickly. Before I know it, they've moved on to discussing some kid on the basketball team who, allegedly, knocked up an underclassman's mom over summer.

Twisted shit.

I stand to grab the small bottle of body wash from the top shelf of the locker, but my brothers block my path before I can take another step. Sterling grills me with a look but doesn't say a word. It's Dane, though, who steps up to speak his mind.

"There's obviously a lot you aren't saying," he starts. "Don't you think it's time to tell us what's up between you and this girl?" There's a brief hesitation before he says more. "I hate to bring her up, but does this have something to do with the whole ... Casey situation? Are they connected in some way?"

First, the question makes me wince, and then it turns into a scowl, adding to the tension already locked in my shoulders after a tougher-than-usual practice.

"No, it's not about that," I respond, vaguely addressing the latter part of his question. "But it sure as hell isn't what everyone *thinks* it is, either. You know that," I remind him. "My response to Austin wasn't some weak-ass attempt at cock blocking. I just need the lines to not get blurred. Southside has to understand she's alone here, as far from home as she can get. If the guys start moving in for the kill, the whole plan falls apart."

They're both quiet now, which I wasn't expecting.

"And you're ... sure you want to keep this going?" Sterling asks gravely, keeping his voice low so the words don't go beyond us three.

I'm tempted to tell them why this girl isn't deserving of this sudden onset of pity but refrain. It's bad enough *I* have to live knowing what I know. I can't justify filling their heads with this shit, too.

Never could.

"I'm sure," I answer through gritted teeth. It's all I can do to keep my cool as I push between them, finally moving toward the showers. They don't try to stop me, but it's not lost on me that they want to.

This little conversation has made several things clear. If left to their own devices, my teammates will bone anything that moves, which means I have to be hyper-vigilant to keep them off Southside.

Literally.

But this convo also showed me something else. That my brothers aren't all the way in. Generally speaking, they're good guys, mostly because they haven't seen the things I've seen. Haven't become so jaded. Their good nature is causing this mission to take its toll on them already. I won't force them into being a part of my plan if they want out, but there's one thing I will not bend on.

Come hell or high water, I *will* see this thing through.

Even if I have to blow up Southside's shit on my own.

Chapter 11

BLUE

"Did you hear?"

I can barely make out Scarlett's words as she inhales another handful of fries.

Jules peers up from her burger. "Hear what?"

"Blue's NewGirl! The one Pandora thinks has a thing going with KingMidas!"

It stings particularly bad hearing the excitement in my sister's voice. She lives for the idea of climbing the social ladder, and to her, being with West sounds like a dream come true.

Shane's ears perk up, but he continues to hover over his spaghetti, actively pretending he's uninterested.

"And to think, the only update *I* got this week is that you joined the Journalism Club," Jules points out, turning to face me.

Taking a sip of my water gives me time to think of a suitable response. "I *did* join journalism club. And I'll have you know it's very fulfilling," I lie.

Actually, Mr. Dansk kind of blows and it only makes my time there suck even harder that I've been tasked to handle the sports segments. Which means I'll get to spend even *more* time with West and Co.

Fun times ahead, right?

"Cut the crap. Is this true?" Jules practically sings. "You been holding out on me?"

"It's not like that," is the best response I can come up with.

Her brows shoot up, which means she's not buying it. "Clearly, we have one heck of a heart-to-heart in our future," she decides.

We seriously don't, though. Not unless I suddenly decide to share with her that, for my first full week at Cypress Prep, I've been bullied by their gang of elites. But that'll never happen because I know Jules, just like I know Ricky. I purposely keep both in the dark about what really goes down at CPA. Protective as they are, they'd never stand for it. First chance either got, they'd call out West and the others, resulting in the world crumbling right on top of me. Not the ones who actually deserve it.

No thanks.

Putting up with their shit is not only embarrassing, but it isn't like me. On my side of town, the last name Riley is synonymous with having a short fuse, taking on whoever stupidly gets in our way. I'm a fighter by nature. To the point that it nearly cost me admission to CPA. But the difference is, I know what's at stake now. It's the reason I keep my head down and *try* to mind my business.

Only, that doesn't really fly with West.

This week alone—in addition to the poster thing—I'd been shoved in the halls by randos I'd never seen before, locked inside a bathroom stall, and I had my backpack disappear from my locker during gym, only to *reappear* on top of the basketball rim.

Mostly, it's amateur shit, but still annoying as hell.

I peer up at Uncle Dusty when he hovers over our booth, whistling the tune to whatever oldie is playing through the sound system. He's exhausted from being on his feet cooking all day, but still managed to prepare each of our favorite meals for dinner. Mine was in a bag beside Scar so I could enjoy it later. If I started in on it now, I'd have to finish my shift in a food coma. Nobody wants that.

"You guys have enough?" he asks.

Shane belches into his fist before answering, "I'm stuffed." Afterward, he leans back and places a hand on his stomach, looking so much like Ricky it's scary.

"That's what I like to hear," my uncle adds, checking his watch before his eyes lock with mine again. "I'm gonna need you back on your section, sweetheart. You know we get a little bit of a rush around this time. Plus, Becca *and* Joanne called in tonight."

"I'm on it," I answer, sliding out of the booth.

Scar, Jules, and Shane follow, collecting their phones from the table. When Scar scoops up the bag with my dinner inside, I nod toward it.

"Do *not* let Mike eat my sandwich," I warn.

"And if he does, let me know," Uncle Dusty chimes in. "It'd give me a good reason to kick his ass. Been almost a decade since I had the chance."

He walks away after that, with the four of us laughing because he means every word. As my mother's older brother, he's never taken to my father, and for good reason.

"Homework and then clean your room," I say to Scar as she moves toward the door.

"But I need to start baking tonight!" she snaps. "Or did you forget about the block party tomorrow."

Of *course* I forgot, but I'll never tell *her* that. Not with how important this bake sale is to her.

"The party is all the more reason for you to get your work done tonight. If I let you put it off, you'll start on it at 11:59 Sunday night. So, homework first, *then* baking. Deal?"

This time I get an eye roll as I tug the end of her pink ponytail, but she doesn't object.

"If it's the math assignment, I can help you," Shane offers. "I got mine done in class."

The very thought of these two being left alone makes my heart race a mile a minute, wondering how I can cock block from here at the diner.

I mean *actually* cock block.

Jules sees me scrambling and intervenes. "Tell you what, I'll hang out at the house until you get off. That way Scar can get help ... and you don't have a heart attack," she adds only loud enough for me to hear.

I discreetly mouth a heartfelt *"Thank you"* in return.

"Hold up a sec."

We all turn when Uncle Dusty rushes out of the kitchen again.

"Almost forgot to have you take these for Ricky and your aunt Carla," he says with a warm smile as he hands two bagged carryout containers to Shane. "If you have other plans, make sure you stop home to drop those off first. Made 'em fresh."

"I'll get it there," Jules promises.

"Thanks, Dusty." Shane offers a polite nod as my uncle makes his way back to the kitchen.

"See you guys when I get off. Shouldn't be too late," I add.

They wave and I watch until they leave the lot, then slip behind the counter. Uncle Dusty is putting the finishing touches on a phone-in order when I lean on the ledge cutout between the kitchen and dining room.

He catches me and flashes a smile from behind his gold-toned beard—one so big I often tease that it's been fertilized with the tears of lesser men. Tall, broad, and looking like he'll put a guy through a wall if he needs to, you'd never guess that when it comes to me, Scarlett, and even Hunter, our uncle is a big softy. One who's actually given a stranger the shirt off his back once.

"Something I can do for you, Blue-Jay?" he asks, flipping the spatula just because he's a show-off.

Shrugging, I smile back. "If you're taking requests, I'll take a yacht with a million bucks stashed inside."

His smile turns into a quiet laugh. "Well, make that a double. When you find this mythical genie granting wishes, point him in my direction."

The door chimes again, ending our conversation. Dusty glances over my shoulder and then goes back to scooping mashed potatoes into a to-go container.

I tighten my apron and start toward the door to greet the customers who entered, but I stop dead in my tracks when I finally look up and see who said customers are.

My first instinct is to ball both fists at my sides, and my next is to *swing* them when West flashes that wicked grin at me.

How on Earth did he know where to find me?

The group of twenty-plus make their way toward the booths lined along the window, but not West. His steps are steady and brimming with confidence when he strides over to me, stopping only when there's a foot of space between us. Naturally, my body goes rigid being so close to the enemy.

Among the many things I take note of within the first few seconds of laying eyes on him is his hair. The unruly, loose curls are tame tonight, wet and darker than normal. The wifebeater beneath his white tee is visible, highlighting the breadth of his shoulders. A scent permeates from him and I hate that I enjoy it so much. It's clean and crisp, not at all overpowering.

West's height gives him an advantage and he uses it, staring down on me like he loves to do. And like always, I can barely breathe in his presence, doing my best not to show any sign of weakness.

"You have to go." The words are biting, and every bit as scathing as I intend for them to be. "Two of our servers called in sick, so we're understaffed. There's no way we can wait on all of you."

His head cocks to the side and his eyes dim. "And here I was, thinking you'd be *honored* to serve me, Southside." The tip of his tongue slides between his lips, wetting them, and my attention goes there before meeting his gaze again.

"Sounds like you've confused me with one of your groupies."

After speaking, I nod toward the handful who followed the team in tonight. The train of sickeningly feminine perfection that filed through the door with them.

They're all from the dance squad, I imagine, but the only three I recognize are Joss, Ariana, and Heidi. Parker's fall turned out to be worse than anyone thought. The sprained ankle she sustained would keep her on the sidelines at least a few weeks.

Whoops. My bad.

On cue, bubbly laughter flutters from their pink, glossed lips and I prop both hands on my hips.

The motion grabs West's attention and his gaze slithers down my body, inch by inch. Realizing he's checking me out, I swallow hard, feeling an unexpected degree of tension explode between us. It swirls in the air like a hot, thick fog.

It isn't lost on me that he's hot as sin, but it's easy to overlook when he's calling for his minions to make my life a living hell.

Suddenly coming to himself again, his gaze flashes toward mine.

"I think we'll stick around," he declares. "And I expect you to be on your best behavior, Southside. Wouldn't want anybody to cause a scene, now would we?"

Chapter 12

BLUE

"Blue-Jay?"

My eyes fall shut when Uncle Dusty approaches from behind.

Well, there goes keeping West out of my business. Didn't exactly want him to know the diner belongs to a relative. In fact, the less this dick knows about me, the better. An enemy should never know your vulnerabilities, the chinks in your armor.

In my case, those vulnerable spots are my family.

"This one of your new friends, sweetheart?" Dusty steps closer, wiping his hands on the towel draped over his shoulder.

"Yes, sir. Name's West."

Hearing him answer for me, I shoot him a look. One I wish could kill his ass in real life. We're nothing even remotely *close* to friends.

"Nice of you to stop by, Son. What brings you kids in tonight?"

Son? What type of upside-down dimension am I living in right now?

"Cypress Prep played South Cypress tonight," West answers, doing his best to charm the pants off my uncle. "We just stopped in for a bite to eat."

"Ah, Friday night football. Good memories." Nostalgia marks my uncle's gruff voice. "Hope you didn't put too bad a whoopin' on our boys, though?"

The two laugh together, and I throw up in my mouth.

"Only enough to pull out a win, sir," West answers, being all sweet. "It was a close game, but we turned things around in the last quarter."

"Good for you. And no offense but, as nice a kid as you seem to be, I'm still hoping we can give you boys hell this season."

Another fake laugh from West has me wanting to sprint out into oncoming traffic.

"May the best team win," he answers with a grin.

"Absolutely," Dusty agrees, peering around West to glance at the rest of the team. "I see you brought a few friends with you."

Continuing with the good guy act, West chuckles. "Yeah, a few. I hope it's okay that we stopped in. Blue just explained you guys are short staffed tonight. We wouldn't want to inconvenience you."

Dusty shoots West an incredulous look and waves off the concern. "Nah, my niece here will take good care of you. Ain't that right, Blue-Jay?" He nudges me forward playfully, but I'm standing awkwardly and lose my footing. Stumbling very ungracefully, I nearly face-plant right in the center of West's chest.

Blazing heat radiates from his palms when he catches me by my waist, sending a wave of warmth right through the fabric of my uniform. His hands slip lower, toward my hips, but I quickly reestablish the necessary distance between us.

My stare tangles with his and I smooth both hands down the powder-blue monstrosity Uncle Dusty insists all the waitresses wear.

"We'll get you boys fed in no time. Sound good?" he promises.

"Yes, sir," West replies, sounding a bit less focused than before.

Dusty leaves us and, ugh! Talk about a punch to the gut! He just practically ate from the palm of my nemesis.

There's more of that weird energy reverberating between West and me, potent enough that it recharges my frustration.

"Just ... go sit," I hiss, realizing this is about to happen whether I like it or not. I move to brush past him, but halt when his fingers encircle my arm.

Peering up, the deep crease at the center of his brow makes it clear he didn't appreciate my sharp tone. In fact, it seems to have refueled his rage.

"Don't provoke me, Southside," he growls. "You haven't seen me off my leash yet." The freakishly deep tone of his voice radiates down to my bones.

I have his undivided attention and take full advantage of it by leaning into him. His gaze slips down to my lips when they part to speak.

"Careful, KingMidas," I warn. "In the wrong hands, a leash can quickly become a noose."

I feel his eyes glued to me when I leave him behind, slipping the notepad from my pocket.

"Can I start everyone off with drinks?" I ask, approaching the first booth.

In my peripheral, I am more than aware of West when he eases into a seat at the table with Dane and Sterling. Mostly, I ignore him and write down the order that's spoken, before moving on to the next table.

It isn't until I get to *his* that I'm unable to pretend he doesn't exist.

I don't fight the scowl that overtakes my expression. "Drinks?" I ask flatly.

The brothers keep it simple with sodas, but not West. KingDick decides to be difficult.

"I'll take a float. Half root beer, half ginger ale."

I roll my eyes but keep my thoughts to myself. Instead, I head to the drink fountain and get started. I fill the order by table and then make the deliveries, but when I get to West's, I make it extra special. Just for him.

Glancing around to make sure there aren't any witnesses, I suck my finger and then use it to stir his float. He'll never know, but it makes me feel a whole lot better about having to put up with him tonight.

As much as I want to smile setting the glass down in front of him, I refrain, knowing he'll sense something is up if I let it slip. Dane and Sterling actually thank me when I hand them theirs. The polite reaction earns both swift rebuke from West, in the form of a sharp, daggerlike look.

Only now does he glance down at the tall glass I placed on the table, and then he peers up at me.

"You did something to it, didn't you?" His voice is low and steady, but suspicious.

Pretending this is all an overreaction on his part, I prop the tray against my hip and feign innocence.

"What are you talking about? I made it just like you said to."

His stare is hard and unrelenting, but I don't fold. Not even when he stands and steps so close his solid chest and torso press against my shoulder.

"Make ... another one," he demands quietly. "And this time, I'll watch."

For some reason, I'm insulted. Despite being one-hundred-percent guilty.

"Paranoid much?" I ask with a grin.

"Don't fuck with me, Blue."

His quick response comes as a shock. "Just Blue?" I ask. "Not Southside?"

I've never gotten so deep under his skin before, and I have to say, I like it here.

"Tell you what," I lean in to say. "If you want a different drink so bad, walk your arrogant ass behind the counter and make it yourself."

"Daaaamn!" Is Sterling's helpful interjection. Meanwhile, Dane chokes out a laugh when his drink goes down the wrong way.

I'm probably lucky no one heard but his brothers. I don't gather West is the type to tolerate being put on the spot.

Hellfire fills his eyes and it gets to me. I mean, really gets to me. I feel bold and untouchable, which, historically speaking, can be quite the deadly combination.

"Get your ass to the bathroom," he growls.

I stand tall, holding his gaze. "No."

"What'd I just tell you about provoking me?"

We stare one another down and, feeling defiant, I lock both arms across my chest. "And if I don't?"

The rims of his nostrils flare with anger. "If you don't, it's possible this place could burn down overnight, and no one would even bat an eye. That kind of thing happens all the time."

His gaze flickers toward mine and there's darkness within it.

"It'd be such a shame," he teases. "Your uncle being such a nice guy and all."

The threat lingers between us before he storms toward the back of the diner. I hesitate a moment, volleying a look between his brothers.

Dane glances up when I don't move right away.

"Might want to do what you're told," he says, warning me with his eyes. "West isn't known to bluff."

An image flashes in my head. One of my uncle's diner going up in a roaring blaze. Not to mention, his small one-bedroom where he lives above. A disaster like that would ruin him if it didn't kill him, which is precisely the reason I wanted to keep West at arm's length. The less he knows, the less he can hurt me, the less he can hurt the people I love.

I feel Dane and Sterling's gazes on my back as I stomp toward the bathroom to join their evil triplet.

I burst through the door of the men's room to find West pacing, steam practically rolling off him now. My heart races double-time, and only quickens when he snatches me all the way inside, and then turns the main lock.

He has me trapped. In so many ways.

Just above the door, a speaker cranks out an oldie I've always loved—*'Time of the Season'* by the Zombies. It echoes loudly in the small space and I have a feeling I'll never hear it the same again after tonight.

"What do you want?" I ask as boldly as I can.

A cold, jarring look snaps toward me. "You still don't get it do you?"

The question sets my nerves on edge.

"Of course, I don't get it!" I yell. "That's what I've been saying this whole time! Every chance you get, you're in my face, giving me shit, but you still don't have the balls to say what I've done to deserve it."

There goes that stupid tremble in my voice again. The one I'm sure West has mistaken for weakness, instead of what it *really* is.

Rage.

Frustration.

"All you need to know is I own you. So, when I say jump, your only response is how fucking high," he roars, coming toward me with quick steps.

Startled, I back toward the green-tiled wall until there's nowhere else I can go. But he doesn't stop. He comes closer, until we're breathing each other's air, and I'm suddenly at a loss for words.

"Now, talk back again," he warns. "When I'm done with you, you'll wish your ass had stayed in line."

I struggle to look into his eyes, but force myself. I'm not his pet, or one of his mindless followers.

"You think you're hot shit because you have these assholes falling at your feet? Because you rule Cypress Prep with an iron fist? Well, newsflash, I've lived with a bastard just like you my whole damn life, West. One who thinks the louder he barks and the more shit he breaks when he rages out the more of a man he is. And, just so you know, I'm not scared of *his* ass either," I snap. "So, whatever you *think* I've done to you, you can either man up and say what you need to say, or get the hell over it," I declare. "But pushing me around? Having your groupies do your dirty work? Threatening to burn this place down? ... Bitch moves, West. All of them."

I just struck a nerve. The vein throbbing in his forehead tells me so.

"So, what's it gonna be?" I ask. "Are you ready to tell me what I've done to piss you off? Or should we just continue with the games because you're weak?"

The steady glare that's trained on me is impossible to escape. *He* is impossible to escape.

"Weak?" he groans, challenging me with his tone. "That's what you think of me?"

The deep rasp causes me to freeze. Even when there's suddenly no gap between his body and mine, I don't move.

Massive hands press into my hips when he grabs me rough, but I say nothing, show no sign of being affected by his touch at all. Especially not the sick, twisted part of me that doesn't hate it entirely.

I even stay quiet when his sadistic power-play becomes something more.

Something I didn't see coming.

The dark centers of his eyes turn even more sinister as a smirk takes over his expression. A smirk that touches his hot, fleshy lips ... just before they're on mine, moving against them.

Heat is coming from everywhere, burning me up, making me perspire a little. I manage to keep my hands hanging limp at my sides, but it isn't easy. They're twitching with lust, aching to touch every inch of the beast I hate more than words can ever express.

And he smells so damn good, freshly showered after dominating on the football field. No, I wasn't there to witness for myself, but I know he'd have it no other way.

I breathe him in deep and it's my undoing, the reason I'm not lucid enough to protest when his tongue pushes between my lips. A taste of mint lingers in his mouth and I'm keenly aware that this is something I shouldn't know about him. It's wrong on so many levels, but there's no use fighting. It's a lost cause. *I'm* a lost cause.

Feverish sucking and tugging on my lips has my head hazy, until I barely know who I am anymore. He's stolen all traces of flavor from my gloss and still isn't finished with me. A dangerous feeling builds in the pit of my stomach—the realization that I want more of this.

More from the wolf who's made it crystal clear he intends to do *more* than just blow my house down.

He wants to level my entire world.

A slow, deep push of his hips toward mine reveals something else. He's rock hard and isn't bothering to hide it, isn't ashamed that I now know for sure there's more than one kind of tension steeping between us. It's there, it's real, and in a flash ... he takes it all away.

Everything.

The sound of our sharp, rapid breaths is all I hear. He's still flush against me, and still very much turned on. There's something different about his eyes, though. They're softer, kinder as he searches my face for something I'm not sure he's found. An explanation for the energy that just surprised and then wrecked us both a second ago.

With my chest heaving against his, neither of us rushes to move, which is telling in and of itself. But then, just like that, he flips the switch again, appearing to have felt nothing. The moment I realize he's reverting back to his d-bag default setting, I snap back to reality, too, straightening my uniform when he backs off.

He's still West—my tormentor, my worst nightmare.

Brushing the back of my hand over my hot, damp lips, my eyes fall closed. Even with everything he's done and said fresh in my head, I still let this happen. It seems like as hard as I try *not* to become my mother, I'm more like the woman every day. I'd watched my dad walk all over her for years. And now, I'd just allowed West to do the exact same.

He steps back further, and I won't even look at him. I hate myself enough already.

"You were right; one of us *is* weak," he rasps. "But are you still sure it's me?"

The lock on the door twists and my head is clear enough to understand exactly what just happened—the transfer of power. By allowing him to handle me this way, I've unwittingly made it clear that, even with all he's done, I'm drawn to him.

He pulls the door open and then I'm alone.

If his goal was to make me see I ought to have hurled that particular insult into a mirror, right at myself, mission accomplished.

West

"That's red-light number three you just ran," Sterling points out, bracing a hand against the dashboard.

His words barely register, though, because … what the actual fuck just happened?

My intentions were clear-cut. I had one goal in mind—to teach Southside a lesson. But now, I'm sweating bullets, hoping she didn't get the wrong idea, didn't misunderstand me touching her like that.

Like … I enjoyed it.

This is the whole damn reason I never kiss chicks. They read way too much into things. I should've been smarter, thought things through.

Not to mention, she had me hard as a brick—a sign I'd let her inside my head. *Deep*. The loss of control happened almost the instant I tasted that sticky, orange-flavored gloss on her damn lips. As pissed as I am at myself, I'm aware of the fact that, if I didn't know her secret, things would've gone a lot further than they did tonight. Right there, with her pinned against that wall, knowing her uncle and all the customers would be a few yards away listening.

"You owe me dinner." Sterling's gripe pulls me out of my thoughts. "Seeing as how you spazzed before we even got to order," he added under his breath.

I know I just caused a scene, making my brothers clear out of the diner without explanation, but leaving was an absolute must. If I didn't go right then and there, I couldn't guarantee she wouldn't have seen what kissing her had done to me.

I pegged her right; she's pure poison. But I have the perfect remedy.

"I'm texting Joss," Dane jumps in. "She says her mom cooked a huge dinner and we're welcome to whatever we want."

I hear him, but have something else in mind.

I'm already shooting a text of my own before answering him. "Can't. Just made plans," I reply. "Besides, her dad hates your ass. Remember?"

He doesn't laugh when I do.

"Hate's such a strong word," he counters.

"Maybe, but it sure as hell isn't the *wrong* word," I say back. "You guys are on your own tonight, though. I'll drop you off to get one of your cars."

"Got other plans?"

I smile at Dane through the rearview mirror when answering, "Parker's."

Both he and Sterling laugh. "How's that gonna work? She's on crutches," Sterling points out.

I take off into the intersection and shrug. "There's nothing wrong with her mouth."

Yeah, the head is terrible, but practice makes perfect. Even the worst can be great with the right teacher on the job.

Ten minutes later, my brothers are out of the car and I'm on my way to get Southside's taste out of my mouth.

The best way I know how.

Chapter 13

WEST

"Explain again why we're spending a perfectly good Saturday night out there?" Sterling asks, slipping on a pair of brand-new kicks.

"Who cares why? Just think of all the photo-ops," Dane cuts in, answering Sterling's question before I have the chance.

And not at all in the way I would've answered it.

Joss rolls her eyes from the armchair beneath my window, shaking her head at Dane's vain ass.

"Do you make *any* life decisions without thinking about selfies?" she asks.

Gazing at himself in the floor-to-ceiling mirror opposite my bed, Dane smooths his eyebrows. "I gotta give the people what they want," he teases, knowing it'll get under Joss's skin.

It does. She stands, pushes both hands down the front of her jean shorts, deciding she's had enough of us already.

"I'll be down in the car when you three prima donnas are done getting ready for the ball," she says with a playful sigh. "Not being the prettiest girl in the room is getting kinda old."

We laugh, but the moment she passes to walk into the hall, Dane's eyes are lustfully glued to her in those tiny shorts, taking it all in.

"I don't know why you don't just hit that already," I say with a sigh.

He faces the mirror again, fixing his collar.

"It's simple," he reasons. "I refuse to be the asshole to ruin something so perfect."

His honesty catches me off guard and I pause, rolling the sleeves of a black button-down to my elbows. "Well, damn. I think that's the realest thing you've ever said."

"Which is fuckin' sad," Sterling chimes in, shoving his wallet into the pocket of his jeans.

Then, we're ready.

I kill the lights in the penthouse on our way to the elevator. It's not until the doors close and seal us in that Sterling revisits his earlier question.

"So, we're slumming it on the crap side of town for … what reason again? Sorry, just still trying to wrap my head around this."

My back rests against the wall as we descend twenty-plus floors. "Because I have a message to send," I explain. "Can't have Southside thinking she can escape me. She needs to know I'll be everywhere, until *I* say she's had enough. Her job, her hood, everywhere," I add.

I don't mention it, but showing up and pissing her off again serves a secondary purpose. Like fixing whatever malfunction I had last night when I touched her. I just need to remember how much I like seeing her broken, and all will be right with the world.

My brothers are silent, probably because I've never gone this dark. But if they knew what I found, knew what I'd seen in the past, they'd be raging, too.

There's an unknown history between my dad and me, information only the two of us share. Well, us and the cunt I caught him with exactly a decade ago. He always had a soft spot for young blondes and seeing Blue in his phone only proved he hadn't changed. The only difference is, unlike the first time I caught him cheating, I'm old enough to do something about it.

Like, break his newest conquests soul in two.

"You can't defeat an opponent unless you know what makes them tick," I explain. "So, to answer your question, *that's* why we're going tonight. Once I know what's important to her ... I can go in for the kill." I add.

And in case it isn't already clear, I'm going to enjoy that shit.

Chapter 14

BLUE

Music, dancing, good food.

Southside block parties never disappoint.

Peeking around Scar and Shane's baked goods booth from a lawn chair, I take in the glittering lights that zigzag from one side of the street to the other. They burn bright against the dark sky. A neighborhood committee had carefully hung them just this afternoon, having taken on the challenge of making this year's celebration a little more festive than in the past.

The lights, the hired clowns and face painters, a professional DJ posted at the end of the street. Mostly, he played hip-hop from the 90s and early 2000s, which has the neighbors dancing beneath the lights. Young and old. All races.

A lot of work went into pulling this off, and it shows.

"Get those away from me," I cringe, turning my face when Jules bounces to the table with the last batch of peanut butter cookies from her oven. She volunteered to bake them for Scar, since preparing them in the house could end badly for me.

"Oh, relax," she teases. "I even wiped down the outside of the container and washed my hands before coming over here, so—"

She takes my face and plants a big kiss on my forehead.

"Cut it out! I know the many, many places those lips have been!" I joke.

She shoves me playfully and I do the same to her once she takes the seat next to me.

"Hopefully, we made enough," Scar huffs, surveying the several dozen cookies and brownies she slaved over last night, as well as most of this morning and afternoon.

"We've got *way* more stuff than last year," Shane assures her. "You're gonna make a ton of cash." I glance up at the sound of his deepening voice. He's not much of a kid anymore, which feels strange, seeing as how I've known him his whole life.

Year after year, he looks more like his big brother—jet black hair, killer gray eyes, and dimples that make me fear for my sister's chastity. Lord knows I happily let his brother decimate mine. Shane's gotten tall, too, towering over Scar by a few inches already. They laugh together like innocent friends, but I'd been down that road once with a Ruiz brother, and we all know how that ended.

"Everything turned out perfect," Jules beams, surveying the party. "Mr. Huang even sprang for a bouncy house." I follow her gaze when she points to the long line of kids waiting to jump on the large, inflated castle a few doors down.

"The amount of germs in that thing makes me want to bathe in a vat of bleach," I joke, which earns me an eye roll. "Seriously, that's a ringworm outbreak waiting to happen."

"Pessimist.

"Realist," I counter.

Her phone chimes and I no longer have her attention.

"Things are about to get *real* interesting," she says with a smile. "A bunch of kids from the north side are headed this way. Pandora's been posting about the block party all day."

I hadn't missed her updates, nor that my moniker had been stated in most of them. While some might argue she's only trying to bring unity between their side and ours, I feel differently about it. Almost like we southside dwellers are some kind of sideshow, an exhibit for the rich to come gawk at for a few hours, and then return home to their mansions.

Needless to say, I hope to blend into the crowd tonight, flying under the radar of anyone from Cypress Prep.

"This seat taken?"

I peer up to find Ricky peering down on me, that same killer smile his brother likes to hit my sister with.

"Free country," I reply, which draws a laugh out of him as he gets comfortable in the seat beside me.

"Take you all day to come up with that one?" he teases.

It's been a solid week since we've spoken, and it didn't end on a good note, but he *is* the reason our electricity is on. I smile a little when he nudges me with his knee, although I don't mean to.

Behind us, the screen door of my house creaks open and I don't even turn to see who's staggering outside.

Freakin' Mike—Daddy Dearest.

"Maybe if we don't stare it right in the eyes it'll go away," Jules jokes under her breath, which makes me choke out a laugh.

"I've been trying that for years. Doesn't work," I whisper back.

"If you're gonna talk shit, do it in front of someone else's house," Mike gripes, the words partially muffled by the cigarette dangling from his lips. His lighter clicks a few times and I can't help but to wish we *had* set up in front of a different house.

When I finally turn, a tall, slender frame steps into my peripheral, wearing the same jeans and wifebeater he's had on the past four days. His fingers slip through his stringy, shoulder-length hair while he scans the street, scowling.

"Damn music's so loud it's rattling my windows," he manages to get out before an ugly cough chokes him out.

He steps toward Scar's booth and I'm immediately on high alert. Sure enough, he reaches his filthy hand toward a stack of snickerdoodles and I'm not having it.

"Got a dollar?" I ask, getting to my feet as I stare him down. "Because that's the only way you're taking *anything* off that table."

His hateful glare lands on me and I give it right back to him.

"Where the hell do you think this shit came from? My damn kitchen," he declares, making my blood boil.

"Mike, you haven't spent a dime on groceries in years and you and I both know it," I seethe. "So, if you don't cough up the cash, you get nothing."

And I mean that with everything in me. All he's ever done is take, and I refuse to let him belittle what Scar's doing here tonight. To help out with bills, no less.

A long, intense silence passes between us and I'm fully committed to sucker punching him if he touches a single chocolate chip.

His gaze slips back toward Scar's merchandise, and then to me.

"You're just like your mother, you know that?" he asks. "A world-class bitch."

He turns to walk away and, without even thinking about my actions, I lunge at him. Had it not been for the arm that catches my waist, I would've knocked Mike right on his drunk ass.

"Whoa, whoa, whoa," Ricky says in my ear, holding my back flush against his chest until Mike's made it inside again. "You know he's always talking out the side of his neck. He'll forget everything he said when he sobers up."

But the problem is *I* never forget. I carry every hateful thing he's ever done or said with me like an old suitcase weighing me down.

"I'm fine," I snap, snatching out of Ricky's grasp. But he knows I'm only pissed at my dad, not at him.

Scar's trying to pretend our father's antics don't affect her, but I know better. I realize Shane's aware of it too when my gaze lowers, to where his hand is linked with my sister's.

"Why don't we walk until you cool off?"

Ricky barely has the suggestion out of his mouth when Jules agrees. "Yep, go. I'll keep an eye on the kiddos."

"We're not kids," Scar sing-songs.

"You're whatever I say you are," Jules teases in the same tone.

I feel hot all over, brimming with anger as I glare at the house. Knowing he's inside makes me want to burn the damn thing right to the ground.

"Know what's better than walking?" Ricky asks. "Dancing."

I throw my head back. "Absolutely not."

Even as I'm protesting, he's dragging me out toward the street, closer to the gigantic speaker set up by the DJ. Since I refuse to move, Ricky takes my hands and makes me sway awkwardly to the beat. It's only a matter of time before I can't take it and a laugh slips out.

I meet his gaze and the negative energy starts to burn off. He tends to have that effect on me often. It seems he notices when my mood lightens and drops my hands, placing his own on my waist.

Too much. Way too much.

"We should go back." I *sound* casual, but I'm anything but that at the moment.

He smirks and draws me even closer to speak over the music. "Why? Because your boyfriend's watching us?"

At first, I don't know what to make of that, but then, as I scan our surroundings, I put two and two together.

The Golden boys.

They're posted on the other side of the street, but Dane and Sterling are focused on their own conversation with Joss and a couple players from the team. However, there's no question who has *West's* attention.

Lucky me.

Chapter 15

BLUE

West's heinously dark stare burns right through me.

I can't escape it.

The tension in his jaw, the sharp flare of his nostrils, both only add to what I already know. He's still just as wicked as the first time our paths crossed.

And even knowing this, I don't quite look at him the same. Not since the kiss.

Feeling the moist heat of his mouth covering mine, the taste of it … I haven't been able to shake the memory. Believe me, I've tried putting it out of my head, because I know exactly who I'm dealing with.

But that's been easier said than done

He's not the boy next door, or the kind you trust with your heart. West Golden is a devil in designer jeans, with all the charm of a bona fied psycho. Still, even with all the hatred I hold for him, I swear I feel him all over me.

Like a ghost.

"Should I go?" Ricky isn't one to be easily intimidated, so I know he only asks because he thinks it's what I want.

"It's fine," I answer casually, but heat creeps up my spine as my eyes lock with West's. So much that I quickly turn away.

"You sure about that?" Ricky adds with amusement in his tone, "because he's on his way over here."

Balls.

I snap my head that way again and a quiet, inward gasp hisses in my throat. All because that confident stride of West's, the rhythmic dip and roll of his broad shoulders, has brought him right to me.

"Sooo … Enjoying yourself, Southside?"

There's a cocky smirk on his lips as he eases both hands inside his pockets. First, he stares *me* down, and then drags his gaze toward Ricky. The usual bright green of his irises seems to darken then, as the two stand eye-to-eye.

My fingers tighten into fists where they rest on Ricky's shoulders, but we aren't dancing anymore. He seems to sense that I'm *highly* uncomfortable at the moment, and misreads it completely. I fear he thinks my concern is that West will get the wrong impression about us, when I honestly couldn't care less about that.

"I'll uh … I'll go check on Shane and Scar," Ricky offers, but something in his tone is off.

Way off.

Unlike most guys in West's presence, Ricky shows no sign of being shaken, which means he's only backing off for my sake. Thanks to Pandora's misguided posts, the world—those living outside of West's circle, anyway—seem to think I'm his property.

Which I definitely am not.

There's a loaded stare that passes between the two guys, but then Ricky turns to walk toward my front lawn, never looking back. My gaze flashes to West again, and I hope he can feel the hatred burning within it.

"Why are you here?" I practically growl.

"That your new boy-toy?" He tips his chin toward Ricky, asking the question through gritted teeth. That's when I notice I don't have his full attention.

Ricky does.

"You don't belong here," I snap.

A furious glare falls on me. "What's the matter, Southside? Not a great feeling when someone weasels their way into your world, is it?"

I hate him. I mean absolutely, positively hate him. From the bottom of my heart.

Both fists tighten at my sides and, for the second time tonight, I want to punch someone.

Something dawns on me then. Unlike when we're at school—West's kingdom—I don't have to put up with his shit. I can walk away, so that's what I do.

He doesn't seem to get the hint when I start putting distance between us, because he's right on my heels. I step up onto the sidewalk and the second Scar spots who's hawking me, her entire face lights up.

Jules notices him and stops mid-chew to stare at West, leaving a hunk of cookie dangling from her lip. I'm reminded of something she said the night at the bonfire. Something about being willing to trample her own grandmother for the chance to lick him?

Apparently, I'm the only one who isn't a fan.

"This your place?" West's voice is deep and quiet when he leans closer to ask, letting his chest bump my shoulder.

Frustrated, I bump him back, which only makes him laugh. But then, my eyes slam shut, because I realize what I've just done in my desperation to get away from him.

"Nope," I lie. "Just a neighbor's place."

He doesn't say more, and I don't *offer* any details other than that. Hopefully, he bought it.

"Brownie?" Scar's voice is bright and chipper as she grins at the devil.

He, of course, soaks it all in. "Sure. How much?"

Scar waves him off, like I knew she would. "For you, it's free."

Shane and I both shoot her a look.

"What she *meant* to say is it's five bucks," I interject, casting a bitchy smile toward West. He can afford the upcharge.

Being the freak he is, he smiles back and it grates my nerves.

Without protest, he digs out his wallet, and drops a hundred-dollar bill into the fishbowl where Scar's been stashing her earnings.

"That cover it?" West asks.

Scar's eyes widen and I hate the idea of her idolizing him. And also the idea of him winning over yet another of my family members.

"Oh my gosh! You're awesome!"

Before I can stop her, she's bounding around the table, squeezing West around his waist. Surprised by the attack, he lightly hugs her back.

"I'm Scarlett by the way," she freely shares. And just like that, the thin lie I told is blown to hell. No way he'll buy that I don't live here now.

"Scarlett," West repeats, looking directly at me. "Your sister, right?"

He remembers, from when I stupidly told him too much about my life after orientation. Before I knew he was the devil himself.

I don't answer. A searing hot glare is my only response.

"Yep! The one and only," Scar happily confirms, pushing pink strands behind her ears as she returns to her post.

She tries to play it cool, but I know my sister. She's getting ready to put her foot in her mouth and I see it coming from a mile away.

"So … are you two, like, dating?" There's so much hope in her eyes, all at the mere idea of me dating someone she equates to a celebrity. "I only ask because that's what Pandora seems to think."

Of *course*, she does …

In my peripheral, I'm aware of the moment West casts a slick grin down on me. Right before he answers my sister's probing question.

"Yeah," he lies. "You could say that."

My heart sinks to the pit of my stomach and my focus instantly shifts to Ricky, who's overheard everything. I'd made it a point to squash Pandora's rumor when he first asked, and again a moment ago when we were dancing. Only, now, with West opening his big mouth, I'm sure Ricky thinks I'm a liar.

Awesome.

Ricky turns to face the street instead of looking at me. He's pissed and I see it all over his face.

My skin comes alive at the feel of hot fingers slinking across the small of my back. In the sliver of space where my high-waisted shorts and the t-shirt I've knotted at my ribs meet. West draws me close in a smooth motion that smashes me against his rock-hard body.

For a second, I forget that I hate him, but those feelings come rushing right back when he peers down at me.

"You said something about showing me your room, didn't you?" He slipped the question in so smoothly I have to do a double-take.

"What? I—"

Before I can even form an answer—which would have been a resounding, *'Hell no!'*—his hand eases into my back pocket and I'm ushered toward my front door.

Don't make a scene Blue. You can light into him as soon as you cross the threshold, but don't ... make ... a scene.

I still hadn't forgotten West's threat from the night before. Challenging him in front of his brothers had been enough to stir up talk of burning down my uncle's diner. I could only imagine how much worse his reaction would be if I called him out right here, in front of everyone.

Fear of how far he'd take things is all that keeps me from breaking that hand now gripping my ass as my sister and friends watch him follow me into the house.

The second I close the door behind us, I shove him hard. I feel so much satisfaction when his back slams against the wall, rattling the pictures hanging beside the window.

Even if he *is* completely unfazed and laughing.

"Feel better getting that out your system?"

"What do you think you're doing? Why'd you lie to them?" I cut in, ignoring his snarky comment completely.

He steps away from the wall and straightens his shirt while staring me down. "I think an even *better* question is why you didn't correct me."

I'm seeing pure red. "You think I don't know how that would end?"

The smile on his face broadens, but it's turned wicked. "Well, *somebody's* learning," he croons, seeming pleased with the idea of me finally understanding my place.

"Congrats!" I shout. "You're rich, I'm poor. You have this entire town on your side, and to you I'm nothing. Got it, asshole."

I cross my arms over my chest after speaking and can't even look at him. It's then, in that moment of silence, that I glance around. The place is a wreck. Scar spent her day baking while I worked an early shift with Dusty. There had been no time to clean and, honestly, with school, work, and journalism club all week, it'd been more than a few days since anyone had straightened things.

The frustration that dominated my mood a moment ago is replaced by something else.

Embarrassment.

From the old couch that dips in the middle—thanks to the many nights Mike has chosen to sleep *there* instead of his actual bed, to the collection of empty beer cans and overflowing basket of laundry, to the two fist-sized holes in the wall from a recent episode where my father couldn't control his temper.

West is worming his way into areas of my life I hardly allow the people I trust to enter, let alone my enemy.

"Just ... go," I say softly, feeling the weight of shame holding me in place. I can only imagine the things he'll take back to school about me, about my home.

Before he can even say anything ugly, a door creaks down the hall and my stomach plummets.

"What's all the damn noise about?"

Mike's staggering even more than when he'd come out to terrorize us out front. Meaning, he's downed another bottle or two since then.

"Nothing, Mike," I say as firmly as possible, but my voice is quieter than usual, strained. "West was just leaving."

At least, I hope he is.

Especially as I become aware of the familiar sting in my eyes. The one that usually means tears are on the way. I can't think of anything worse than giving someone who sees me as weak, who believes he owns me, the chance to see me cry.

"Thought I told you bitches not to let any of these hellraisers you call friends into my damn house anymore. You stupid or something?"

I've long-since grown numb to my father's insults, his indifference towards my siblings and I, but it stings especially bad to be treated this way in front of West. Someone who already thinks I'm worthless.

I suppose I don't answer quickly enough for Mike, because his next move is to amble across the living room, coming straight toward me to get in my face. Surprisingly, he's never struck anyone under this roof before, so I don't brace myself for impact, but ... West does.

In what I guess is some kind of knee-jerk reaction, he's suddenly standing between Mike and me. Like a fortress, shielding me from the encroaching storm. Shocked, and very much confused, I'm unsure what to do or say. So, I watch in silence as the two engage in a fierce stare-down.

"Try it, boy," Mike grunts, barely sober enough to stand on his own.

West is unwavering, but his biceps tense when he readies his fists. Just in case, I guess.

"You should back up," is his cold warning to my father. "Maybe go sleep it off before you do something you'll regret ... sir."

Mike doesn't take kindly to threats, but I imagine the polite, and yet stern, tone of West's voice is confusing to him. He certainly wouldn't be the only one with no clue what's going on.

They seem to have reached a stalemate, neither having spoken a word in several seconds. But then, adding to this batshit crazy turn of events, Mike retreats. Yeah, he's grumbling and cursing to himself, but he's doing all those things while slow-walking it back to his bedroom.

There's an awkward silence in the room, hovering between West and me as I keep my stare trained on his back. With each of the deep breaths he draws in, his shoulders rise and fall. But he has yet to face me.

Maybe he can't.

A wall came down I don't think he intended to lower. *Ever.* But what's done is done. There's no taking back what I know—that he just put himself in harm's way for me. If it had been anyone else who intervened just now, I wouldn't hesitate to show my gratitude, thank them, but ... not him.

Never him.

Instead, I'm bitter as hell that he's pushed himself into this corner of my life, seen the dark parts I keep hidden at all costs.

Furious, I can only get one word out of my mouth. "Leave."

I don't regret the chill in my tone. Not even a little. He has no right to be here.

What could have been an act of valor, only feels like an invasion of privacy to me and I want him gone.

Opening the front door makes it clear I mean what I said. And I don't breathe again until West brushes past me without either of us even attempting to make eye contact. Then, he storms down the steps of my porch, hopefully knowing better than to ever come back here again.

The Golden Boys

#FollowMe

@QweenPandora:

Hold up ... RED ALERT: Fellas, hide your ladies if you intend to keep them. It looks like there's a new player in the game. My sources identified this bringer of hotness as Ricky Ruiz. However, his official, Pandora-issued moniker tells you everything you need to know about him—SeXyBeAsT.

If my eyes on the street are right, it seems he may already have his sights set on a prize. Perhaps, ... a prize fit for north side royalty.

Looking at you, KingMidas.

A little friendly advice for our beloved QB-1: It might be time to channel that energy you bring to the field, because from where the rest of us are standing, NewGirl's got options. And since it's my job to express my completely unbiased opinion, I'll give it.

The King might already be too late.

Later, Peeps! 😼

~P.

Chapter 16

BLUE

Today's been quieter than expected. I mean, sure the Golden boys' followers are still on a hundred—whispering insults, purposely bumping me in the halls—but the boys themselves have absolutely nothing for me.

Which should come as a relief, but instead, I'm paranoid as hell.

I make it through lunch with no drama, and I'm admittedly confused. There's been no commentary about my house or my hood. No petty jabs about my drunk-off-his-ass father. The only thing I can come up with for the fight being taken out of West is the weirdness between us over the weekend.

Friday, the kiss that practically made my underwear catch fire.

Saturday, West shielding me from my dad.

Because I've been around Mike all my life, I know he only intended to get in my face about defying his BS rules. No, that's nowhere near okay, but I knew I wasn't in danger. However, to West it looked like more than that. It looked like my raving lunatic of a father was about to haul off and hit me. That is, until my knight in blindingly white Nikes stepped in.

Apparently, no one's allowed to push me around but him. But who knows what goes on inside that sick bastard's mind?

I'm the last one to make it into the girl's locker room to change, and every set of eyes shifts to me when I walk in. I bypass all the chatter and head straight for Lexi, seated at the end of a bench, already wearing her bathing suit.

I'm dreading this for too many reasons to name, but I need the grade. Failure is not an option.

"I vote we skip and go smoke a joint behind the athletic building," she suggests.

"Don't tempt me."

Right after answering, I grab the bathing suit from my duffle bag. Jules loaned me hers, seeing as how I've never had reason to own one.

I disappear inside a stall to change, then return to close my things in the locker. It's not lost on me that Parker's girls haven't taken their eyes off me once. I think it's pretty safe to say whatever they've been discussing since I walked in is likely about me.

Still, I can't find it in my heart to regret what I did to her, their queen. She tried to take me down, so it only seemed fair that I do the same to her.

Not *my* fault I succeeded and she didn't.

Lexi stands when I start toward the door. Already, the heavy scent of chlorine is freaking me out. I've avoided situations such as this my entire life, but Cypress Prep has a knack for shoving me into the worst possible scenarios, which I couldn't hate more.

The heavy door slams behind Lexi and me, and I observe my surroundings. Pale turquoise tile covers the floor, nearly matching the color of the water perfectly. Gigantic windows make up the upper half of the two-story addition off from the school's main building. Bright lights hang from the metal beams above and I accept that this will be the setting of my nightmare.

"You okay?" Lexi asks. "You're shaking."

I glance down at my hands before tightly crossing both arms over my chest.

"I'm cool," I lie.

She shoots me a weird look and then smiles. "If you say so."

Our gazes shift to Mrs. C. as she begins explaining what's

expected of us. However, she only has my attention for the fraction of a second because the door to the boy's locker room has just burst open.

Like every teenage girl's wet dream just spilled into reality, out walks more bronzed skin, ink, and muscle than any girl can reasonably handle. The Golden boys and a handful of their teammates line up on the opposite side of the pool and I swear the temp shot up ten degrees. Their quiet conversation lowers to a hum now that they've joined the rest of us, but a smile still ghosts on West's lips.

Of *course*, I've singled him out from the rest.

His dark hair is lightly tousled on top of his head like always. But without a shirt to cover the superhuman physique marked with the dark images adorning his arms and chest, I barely notice much else.

"See something you like?" Lexi teases, letting me know I'm not being as discreet as I think.

"Not at all," I lie. Truth is, I see *plenty* I like. Just sucks he's so ugly on the inside.

Before averting my gaze, I watch West scan the line where me and the rest of the girls have lined up. There's a slow burning fire in the pit of my stomach, and with it comes a growing need to know for sure I'm the one he's searching for. It's sick and stupid to need confirmation, but I do. In fact, the second his eyes land on me, I glance away, satisfied knowing I was right.

Kissing him has obviously screwed with my head. I've thought about it more than once, and what's worse is that I know it meant nothing to either of us. It was a power play. One that proved his point more than I'd ever let him know.

My eyes are locked squarely on Mrs. C. now, but it isn't easy to do. Not with *him* standing on the other side.

"Okay, jump in and warm up," Mrs. C. announces. A cacophony of screams and splashes follows. Lexi joins the others, but I've decided it's probably time to speak up about my limitations.

The whole *'I can't swim'* thing might present a few problems.

With most in the pool, the group has thinned enough that I notice Parker seated in a chair near the wall. Her ankle is neatly bandaged, her crutches are propped beside her, and she's staring right at me. I probably shouldn't, but I smirk at her, just to make it known that I regret absolutely nothing.

Mrs. C. glances up when I approach, and I note the weary smile that flashes across her face. I'm guessing she's still on the fence about whether Parker's accident really was one.

Nervous, I pick at the end of my braid as I begin to speak.

"Can I ... talk to you for a sec?" I force the words from my mouth.

Her brow quirks. "Of course. Always."

Breathing deep, I just spit it out. "I can't swim. I had a ... *thing* happen when I was a kid, so I never learned."

Her head tilts slowly. "You aren't the first newbie I've had," she shares. "It just means your milestones will be a little different than the others'. Instead of working on timing and technique, you'll have until the end of the unit to learn how to actually swim. I'll need to see you get from end to end to earn a passing grade. I can work with you, but would you prefer that I assign a classmate to help instead?"

I hated the idea of *anyone* having to babysit me, but especially a classmate.

"I'll figure it out," I answer, offering a tense smile right after.

She passes another weary look my way, then goes back to taking attendance on her tablet. Meanwhile, I turn to hightail it back to the shallow end.

A deep breath leaves my mouth and I'm trying to wrap my mind around facing my biggest fear. My eyes are focused on the intermittent tiles I step across, counting down the numbers printed on them.

Thirteen feet.

Twelve feet.

Elev—

"Payback, bitch."

A hard shove to my shoulder knocks me off balance, and those are the last words I hear. There isn't time to catch myself or even *scream* before going under. First, there's the shock of the cold water rushing over my skin, but then there's only panic as I struggle to break the surface.

Still, for all my effort, it's no use. My limbs flail wildly as I try to grab ahold of something or *someone*, but nothing helps. Every move I make pulls me under deeper and deeper. It doesn't make a difference that I'm surrounded by bodies bobbing in this deathtrap, because there are none close enough to touch.

None who notice I'm in trouble.

A large gulp of water fills my lungs and immediately feeling the situation become more dire, I fight harder, but it still doesn't matter.

I'm going to die here, in this gigantic pool, and no one will know the difference until it's too late. My vision starts to darken and I'm blacking out. The thought that comes to mind is of Scar. It's my only comfort.

I'm starting to fade, but I'm aware of an arm slipping around me, looping across my ribs. Suddenly, I feel weightless and it dawns on me that I'm floating toward the surface.

Apparently, my appointment with death is now postponed.

"Move! Get the fuck out the way!"

The deep voice booms only inches from my ear. And sure enough, at his command, the crowd that's gathered near the edge of the pool backs off.

My hands are taken, and someone pulls. Meanwhile, whoever just dove eleven feet down to save me has both hands planted on my ass, hoisting me over the edge. I collapse there on the tile, hacking up both lungs, gagging on the mouthfuls of water I swallowed before being rescued.

"What's going on?" Mrs. C. races closer, lowering to her knees to look me over while the sound of rushing water signals me when my savior finally emerges from the pool.

I'm still too choked up to talk, so someone speaks *for* me.

"She fell," the deep voice answers, sounding winded.

Despite myself, I turn to confirm what I suspect. That the voice does, indeed, belong to West.

He's pretty close, sitting sideways right behind me. His knee gently settles against my back. Slowly, as if suddenly aware of my gaze being set on him, *his* rises to meet mine. Two emotions seem to be at war within him, if that look on his face means anything. There's the clear presence of concern, but just beneath it, is anger.

As if he's furious because me nearly drowning has been an inconvenience.

I face forward again, still struggling for air.

"I watched for her to resurface, but ... she never did," he continues, telling a bold-faced lie. Either he's just made a monumentally horrible guess, or ... is he protecting them? Lying to cover for his cunt of a girlfriend?

"Good work, Golden," Mrs. C. declares. "You likely just saved her life."

Lexi settles in front of me and this is when I realize she'd been the one who pulled me out a moment ago.

"Shit, Blue. You okay?"

"Language, Rodriquez," Mrs. C. reminds her.

"My bad, but ... dude, you almost died," Lexi says, stating the obvious.

Her very accurate depiction of what just took place has me scanning the small crowd. And right there, flanking Parker at either side, are Heidi and Ariana. All three are grinning, satisfied with having nearly killed me.

One word spoken as I was shoved into the pool comes back to my memory.

'Payback'. The attacker said *'payback.'*

Ariana flashes her middle finger at me, and their cackling grows louder, but apparently not loud enough to catch Mrs. C's attention. Instead, she's focused on dialing down to the office, asking the nurse to come check me out.

"I'm fine," I assure her. "Really. You don't need to do that."

She casts an uncertain glance toward me, but after giving me a quick onceover, concedes.

"Are you lightheaded at all? Feeling out of sorts?"

I shake my head to that question. "No. None of that."

That answer apparently satisfies her, because she dials the

number back a moment later, letting the nurse know her assistance won't be needed. Then she casts a look toward West.

"Golden, I think I have a special assignment for you this term," she says with a grin. "Ms. Riley here has until the end of this unit to learn how to swim. And seeing as how you've just proven you're capable of handling her, I believe you'd be just the man for the job. What do you say?"

"Wait. What?" I croak, still struggling to find my voice.

"You need to master this by the end of the marking period, and I trust West will look after you. He's a good kid," she adds, and I can't fight the scowl that twists my mouth.

"So, what do you say West?" Mrs. C. asks.

My eyes shift to him again, staring as he searches for an answer.

"Sure," he says begrudgingly, clearly unhappy with his new assignment.

"Good. It's settled then," Mrs. C. adds, standing to her feet again. "Can you look after Ms. Riley for a few minutes? Make sure she pulls it together?"

I listen as she asks, wondering just how much West hates me right now.

When he finally does answer with a polite, "Sure," there's a hint of frustration hidden within it.

Mrs. C. turns toward the onlookers and points to the pool. "Okay, show's over. Hop back in and get to it."

The next second, it's just us. The crowd has thinned, and West and I are thrust into an awkward silence. Of course, because I'm trying *not* to think about that kiss, now it's *all* I can think about

He draws his knees toward his chest and props both elbows there, staring out across the pool while I shift beside him to sit cross-legged. Not as close as a moment ago, but still close.

"You gonna thank me? Or are we gonna just sit here and pretend I didn't save your life?"

The corner of my mouth twitches with a smile, hearing him jump right back into character, turning back into the *real* West.

"Maybe I'll thank you when you call off your dogs," I counter.

"Seeing as how someone from your crew is the whole reason you had to ... as you say ... 'save me'."

He smirks, too. "For what it's worth, I didn't give the okay this time."

"Ah, so they've gone rogue. Telltale sign of poor leadership," I deduce, hoping he senses that I'm being smug as hell right now.

"Maybe," he teases with a shrug. "But let's say I do like you said, and call them off, who on Earth would keep me entertained all day?"

I swear, if I didn't think he'd catch my fist in midair, I'd knock that grin right off his face.

"Besides," he continues, "you know what they say. What doesn't kill you only makes you stronger. So, in *that* sense, I'm doing you a favor, Southside."

There's the callous dick I love to hate.

My eyes rise with him when he stands, and I'm still dumbfounded by his logic. Or lack thereof.

"On that note, I'm out," he announces, watching our classmates instead of making eye contact with me. "And if you, somehow, find yourself in any more trouble, you're on your own from here."

"I didn't ask for your help in the first place," I snap.

Also, it goes without saying, but I hadn't asked for his help when he stepped between me and Mike either.

At the sound of my words, West's head tilts back until he's facing the ceiling. He lets out a cocky chuckle that fries my nerves.

"Well, if it makes you feel any better," he scoffs, "I was *this* close to letting your ass drown. So, suffice it to say, we're *both* a little disappointed with how things turned out."

My blood is starting to pump faster, rushing through my veins like a surging river.

"So, that's your plan? You're just gonna cover for them after I nearly drowned out there?" I call out. "You're fine pretending it wasn't one of *your* girls who pushed me?"

"Got proof of that?"

"Nope, but I have an ass kicking with all three of those bitches' names on it. That good enough?"

He's standing a foot or two away, with his back partially toward me, but I see his smile. The sight of it makes my stomach twist in a way I don't approve of, because it's not completely coming from a place of hatred.

"Do what you gotta do," are his final words, leaving me to watch as he gracefully dives into the water, showing off for those of us whose swim style is similar to that of a rock.

Mrs. C.'s decision to pair me with West is the icing on the cake. Seems the more I try to distance myself from this guy, the more the universe pulls us back into one another's space. I'm not sure what it is, but it's a cycle I need to break.

Quickly.

Chapter 17

BLUE

Thank you, Dr. Pryor. Thank you *so* freakin' much for making me join journalism club.

Insert sarcasm here.

I like the lady and all, but this has to be the worst fit she could've ever chosen for me. It's bad enough the other students have no sense of time, accounting for our half-hour, afterschool meetings turning into a full hour most days. But Mr. Dansk assigning me to cover sports this quarter is going to be the death of me.

I had to bail on Uncle Dusty to be here, taking stupid pictures at Cypress Prep's first home game of the season. Friday nights are our busiest at the diner, but he assured me he can get by without me. Doesn't change the fact that I'd much rather be there, waiting tables, than sitting here on these cold bleachers.

Jules and Scar, on the other hand, love it. Scar even dragged Shane out here to watch. From the looks of it, I'm the only one who's miserable. Nothing like enduring the chilled rain and being forced to snap pictures of my nemesis to kick off the weekend.

Thank God I listened to the forecast. First thing I did when I rushed home between school and the game was grab one of Mike's oversized jackets from the closet. Which is when Scar and Jules begged to come watch King Midas and crew likely bring in another win.

These are difficult waters to navigate. So far, I've successfully hidden the true nature of my dealings with West. The last thing I need is Scar and Jules intervening. Not when I've worked so hard to stay off school administration's radar. This may stem from some deep-seated trust issues with authority, but I could see it now. I turn West in, his parents strike back, next thing I know I'm finishing out the year at some random, alternative school for troubled children. Goodbye college plans.

Long story short, I've settled on suffering in silence for the remainder of my time here.

It only helps that West seems resigned to let the world believe Pandora's ruse—that there's some sort of romantic involvement between us. Although, for his own reasons, I imagine. Most likely because he knows how the idea of it sickens me. In fact, aside from setting the girls loose on me, no one else seems to know about the toxicity between us. This reminds me of a statement he made last weekend. The one about my only response to being told to "jump" should be "how high". With how the girls haven't spread the truth around school, I can only imagine they'd given in to that twisted rhetoric.

But I digress. Apparently, I've got pictures to take.

West snaps a pass across the field and I capture the image with my phone just as the ball leaves his hand. We're deep into the fourth quarter and I hate to admit it, but he's managed to impress me tonight. Although, not nearly as much as he's impressed Jules and Scar. Both will be hoarse by morning with how they've screamed for the team.

For West, in particular.

Ugh ... traitors. Even if they don't have a clue that I hate his guts.

My phone buzzes and, glancing at the screen to see who's texted, I stare at a snippet of the tenth message Ricky has sent in the last hour. Without opening it, I'm certain it has nothing to do with me having

Shane in my care. Because, if it *is* about that, he'd text him directly. This is something else.

Like, the same conversation he's been trying to have with me for weeks.

I'm jarred from my thoughts when Scar jumps to her feet, screeching in my ear. Dane—who I've come to learn is wide receiver extraordinaire—has been on fire tonight. The throw West launched was plucked out of the air so gracefully the whole thing played out like a choreographed dance. They're graceful and yet fierce, in tune with the game. In tune with each other as they move across the field. It's no wonder they went undefeated last season.

"Do you think you can get the Golden boys to sign my t-shirt?" My sister, the turncoat herself, asks. "I mean, since you and West are basically a thing," she adds. "Their autographs will *definitely* be worth something one day. Just look at them out there!"

She's trying to gut me. She *has* to be.

Jules catches my gaze and cracks up, but Shane isn't nearly as amused by Scar's newfound obsession with the triplets. If I'm not mistaken, he looks a little bothered by it. Poor kid.

When Scar turns to face the field again, I don't miss that those stars are back. The ones I've seen in our mother's eyes over the years. The ones that make me worry Scar will fall victim to some of the same snares.

The crowd explodes in a deafening roar when Cypress Prep scores another touchdown, bringing the final score to an embarrassing forty-eight to twelve.

Well, embarrassing for the other team, that is.

However, our guys aren't celebrating like I would expect. Instead, they're surprisingly subdued as the stands empty and fans rush to the sidelines. And the center of their attention seems to be QB-1. West.

For the sake of my role with the paper, I focus the lens of my camera on him, zoom in, and snap a picture just as he flashes a smile at some kid who's brought his football to the field to be signed.

"See? I'm not the only one!" Scar pleads. "Even *that* kid knows we're witnessing history in the making."

I barely get to roll my eyes when another message comes through. This time, I open it and Jules must see my expression shift, because she speaks up.

"Everything okay?"

I don't answer right away, because I'm suddenly distracted by the roar of a motorcycle engine. Ricky revs it when he spots me from the parking lot, letting me know the text stating that he wasn't afraid to show up here if I didn't answer hadn't been an empty threat. Guess he wasn't in a mood to be ignored today.

Jules lifts a few inches out of her seat, just enough to see what I see—a very frustrated Ricky Ruiz pulling off his helmet, likely headed toward these bleachers to speak his piece.

"Um ... need me to keep an eye on these two while you take care of that?"

Frustrated, a heavy sigh leaves my mouth. "Please."

The next second, I'm storming down the bleachers, but not without King Midas taking notice. Amidst a sea of his adoring fans, his gaze is set on me. Already pissed and wondering who Ricky thinks he is showing up here, I take it out on West by giving him the finger. Of course, the bastard finds it funny, lowering his head when a smirk touches his lips.

Whatever.

I swear, I'm beyond fed up with the cocky, domineering men in my life.

Ricky's eyes are on me the entire time I trudge across the grass, and his glare hardens when I make it to him.

"What the hell do you think you're doing here?"

"Didn't you get my messages?" he snaps.

Sighing, I fold both arms over my chest. "I was busy."

Something I say makes him scoff, looking out toward the field when he tips his chin.

"Yeah, I bet."

It isn't until I follow his gaze that I understand what that means. Apparently, not only do we have West's undivided attention, but he's trudging this way—drenched in sweat, toting his helmet in hand.

"Not that. Not ... *him*," I say softly. "I had a school thing and ... wait. Why am I even explaining this to you?" I ask, remembering that I have zero obligation to Ricky whatsoever. Haven't for a long time.

West draws closer and I'm holding my breath, unsure what his intentions are as he approaches, but then he passes by like a storm I narrowly dodged. However, I don't miss that deadly glare in his eyes. Only, he doesn't cast that look at *me*.

It's for Ricky.

It isn't one of those looks that comes and goes quickly. It lingers between the two until West makes it to the fieldhouse and slams the door behind him.

It doesn't come as a surprise when Ricky's shoulders square with tension. I see it through his dark t-shirt, in the way the veins on his arms protrude, in the tension held in his jaw.

He won't even look at me now.

"I didn't come here for trouble," he states first. "Just thought you should know Hunter's getting transferred. They're moving him upstate."

My eyes widen with the news, as a flash of sadness shoots through my chest. No, I haven't found the courage to visit since he got locked up, but there's some small measure of comfort in knowing he's not so far away. But to move him upstate? That feels like having him taken away all over again.

I'm aware of the emotion bleeding through my expression, so I correct it before Ricky might notice. Because, truth is, this changes nothing. Hunter's still gone, I'm still doing this all on my own, and I'm still not ready to see him like that.

"Okay," I finally respond. "Thanks for letting me know."

Ricky's brow draws together as he takes that in. "Thanks for letting you know? That's all you have to say, B? Thanks for letting you know?"

"What more do you want from me?" I snap.

"I want you to stop being selfish!" Those words hit me square in the chest, like a searing hot knife, breaking skin.

"... Selfish?" I feel like the wind has been knocked out of me. "Name one thing in my life that's completely about me?"

When his expression softens, I imagine he regrets his choice of words, but they're out there. No taking them back.

"You know I didn't mean it like that. You do a lot for Scar. I only meant that—"

"This isn't your business," I remind him. "Nothing concerning me, or my family is your business. You've done enough already, haven't you?"

My words seem to have struck him, like how his hit me.

"What the hell's *that* supposed to mean?"

A group of girls cackle as they walk past and I hold my tongue until no one's around to hear.

"It means you were the one who got Hunter into all this. You were the one who linked him up with your Uncle Paul, got him started on this path."

I'm fighting tears, but I'm not so sure I'll win.

"That's what you think?" Ricky snaps.

"All I know is, Hunter used to be good," I remind him. "Once upon a time, he was responsible, and then he got caught up with you and—"

"That's what you think happened?" he interrupts again. "First of all, I've known your brother since we were little, Blue. So, your logic doesn't even add up. I didn't just come into the picture the day before Hunter started getting into shit."

There's a familiar pain in my chest and I know it well. It's the ache of abandonment. The sting of loneliness.

"Now, I'll be the first to admit I'm no angel," he continues, "but I've only ever looked out for Hunter. He's as much a brother to me as Shane."

Guilt. It slams face-first into me, because I know what he's saying is true.

At the first sign of water pooling in my eyes, I turn to walk away, but halt. In part because of the sudden, light hold Ricky now has on my wrist. But I'm also frozen in place because West is back, and his eyes are laser-focused right where Ricky's got a hold on me.

Still sporting the all-black uniform with his number embossed in gold, right in the center of his chest, he doesn't move. My guess is that he's heading back toward the field where some of his team still lingers. But now, the only thing he's aware of is me.

Something's clearly sparked anger within him and I admittedly don't understand. Is it because he wants to stamp out any sign of happiness in my life? And, in his mind, Ricky is a potential source of happiness for me? Something he needs to kill before I get too high and mighty, thinking I can have one single thing in this world without him screwing it up?

It's the only thing that makes sense.

I'm lost in thought until Ricky's hand slips down from my wrist, linking his fingers with mine. Cool gray eyes lock me in place, and I push aside thoughts of the brute seething behind me.

"I'm not saying Hunter was never good. All I'm saying is, I'm not the one who turned him bad," Ricky declares. "Might want to look a little closer to home if you need someone to blame."

I'm not quite sure what that means, but neither my pride nor my pain will let me ask. There's a stretch of silence between us and when his gaze flickers over my shoulder, I know exactly who he's staring at.

Frustration sets in and I snatch my hand from his, using it to wipe the tear that's escaped.

"I need to go check on Scar and Shane. Anything else?" I ask, forcing my tone to go cold.

He's quiet, like there's something more he wants to say. "Nah, just tell Shane I won't be home when he gets there. I have things to take care of."

I nod but don't say a word.

More than aware of both sets of eyes locked on me, I refuse to look at either. Ricky's bike thunders when he climbs back on and revs it. Then, he leaves just as quickly as he swept in. I've already made up my mind to call and apologize later, because I know he catches the bulk of my bitchiness, but my emotions have to settle first. Even knowing he always means well, I'm honestly starting to resent him coming around. Simply because he never seems to bring any good news.

Ever.

Chapter 18

BLUE

I haven't seen Scar this happy in weeks. Yeah, she loved being at the game, but it's also clear that we needed this time together. She misses me, hates that I'm away from home so much, but I never doubt that she understands why. It doesn't go over her head that I'd be around more if I could.

First thing in the morning, I'll be waiting tables at the diner, but tonight is all about her.

A phone call from Uncle Dusty takes us on a slight detour. It only takes him saying he's made us dinner to bring home and we eagerly deviate from our path. Despite likely being overwhelmed with customers in my absence, he still made time to take care of us.

Like always.

I hadn't made either Scar nor myself much of a lunch, and didn't have money for concessions at the game, so it goes without saying that we're starving by the time we reach our side of town.

We drop off Shane and Jules, then I make the quick drive home, going as fast as I'm legally permitted. The second Scar and I burst through the back door, laughing loud enough to wake the dead, we race for the kitchen sink.

"Respect your elders," I yell, yanking her backward by her shirt.

A shriek leaves her mouth and she playfully shoves me aside. It's a fight to the death, both wrestling to be the first to wash our hands and dig into whatever Uncle Dusty sent this time.

One solid hip bump knocks Scar into the cabinet and I'm in the lead. By the time she finally catches her breath from laughing, I'm done rinsing and grabbing two forks from the drawer.

"You cheated!" she yells. "No one stands a chance against those hips."

"Hey! Watch it," I warn her, laughing at the well-timed insult.

She ignores me, opting to forego an apology, and drops down in the seat across from me.

"Ah, burgers," she sighs after flipping open the lid of her to-go container. A second before digging in, she dramatically inhales the aroma.

"I know you thanked him when we stopped into the diner, but don't forget to shoot Dusty a text later, too," I remind her.

"Always do."

The only thing that keeps me from wolfing down my food is that I'm now caught up watching my sister. Not only is she breathtakingly beautiful, she's also the best kid I know—good grades, responsible. I probably shouldn't take credit for that, but I can't help feeling like I kind of had a hand in her being so awesome. Of all the things I've ever done, helping take care of her is the most meaningful.

"I was so hungry my stomach was two seconds from eating itself," she says with her mouth full. "Only thing missing is ketchup."

She hops out of her seat and I watch as she bounds over to the fridge. From down the hall, the floorboards creak after Mike's door slams, and I know he's coming this way.

Scar doesn't say a word, but she rolls her eyes in anticipation of good ol' dad joining us in the kitchen.

"How come no one told me it was dinnertime?" His speech is slurred, which doesn't come as a surprise.

"Because there's no dinner for *you*," I answer.

Scar takes her seat again and our gazes lock across the table.

My gut tells me it's time to gather our containers, grab a blanket, and eat picnic-style on my bedroom floor. It's what we used to do when our parents would get into it back when we were kids. I'd lock the door and turn the radio up to drown them out. She was young enough that it worked—out of sight, out of mind—but Hunter and I knew all too well what went on beyond that bedroom door.

"Let me have a fry," Mike grumbles, reaching toward Scar's food without asking.

"Touch anything on that plate and you won't live to taste it." My warning earns me a hard glare from my father.

A haughty laugh leaves him, and he folds both arms over his CPPD t-shirt—a throwback to when he was still on the force. You know, when he was still a respected citizen of this town.

"You think you're real hot shit, don't you?" he asks. "Walking around here acting like you're better than everyone else, when the truth is—"

"Please," I begged. "Please tell me what you think you know about me. Seeing as how you've never in your life taken any interest in any *one* of your kids, Mike."

His glassy stare levels on me again and I sense a challenge in his eyes. Another humorless laugh leaves his mouth and I'm tense all over, ready for whatever insult he's prepared to hurl at me next.

"Your just like your mother. You know that?"

This is his favorite insult, and the way those words leave his mouth, there's no mistaking he believes them to be the most hurtful thing he could possibly say to me. Which speaks volumes about how he feels about her. For now, anyway. Were she to come home today, he'd welcome her with open arms. No questions asked.

"Well, maybe it's because Mom and I have *one* thing in common," I reply, staring him straight in the eyes. "We both hate *your* sorry ass."

The muscle in his jaw hardens as my words cut deeper than I realize they will. And to push me to my limit, he swipes his hand across the table, knocking both mine and Scar's dinner to the kitchen floor.

"There!" he chuffs with a big, satisfied grin. "Now you two bitches can eat it off the floor like the dogs you are."

My blood is boiling. I've had my share of bullying already. The difference is, at school I can't do anything about West Golden. But here, on the southside, under this roof, I can do whatever the hell I want.

"Blue, no!"

Scar's voice sounds so faint in my ears when I lunge out of my seat. Mike tries to take off when he realizes I'm coming for him, but I'm too quick and he's too drunk.

"Let her go!" Scar screams next, when Mike reaches behind his head and grabs me by my neck. I'm clinging to him like glue, though, while he spins wildly, trying to fling me off him. But I won't let go. Especially now that I have a tight grip around his throat with my forearm.

I don't know what my plan is. To choke him out, maybe? To drag an apology out of him for being the reason my sister will go to bed without a meal? I'm not sure, but I do know I want him to suffer like we suffer every day of our lives, simply because we were cursed to be born his children.

"I'll kill you," he chokes out with saliva gurgling in his mouth. He's clawing at my arm now, but even with the deep scratch marks he leaves, I'm nowhere close to giving up.

"Tell her you're sorry," I roar. "And give me your wallet, so I can buy her something else to eat and be the parent you never were."

My demand only seems to anger him more. Pissed off and gasping for air, he rears back with all his might, slamming me hard against the wall.

"Stop it!" Scar screams. She's hysterical now and I can only pray Ms. Levinson doesn't hear her.

"The hell are you yelling at *me* for?" Mike forces from his mouth. "Crazy bitch attacked *me!*"

For once, I didn't totally disagree with him. I *am* a crazy bitch, and he's the one who made me this way.

I tighten my grip and my action draws an even stronger reaction from him. One that doesn't just leave me breathless, but sends a sharp pain shooting through my shoulder. With every ounce of strength I haven't choked out of him, Mike charges backwards toward the wall, ramming me right into the sharp corner.

As badly as I want to take him down, *I'm* the one who gives in.

My arm loosens from around his neck and with a loud thud, I'm on the ground. He staggers away, pawing at his throat like he's on the brink of death, finally teetering clumsily into a chair.

"You've lost your damn mind!" he croaks, sounding hoarse. Knowing I managed to hurt him is some small consolation for the pain I feel spreading through my back and shoulder. If it hurts this bad now, I can only imagine what it'll feel like by morning.

"Are you okay?" Tears are streaming down Scar's face when she asks me this question, which makes guilt spike in my stomach.

She needs reassurance, so I nod, even though the last thing I want to do at the moment is move.

A pink ponytail whips through the air when she casts a sharp glare toward Mike.

"What is *wrong* with you?" she screams, calling the tears to come faster. I lift a hand to push them away, but it doesn't matter, because they're falling in sheets now.

Mike volleys a look between the two of us, working his jaw in anger, and then stands. He casts a gaze around the kitchen as he kicks over his seat as one last pathetic show of dominance.

"Pull yourself together and get this mess cleaned up."

He leaves us with those words, and I feel anger I didn't even know I had in me, bubbling up from my gut, urging me to launch another attack on him. Pain and all. The only thing that stops me from leaping onto him again is Scar. She's a sobbing mess and it's on me to fix it.

Mike has a way of foiling my attempts at creating the illusion that we have a normal life here. Tonight is a shining example of that.

When Scar takes her phone from her pocket, I'm confused at first, but see that the first two numbers she dials are nine and one.

"Scar, no!" That plea leaves my mouth much harsher than I mean for it to, but it was one-hundred-percent necessary.

"He can't just do these things," she belts out from some broken place within her. It's someplace hidden, so deep down I fear it's *too* deep for me to mend it.

Her statement isn't wrong, but there are things she doesn't understand. As calmly as I can, I place a hand on her phone and lower it.

"Scar, if you involve the police, they won't just arrest Mike and go on their way," I explain. "They'll take him away, then take *you* away, and … that can't happen."

As much as I like to think *she* needs *me,* I'm well-aware that this works both ways. I need my sister. She keeps me sane, gives me something to fight for, something to *live* for.

There's a short pause that leaves me worried. Sure, Scar might not call the cops on Mike today, but what if she says the wrong thing to the wrong person at school and—

"Promise me, Scar," I plead as it plays out in my head. "Promise me you'll keep anything that happens here between us."

She glances down when I knock her phone aside and squeeze both her hands in mine. I can't say for sure she understands completely how these things work, but I do believe she can see the desperation in my eyes. It's proven when some of the blind emotion clears from her expression and she gives a solid nod in response.

I know that look. Because I'd given it several times myself growing up. It's the look of a kid who's seen too much.

"I promise," she finally concedes, and I pull her into a tight embrace.

Although this evening has been nothing like either of us expected, I kept my word. I said tonight would be all about her and it is. Everything I do—even the things that make me look insane—are because of one truth I will never outrun.

Out of all the things I've ever loved, Scarlett is the only thing I have left.

Chapter 19

WEST

Scratch marks down one arm.

A huge bruise on her shoulder.

What the hell is going on with this girl?

She notices me staring and adjusts the strap of her bathing suit. Sure, like *that'll* hide it.

Hard fail.

I'm so distracted by the deep, purple mark she's sporting, I hardly hear Mrs. C.'s short lecture about pool safety and being mindful of our surroundings. Even when she dismisses us to jump into the pool, I'm one of the last ones to move.

The only one more hesitant than me is Southside. Likely because of last week's incident that resulted in her nearly drowning.

"Up for this?" Mrs. C. asks, approaching me from behind. I glance at her and then follow her gaze back to Southside. "She's gonna need a lot of work, but you're probably the strongest swimmer I have."

I wipe the concern from my expression and nod. "It won't be a problem."

Mrs. C. offers a tight grin. "Good. Today's your first day on the job."

She turns and leaves me to it, and I'm aware of what a huge

opportunity this is to further get under Southside's skin, but for some reason, I'm not feeling it today. Maybe it's the bruises and cuts she's wishing desperately to hide. Whatever the case, I can't shake the notion that she's probably had enough hell over the weekend.

As I approach, she casts a weary gaze toward me. One that spurs a feeling I wasn't quite expecting.

Guilt.

There's real fear and mistrust in her eyes and I did everything in my power to put it there.

"Not today, West," she groans. "I know what Mrs. C. said, but I'm just going to walk the pool for the hour, so you're relieved of your duties."

My eyes are on her as she descends the steps, wincing as the cold touches new parts of her skin. As a closeted admirer of her figure, I notice when the chill reaches her tits, hardening her nipples beneath her bathing suit.

Focus, asshole.

"Not my call," I answer, hiding all traces of sympathy and lust from my tone. "I'm not failing one of the easiest classes I have because you don't feel like putting forth the effort."

Her stare darkens as I join her in the water, keeping a fair amount of distance between us. Mostly to make sure I'm not tempted to eye-bang her like I just did a second ago.

"So, how much do you actually suck at this?" I ask. "Can you at least float?"

She's full-on glaring at me now. "Hmm ... let's see. Did it *look* like I could float last week? You know, when I practically drowned?"

A smirk slips. She's sassy, and in a world where everyone puts on their best face to make sure they stay in my good graces, it's surprisingly refreshing. She keeps it real when no one else has the balls.

"Smart-ass," I mutter.

"Dumb-ass" she shoots back.

She's fighting it, but one corner of her mouth tugs up. She *wants* to smile, even if pride won't allow it.

"Let's just get this over with," she says with a sigh. "What do I do first?" Her tone is cold and indifferent, but I have reason to believe she's anything but that.

"Well, seeing as how you have the skillset of an infant, we need to start with the basics. You've gotta get comfortable holding your breath underwater."

A look of sheer terror fills her expression.

"That ... gonna be a problem?" My brow quirks with the question.

There's a brief moment where she doesn't speak. Then, a sharp breath leaves those full, pink lips I hate that I still think about from time to time.

"It's fine," she concedes. "Just explain what I need to do."

I suppress a laugh. "There's nothing to explain. Just breathe in deep, hold it, then lean into the water until your face and ears are submerged. I'll count to ten, then you come back up."

That distrust in her eyes grows.

"No funny shit, West. I mean it. If I feel you trying to hold me under, I'll junk punch you so fast you'll—"

"Relax, Southside. My grade depends on this, too, remember?"

She doesn't give in easily but, eventually, she calms down a little.

"Ten seconds," she reminds me. "Not a second longer."

"That's the plan."

Another of her death stares and she does as instructed.

I count her down as promised and she pops back up, drawing in a dramatic breath like she's been under for minutes, not seconds.

Trying not to laugh at her is going to kill me, I swear.

"Relax," I say to her again. "You're fine."

Without thinking, my hands are on her waist, trying to remind her she's safe and isn't alone. However, the second I realize what I've done, I pull back.

"Try it again."

I've earned myself one of her familiar *'Are you crazy?'* looks and nod at her.

"Come on. This time we're gonna double the time."

She's already shaking her head before I even finish. "No way. I barely made it ten seconds," she protests.

This girl who's, literally afraid of nothing, is terrified of four-feet of water? Something's up.

"What is it? You fall in your pool trying to reach one of your Barbies as a kid?"

I'm laughing, but she isn't. And judging by the scolding look she just passed my way, I'm guessing there *is* a story. And it isn't nearly as funny as I just assumed.

"You've seen where I live and you've met my dad, so if you think there's anything but weeds and a couple broken lawn chairs in my backyard, you're sadly mistaken."

That usual sassiness is there, but it's buried now, beneath a ton of emotional baggage. Her walls have never been low enough for me to notice before, but I see her now. Enough to know she's a girl who carries a lot and doesn't have much to show for it.

Perfect prey for a man like my father.

A spark of sympathy tries to ignite within me, but I don't allow it. There's no excuse for getting involved with a married man. Not even having a piss-poor life you'd do anything to escape.

"Again," I command coldly, remembering exactly who she is and why I can never forget it.

She rolls her eyes and groans, but does what I told her to. The twenty seconds pass quickly and, like I said, she didn't die.

"Better," I admit. "Now, let's try getting you to float. Then, maybe we'll have time to try some kicking and arm movements."

Her gaze shifts down to the water then, but she doesn't immediately protest, which isn't like her.

I'm already feeling frustrated with her lack of cooperation. "What now, Southside?"

Her eyes flash toward my chest when I cross my arms over it.

"Nothing," she forces out. "I just ... I did something to my shoulder, and I can't really move it all that well."

Half-surprised she even mentioned it, my eyes are drawn there. Although the bruise isn't visible from this angle, I haven't forgotten. Nor have I stopped wondering how it got there.

My gaze flickers to hers when I have a flashback to Friday night, when I spotted her in the parking lot with that dickhead with the motorcycle. He was all over her at the block party, so I can only guess there's something going on between them.

"Your friend do that to you?"

Confusion flashes in her gaze. "What friend?"

My brow quirks. "The one who seems to make it a point to be wherever *you* are."

Damn ... I sound bitter as hell. Check that shit.

When it takes her a few seconds to answer, I'm starting to think she read more into my tone than I meant for her to.

"You mean Ricky?"

"Fuck if *I* know his name," I snap. "The asshole who grabbed your wrist when you were crying after the game."

She seems shocked that I remember the details so clearly, but I ignore what that probably implies. Instead, I maintain my cold expression, waiting for her to answer.

Her eyes close and stay that way a few seconds. "No, Ricky would never lay a finger on me."

What about his dick? Does he lay that on you sometimes?

I catch myself before letting those very words leave my mouth, choosing instead to stick to the script.

"If not him, then who?" I ask. "Because you and I both know you didn't do this yourself. So, before you feed me some bullshit about slamming it on a cabinet or falling down the stairs, know I'm not buying it."

There's a standoff between us. One in which I find her incredibly hard to read.

"Why are you doing this?" she asks, pushing strands of her drenched hair behind her ears. "We both know you don't care what happens to me one way or another. So, why is it so important that I answer you?"

My chest moves steadily with the deep breaths I draw in. This conversation has left me feeling exposed, like I've let her see the man behind the mask. This realization is the perfect opportunity to correct my own wrong, but I forego it to ask another question.

"Your dad. Was it him?"

There's a measure of surprise that briefly fills her expression and I didn't miss it. It's enough to leave me thinking I just hit the nail on the head. And to drive that point home, she didn't jump to his defense like she did this Ricky guy.

"He do shit like this often?"

She rolls her eyes before answering. "It wasn't him," she insists. "Now would you just drop it? Please?"

I study her for a long stretch, wishing I had already unearthed her tells, the signals she gives when she's lying. But I don't know her like that.

"So, thirty seconds, right?" she asks, trying to shift the subject back to her swimming lesson. She passes me an impatient look and I hold back from asking anything else.

"I'll count," I say instead, mulling over the sparse details as Southside goes under.

The conversation did nothing to expose her secrets, but it's shined a light on several of mine. Like, how I'm a little too concerned with what happened to her over the weekend. As the one who swore I wanted her to suffer by my hand, why is it so hard to let this go?

I should be ecstatic that someone else is making her life a living hell, picking up the slack when I'm not around, but I'm finding it hard to get off on her misery today. Which I had no problem with just one short week ago. Somehow, I'd let her get under my skin, and I hate it. With a passion.

She pops above the surface of the water again, doing that same ridiculous gasping routine as before. As I watch her overreact, and nearly smack some unsuspecting nerd girl in the face as she swims by, I'm aware of the damn soft spot forming for the one I swore to ruin.

It was never a secret that the sexual tension between us was blistering hot, from that first time I laid eyes on her at the bonfire. But what comes as an unwelcomed surprise is that I find myself drawn in by more than just her looks. Even the dorky mess I'm staring at *now* gets to me.

Something about this girl ... it makes me want to pull her close and block out all the bad things she seems to draw to her like a magnet. People like me, her dad.

My dad.

Don't get distracted. This changes nothing. She's still the enemy.

The short pep talk I give myself brings me back to my senses. I chose my side weeks ago, when I found the pic in the safe. I decided then that I'd find and destroy her. It's a means to righting my own wrongs from the past, starting with being too young to do something about the *first* affair I found out about.

If being attracted to Southside is the only thing that stands between me and making things as close to right as I can—without simultaneously tearing my mother's world apart—I can manage that.

From now on, I'm keeping the blinders on. Her problems are just that. *Her* problems. Including me, the biggest, most resilient problem of them all.

And as God is my witness ... I'm not going anywhere.

Chapter 20

WEST

"So, you boys already have dates to Homecoming?"

Mom's smile is bright when she asks, contrasting the tension at the dinner table tonight. It isn't often we actually join her and Dad for this Brady Bunch bullshit, but she asked nicely, so …

Not to mention, I figure she needs a break, after dealing with my father on a daily basis.

"Dates?" Sterling counters with a laugh. "Nobody really does that anymore, Mom. You go alone, then hook up with friends when you get there"

Our mother's tiny, manicured hand slams to her chest. The southern belle of the family seems genuinely horrified by that answer.

"Are you kiddin' me? Part of the fun of going to these things was waiting for '*the boy*' to finally get up the nerve to ask," she shares. "Can't believe your generation's done away with all that. Some traditions are worth keeping."

"And some are nothing but pretty little fantasies that twirl around inside you women's heads," Dad interjects with a gruff laugh. "It's nonsense. You, of all people, should know this."

He barely notices that we're all staring as he stacks potatoes on his fork.

I've never known him to miss a chance to belittle her, the woman who bore his sons and stood by him while he built his empire from nothing. Seems like, to him, she's only an armpiece these days.

You know, when there's not some underage gold digger swinging from his nuts.

"Well, just seems like a missed opportunity is all. It's the perfect chance to show whatever young ladies you three have eyes for that they're special to you," Mom adds. After speaking, her gaze lowers to her plate and she leaves it at that.

"Pam, please. These boys are star athletes. They can have any girl in this damn city. It'd be stupid to walk into some dance with chicks on their arms. Talk about taking sand to the beach," he barks out with a laugh.

There's an uncomfortable silence that follows, but my dad seems to completely miss that he's killed the vibe as usual.

"What's the verdict on South Cypress?" he asks, taking a sip from his glass of wine while changing subjects.

"We're solid this year," Sterling answers. "We pulled out the win against them a couple weeks ago, like we knew we would."

"Barely," Dad shoots back. That one word is spoken sharply, and a displeased look passes over my brothers and me.

"It was a clean win and—"

"You're Goldens," he says, cutting off Dane. "You boys are good. *Damn* good," he adds. "It's the reason each of you got a full ride to NCU. So how do you think the coach over there feels about his future stars narrowly stealing a win against a poor, gutter-trash school like South Cypress?"

Mom glares up at him but doesn't dare interrupt.

"Whoever this punk kid is that they've staked everything on, squash him," he declares. "The next time you go up against him, show him why he should've stayed in Ohio. Or wherever the hell he came from. Understood?"

Dane and Sterling pass one another frustrated glances, but don't speak or agree with his B.S. logic.

I, on the other hand, am in no mood to keep quiet or play pretend. I know who and what he really is, and I know so many of his secrets.

"We won. Get over it," I grumble. "For someone who hasn't shown up to a single game in three years, you sure have a lot to say."

A hush falls in the room and I feel my father's gaze locked on me. Still, I don't look up to confirm that I have his full attention.

"What'd you just say to me?"

"Vin, honey, relax," Mom says sweetly, trying to diffuse a situation she doesn't realize is already beyond her control.

He doesn't speak directly to her, but holds a hand up, which silences her instantly. I swear, I hate that he's broken her down to nothing, made her so weak. It's not unlike the control he's tried to place over me, Dane, and Sterling. We're just all too pigheaded to be ruled by anyone.

Just like him.

"There anything else you want to say to me?" he asks, staring me down again. "Now's the time to get it off your chest."

"If I did, you'd know." I stuff a forkful of green beans into my mouth and don't bother softening my tone.

If I cared to look at him, I'm sure his face would be bright red right now. His tolerance for disrespect is uncommonly low, which is why I'm only mildly surprised when my plate is snatched from in front of me.

"You're done. Come with me," he asserts, being the supreme dick he is.

"Vin, he's barely even touched his food," Mom jumps in.

Another of those cocky laughs leaves my father's mouth.

"Then, worst case, I just saved him from having to choke down the rest of that tough steak," he adds callously, and then stands, leveling another glare on me. "We're leaving. Now."

I could fight him on this, but I know it's no use. The guy has a way of getting what he wants out of people.

So, hungry and pissed off, I oblige. Within minutes, we're seated in his SUV and I'm staring up at the bright lights of the high-rises as we drive past. At first, there's no conversation, but then that all changes.

Unfortunately.

"Do you even realize how much I do for you boys? Do you realize the sacrifices I make to ensure you three and your mother have everything you want and need? Meanwhile, you're bitching about me not showing up at your games," he rages. "Tell you what. Do well, get drafted, and you have my word I'll be at every single game."

He goes from trying to draw sympathy to just being a dick. Neither action is surprising. So, unfazed, I stare blankly out the window.

"You've *really* got balls on you to disrespect me after that pricy little toy I spotted on my credit card statement this month."

I should feel guilty knowing I'm caught, or at least worried, but I don't feel *either* of those emotions. Only empty, hollowed out on the inside.

"Where'd you stash the car? Some hole-in-the-wall garage again?"

Actually, I stashed it in Trips pole barn for now, douche-knuckle, but you'll never know that.

His gaze volleys between me and the road. "Still nothing to say? No, 'sorry I screwed up again, Dad'?"

"Goldens aren't big on apologies," I say dryly. "But you already know that."

In my peripheral, I see his grip on the steering wheel tighten. Next thing I know, he's pulling over on the side of the road. Traffic whizzes past and I feel the weight of the statement that follows.

"You used my card," he states, "which means you got into the safe."

And there it is. Asshole knows he's busted. He's trying to sound cool, calm, and collected, but he's anything but that. In fact, I'd bet money this little drive is *only* about what I might've found in that safe. My smart comments just made it easy for him to get me off by myself without Mom getting suspicious.

With him, there's always an angle.

"How'd you crack the code?"

I shrug. "You're smart when it comes to business. Not so much when it comes to common sense."

He snorts a laugh. "Fair enough."

The long, awkward silence that comes next only means there's more he wants to say but hasn't quite figured out how to go there.

"Son, you know there are a lot of layers to my business," he begins. "Which means there are bound to be aspects of it that you don't quite understand. So, if you—"

"I saw the phone," I reveal, putting him out of his misery.

"...And?"

It's rare to humble Vin Golden, but that's exactly what I hear in his tone right now. Humility.

"I didn't look through it." This lie is particularly easy to tell because it suits me to have him think I'm in the dark.

"It isn't that there's anything on it worth hiding. I just—"

"Save it."

He drops his sentence at the sound of my voice, and I'm relieved not to have to listen to his bull anymore.

A heavy hand falls on my shoulder and I glance toward it, choosing not to make eye contact with the man I just lied to.

"I love you and your brothers equally," he shares, "but I've always held you to a bit of a higher standard, West. By you being older and all."

"Didn't realize being born two minutes earlier than them granted me infinite wisdom," I snap.

He doesn't immediately react to the tone I've taken, probably because he's on super thin ice right now, knowing I at least know he keeps a secret phone.

"It's more than that," he continues. "You're just a natural-born leader. I've seen that in you from day one."

My focus is honed in on the sleeve of the dress shirt he wore home, and I barely hear what he says next.

"You do know that everything I do is for you boys and your mother, right?"

The question echoes in my thoughts, and his brow tenses when I reach toward the studded cufflink on his wrist. His gaze follows me as I pull a long, blonde hair off him.

"What about her?" I ask, placing the strand on the dashboard. "You do her for us, too?"

His hand falls away from my shoulder and he slumps in his seat.

"Guess I know why you were an hour late getting home," I add.

Of all the reactions the man could've had, he laughs. Because our family is such a joke to him. The sound of a defeated sigh follows, which means he's about to forego the obvious route—lying—opting instead for the truth. So, I brace myself.

Here it comes.

"Listen, I never pretended to be perfect, West. *None* of us are perfect. I'm a man and I do what all men do," he claims. "Is it right? No. But it's just the way things work. Live long enough. You'll get it one day."

A memory flashes in my head and I'm forced to close my eyes. It's a vision of the time I wanted to spend his fortieth birthday with him—back when I still thought he was the greatest dad in the world. I was only eight, but remember it plain as day. Down to every detail. Even the moment I climbed into the back of his truck, smelling his cologne still clinging to the interior. But what's most important is that I remember the chick he drove to see, not realizing I hid in the back.

They talked for a little while. Long enough for me to gather they'd been involved for a while. Long enough to know she was an attorney somehow associated with my father's firm.

Too shocked and emotionally raw to turn away, I sat by as she proceeded to suck him off in the front seat.

I watched in silence from the shadows, listening to the combination of his lust-filled moans and her loud slurping. All the while, eight-year-old me was trying desperately to wrap my head around how he could do something like that. Mom loved him so much, and always had.

Naturally, I never got that explanation.

When the woman finished, she spit his remnants into an empty fast food cup she grabbed from the cupholder. Then, after attempting to kiss him and getting rejected, she climbed out and disappeared inside a tall office building.

I got found out when I moved and accidentally kicked the windshield scraper into the side panel. Suddenly, he realized I'd been there the whole time, realized I'd seen him cheat on my mother with my own two eyes. And maybe he even knew he didn't deserve the pedestal I put him on.

His response to this flagrant fall from grace?

His response to seeing me bawl my eyes out?

A lecture.

Mostly, he insisted that me telling my mother would ruin our family and break her heart, convincing me that her pain would be all my fault. According to him, our family dynamic was a bit more complicated than I understood, and me telling what I'd seen would cause it all to fall apart. At eight, I believed that shit, and the bastard bought me ice cream before taking me home. As if that fixed everything.

To this day, I'm still broken in places no one can ever possibly repair, carrying the guilt of not doing more back then. But one thing my father said that night was not a lie. My mother is every bit as fragile as he said she is. Only, that doesn't change the fact that someone deserves to pay.

So, if not my father—for fear of it inadvertently breaking my mother when his indiscretions come to light—it has to be the women.

Every single one I'm made aware of if I can help it. Now than I'm older, I can at least do that. My mother deserves that much.

"Tell you what," he pipes up again. "How about we resolve this whole thing right here, by just calling it even. You keep this whole little talk between us, and I don't raise hell about you using my card. Sound like a plan?"

I say nothing because I have nothing for him.

"I'll take that as a yes," he concludes. I don't miss the confidence in his voice, either.

Like nothing happened here tonight, he reaches to turn up the radio. Then, after checking for traffic, we merge back onto the road.

He was with Southside tonight, before coming home to sit at the dinner table where he pretended he'd done nothing wrong. Pretended to be some kind of family man. An act I never bought.

I could only imagine what kept him so long, what kept him out an hour late tonight. I know I'm not wrong. Especially with what I know about south side girls.

They're only good for one thing.

And, apparently, my father knows this all too well.

Chapter 21

BLUE

"I hate everything about this school. Literally," I add, just to make sure Jules gets the point.

"You have a thing going with one of the hottest boys at Cypress Prep," she reasons on the other end. "How bad can it really be?"

"You have no idea."

Her view on my experience here is incredibly distorted, due to a number of factors. Starting with Pandora getting the rumor going about me and West. Then, he only made things worse when he stopped by uninvited during the block party. No one knows what he actually puts me through.

"And to add insult to injury," I go on complaining, "I'm stuck doing this stupid journalism crap, which I have *zero* interest in, by the way. So, my day is even longer on the afternoons we meet."

"Well, at least you don't have to double-down by working at the diner, too, right?"

I know she means well, but I'm not in the mood for her upbeat outlook on life today. So, "I guess," is my only response.

The halls are completely empty as I turn the corner to my locker and grab my backpack. All I want to do is go home, eat something, then crash.

"You still there?" Jules asks as I push through the metal door that leads to the parking lot.

"Barely," I say with an exhausted laugh, fishing my keys from the pocket of my jeans.

"Things won't always be so bad," she assures me, and it's exactly the reminder I need. But, as I get halfway to my parking space, a sizable cluster of football players surrounding my car makes my anxiety spike.

"Jules, I'll call you back," I say in a rush, hanging up as I pick up speed.

The fatigue I felt a second ago evaporates as adrenaline replaces it. My feet thud against the pavement as I full-on sprint now, hearing laughter coming from the guys. It isn't until I'm within a few feet that I see what they find so funny.

Several of them back off, and Austin raises his hands in the air. "Hey, wasn't us," he says in surrender. "You and Golden get into it or something?"

I don't bother answering as I stare at my car—a hand-me-down from Uncle Dusty, and the only thing in this life that's completely mine. It's sitting on bricks, and to make sure I know he's proving a point, and that this *isn't* some criminal act, all four tires are stacked neatly on the trunk. Beside them, the lug nuts rest neatly in a pile. The bastard even left me a jack and a four-way lug wrench to reassemble it all myself.

Heat sweeps up my chest and neck, finally reaching my face. I'm seeing red as I take it all in, consider the time and energy that dick put into this stunt. After football practice, at that.

"Where ... is he?" I ask through gritted teeth.

Five of the players standing by point toward the field house, but not Dane and Sterling. Instead, Sterling sprints to step into my path when I start toward the building to kill their brother. He towers over me like West, and he even stares down on me with those same green eyes like him. It only infuriates me more that he looks so much like him.

We're out of earshot now, so no one can hear me snap at him.

"Move."

"Just thought you should know it's a bad idea for you to go in there," he warns with a smirk. His voice drags over the words, unhurried, making light of my car sitting on freakin' bricks right now.

It's so clear he doesn't care, has no idea how exhausted I am. I worked nearly every day after school last week, on days I didn't have Journalism Club, that is. Then, on top of it all, I had to be at another game this past Friday to get pics for the paper. Add to that the two double shifts I worked Saturday and Sunday, and I feel like I haven't had a break in forever.

I glare at him when his massive hands land on my shoulders, holding me in place.

"If you're fond of your nuts not rolling across this parking lot like tumbleweed, I suggest you get your hands off me and get out of the way," I hiss.

His brow quirks in that smug way West's does, and I want to do him bodily harm. But he does let go, so I don't make good on my threat just yet.

"I'm looking out for you," he insists. "Not sure if you've figured out how things work around here yet, but the more you screw with West, the worse you make things for yourself."

"Your brother isn't some sort of god," I remind him. "He doesn't scare me."

I pray he bought that, because some days I'm not so sure it's completely true.

"Just sayin', if you're smart, you'll just piece that death trap back together and take your ass back across town," he adds, pointing at my car.

The nerve of these dicks is unbelievable. Does he really think I'm just going to let his brother get away with this? Absolutely not.

Sterling freezes when I lean closer, invading his space like his psycho brother loves to do. As much as I hate it, the rush of power I feel in this moment explains why West uses this as a tactic.

"Not sure who your brother thinks he's dealing with, but he can count on one thing," I warn. "When someone fucks with me, they can expect me to throw it right back at them. And that *especially* goes for your brother."

My shoulder slams Sterling's when I push by him. He doesn't bother trying to stop me this time, and I don't miss the half-cocked smile set on his lips when I glance back.

I storm toward the fieldhouse and drop my bag in front of the door the second I enter. My sneakers squeak across the white tile and I hype myself up while passing rows of benches and lockers where some of the team still linger, but no West. I don't acknowledge the sideways glances and questioning stares I pass, because I have one goal in mind.

I'm going to find and hurt West Golden.

Stomping toward the back of the locker room, I try to ignore the fact that I hear running water. It's a wonder I've made it *this* far without their coach spotting me from his office, but he's nose-deep in what I guess to be the team playbook and doesn't notice.

For a fraction of a second, I'm tempted to turn back, imagining what I might walk in on when I reach my destination, but fuck that.

I force myself to charge full steam ahead, but I can admit I'm not nearly as confident as before. For some reason, it hadn't dawned on me that some of the guys might not be decent. I'm too deep in to quit now, though.

Then, I soon realize I should've followed my gut and waited in the parking lot. Because when I turn the corner, I walk in on several members of the team still showering. Even with them all fully exposed, I swear I barely even notice once I spot West.

All ... of West.

His back is to me, but I see enough. Skin that still holds his summer tan, ink that wraps around his solid biceps and across his shoulder blades. There's hard muscle everywhere. I sigh a little, releasing the pressure that's built up inside me. However, it doesn't help at all because I still haven't turned away.

He's soaked and lathered from head to toe, like some sort of wet dream playing out before me, in real-time. Half a second passes before I gather myself and remember why I'm here. Then, the soles of my shoes slosh through water that pools near the drain, and the second I'm within arm's reach, I gather all my rage and frustration from the past few weeks and slam my fist right between West's shoulder blades. Having been taught to fight, I know I'm not weak by any means, but the hit barely moves him. However, it does get his attention.

Pissed and confused, he whirls to face me. I know he doesn't miss the fury in my expression, either.

"Too far!" I shriek, and before I can stop myself, I swing on him again, but this time I aim for his face.

Just as fast as I fire off, his hand catches mine in midair and I'm not sure what pisses me off more. That I swung and missed, or that I'm having to try so hard not to look down at his junk. Even not lowering my gaze, I see way more than I should.

His chest heaves with rage and his eyes reflect it. A sharp tick in his jaw has me equal parts angry and turned on.

"Get the hell out," he growls, but the command isn't meant for me. It's meant for those who were just showering in peace before I strolled in. But now, they've taken heed to their king's orders and I'm left alone with the magnificent beast himself.

The rims of his nostrils flare with anger and mine at *least* matches his.

"You ruined my car!" I shout.

A sick, twisted grin slowly touches his lips, but he doesn't let my fist go.

"What's wrong? Didn't like my little surprise?" he teases. "At least I left the tools you'll need to get that piece of shit back on the road."

My chest tightens and I've, without a doubt, never hated anyone more. Which makes it super confusing that I'm finding it more difficult not to peek at his package by the second. To fight the urge, I swallow hard, staring instead as water rinses down his face and chest, washing away the soap that once covered him.

Dark strands of hair cover his forehead, drawing my attention to the pair of eyes now blazing a hole through me.

"You must be used to this," he rasps, "coming outside to find your car on bricks? Has to be a regular thing in your hood, right?"

He's so damn snide and arrogant. It's amazing he can even stand it himself.

"You crossed the line," I hiss.

His grip on me tightens and, before I can react, he has my other wrist and yanks me forward, bringing me beneath the scorching water with him. It rushes down my arms, soaks my hair and clothes, but I don't even flinch.

"Do I look like I give a shit what you think?" he seethes.

"Fuck you, West," I say back, and the statement leaves my mouth with a rough edge.

There's so much hatred in those words, mine and his. In his eyes, even. But, for some reason, amidst all this swirling tension and negative energy, this is the precise moment I lose the battle, glancing down the rolling hills of his abs, blinking droplets of water from my lashes as my gaze slips lower.

I only gawk for a moment, admittedly startled by his impressive size, but when I lift my eyes again, that wicked smirk of his is back. I'm already rolling my eyes before he speaks, at the mere idea of what his reaction will be to catching me in the act.

"See something you like?"

His deep voice is low and penetrating. I feel it everywhere when he leans in to speak.

The words, "Go to hell," pass between my lips.

He's close, staring down his nose at me, and I see the war. It rages inside him. He hates me, yes, just as much as I hate him. But there's more to it than that.

More to *us* than that.

It's uncomfortable to even think that word—us—but it fits. Because there *is* an us. Even if what we are is warped and ugly, lust wrapped in such intense loathing that it runs bone-deep.

But ... it's still real.

As real as the monster standing before me. The one who's just brought me another step closer, making this space feel small and suffocating.

"You didn't answer my question," he says, his voice rumbling low. "Do you see something you like?"

My lips part, but no words come out.

"Or is 'like' the wrong word?" he questions. "Maybe you see something you *want*."

These words fall from his lips and I swear the water gets hotter as we stand beneath it. Unprepared for such a bold statement, I, again, don't immediately have a response. The effect of being called out passes quickly, though, and I come up with a snide remark.

"I didn't answer because there isn't much to see, King Midas." My brow quirks with the lie I've just told.

The cocky smirk that follows means he knows I was only protecting my pride.

"Come on, Southside," he says against my ear, "just admit it. You *love* this."

I scoff, and with how he's invaded my space, my mouth nearly touches his shoulder.

"What kind of sick person loves being tormented? Loves coming outside to find her car in pieces?"

A low, primal laugh vibrates in his chest and, for some reason, the sound of it sends a chill streaking down my spine.

"The kind of girl who's just as fucked up as I am," he answers. "The kind who always wants who and what she shouldn't."

I feel exposed, like he dug down to the core of who I am, found the strands of depraved DNA my mother marked me with, and forced me to own it. Only, his statement has the opposite effect I think he intends for it to have. It jars me out of the trance our bizarre energy always puts us in when we make the mistake of venturing too close to one another. For once, I'm the one who breaks the spell, putting distance between us.

I don't miss the flash of disappointment that leaves his expression as quickly as it revealed itself. He's a wizard at using that mask, the one that paints him as a one-dimensional jock, but it doesn't fool me anymore. If there's only bad blood between us, this wouldn't keep happening. These moments of letting our guards down. These moments of craving something from one another neither of us is prepared to handle.

But I'm smart. I know my limit, and I've reached it. So, instead of lighting into him again with my fist to prove a point, I back off. His guard has lowered some since I first barged in here, but it's far from being down. And because I know it's in me to flock to other wounded birds, I don't let myself get sucked back into his space.

I'm wise enough to acknowledge he's got some small measure of power over me. More than I care to admit.

He stares at my feet as the space between us grows. His gaze flickers up to meet mine, and despite him wanting me to believe he's all cold glares and a hot temper, I know better.

His chin tilts up confidently and he stands there, a godlike statue with water pelting his shoulders before streaming down his naked flesh.

"Guess you had better get going," he teases. "You've got a little work to do on your car, don't you?"

His teeth flash when he grins sinisterly, but I find it difficult to maintain the same level of anger I stormed in here carrying. Because, with one glance, I've suddenly got a clearer perspective of which one of us has the upper hand.

Pointing, I toss a bitchy smile his way. "Well, from the looks of things, I think we both have something to take care of."

His gaze never lowers to his cock and he isn't even a little embarrassed by having a hard-on in front of me. For the second time at that.

"You're welcome to stay and watch," he teases. "I'm into that sort of thing."

I can't help it when my smile grows. "Hard pass," I shoot back, leaving before I change my mind.

He's weak for me and hates that I see it, but I'll never let him live it down. Ever. In this little slice of hell he keeps me trapped inside, I've got to take what I can get. So, if my only consolation is knowing my enemy wants to get inside my pants ... I'll take it.

Chapter 22

BLUE

Thanks to Uncle Dusty, I'm not a complete novice when it comes to common car drama. For instance, I'm not some desperate, lost cause when I need to re-attach tires after some asshole thinks it's cute to remove them.

I was mildly impressed Dane and Sterling had taken it upon themselves to have the rear two on when I came back from ... *whatever* that was with West. However, I screamed at them as soon as I realized what they were doing. Because if they wanted to do the right thing, they should've spoken up when their idiot brother started messing with my car in the first place.

So, as much as I would have loved to let someone else finish the work, I wouldn't allow it. If they feel guilty, then let them. They deserve it.

I'm still pondering their weak attempt at righting their wrongs when I pull into my driveway. Lucky for me, Mike's car isn't parked on the street where it usually is, which means he's at his *real* home.

The bar.

As much as I hate his drinking, I much rather he be there than here. With the last few weeks I've had, a little smidge of peace goes a long way.

I reach to grab my bag from the floor on the passenger side and the sharp pain that shoots through my shoulder serves as a reminder of my last encounter with that man. The bruise had faded to a sickening yellow, green, and brown stain on my skin, but West had given up asking about it. Thank God.

I hate this weird dual personality thing he has going on. Ninety-nine percent of the time, he's a nightmare, but those moments are punctuated by instances of the weird savior complex he has when it comes to me. His mood swings are impossible to keep up with, and I never bother trying.

The motion sensor Uncle Dusty installed over the back door signals the porch light to kick on and I turn my key in the lock. My first instinct is to listen out for Scar, but I hear nothing. She's known to nap after her homework is done, so I'm careful to keep quiet as I stop at the sink for a glass of water.

There's a fleeting temptation to grab one of Mike's beers—one of the few things we actually have in the fridge—but shouldering *one* parent's bad habit is bad enough. I don't need to add my father's vice as well.

Resisting, I drop my things into one of the kitchen chairs and take a sip before heading down the hall to check in on Scar.

Soft music seeps beneath her door and I smile at how much she's like me. Music helps me sleep, too. Still being quiet to keep from waking her, I push the door open. What I expect to find is my adorable, pink-haired sister drooling on her pillow like I always tease her about, but instead, I'm horrified by what I see.

"What the hell are you doing?"

Two completely naked bodies hop out of her bed, scrambling across the floor for their clothes. I'm in total shock, and feeling so many emotions bubbling in my gut, I can hardly decide how to react to finding my fourteen-year-old sister in bed with a boy she's sworn is only a friend.

"I'm so sorry. I swear it'll never happen again," Shane pleads as he slips past me and into the hallway. He's holding a pair of jeans and a t-shirt over his crotch, providing a clear view of the bird chest that reminds me just how young they are.

Too young to be doing *this*.

Way too young.

Tears well in my eyes and I'm panting like *I'm* the one who's been caught. I've had my heart broken before, but none of those breakups or letdowns felt like this. What I just witnessed has absolutely gutted me.

This is my fault. I'm gone all the time. Knowing what a shit parent Mike is, I should have been here to keep an eye on Scar. She's been lonely and I know that. It's the reason she wants Shane here all the time, to make this house feel a little less empty with Mom, Hunter, and me being absent.

This is my fault.

It's on me.

The back door closes after Shane hops into his clothes and bolts.

I still haven't completely processed the fact that I just walked in on my little sister having sex, but my back hits the wall as I try to make sense of it. Scar hasn't said a word. She slips into her t-shirt and shorts and then lowers to the edge of her bed. After a few seconds, I can only guess shame has set in, because her hands come up to cover her face. I'm aware of the quiet sobs she releases behind them, but don't quite have it in me to go to her.

I study her—the tousled ponytail on top of her head. The chipped polish on her nails. The studded earrings I passed down to her as a Christmas gift last year because I didn't have the funds to spring for anything new. All I see when I look at her is my baby sister. She has no idea what she's getting herself into, and as much as I blame myself for her growing up way too soon, I blame the other members of this family as well.

Sniffling, I push tears from my cheeks and set my emotions aside. I can deal with them later, on my own, behind my bedroom door. But for now, I have to step in and be the mother neither of us ever had.

"Did you use protection?" I ask, feeling sick to my stomach that I had to form my lips to string those words together into a sentence.

She takes a moment to answer, but nods eventually. "Yes."

I swallow the lump in my throat, grateful at least for that.

"Was this the first time?" This time, I hold my breath, unsure I'm ready to hear just how hard I failed her. For all I know, this has been going on for months.

She takes a deep breath and finally lowers her hands to her lap. "No," she answers, ripping my heart from my chest. "The third."

Bile rises in my throat and I'm suddenly more exhausted than before, at the idea of having to be present more, while also keeping up with the many other responsibilities that have been dropped on my shoulders.

Still, among all those things, Scar is the most important.

"Three times," I force out. "The other two times, were you careful as well? Did he wear a condom?"

"God, Blue!" she snaps, still choking back tears. "Is this really necessary?"

"If you're not mature enough to have this conversation, you sure as hell aren't mature enough to be having sex."

She rolls her eyes when I say that word. "You act like you're an angel, but you're not," she shoots off, passing a hateful glare toward me.

"And I've never claimed to be, but that doesn't change the fact that you're not old enough to handle this, Scar."

A frustrated growl leaves her mouth. "Yes, we were careful all three times. Are you happy? Can we stop talking about this now?"

"No," I shoot back. "Did he force you into doing this?"

She gets to her feet and starts pacing when my line of questioning makes her more uncomfortable than she already was.

"You cannot be serious," she grumbles to herself.

"I am serious. Now answer the question."

Another hateful glare passes my way. "No, I wasn't forced. It's something we talked about all summer, so it wasn't just some snap decision. And we didn't do anything until we were both ready," she hisses. "And for the record, I'm not a child."

We clearly disagree on that point, but it won't help anything to start an argument.

"What happened to you two just being friends?" I ask.

I feel wounded, like I've been lied to by the person I love and trust most in this world.

"We *are* just friends," she insists. "This is just ... something we wanted to do. Lots of kids in our grade have already done it, so we decided our first time should be with someone we trust."

My head is spinning. While I believe this makes perfect sense in her mind, I can't understand it.

"Your first time shouldn't be because you want to get losing your virginity out of the way."

She's quiet and, as a change of pace, she's actually listening. There's a long stretch of time that she simply paces back and forth across her floor, but some of the fight seems to leave her and she sits again.

It isn't lost on me how uncomfortable this must be, but it's uncomfortable for me, too.

There's something she wants to ask. I can tell by how she lowers her gaze to her nails as she fidgets with them.

"I'm listening," I remind her, hoping to make it easier for her to speak openly.

She hesitates a few seconds longer, but eventually softens.

"How old were you *your* first time?"

I glance down at the floor, unable to hold back images of that night.

"Sixteen and a half," I answer. "Nearly two years ago."

She nods and some of the tension leaves her shoulders. "And ... have you done it with a lot of guys since then?"

A small laugh slips out despite the tears still falling from my eyes. "Nope. Just the one guy."

Finally, her gaze wanders to meet mine. "Ricky?"

I nod thoughtfully. "Yep."

She nods, too, when my answer seems to confirm what she already knew. "Did you love him?"

A sharp breath puffs from my lips.

"I did," I admit, "but it will never work between us. He's set in his ways, in his lifestyle, and I'm not willing to accept that. Not after seeing how quickly things turned bad for Hunter."

Instead of firing off another question, Scar just sits and thinks for a moment, giving me a chance to brace myself for the next one.

"What about West?"

Her tone always softens when she mentions him. It's innocent and mostly harmless that she seems to think the world of him, but it does concern me that she's not a better judge of character.

"What about him?" I fire back.

She shrugs. "I don't know. Do you think you guys might ... you know?"

There's no hint of laughter in her tone, only genuine concern and curiosity. We don't talk about stuff like this often, so she seems to be feeling me out.

"Things with West are ... complicated," I answer honestly. "So, I can safely say the answer to your question is no."

When I smile at her, she smiles back. Answering questions about me and Ricky was not how I wanted to spend my evening, but if being transparent with my sister makes it easier for her to open up, then I'll do it.

"What about you?" I ask. "Do you think you love Shane?"

There's a long pause and I'm not surprised she doesn't have an immediate answer.

"We've been friends so long, sometimes it's hard to tell *what* I feel for him," she admits. "I do know I care about him. And that I'd feel weird if he decided to be with some *other* girl."

I watch her as she sorts through her feelings.

"That's normal," I assure her. "Sometimes, the traits that draw us to a guy as friends blur the lines a bit. That's kind of what happened with me and Ricky."

She seems to understand, and I hope she does. I don't want her to feel ashamed about this, but there is definitely a lesson to be learned.

"You know this can't happen again, don't you Scar? Not until you're much, *much* older."

The messy ponytail bobs when she nods. "I know."

"Because having sex is more than just the physical. It's emotional and can really screw you up inside if you aren't careful," I warn gently. "What feels right today can feel like the biggest mistake in the world tomorrow."

While I don't regret Ricky, I've known enough girls who *have* regretted their first to know there's truth in that statement.

"And you can always talk to me," I remind her. "About anything. Whenever you need to."

Her head bobs again and I smile at her. When I stand, she does too.

"Not sure about you, but I could use a hug," I admit with a quiet laugh.

She meets me in the middle of her room and wraps both arms tight around me. I kiss the top of her hair and question whether I said enough, whether she believes she can come to me about anything, and imagine this is what parenting *always* feels like.

"I love you. You know that don't you?" I ask.

She nods against my shoulder. "More than anyone."

Those words break my heart a little, because I wish she had more than just me—a barely making it, almost adult who hasn't quite been able to get things right—because she deserves more. But the best I can do is be consistent.

Keep loving her.

Keep showing up.

Keep fighting to give her everything.

"Are you mad?" she asks, still holding on to me.

"No, I'm not mad," I answer, "but just know; as soon as I can afford it, this whole house is getting nanny cammed. Not even kidding."

She laughs quietly and squeezes tighter. "Fair enough."

Chapter 23

WEST

I can barely hear myself speak with all the shouting. Mostly, they're screaming for me, Sterling, and Dane, but there's fanfare for Austin, Trip, and Marcus, too. We've just been announced as this year's Homecoming Court, but it's an expected nomination, so we're only pretending to be excited about it.

Pep assemblies have never been my thing, but especially not ones held at the end of an already long day, and with tonight's big game ahead of us.

Trip is the last guy to storm down the bleachers, coming to join the rest of us on the basketball court while the entire school watches from the stands. He gives Austin a quick fist-bump and then we all face forward as things settle down.

The six chairs seated in front of us are for the girls making court this time around, and that's predictable as hell, too. Kids always vote for the ones they either idolize or fear, and my crew has both markets on lock.

"Parker Holiday," Headmaster Harrison calls out, and the volume in the gym goes wild again.

Parker hobbles down the steps, having finally been downgraded from crutches to an ankle brace. The tiny little shirt she's wearing doesn't hide much. If her family didn't practically fund half this school's auxiliaries, she'd be sent home for wardrobe violations daily. Guess it pays to have the powers that be by the balls.

She flashes a cheeky grin at me before dropping down into the seat right under my nose.

'Just sit the hell down and play the role,' I think to myself. She's always over the top. About everything.

"Next up, we have Josslyn Francois," Harrison announces.

Glancing left, I'm not surprised to see Dane holding back a grin. His eyes are glued to her as she descends the bleacher stairs in tight jeans and an oversized sweater that hangs off one shoulder. Wanting her is gonna be the death of him.

I smile and turn straight forward again, waiting for Harrison to finish. The girls we're paired with are the closest thing any of us will have to dates, so it looks like Mom got her wish after all. Only difference is, first chance I get tomorrow night, I'm ditching Parker to prowl for something new. The girl brings nothing interesting to the table. In bed or otherwise.

Heidi and Ariana are called next, then two other chicks from the dance squad, but I can't remember either one's name. Despite banging one of them once after a party. At least, I *think* it was her.

Probably.

Maybe.

Anyway, the production finally ends, and we move into a speech about how we're expected to conduct ourselves should tonight's big game be a win. The usual—no excessive celebrating on the field or any other displays of poor sportsmanship. Of course, we're gonna win. With four games under our belts in four weeks, it's inevitable.

Next, Harrison starts in on the rules for tomorrow night's dance. He starts with *'no twerking, no bumping and grinding'*—his words, definitely not mine—and *'no smoking on the premises'*. In short, I'm positive everyone's tuning him out right now. We'll do all those things and he won't do shit about it.

I zone out and scan the crowd, and it doesn't surprise me when my gaze lands on Southside. She's watching me, too, and damn if I'm not still thinking about her storming into the locker room a couple weeks ago. I'd never been naked in a girl's presence without things escalating. Definitely had never had one walk out on me, leaving me hanging.

Literally, in this instance.

But Southside isn't like other girls. For one, I've never hated and wanted someone at the same time. She's the ultimate forbidden fruit. The one I've sworn off.

An innocent smirk touches her soft, pink lips and I hate that I know how they feel. Hate that I've wanted to have them on mine again more times than I can count.

She stands and my brow tenses. In the middle of Harrison's speech, she walks down the bleachers, and then as soon as she makes it down to the floor, my eyes are glued to her ass. It's round and perfect and …

Shaking my head, I get my thoughts straight. She doesn't get to do that, distract me from hating her. Not when I have such a good reason behind it.

She casts a look over her shoulder and it lands right on me. That sassy up-to-no-good grin is still there and if I weren't standing at the center of attention right now, I'd see what she was up to.

She disappears and Rodriquez follows right behind her. There still hadn't been any repercussion for the stunt I pulled with her car a couple weeks ago and I can admit I've been on edge ever since. She doesn't take anything lying down, which, if I'm being honest, I find hot as hell. Even if it's also her most annoying trait.

Whatever the case, I'm stuck standing here, playing the part of North Cypress royalty. Smirking to myself, I'm positive she'll soon be evening the score, and I'll know soon enough.

If I'm right, she already knows I'll be giving that shit right back to her.

Blue

I haven't felt this good in a really, *really* long time. Driving down my street, it even seems prettier than usual. Maybe it's the changing leaves or the Halloween decorations all the neighbors put out the first day of October, but I'm definitely in a great mood, seeing my surroundings in brighter colors.

Then again, it could have something to do with the two garbage bags in my backseat, knowing I just scored myself a huge win.

Getting to witness the outcome of my well-played move during tonight's game will be the icing on top. The thing that makes what I risked today all worth it.

I tap the brake and turn into my driveway, only to find someone else parked in my spot. Ricky's posted against his sleek, black motorcycle, both arms crossed over his chest. His gaze is locked on me through my windshield, but his expression's hard to read.

Killing the engine, I climb out and approach him with caution. I never did get around to apologizing after our last conversation, when he showed up during the game a few weeks ago. Since then, the tension between us has only grown. So, standing face-to-face with him now, I feel super awkward.

"Hey," I say a little quieter than usual. And a little less sassy, too.

He nods but doesn't return the greeting. Instead, his gaze lowers to where I have my thumbs hooked on both pockets of my jeans. When his eyes narrow, I look there, too.

"Art class?" he asks, referring to the pink spray paint staining my fingers.

I tuck them behind my back and feel grateful *he* was the only one who noticed. Would've sucked if someone else had peeped the evidence tying me to what I'd done.

"Uh ... no. Not exactly," is the only answer I give. "What's up? Why'd you stop by?"

His gaze flashes to mine again and his head cocks. "Why am I *always* here?"

Rolling my eyes, I move to step past him. "I'm not doing this with you anymore, Ricky. I ca—"

"Blue, he's out of here in less than a week," he cut in. "If you don't go now, you're gonna be making an eight-hour drive north if you ever want to see him. And you and I both know that ain't gonna happen. Not if you aren't even willing to drive thirty minutes."

A breeze sweeps past then and I hug myself through my hoodie, thinking deeper.

"Trust me," Ricky continues. "If I could drag out of Hunter whatever it is he needs to say to you, I would've done it already. But he isn't talking. Not to me. Not about that, anyway."

My gaze shifts toward the house where I know Scar is waiting inside. I've made it my business to spend more time with her, which means making time for Hunter is even more of a challenge, but ... he's family, too.

I meet Ricky's gaze and I don't miss how differently he's looking at me. It's not like usual. If I'm not mistaken, he has his guard up with me, which has *never* been the case.

"I can't go this evening," I share, giving in. "But I'll make time tomorrow morning."

He does that thing with his brow again, where it creases in the middle.

"You got something more important to do?" There's judgement in his tone, and I feel it.

"There's a school thing I have to attend, but I don't work in the morning. I can head out to see him then," I answer.

It's not until Ricky lowers his gaze, shaking his head, that I think I've figured out what his problem might be.

"Let me guess," he grumbles. "Can't afford to miss your boyfriend's game. Am I right?"

I can't even begin to explain all the things wrong with that statement, but I'm going to start with it being none of his business where I'm going or why I'll be there.

"You and I aren't together, Ricky. Have you forgotten that?"

There's a humorless smirk on his lips when he answers. "Nah, I'm pretty sure I got that message."

For so many reasons, I don't have time for this. When I finally push past him, he's on my heels.

"This isn't like you, Blue. Never known you to be some dude's doormat. And if I'm being honest," he adds, "it's not a good look."

Feeling heat sweep up my spine, I turn to face him.

"What the hell are you talking about?"

He rubs a hand down his goatee and looks everywhere but at me. "I saw the update about him leaving your car on bricks," he shares. "Now, you're putting Hunter on hold to show up at this asshole's game? Shit just doesn't add up."

I'm so sick of people assuming they have me pegged. Only, Ricky being one of those people is completely new to me.

"For your information, dickhead, the thing I have to do at school is for Journalism Club," I admit through gritted teeth. "Yes, I have to be at the game, but only because I'm required to submit pics from every home event, and it just so happens that tonight's Homecoming game is on Cypress Prep's field. Is that okay with you? Or do you need me to make a presentation on what my entire schedule is looking like this week?"

I sense it the moment he backs down, realizing he messed up. Now that I've gotten my point across, I steer my angry glare from him and take a breath.

"I didn't mean to piss you off," he concedes. "It's just that, when I saw what he did, and knowing you're supposed to be together or whatever, I just—"

I don't have anything else to say and it seems he doesn't either. I'm simply counting down the days until I can put high school behind me and move on with my life. The drama is exhausting. Drama I desperately tried to avoid, might I add.

"I um … I showed up at the school that day," Ricky eventually admits. "As soon as I saw the post about what happened. But the lot was clear when I got there, so I figured I just missed you."

My eyes dart to him and, for obvious reasons, I'm not glaring quite as coldly as before.

"Not sure which I planned to do first—put the tires on for you or beat that guy's rich ass, but … I just knew I should be there."

It's things like this that make me forget why I ever put distance between us, but one glance at the tattoos on his knuckles—a reminder of the crew he hangs with—and I remember.

When it came down to choosing me or embracing the lifestyle here in South Cypress, I never stood a chance of winning that battle.

"You shouldn't worry so much about me," I say calmly, which brings his eyes to mine. "We've got bigger problems than that."

His brow quirks. "Like?"

I take a deep breath and glance toward the house to make sure the windows are closed so Scar doesn't overhear.

"Has Shane ... said anything to you lately? About anything major?"

Ricky's thoughtful for a moment, and then shakes his head. "Nothing that stands out. Why?"

I swallow hard before speaking. "A couple weeks ago, the day of the whole ... tire thing," I explain, "I came home and found Scar and Shane in her bed together. And they weren't taking a nap."

Ricky's expression is blank, and then he stares off, gazing down the alley instead of at me.

"Damn..."

I breathe deeply. "Precisely my thoughts."

I'm not sure what he's thinking, but I'm sure he's at least as shocked as I was.

Well, maybe not *as* shocked. Seeing as how I was the one with a ringside seat of the whole thing.

"I'll talk to him," he promises. "And I'll tell him not to come around anymore."

"It's probably best that he wait until I'm home, but I don't think keeping them apart indefinitely is the answer. With our luck, that'll only push them together," I say with a quiet laugh that has him smiling. "They're friends before they're anything else, so ... I think it's just on us to steer them in the right direction, explain why moving too fast too soon isn't healthy."

He nods. "I can agree with that."

"And in case you're wondering, they were careful all three times."

"Three?" He flashes a surprised look my way.

I nod. "Three. After we talked things out, she showed me the box of condoms she had hidden under her bed to ease my mind. I counted and only three were missing, so she didn't lie about anything."

When I peer up, I'm shocked to see Ricky smiling even bigger than before.

"What could you possibly be smiling about right now?"

He shrugs and his dimples deepen. "It's just crazy how you Riley girls seem to be me and my brother's weakness."

I roll my eyes playfully and start up the steps of the back porch. "On that note, I'm going inside. Gotta grab Scar and Jules before the game starts. And I guess washing my hands wouldn't be a bad idea either."

Glancing down, I observe the pink paint I'm still sporting.

Ricky's gaze lingers on me, and he nods. "Yeah, you do that. And if you need someone to vent to after seeing Hunter tomorrow, you know how to get a hold of me."

"Ok," I answer, but as he's walking away, I stop him to say more. "I haven't said it lately, and I know I've been kind of a bitch to you these past few months, but ... thank you for being such a good friend."

The smile reappears and so do the dimples. "Anytime. You know that."

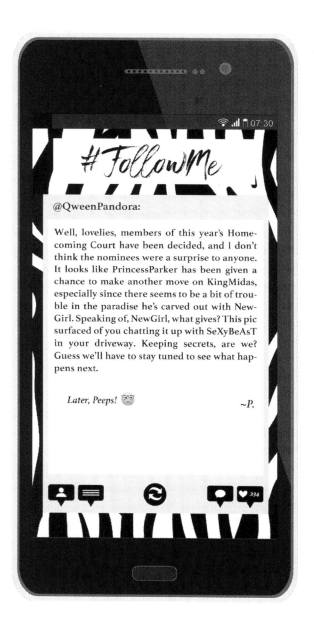

Chapter 24

BLUE

We make the ride back to school with the windows up. The temp has dropped quite a bit since school let out. Scar and Jules are just as bubbly about being here as before, but neither has said a word to me about West. They had plenty of questions when they first heard he'd vandalized my car—via Pandora, of course—but I sidestepped each one until neither Scar nor Jules knew what to make of it. For now, no one has any idea how volatile things between us really are.

Even then, people aren't sure what to believe.

Had West really done it? Or was it someone else?

Those are the whispers on the wind. Some assume it's the result of a nasty fight that has since blown over. Which, ironically enough, has led them to believe West and I are more serious than anyone originally thought. However the heck *that* happens. Others question whether it has all been some sort of bitter retaliation on Parker's part, for me stealing her guy or some shit like that. Guess this is what happens when there aren't any pics, but only eye-witness accounts.

I'm sure the reason there are no pics is because whoever saw West tampering with my car was too afraid of *him* to take any.

Either way, whatever conclusions people have drawn, they're wrong. That's all I know.

I catch myself smiling when I turn into the lot, thinking of what I pulled off earlier, and also praying I covered all my tracks.

Scar looked at me like I was crazy when I went back to my car after scrubbing spray paint off my hands, then came into the house dragging two garbage bags filled with the football team's extra pants. I'd return them eventually, but for now they're mine.

I snagged them from the storage room in the field house during the pep rally. Actually, Lexi did that part, when she decided I had too much to lose if I got caught. Whereas she, on the other hand, could use the few days off if she got suspended over this. So, while she did *her* part, I did mine.

Which everyone attending this game will see soon enough.

I spot her just after I park, and the lot is already full. This year, the athletic department decided to hold the game earlier in the day, so students could just stick around after school to make sure the stands are at max capacity.

Good for optics. Good for funding.

Lexi waves me down and I usher Scar and Jules that way, introducing the three for the first time. Lexi admits she usually avoids these kinds of gatherings like the plague, but tonight's extra special.

"Jules, Scar, this is Lexi. The one good thing about this godawful place," I add.

Jules rolls her eyes, likely thinking I'm exaggerating, but she has no idea.

"Hey," she says with a bright smile.

To which Lexi responds with a nod. "Hey."

Scar waves and the next second, we're on our way to the bleachers. My heart's racing a mile a minute, but I play it cool. The crowd is already fired up, and there's standing room only. However, our seats are reserved with a laminated sign for members of the paper.

Guess there's *one* perk.

The crowd goes wild when the announcers talk over the loudspeaker, getting everyone hyped up about tonight's big game.

The dance squad do their part to get fans riled up as well, and I'm holding my breath at the sight of the first black and gold helmet that takes the field. My eyes are glued to them all, waiting for West to make his appearance, and as expected, he's last in line.

Then, a hush comes over the crowd when they lay eyes on him. Quiet murmuring follows as confusion spreads. My guess is they're staring at the bright pink letters painted vertically down West's pants that read: BITCH.

Seeing him out there, wearing my handiwork, I can't possibly be more satisfied. It was the perfect storm. First, with the earlier than usual game time preventing anyone from coming to West's rescue with a spare pair, and Lexi's willingness to steal the extra uniform pants from the storage room, West was left with two options.

Sit this one out ... or let the world know what he really is.

My bitch.

It takes everything in me not to glance over toward Lexi and smile. Especially when Scar starts asking questions about who would do such a thing. Jules passes me a knowing look, though, then lifts a hand to cover her laugh.

"Well, ladies and gentlemen, it appears we have a wardrobe malfunction of some sort on our hands," one announcer explains.

I snort then. Can't help it. While I would've liked for this to have stolen just an ounce of West's confidence, it clearly has not. His head is still just as high as always, and he doesn't look any less focused. But it wasn't about that. This move was simply about me getting the win. And thanks to being on the newspaper, it will be memorialized.

Raising my phone, I snapped a pic. Whether I'm allowed to publish this baby or not, this is *definitely* my best scoop yet.

Cypress Prep sweeps the opposing team, like everyone knew they would. All with their beloved QB-1 sporting my pink paint job the entire game.

At one point, a woman I guessed to be his mother arrived with spare pants, but shaking his head, West refused them. Being the cocky bastard I've come to know him to be, it was probably a power play. His attempt at proving to me that I hadn't gotten to him. A chance to show me that what I'd done couldn't stop him being a beast on the football field.

Whatever the case, seeing how unshaken he was out there, *still* making plays with confidence, I liked it a little more than I should have.

Because I'm an idiot.

Scar's already making her way back to the car, clutching her phone close to her face while she texts. Probably Shane, which is something I've been keeping a close eye on. Jules spots a couple girls she knows from volleyball, so it's just me and Lexi, silently stewing in satisfaction for having pulled this whole thing off without a single hitch.

The smug grin I'm wearing has me feeling good for a while, and it's only *more* pleasing when I spot West.

"Uh oh. Here come's trouble," Lexi announces, and then takes off before the storm in cleats and shoulder pads approaches. He's with the team after having been bombarded by fans, but I have one hundred percent of his attention. And, like him, I can't stop staring.

Soaked with sweat from head to toe, and keeping his eyes trained right in my direction, West reaches me. I'm not even shocked when he breaks from his team to step to me, invading my personal space like always. Only, he isn't angry like I expect him to be. There's something else that has his eyes wild this time.

Heat from his breath grazes my neck when he leans in to whisper.

"Well played, Southside," he admits with amusement in his tone. "But you got one thing wrong."

I'm shivering and it has nothing to do with the slight chill to the air, but has *everything* to do with inhaling the scent of his sweat. There's something raw and primal about it that I'm not exactly hating.

"What's that?" I finally ask, peering up into his bold eyes, feeling weak in all the wrong ways.

His lips move and I'm all ears.

"We both know which of us is *really* the bitch, don't we?" he growls with a smirk.

I'm barely able to process the words when wet heat presses to my lips. The undiluted taste of him is everything to me in this moment, and I don't even know what's happening. Unsure of what to do with my hands, they move on their own, and the first place they go is into his warm, damp hair, drawing him closer as the helmet he carried settles against the small of my back.

His tongue pushes inside my mouth and, on instinct, I lean into him, proving him right yet again. He may be the one with the words printed on his uniform, but letting him kiss me like this—*enjoying* the kiss like this—says so much about me.

He pulls away and his dark stare burns through me, leaving me hot and flustered when he backs off. But he doesn't leave without smacking my ass first, in front of everyone, marking his territory.

He wants them to think I'm his because he believes I find nothing more repulsive than that, but ... I'm not sure *what* I'm thinking at the moment. However, I'm suddenly aware of having so many eyes on me now.

Most notably, *Parker's*.

There's more hatred in them than usual, more of that icy vibe that's always bouncing off her. She passes by without a word, but I feel exactly what she's thinking: I'm in her way, blocking her path to West.

Even though the attention I get from him is pretty damn negative, it's more than she thinks I deserve.

More than she'll allow.

Feeling self-conscious having everyone's attention, I cross both arms over my chest and chew the side of my lip. Then, I start fast-walking it to my car.

What is wrong with me?

I'm screwed up in ways I didn't even realize, but what's surprising is ... I'm beginning to think West and I suffer from the same strain of stupidity. And, as wrong as I know this is, I'm finding the idea of exploring our warring, explosive natures less and less appalling.

The Golden Boys

Call me crazy.

Chapter 25

BLUE

I swore I'd never step foot inside this place. It's cold, it's heartbreaking. It's also my brother's home for now.

Well, at least, until he's transferred in a week.

The process of getting signed in, waiting for my number to be called, and then getting screened took nearly an hour and a half. Now, here I sit, waiting for Hunter in what looks like my old cafeteria at South Cypress. Small, square tables are spaced out across the room, anchored to the ground with chairs attached. Everything is drab, sterile, and just downright depressing. Everything about this place makes me want to stay on the straight and narrow for the rest of my life. Which, I suppose, is the point.

My knee hasn't stopped bouncing since I was escorted here by a guard. It'd be nice to check in with Jules, Scar or Lexi while I wait, but seeing as how I had to store all my things in a locker, it's just me here.

Me and my anxiety.

Every time a figure moves past the reinforced glass on the far wall, I perk up, thinking it might be Hunter. Only to be let down every time. I'm feeling equal parts excitement and dread. It's been so long since I laid eyes on him, but I know it'll gut me seeing him in a place like this. Wanting to spare Scar the heartache, I asked Jules to head over and keep an eye on things. I got a ton of pushback from Scar about leaving her behind, but as I sit here, listening to a woman sobbing her eyes out to my left, I know I made the right choice.

This time, when someone passes the glass, it isn't a false alarm. My heart races faster than I think it ever has as I lay eyes on my brother. Already, I'm fighting tears and I haven't even gotten a good look at him. What I'd give to just *hug* him, but I know it isn't allowed. No touching.

I breathe deep and decide to stand when the guard pushes the door open. Then, in walks Hunter, wearing the bright orange jumpsuit I've only imagined him in before today. Now, I'm certain this will be the only way I'll see him when I close my eyes.

His back is to me for a moment, while his cuffs are removed. Then, I see his face for the first time in far too long, but ... there are cuts and bruises on one side. And his eye is practically swollen shut.

My chest tightens and I force air into my lungs, trying to keep my emotions in check. He catches my eyes and his own well with tears and relief. Immediately, guilt sets in for making him wait so long, but among the many things I'm feeling right now, I'm angry.

He's better than this, better than this *place*. Plus, Scar and I should've been enough of a reason for him to make sure he never ended up here.

"You made it," he says breathlessly, clearly trying to be strong, but his lower lip quivers when he reaches me.

I'm at a loss for words at first, but then pull it together and manage a smile. Albeit a faint, *fake* smile, but it's a smile, nonetheless.

"It's good seeing you," I finally say back, lowering into my seat when he does the same.

"Black eye and all, right?" I hear the embarrassment in his tone when he makes the joke.

"It's ... Are you okay?" I stammer.

A casual shrug doesn't have me fooled. The angry wounds on his face tell me everything I need to know.

"Depends on how you define *'okay'*."

That's a fair response, considering.

To lighten the mood, I grin at him. "Did you at least get a couple hits in on the other guy?"

A small laugh leaves him. "One or two, but nothing like the beatdown Ricky told me you put on Loren Pete. What the hell was up with that?"

An easy laugh slips out. "She opened her big mouth at the wrong time."

"Clearly." The lighthearted expression on his face begins to fade as we settle into a strange silence.

The culprit? The huge elephant in the room. He'd put Ricky up to harassing me until I showed up here today. Now, here I am, and it hasn't come up.

His gaze lowers to the table and he drums his fingers nervously on top of it.

"You uh ... you and Scar been okay?" He peers up then and I don't miss the raw emotion he's carrying.

I shrug. "Depends on how you define *'okay'*."

When I repeat his response, he chuffs a quiet laugh before lowering his gaze again.

"Mike been staying in line?"

The question brings an eye roll out of me. "Mike is Mike."

Hunter nods knowingly. "Sounds about right."

Turning to peer over his shoulder, he makes eye contact with the guard who brought him to me, then scoots to the edge of his seat when he faces me again.

"Listen, Blue-Jay, there's something I need to tell you, and I know you're gonna be pissed, but you can't react by asking a shit-ton of questions, okay?"

I'm reluctant, but I nod. "What is it?"

He does that shady glance over his shoulder a second time before I have his attention again.

"You have to be careful out there. I mean, lock the windows and doors behind you, keep an eye out for strange vehicles following you a little too long, people walking up on you in the street."

My brow furrows and I quickly disregard his wishes to question him. "What are you talking about? Who wants to hurt us? Why would someone—"

"You gave me your word you wouldn't ask," he cuts in.

"Well, I'm sorry, but that was *before* you made the job of looking after Scar a million times harder," I shout, earning the attention of those seated at the tables around us.

Hunter gives a discreet glance sideways. "Don't make a scene," he whispers.

"Are you kidding me?" I'm still a little too loud, but it can't be helped.

He reaches for my hands to calm me, but quickly draws back when he remembers that's not allowed.

"Blue, I just … I know everything's on you right now. I know Mom took off. I know Mike is more of a burden than a help. Trust me, I beat myself up about leaving you to hold everything down every day I wake up in this damn place. But I just need you to trust me," he pleads. "I hate that the shit I've done always seems to hurt the only two people in the world I owe anything, but what's done is done. Now, all I can do is protect you as best as I can from in here."

I stare at him with burning eyes and tear-blurred vision. How dare he drag me here to dump even more responsibility on my shoulders, and not even tell me why.

When I stand, he forgets about the boundaries and takes my wrist.

"Riley," one of the guards calls out, causing Hunter to release me abruptly. There's so much frustration pent up inside him, but he's trying to contain it. Trying to keep his cool.

"Blue, I just … I know you hate me right now, and you have every right to, but all I ask is that you watch your back."

I stare down on him while he sits there, red in the face and fighting tears.

"Is it her family?" I finally manage to ask.

We don't talk about her ever—the girl whose life he took—but it looks like we've run out of options. His eyes slam shut when I fold both arms across my chest.

"Answer me," I seethe. "This is about Robyn, isn't it?"

He winces when I speak her name aloud. "It's not that simple, Blue. I—"

"I shouldn't have come here." The words leave my mouth at the precise moment the realization occurs to me.

"Blue!"

I don't turn because I'm barely even able to walk right now. Everything hurts, inside and out. Life just keeps throwing me one hard blow after another and I'm not sure how much more I can take. As I put distance between my brother and me, I feel more fragile than I've felt in a long time. And if I'm going to keep from folding under the pressure, something has to give.

Fast.

Chapter 26

BLUE

"That was it? No explanation? Just *'Watch your back'*?" Jules asks, staring at my reflection in the mirror, waiting for an answer.

"Yep. Pretty much."

My gaze lowers and my thoughts are all over the place. Jules has been a welcomed distraction tonight, even if the reason for her visit still has me wanting to slam my head against a wall.

I had zero plans to go to the Homecoming dance, but she has a way of pressuring me into things I don't want to do. Naturally, that got us both into a lot of trouble growing up. She offered to buy our tickets at the door and promises we'll have a blast, but I'm almost positive we'll have whatever the opposite of that would equate to.

She made it hard to shoot down her idea by having Scar already settled at Uncle Dusty's for an overnight visit tonight. Plus, there's an array of dresses, makeup, accessories, and hair tools laid out on my bed that all look like torture devices to me. After crying my eyes out on her shoulder without explanation after returning home from my visit with Hunter, she instructed me to shower and leave the rest to her.

So, this—me seated in a chair while she does a professional-level makeup job on my face and hair—is me leaving the rest to her.

"There," she says with a smile, pushing a bundle of beach waves forward over both my shoulders.

I can't help but to stare because, with the glossy red lipstick she added, it's hard not to see my mother staring back at me.

"Now, the dress," she adds with a chipper grin.

I stand in my robe and follow her over to my bed where she's laid out everything she hauled over from her house.

"Take your pick," she insists.

I scan the lot and can't help but notice that *every* dress looks like I'll get sent home for indecent exposure, which is when an idea occurs to me. Getting sent home isn't such a bad plan. At least Jules would feel like I tried to be sociable, while all I *really* want to do is sulk under a blanket.

"I'll take this one."

She eyes me as I grab a black, bodycon number with modest, long sleeves, but the modesty ends there. It's sure to be tight and short, which should get me kicked out of there and back home in no time.

"Awesome," she beams. "I've got the perfect silver lariat necklace and black bondage booties to go with it."

"Bondage booties? Sounds like pirate porn."

Laughing, she rolls her eyes seconds before another wave of excitement hits her. "Oh! And I'll wear black, too. That way we'll complement each other when we're side by side."

Our gazes lock and she grabs my hands.

"Get excited, girl! You're about to steal the show tonight." She pops a brow before saying more. "And if West has a pulse, he'll be eating out the palm of your hand within seconds of seeing you in this dress. You know, assuming he isn't already." Her brow wiggles again, being anything but subtle.

I force a smile, and let it fade the moment she turns her back to gather accessories.

Why on Earth did she have to mention his name?

Right away, last night's kiss sends a burst of heat up my torso and chest, bringing warmth to my neck and face. This boy burns me up on the inside. With rage, lust.

Our game of cat and mouse is beginning to take a turn, losing some of its predictability, leaving me to wonder if he hates the things I do and say in retaliation or ... secretly gets off on them.

Hell, maybe we *both* do to a degree.

I need so much help.

A heavy sigh puffs from my lips as I peel the dress off its hanger, heading toward the bathroom to change.

Dear, Lord. Please let this night be over as quickly as possible. Before I do something stupid that I'll definitely *regret later.*

West

Two hours in and I'm still scanning the gym every few seconds.

Damn girl is inside my head.

Deep.

She probably won't even show, being a social outcast and all. Her one and only friend at Cypress Prep would never be caught dead anyplace you can't show up in jeans and a t-shirt. So, yeah, pretty good chance I'm on the lookout for nothing.

Why am I looking for her ass anyway?

Fuck that.

A squeal leaves Parker when I grab her and bring her close, tonguing her down just to help me get that other one out of my head. It won't work, but I'm committed to trying.

I let Parker go, but she stays in my space, holding me around my waist as she stares up with a sweet grin. *Too* sweet. I hate that shit.

She's practically got hearts in her eyes, dreams of a white picket fence and two-point-five kids. With *my* ass strapped to a leash.

Never gonna happen.

All this thing between us has ever been is a means of killing time. She's been something to do this past year, but I've been bored for months now.

She's too ... perfect. Too neat and clean around the edges. Might just be me, but I like my girls a little bit rough, a little bit crazy.

Like Southside.

My eyes slam shut when the unwelcomed thought hits me hard and fast.

"Something wrong?" Parker pipes up to ask.

I shake my head and lie right through my teeth. "No, just a headache."

"Need me to get you something? Water? I think I have pills in my purse if—"

"I'm fine," I manage to cut in. Girl's mouth runs a mile a minute.

She settles down and turns her back to me, pressing her ass against my dick as she gets comfortable. I pass a sideways glance toward my brothers and they're already laughing.

This chick's harder to shake than a leech.

The music is loud, so Parker's none the wiser when Dane leans in. "Why don't you ditch her and go get what you *really* want?" he asks.

Tension spreads across my brow. "What the hell are you talking about?"

He doesn't answer with words, but nods toward the door. To where sex in heels and red lipstick has just walked her sexy ass into the gym. She's way over dressed—like she's hitting a *club* overdressed—but she's hot as hell and she knows it.

Parker thinks my growing hard-on is for her and glances back with a discreet grin.

I haven't taken my eyes off Southside yet when Dane's in my ear again.

"Five-hundred bucks says you end up walking your brooding ass over there to talk to her at some point."

Hearing his bet, I'm aware I'm still watching her like some sort of lost dog.

"Easiest money I'll ever win," I answer.

He turns to gawk at Southside again, grinning as he takes a drink from his cup. "Okay. Just remember you said that."

Chapter 27

BLUE

Jules and I wait out the long line to buy our tickets. Of course, the moment we step foot inside the dark gym, I spot the devil himself. Like usual, he's posted between his brothers, but to my disgust, Parker's glued to his chest. She doesn't see me yet, but West does.

Somehow, he always manages to find me first, like his default reaction is to be on the lookout for the moment I enter a room.

Stalker.

Even from this distance and with the lights low, I notice everything about him despite Parker partially blocking my view. The tight-fitting, white shirt that buttons down his chest and torso, sleeves rolled halfway up his forearms, showing his ink. The watch that catches the colorful lights swirling above. The thin, dark tie around his neck.

Even that look in his eyes, challenging me to pretend I feel nothing.

I see you, King Midas. But you don't run me.

"This puts South Cypress's dances to shame," Jules says, cutting into my thoughts.

I smile, having to agree with that. The budget there for things like this may as well be zero.

"Where's your girl, Lexi?" she asks.

"Home," I answer with a laugh. "She doesn't do the social scene thing."

Jules nods. "Too bad. She seems cool."

I smile, thinking of how Lexi had my back yesterday, helping me get some small measure of revenge on West.

I scan the room, purposely not looking *his* way. The party is in full swing, seeing as how Jules and I missed half of it because I dragged my feet getting dressed. The dancefloor is flooded, jampacked with bodies moving and grinding to the beat. Bass vibrates my chest and I'm reminded of a time when I used to enjoy things like this.

Back when life was considerably easier.

"Let's get out there!" she belts over the loud music. "It'll be fun."

It's on the tip of my tongue to say I'm not in the mood, but as usual, I can't tell her no. A deep sigh leaves me when I nod, agreeing to yet another measure of torture.

Jules pulls me out to the middle, then her eyes fall closed as she moves in rhythm. I'm kind of stiff, but trying to have fun.

Trying.

Images of Hunter in that jumpsuit—with all those gashes and bruises—keep flashing in my head and I have to force them out. I've been pretending to be okay all my life, I can do that again tonight.

I let go just a little. Loosening up, I start to get into it, feeling the B.S. I've carried with me all week begin to lift. But then, a second later, I'm no longer dancing alone. A massive body bumps into me from behind and, at first, it seems like an accident, but then large hands have my waist with a confident grip that can't be ignored. And he smells like a dream.

A wild, hot, sexy dream.

His moves sync up with mine and he's shamelessly grinding against my ass, taking my breath away. It's only now that I glance back, and my heart skips a beat.

A Golden boy is definitely behind me, just ... not the one I might have expected.

Dane casts a dark smile down on me and I immediately feel

conflicted, like I've done something wrong. But ... that doesn't make sense. I'm completely single, not attached to anyone. Not *obligated* to anyone.

Still, it feels strange.

He must sense that I'm flustered when I freeze up a bit, because he leans toward my ear and slow, deeply spoken words go straight to my head.

"If you want him to own his shit, just go with it."

My brow tenses with confusion, but I'm not given more of an explanation than that. And as soon as the statement is made, we're dancing again—close, intimate, steaming hot.

Taking Dane's lead, I relax, leaning forward just a little, pushing my hips back against him, still *very* confused about what's going on.

Is he trying to provoke his brother? The King of Cypress Prep himself?

Jules passes me a look and I already know what she's thinking. That I'm dancing with the wrong brother, but that's because she doesn't know that *any* of the Golden boys are the wrong brother.

Especially West.

Only, now that Dane's raised my curiosity, I can't help but to glance over, not the least bit surprised to find West's angry glare locked on us. In a blazing display of hypocrisy, Parker is all over him. He's dancing with her, but he seems distracted.

As if he's aware of having his brother's attention, Dane's hands move down my hips, controlling them with his touch. Then I feel the smooth heat of his fingertips slipping to my thighs, where the dress I picked barely covers anything.

My heart races on its own, completely against my will as I start to enjoy dancing with him for two very different reasons. One is super obvious—he's hot—but mostly ... I *love* what it's doing to West.

For a guy who rarely gives anything away with his eyes, I see *everything* in them now—confusion, anger.

Jealousy.

I turn away from him and lean deeper into Dane, slinking my arm behind his neck, then push my fingers up through the back of his hair.

He feels just like West, which is a relatively high compliment, considering. Heat from Dane's breath rushes over my collar bone when he leans into me, too. Then, his lips touch me there and my eyes fall closed. I'm completely immersed in him now, the way his hands feel on me, smoothing their way down the clingy fabric laid over my skin.

I've all but forgotten anyone else is in the room when I'm jarred out of the fantasy he's seduced me into.

There's a firm grip on my wrist and a sudden jerk pulls me from Dane's grasp. When I glance back at him, he's wearing a devious grin and hangs onto my hand a moment before I'm out of reach. West has, apparently, trekked across the gym for this, to yank me away from his brother, leaving Parker glaring from afar.

All eyes are on us and I'm surprised he's making such a scene. Typically, he's all about being Mr. Cool Calm and Collected. But, from what I can tell, I've pissed him off, pushed him to the point that he doesn't care who sees he's coming unhinged.

He hasn't said a word as I'm dragged across the gym by my wrist, like a disobedient child. Meanwhile, I can't stop smiling. Maybe it's just knowing that *'THE West Golden'* isn't a god. He's human, hiding flaws and scars just like the rest of us.

It's not until we turn two corners and stand face-to-face in a semi-lit hallway that he addresses me.

"What the hell was that?"

The smirk on my face only drives him crazier. "We're at a dance," I remind him. "I was dancing."

"Not with him," he seethes. "Not like that."

A laugh bubbles in my throat and I can't hold it in. "You sound like such a prude. Haven't you ever seen two people—"

"Not. With. Him," he repeats. Only, this time, the tone he takes steals some of my boldness.

A stormy gaze is locked on me, but it feels different this time. Yes, he's angry, but not his *usual* brand of anger. There's something more to it.

My gaze is trained on his lips when they part, but words don't escape them. There's something he wants to say or do, but I think he's fighting it.

Or maybe he's fighting himself.

I'm no stranger to the heat that seeps from us both when we're close, and it's alive and well right this moment. I let my eyes drift lower, to his throat, down to his swollen pecs that stand out compared to the narrowness of his waist.

I'm aware of how his breathing deepens. I hear it over the lull of bass throbbing from the gym. He steps closer, signaling me to peer up half a second before his taste is in my mouth again.

A deep surge of air fills my lungs and my fingers hook through the beltloops at his hips, pulling him in closer. We've given in to each other like this before, but both those times were about proving a point, manipulating one another as a means of strategy, but ... this isn't the same.

This is all about want.

Need.

Warmth moves up my thigh and I'm so into him it takes a moment to realize he's pushing his hands beneath my dress, squeezing my ass hard. Dizzy from whatever this effect is he has on me, my tongue wanders inside his mouth, kissing him deeper than I've ever done in the past.

His teeth drag across my bottom lip, tugging it, leaving me to want more.

We breathe one another's air and his face is still touching mine. He lifts his hand to push the edge of his thumb across my tender lips, and I feel myself slipping, freefalling down a dangerous slope when it comes to this beast.

My eyes open when he backs off a few inches. At first, he's focused only on me, but then he casts his attention toward the dark, empty classroom beside us. When he stares me down again, I know exactly what he's thinking.

What gives him away is that suggestive grin set on his lips. I bite my own, hardly able to contain myself, thinking of how soft and hot his are.

"You should follow me," he groans, looking like he'll pass out from lust overload.

"Why on Earth would I do a thing like that?" I ask with a smirk.

He passes a sweeping look down to my breasts, and then flashes back to my eyes. "Because I want you." He admits that so freely it knocks the wind out of me.

For several seconds, I consider his offer, but then I come to my senses. His gaze flickers to my lips when a faint smile breaks through.

"Absolutely not. Never in a million years, actually." I *sound* confident, but I'm only half-thinking I have the will to resist.

Whereas most guys would feel defeated by being rejected, not West. I swear it seems he's even more turned on than before.

"Come on, Southside," he croons in my ear.

Something about his tone makes me think I'll be missing out if I don't take him up on what he's offering.

"Imagine how good it'll feel to stop pretending; how good it'll feel to just ... fuck and get it out our damn systems." His breath moves strands of my hair and I swear I can't feel my legs.

I smile and am now thoroughly convinced I'm equally as psychotic as him, because I don't disagree with anything he just said.

"West, we don't even like each other," I remind him. "Hell, most days, I kind of want you dead."

He leans away to catch my eyes. "And if any of that shit really mattered, you wouldn't be thinking about giving in right now."

I hate that he reads me so well, calling my bluff more often than I care to admit.

He invades my space even more, pressing into me so I feel him completely, ending all doubt as to whether he intends to go through with this.

"You know why this works?" His tone drags as his lips move against my ear. "Because we're *both* fucked up."

I'm hazy all over again, feeling my eyes flutter closed.

"You've put me through hell this past month," I remind him, which draws the sexiest laugh out of this bastard. And what does my sadistic ass do? I melt against him.

"And you ruined my shit before the game, making us even. So, why don't we just call all that what it is."

Breathless when he grinds into me, a question falls from my lips. "What's that?"

The tip of his tongue slowly passes over the tendon on the side of my neck, bringing his mouth back to my ear to utter one word.

"Foreplay."

I didn't realize it was possible to want something more than air, but on this night, West taught me that this feeling does, indeed, exist.

"Just give in, Southside."

If he has any idea how close I am to letting him have his way, he'll tip me over that edge for sure, which is why I have to be smart. Which is why I must find it within me to push him away.

I feel actual pain when my hands land on his chest, forcing space between us. He doesn't resist, giving me a few inches to breathe.

"West, I'm not sleeping with you."

"Who said anything about sleep?"

When I peer up, I find him hard to read. "Despite what you think about girls from my side of town, I don't just open my legs for every guy who asks politely."

After weeks of struggling, I feel a small measure of my power return, but his darkening stare undoes that smidgen of confidence immediately, then obliterates it when he asks a bold question.

"So, who *do* you open your legs for then?"

There's bitterness in his tone that I don't really know how to place. Maybe the sting of having been turned down has finally set in? Whatever the case, something about the way he asked has me defensive.

"All you need to know is they're closed to you," I assure him, folding both arms across my chest.

He glances down, reading my body language and, just like that, anger flashes across his face again.

The monster never strays too far. I see him emerge from the shadows right before my eyes—when West's brow tenses, when he stares down on me like I'm nothing.

He's always so hot and cold.

"What the hell do you see in him?"

My brow tenses when he asks, unsure what he means by that. "What do I see in who?"

Hearing my question, he seems uncomfortable. Like he's suddenly aware of having said too much. He shoves both hands inside his pockets, seeming to mull over how he should respond to my question.

"I'm talking about the shady guy. The one who's sniffing behind you every time I turn around," he finally says.

The words burn with envy and I ease up a bit, fighting a smile. "Wait a second. Are you jealous of Ricky?"

"I'm jealous of no one."

I don't buy that for even a second, and with how he just dragged me away from Dane in front of everyone, I'm guessing he knows that already. So, seeing a golden opportunity to get under West's skin, I take it.

When I reach for his tie, he glances down at it, and then his gaze flashes to mine as I speak. "Since you asked so nicely, Ricky was the first."

Thinking that's pretty self-explanatory, I don't elaborate, but I'm surprised when another question flies from West's mouth.

"And who was the last?"

His tone is still so sharp, reeking of authority he doesn't actually have when it comes to me. He isn't owed an explanation about my sex life, nor is it clear why he seems to *need* this question answered. However, the harsh stare locked on me says as much, and for reasons I don't quite understand myself, I offer up the info he's nowhere *near* entitled to.

"Ricky wasn't just the first. He was the only."

Not only is it super awkward that I've just shared this detail about myself, but I'm frustrated that I complied. Maybe because I'm certain he won't believe a single word of it, with his opinions about girls from my hood. But I'm not ashamed of who I am, and if he doesn't buy that, then it's on him. Not me.

"Swear to me," he presses, and I feel my brow twitch with confusion.

My mouth falls open before I'm able to respond, but I'm keenly aware of there being so much more going on here, something he's not saying despite saying so much.

"I don't have a reason to lie," I state boldly.

There's an uncomfortable pause where he should've spoken, and I feel pressured to fill the void myself.

"Were you seriously ready to judge me if there were more?" I ask. "Seeing as how I'd have to block off my schedule for an entire week to hear your list?"

He doesn't laugh when I do, instead choosing to study my expression. Like a red sign that reads "LIAR" is going to start flashing on my forehead. I imagine this to be how criminals must feel while under investigation, but I don't let it get to me. I'm not crazy, though. Dude got super intense on me out of nowhere.

Redness pools beneath his skin and I imagine his face to be hot to the touch. The crimson color only deepens when I smirk again, and his stare stays trained on me when I slip from between his body and the locker I rested against. I feel his eyes chasing after me as I leave him behind.

"Where the hell do you think you're going? We're not done here, Southside," his voice thunders.

But I don't owe him more of this conversation. Which is why I keep moving and wiggle my fingers teasingly to wave goodbye.

"Oh, we're definitely done here," I say. "I've already told you more about me than you deserve to know."

His stare darkens, but not in a threatening way. All I see there is lust, him wishing he had the power to control me like he does everyone else.

"Later, King Midas. I have a dance to get back to," I add dismissively, which I'm certain is driving him crazy.

He called this game we engage in "foreplay", and I'm starting to think his theory might not be too far off base.

Biting my lips, a smirk breaks free as the distance between us grows.

We're twisted enough apart, but damn if we aren't even worse together.

However, in the spirit of honesty, I have to admit ... I'm starting to like it.

Oh, yeah. Note to self: Thank Dane. Dude's a freakin' genius.

Chapter 28

BLUE

King Midas in a crown? Seems fitting.

I'm not even aware I'm smiling until Jules nudges me.

"Something you want to fill me in on?"

Her eyes bounce toward the platform where West stands beside Joss—the crowned queen—and then back to me.

"I'm all ears if you wanna tell me what happened when he dragged you off, caveman-style." She teases.

To contain the huge, stupid smile that breaks free, I bite my lip.

Don't let him get inside your head. You still hate him. He still sucks.

The pep talk brings a small measure of reality back to me, but it's hard to cling to with him staring at me from the stage. Like he's still ready and willing to finish what we started if I just say the word.

And, wow … I've never wanted to give in to *anyone* as badly as I want to give in to him. But there's a principle I must uphold. What kind of girl would I be if I let my enemy have his way with me?

A pitiful one.

…A *satisfied* one.

I'm a freakin' lost cause.

Jules is still smiling at me in my peripheral, but I'm saved by the bell. Glancing down at my phone, an unknown caller pops up.

"Be back," I say to her, and then run out of the gym as quickly as I can in heels. I make it out to the hall just before my voicemail picks up.

"Hello?"

There's silence on the other end at first, and I plug my ear to listen harder while making my way toward the school exit. Maybe reception is bad in this area.

Cool air sweeps over my legs when I make it outside and lean against the brick.

"Hello? Someone there?"

This time I hear something. And it sounds like crying. Right away, I'm on high alert, thinking the worst.

"Scar? Are you okay?"

My heart's racing a mile a minute, especially with what Hunter shared this morning, but she should be fine. I texted an hour ago and she was safe at Uncle Dusty's.

"It's not Scar," a familiar voice says. "It's me."

A rush of air leaves my lungs, and with it, my ability to process words.

"It's Mom, Blue-Jay."

Music from the gym is faint but serves as a soundtrack to this surreal moment. It's been months—*months*—since she's called. So, why now?

"How are you, sweetheart?" she asks, speaking through her sobs.

I envision the state she's probably in right now—disheveled, pathetic.

"How do you *think* I am?" I snap, feeling my throat tighten with emotion. "Where the hell are you?"

Her voice shudders on the other end and I'm guessing my tone has upset her, but who the hell cares? *'Upset'* has been my default setting for quite some time now.

"I've been around," is the lame answer I'm given. "But, Blue-Jay, I can't talk long. I need … a little favor."

And there it is. This call has nothing to do with wanting to know how the children *she* brought into this world are faring without her. She's calling because she needs something.

"What?" I ask flatly, sounding every bit as frustrated and disgusted as I feel.

She holds back for a few seconds, but then gets to her point. "I could use some cash."

"You have got to be kidding me," I say mostly to myself. Her request has me pacing.

"I'm not asking for much," she insists. "Just a couple hundred bucks. I swear I'll get it back to you by next week."

A laugh slips out. "I'm sorry, but do you have any idea what I could do with a couple hundred dollars right now? For starters, I can make sure I feed *your* daughter something other than bologna and ramen five days a week. Oh! And I could've paid to keep the electricity on myself last month. And I wouldn't have to work so many hours that I'm failing at being the parent *you* were supposed to be to Scar. Do you need me to go on, Mom?"

There's silence on the other end, like I knew there would be. She sniffles in the background and I'm panting like I've just run a mile.

"It'll just be for a little while," she repeats, as if she heard nothing I said.

Despite wanting nothing more than to have some small piece of my mother to cling to, I end the call.

My breath puffs in the chilled air, but I hardly notice I'm cold. At the moment, the only thing I feel is empty, void of *everything*.

Because I've made a habit of giving away everything I have to give, but no one ever thinks enough of me to repay the favor.

West

A set of stiff, fake tits bob in my face as Sandy ... or Sara ... whatever the hell her name is, rides me hard and fast. The headboard slams the wall like she's trying to ram us into the other room and, while I *should* be enjoying this Stacey girl, I can't get another out of my head.

Outside the window, screams from the pool distract me. As far as after parties go, it's a lively one, but I'm not enjoying any of it.

Any of it.

"Get off me."

A confused glare meets mine through the dark. "What?"

"You deaf? I said get the fuck off me."

Sydney scoffs when she slides onto the mattress and grabs her clothes, then slams the bathroom door behind her to make sure I know she's pissed. Not realizing I couldn't care less what she's feeling. She'll be forgotten by morning. Already is.

Which begs the question why one, in particular, is stuck in my head like a bad song.

Or ... a good one.

Damn.

I've rationalized it a million times, a million different ways. Reminding myself why she's off limits. Reminding myself why I should be disgusted by the mere *thought* of touching her, but it doesn't work. Every time I close my eyes, I see that face.

That one face.

Now, with what she claimed tonight, she's gotten even deeper inside my head. She could've said anything. Could've lied and said she was a virgin. Could've lied and said she'd been with a few. But instead, she told me about Ricky—that he'd been the first and only. A very specific response.

One that would blow my entire theory out the water if it were true.

However, because of that seed of doubt being planted, I can't even think straight.

She said something else that stuck with me. The joke she made about my "hit list" being too long to share in a night. While I make no apologies for how many chicks I've been with, I'm not proud of everything I've done. The reminder prompted one ghost, in particular, to resurface. One that haunts me despite her being alive and well, despite there not actually being bad blood between us.

And that ghost's name is Casey.

That One slip up in judgment would make me a shit candidate for holding *anyone's* sins against. Only, where my mission with Southside is concerned, it's never been about me. It's been about the only one who's truly innocent in all this—my mother.

"Just so you know, I'm gonna tell everyone you couldn't even get it up, asshole," Sharon shouts at the back of my head on her way out of the room.

Say whatever you want. My reputation in bed precedes me, bitch.

She isn't worth the breath it would take to say these words aloud, but they're true.

I stand, get rid of the wasted condom, then find my pants on the floor. After zipping them, I grab the half empty beer I set on the nightstand, then walk to the end of the hallway where laughter flows in from an open set of French doors.

"Did I miss anything good?" I ask, leaning over the balcony rail to stare down at the pool. We'll pay for having yet another party here at the Bellvue house, but it'll be worth it.

"Nope," Sterling says with a sigh, slouching lower in his seat, a total of three girls surrounding him. Two perched on the arms of his chair, another in his lap.

If something *did* happen, he would've missed it.

Turning away, I smile.

"What about you?" Dane asks with a grin.

I face him slowly, still pissed with the stunt he pulled a few hours ago at the dance. Not to mention, my wallet is now $500 lighter.

When my only response to his question is to look away, he laughs.

"Heavy is the head that wears the crown," Joss hiccups.

I turn again, just as she drops down into Dane's lap. If I didn't already know she was drunk, I would now. She never lets her guard down with him, never blurs the lines for fear of where it might lead.

He's tipsy, too. So, when he bites his lip with lust heavy in his eyes, then begins to slide a hand between Joss's thighs, I save him from himself.

"Joss, we're calling you an Uber," I offer. "Your dad'll be pissed you're drunk, but more than that, he'll be happy when you make it home alive."

"Good idea," Dane cuts in, seeming to come to his senses.

I grunt when I bring her to her feet with little to no help on her part. This girl is *drunk* drunk.

Dane follows behind her, already arranging her ride from his phone when they leave me and Sterling out on the balcony.

"Our last Homecoming at CPA. You ready to leave all this behind next year?" he asks, sounding sentimental like Mom. I'll ream him for it later. For now, I just shrug and stare out at the crowd below.

"It's time to move on, lay claim to a new kingdom," I tease.

He laughs at that. "I feel you on being ready to move on, but if I'm being honest, it'll be so much sweeter with one last championship under our belt. You know, assuming South Cypress doesn't steal it."

"Fuck Southside."

There's silence for a bit, and he sounds suspicious when he speaks again. "Are … we still talking about football?"

I don't answer. Because I'm not so sure myself.

"Mind giving us a sec, ladies?" he asks, prompting the harem surrounding him to stand and leave.

He leans forward in his chair and I brace myself. It must be serious.

"I overheard something tonight," he starts. "And take it for what it's worth, but I thought you'd like to know."

I'm intrigued, so I drop down into the seat Dane left empty. "What is it?"

Sterling sips his drink first, letting it dangle between his fingers after. "I was out getting some air and Southside walked out to take a call."

Hearing him explain, I remember seeing her rush for the exit right after Joss and I got crowned. Now, I guess I know why.

"She didn't notice me, but I heard her conversation," he explains.

"From what I could gather, it was her mom on the line, but … I got the impression her life's pretty screwed up."

My jaw tenses. "What'd you hear?"

He sighs and keeps his eyes trained on the pool below. "Sounded like her mom was asking for money. Then, Southside got triggered, started talking about how she can hardly pay bills and provide for her sister as it is. They went back and forth like that for a bit, before Southside finally got fed up and ended the call."

I don't say a word, but that doesn't mean I don't feel every single thing he just said to me.

"But anyway," he pipes up again, "just seemed like the kind of thing you should know."

I see right through him. This isn't an act of loyalty toward me, to my cause. This is an appeal, a one-man intervention with hopes that I'll go easier on *her*.

Of course, he'd want that because he doesn't know what I know about her. Doesn't know how our lives are connected to hers.

With that thought, her words creep inside my head again and I hate that I'm not so sure anymore. Hate that she's made me doubt what I had been so certain of not so long ago. But I can't unsee that pic in my dad's phone. It isn't something I just dreamed up; it's real and there's only one explanation for it being there. And while I may not know Southside all that well, I sure as hell know Vin Golden.

Sterling stands and slaps my shoulder before taking the balcony steps by two. Then, he pulls off his shirt and dives headfirst into the pool, leaving me here with my thoughts.

I refuse to feel for that girl. She doesn't deserve our sympathy, no matter how pathetic her life is. The only thing Sterling has done here is expose Southside's motivation, the likely reason she attached herself to my father.

It's simple.

She needs cash, he has tons of it.

My father has a knack for sensing people's weaknesses and exploiting them. This is no different from every other stunt he's pulled.

Anger fills me, but I'm shaken by where it's stemming from. It's not even aimed toward Southside this time, but my father. For manipulating yet another person just because he can. And, as much as I don't want to sympathize with Southside ... I do.

Because I've been in her shoes before. No, not the same situation, but bound to my father because he's good at what he does—negotiating deals.

Despite myself, I can't help but wonder if she simply got entangled in something she didn't see a way out of with him.

God knows I could relate to that.

On so many fucked up levels.

Chapter 29

BLUE

Just a few days ago, it was too cold for Lexi and me to eat underneath what we've dubbed *'our tree'*, but today I wish we were inside, enjoying the AC. Late-October heatwave, I guess. We're stuck out here, though. All because he-who-shall-remain-nameless is sitting in the lunchroom with his crew.

The second I lose the battle to keep my eyes away from the window and sneak in a glance, he laughs, and I'm disturbed by how much I like his face.

Stupid face.

Stupid hot body.

A flashback from Homecoming rushes to mind and I zone out for a sec. Doesn't matter much that it was a few weeks ago, I haven't forgotten. When his hands graze me by accident during our forced swim lessons, we're both quick to back off and regroup. He hasn't been as forward—as *open*—as he was that evening, and I thank God for that every night.

Because I'm, admittedly, kind of weak for him.

Just as I start to turn, he finds my eyes and it's over for me. Right away, my lips feel warmer than the rest of my face, like he's touching them, and I'm completely immersed in the memory now. His voice lingers in my ears, like he's whispering something to me at this very moment.

'Come on, Southside.'

Every second since he asked and I refused to follow him into that classroom, I've regretted it.

"Ok, I give. What the heck is it with you and him? I've played along, pretending not to notice the whole … love-hate thing going on between you and Golden, but seriously. What gives?" Lexi pops a grape into her mouth after asking, and I don't miss the suspicious grin on her face, either.

I swallow the last of my leftovers from Uncle Dusty before speaking. "The short version? He hates me for reasons undisclosed, and I hate him because he's a dick. Mystery solved."

She's already shaking her head, disagreeing. "You two need to just bone and get it over with."

Water sprays from my mouth and Lexi screams, trying to dodge it.

"What the hell, dude?" she asks, laughing as she reaches for a napkin to clean off her arm.

"I'm sorry, but that was all your fault."

"It's true!" she insists.

"Nope. No way. West is a definite no-go for me. For starters, dude's mean as hell, which is generally a turn off."

"Maybe it's like the mean boy in kindergarten," she muses. "You know, the one who's got it bad for a girl, but the only way he knows how to express himself is to pull Little Susie's hair and make her cry."

I lean back to rest on the heels of my palms. "Well, unfortunately for West, that tactic stops being cute once we all learn how to add two plus two."

Lexi shrugs. "Whatever it is, it's weird as hell from the outside looking in."

I imagine that's true. Seeing as how it's also weird as hell from the inside looking out. If that's a thing …

"Let's not talk about him, then," I suggest.

She's thoughtful, then her eyes light up. "We could always talk about costume shopping."

Confused, I pop a brow at her, unsure why she's grinning so profusely. "Come again?"

"Halloween's a week away," she reminds me. Not that I *need* a reminder. Between my neighborhood and school, the over-the-top decorations make it impossible to forget.

"You telling me you still trick-or-treat, Rodriguez?"

She rolls her eyes. "I wish. One neighbor straight up slammed the door in my face the last time I tried. Granted, this was just last year, but still. *Super* rude."

Another laugh slips out and, lucky for her, I don't have water in my mouth this time.

"What I *mean* is, Monster Bash is coming up," she explains. "It's always the weekend before Halloween."

I'm still just as confused. "Um ... Monster Bash?"

"Yeah, it's a massive Halloween party this kid Marcus throws every year. Never in the same place, but it's always someplace creepy and secret. Costumes are required. I don't usually do the social thing, but Halloween's kind of my jam, so I make the exception."

Her face is all lit up with excitement, which makes turning down her invitation that much harder.

"Gonna have to pass. Not only do I not have cash to shop, I also just really don't want to," I admit with an apologetic grin. "Plus, I'm guessing the Golden boys will be there?"

So much for not talking about them anymore.

"They show up to all the parties," she answers, which isn't surprising. "But you won't have to worry about them. You'll be with me and I'll make sure you don't even notice them. Should be a ton of guys there. So, who knows? You might just find someone to sweep West right out of your head."

I'm thoughtful for a second and the amount of time it takes me to think things over doesn't go unnoticed.

"Please, please, please!" she begs. "I'll even buy your costume if you say yes."

Rolling my eyes, I cave. Partially, anyway.

"But there's no time. I have to take pics at tonight's game, and I work tomorrow morning."

"We'll make it work," she insists. "We can hit a few costume shops right when school lets out, and the party isn't until late tomorrow, so it won't mess up your work schedule."

As soon as the words leave her mouth, Parker and crew slow-walk it past Lexi and me. I hadn't even seen them come out to the courtyard, but here they are, staring down on us before exploding with laughter the second there's a little distance between us.

I hate each and every one of those robots.

"Ignore them," Lexi insists, clearly holding out hope she'll convince me to go. "Just say you'll come with me," she begs.

I'm firm on my *'no'* for about thirty seconds, and then give in.

"Fine."

She squeals. "You won't regret this."

"Mm hm. I bet!"

Her response to the sarcasm is to give me the finger before she goes back to eating. Me? I'm filled with dread as I stare at the back of Parker's head. West's entire legion of demons will likely be there, but I kind of owe Lexi. She did help me steal all those pants.

Translation: I'm screwed and there's no way out of it.

Glancing down at my phone, I hop to my feet. "Gotta run. Dr. Pryor wants to see me before fourth hour. I'll see you in gym."

Lexi nods. "For sure. And if your boyfriend comes looking for you, I'll tell him where to find you," she teases.

I roll my eyes playfully. "Yeah, okay. You do that."

There are still a few minutes left of lunch as I approach Dr. Pryor's door. She waves me inside and her expression's blank, giving nothing away.

"Have a seat, Ms. Riley."

I do as I'm told, nervously clasping my hands in my lap. She sifts through a stack of papers until finding what she needs. After scanning one sheet for a moment, she slides it across her desk.

"A permission slip," she announces.

"For what?" I ask while looking over the paper, confused.

"You've been invited to join the football team on a little excursion." She says that with a smile. One I don't even come close to matching.

"I don't understand."

Pinching the bridge of her glasses, she removes them and looks me in the eyes.

"I'm sure you're aware of our boys' record this season," she says. "So, it's not unusual for the athletic department to plan ahead when the odds are high we'll make it to regionals. We've already secured transportation and booked a block of rooms."

During the brief pause that follows, I can't help but wonder what this has to do with me and the permission slip in my hand.

"Listen, I'm going to level with you," she continues with a sigh. "In a perfect world, I'd ask how you felt about this, ask if you were up to it, but ... the school will need photos and you need to do everything you can to stand out in Journalism Club. So, that means this assignment is all yours."

I say nothing, because nothing I say will change this decision she's made. A decision that will stick me with West and his crew for an entire weekend.

"Figured I'd tell you sooner rather than later," she adds, "so you can make the necessary arrangements."

When she lowers her head, closing the discussion with that final statement, it's like a nail hammered into my coffin. On my way out of her office, I reach for my phone to text Jules. If the boys make it to regionals, I'll need her and Uncle Dusty to look after Scar sometime next month.

Here I am, backed into the corner again.

Nice.

West

"Your ma tells me you boys are undefeated. Keep that up and they'll draft you straight to the NFL on graduation day."

My grandfather—the legendary Boone Landry III himself—is the only one who's drawn a smile out of me today.

"Thanks, Grandpa, but I'll settle for making QB-1 at NCU. For now, anyway."

"They'd be fools not to want you," he insists, his thick, southern drawl ringing familiar in my ears.

Based on skill alone I'd agree with that. Only, there are other factors that could blow that chance out of the water and they're never far from my thoughts.

"Guess we'll see next year," I say vaguely, making light of how much I have riding on going undefeated this season. Knowing that it still might not be enough if certain truths come to light.

"I *also* heard on the wind that you had an interesting game a few weeks ago. Something about some choice words painted on your uniform?"

Hearing him ask, I laugh a little as noise picks up in the locker room. "Yeah, *'interesting'* is one way of putting it. And, technically, it was just *one* choice word."

I envision Southside's handiwork and then my thoughts immediately shift to the incident in the hallway during the dance. The one where I'm turned the fuck on, and Southside turns me the fuck down.

Damn tease.

Since then, I've maintained the distance between us, for obvious reasons. It's been weeks since I, personally, brought any hell Southside's way, but that doesn't mean I haven't enjoyed watching Parker and crew put her through the wringer. Once my head is clear, once the lines between us aren't so blurred, I'll be back on my game.

"All right, level with me," Grandpa huffs. "Tell the old man what you did to piss off whoever this poor girl is."

"Not sure what you mean," I lie, smiling because there's no way he believes that. "You know me. Mr. Innocent."

"Mr. Full-of-shit is more like it," he corrects, bringing another laugh out of me. "This girl clearly wanted to send you a message, and that little stunt has *'woman scorned'* written all over it."

I don't answer right away and, in the silence, I fuckin' hate who's in my head again.

"It's ... a long story," I sigh.

"Well, if I were you, I'd shorten it up. And quick. Preferably, before she ruins *all* your clothes." He pauses to let out a gruff laugh. "Take it from me, women don't forget a damn thing, so just apologize, admit you're a dog, and do whatever it takes to clean things up between you."

I take his words to heart, because he always shares little nuggets of wisdom, but in this situation, it'll never apply. I'll never apologize when an apology isn't owed.

"I hear you," is all I say back, but decide to move on to a new topic. "How are the boys? Still raising hell?"

The exhausted sigh that leaves his mouth sheds light on where this is headed.

"Let's just say moving on to high school hasn't changed your cousins in the least. In fact, I'm convinced the more hair they get on their nuts, the worse they behave!"

"They can't be *that* bad," I insist with a laugh.

"Hmph. The little shits have all of Dupont Bayou shuttering their windows just at the mention of their names. Hell, probably the entire Parish!" he adds.

I hold back from laughing again, hearing the stress in his voice.

"It ain't really Beau and Keaton causing trouble, but those other three? Whoo-wee! *Those* hellraisers pull everyone right into the mud with 'em. Every damn time," he complains. "I cannot *tell* you how many good dreams I've been yanked out of by phone calls from angry fathers, informing me they found one of my foolish grandsons sneaking around with their teenage daughters in the middle of the night. At this rate, I'll be a *great*-grandfather or bailing them out of jail before I can even get these bastards to college!"

The statement has me wondering how my own missteps would be judged if he ever caught wind of them.

"If you need me to fly down and put the fear of God in them, just say the word," I offer, pushing my own internal B.S. aside.

"Might have to take you up on that. Just keep that slick-ass father of yours away from my property and I'll be all right. I've had a bullet with that son of a bitch's name on it since the day I handed your ma off at the altar."

Note to self: Let Dad know Grandpa's asking him to stop in for a visit. Should go great.

Hearing my grandfather talk, you'd think he's raising the boys all on his own, but he's just always been involved with us—*all* his grandsons—which makes it seem that way. In truth, all five of the cousins he's complaining about live with their parents. However, my grandfather being *the man* down in Saint Delphine Parish, everyone sees us as *his* boys. Not the sons of his five daughters.

The twins—River and Stoney—are notorious troublemakers, and Linden's anger issues made it easy for him to fall right in step. Then, like Grandpa said, the other two just seem to get pulled into whatever trouble these three are involved in.

"I blame my daughters' godawful choices in men," he cuts in again. "Poor girls couldn't spot a good one if he picked her up and tossed her over his shoulder. Not even my little Rosalie, God rest her soul."

I couldn't argue with him on that point.

"Anyway, enough about all this. The real reason I'm calling is to wish you a good game, but I'm sure you already knew that."

I did. "Thanks, Grandpa. I'll call you after we win."

He laughs in my ear. "That's what I like to hear. Now give the phone to one of your brothers, would ya?"

"Sure thing. One sec."

Dane's already reaching for my cell. As the patriarch on my mother's side of the family, the man's kept this same pre-game phone call routine since our dad put us on the pee-wee league as kids.

Lacing up my cleats, I get my head in the game, knowing Grandpa will be expecting that call from me in a couple hours. Only a few games left in the season, then I can breathe a little easier.

Dane wraps things up, then passes the phone to Sterling. By the time I get it back, it's nearly game time.

"You got a text," Sterling lets me know.

Clutching my helmet, I glance at the message.

'Overheard Lexi and that bitch talking about plans to hit up Marcus's party tomorrow,' Parker wrote. *'Mind if I get creative?'*

She loves this more than she should, and that isn't lost on me. Sometimes, I wonder if she sees it, the weird chemistry between Southside and me. It makes me question whether it's the reason she volunteers for evil shit like this.

Probably.

I shoot her back a message then follow the rest of the team out onto the field.

'Have fun. Just don't almost kill her this time.'

Chapter 30

BLUE

Yep, she talked me into it. And here I am, in the middle of nowhere, walking uphill through the darkness to some centuries-old cemetery.

Condensed version: the whole thing is creepy AF.

"Dude, are you scared or something?" Lexi teases.

I peer up at her as we climb, seeing nothing but the moon's reflection in her round, tinted glasses—the staple to her John Lennon costume.

"First of all, only a psychopath *wouldn't* be scared," I point out. "But there's also the fact that I'm doing all this walking in go-go boots and a minidress. Because *someone* insisted that I come dressed as Yoko Ono tonight."

Meanwhile, she's sporting a white, bell-bottomed pantsuit with matching turtleneck sweater—looking very Lennon-esque. She sprung for wigs for us both, and I can't remember a time I've ever been more uncomfortable in clothes.

"We lucked out with this weather, though, right?" she points out. "Otherwise, you'd be freezing your ass off."

"Doesn't change the fact that I'm trekking up a mountain in platforms."

Laughing at my exaggeration, Lexi loops her arm through mine.

"Come on, Yoko, I've got you," she teases, helping me the rest of the way.

At the top of the hill, the scene has been set. As far as secret, teenage, Halloween parties go, it's pretty decked out. Someone's taken the time to set up and decorate snack tables, and a bunch of pumpkins have been carved with cartoon faces. Others are a bit more abstract. Like, the one of a penis, fully detailed with testicles.

Boys.

From what I can tell, there's even designated security. Granted, those patrolling are merely underclassmen dressed in black t-shirts and jeans, but at least they're keeping an eye on the food and drinks. I imagine this is the closest most of them will come to getting invited to a party like this any time soon. Basically, they're likely elite hopefuls, vying for a spot within the *'in crowd'*.

Poor, disillusioned souls.

Dim lanterns hang on hooks near every other headstone. Most of the markers are aged and leaning to one side, which adds to the terrifying ambiance. Fake hands positioned on some of the graves give the appearance of the dead reaching out from the great beyond. It's in poor taste, but creative, I guess.

Loud music blares from huge speakers at all four corners of the party space, and I refuse to scan for … *him*.

He's definitely in my head, though.

Always.

"How's your aim?"

I glance toward Lexi when she asks. "Fine, I guess. Why?"

Without further explanation, I'm dragged across the grass to a beer pong table. One with LED lights that blink to the bass pounding from the subwoofer beside it.

Lexi turns when I laugh. "It's a little soon to start drinking, don't you think?"

She pops a shoulder. "I figure, the sooner I get a little tipsy, the sooner I'll forget I'm mostly partying with a bunch of losers. Then, from there, the possibilities are endless." A huge grin brightens her face.

She steps up for a turn and I pat her on the back with a laugh. "This one's all you, Mr. Lennon. Rock on."

With another shrug of her shoulders, she takes a ball and it doesn't take long for her to find a willing partner to take on the twosome across the table. After that, the next twenty minutes are a blur of flying ping pong balls and red cups going bottoms up. It becomes super clear super fast that this girl can drink most under the table. It's Lexi's turn and she sinks the ball into one of the other duo's cups with ease, and those gathered around cheer her on.

"I'm gonna go grab a drink," I lean in to tell her. "Be right back."

She catches my wrist before I go. "Don't take *anything* that isn't sealed," is her warning, although that's not something I'd ever forget.

When I salute her and walk away, there's more cheering at my back and I laugh. You'd never conclude she's not the social type. Guess she was right. Get a few beers in her and she's the life of the party.

One of the mini security guards eyes me as I snag a bottle of water from the cooler, and then stop to scoop some snack mix from the bowl into an orange sandwich bag. I shoot him a coy wave and keep it moving. The platform boots make walking over the uneven terrain a challenge, but I'm pretty sure no one sees the couple times I nearly face-plant into a head stone.

The music's good and, so far, no one I hate has ventured too close to me. Parker and her girls are always lurking, but they're mostly concerned with being seen in those red horns and the skimpy, red lingerie they're passing off as costumes. I almost wish we weren't experiencing a mild heatwave, so the sluts could freeze their nipples off right here in the cemetery.

Being so abundantly mature, I imagine it, their nipples slipping right out from underneath those see-through teddies and landing in the grass while each one screams in horror.

Who I *haven't* seen, though, are the Golden boys. My first thought is that they've decided to skip the festivities this time, but no sooner than I think those words—

"Who the hell are *you* supposed to be?" There's a laugh in West's deep voice when he startles me, and it grows watching my snack bag slip from my hand. I only got to eat a few pieces out of it, and now it's in the freakin' dirt.

When I turn, thinking I'll only glare at him, I suddenly wish I'd kept my eyes straight ahead.

Bare chested and solid, he's oiled all the way down to that damn V. He looks like some sort of strip-o-gram fantasy and the thought of it has me rolling my eyes at him. You don't get to be a complete ass and sexy, too. Just isn't right.

He's dressed as Egyptian royalty—black and gold, striped headdress that rests on his shoulders *and* matches our school colors. Then, a black kilt-like thingy, trimmed in gold. On his feet, a pair of black and gold sneakers that don't go with his digs, but somehow make him look even hotter. I'm willing to bet that what's on his feet costs more than my house.

I peer out across the cemetery and spot Dane and Sterling already raising hell, both wearing the exact same getup.

Freakin' hot douche bags. All three of them.

At Dane's side, and dressed as Cleopatra, is Joss. Her braids are down tonight, and they look like part of the costume. She's so pretty it hurts, and I always get the impression Dane thinks so, too. I also find myself hating Joss least of all, because she seems mostly neutral.

Not any help, but not so much part of the problem.

"You gonna answer me or just pretend I'm not standing here?" West perks up again.

He sounds less ... venomous than usual. Almost happy.

Almost.

"Aren't nightmares supposed to disappear if you ignore them?" I shoot back, sipping my water, because it's all I have left.

In my peripheral, I see the gleam of white teeth when he smiles. "Come on. Don't be like that."

I scoff and roll my eyes, but don't engage.

"How's Scarlett?" he dares to ask next, and this time, his comment has earned him a hard glare from me.

"Don't ask about her. Or anyone else in my family," I clarify.

The sound of West's quiet laughter grates my nerves, but I hide it.

"Damn, Southside! You always such a bitch?"

"Only in the presence of other bitches," I shoot back.

He's still laughing, which nearly makes me smile. Only a freak would laugh at being called out of their name.

Something's happening inside me. There's this buzzing, some kind of energy that goes haywire when West is around. As much as I'd like to think it's all bad, that would be a lie. The part of me that's twisted like my mother sort of enjoys the raw, unbridled interaction, neither of us the least bit concerned with niceties or holding our tongues.

Whatever comes to mind, we just say it—sharp edges and all.

"You know what I think?" West asks, cutting into my thoughts as I watch Lexi from a distance. Her hands just shot up into the air, which means she's still on a winning streak.

"What's that?"

"I think you hate that your sister actually likes me," he shares. "You hate that I got inside her head, but most of all, you hate that she missed it."

My gaze leaves Lexi now, landing solely on West as the dim light of the lantern beside us outlines his pecs.

"What are you talking about?" I ask, already feeling heat seep beneath my skin.

He smirks again but takes a swig from his drink before answering. "She missed that I'm not one of the good guys."

A surge of air fills my lungs and I'm looking at him, but not seeing him. Instead, my mind goes back to that night, the block party. I envision how Scar lit up at the sight of him, and even more so when he dropped a hundred-dollar bill into her jar.

"And what you hate even more," West adds, "...is that *you* missed it."

I feel sick to my stomach. Because ... he's right.

I *did* let him slip under the radar. My first impression—even my *second* impression—was all wrong. He's nothing like that scorching hot exterior suggests. Inside, he's nothing but emptiness, haunted corridors, and darkness.

Just like me.

"When are you gonna just admit it?" he asks with a humorless laugh.

My brow gathers. "You care an awful lot about what *I* think, while what you *should* be worried about is your girlfriend staring us down like she wants to set us both on fire," I shoot back.

At those words, West's gaze wanders across the graveyard to where Parker's glaring with the heat of a thousand suns burning in her eyes. I don't hate that it gets under her skin seeing West standing so close. Bitch deserves it.

"Fuck Parker," he says with immeasurable disgust.

Caught off guard by how boldly he's just spoken, I snap a look in his direction.

"Now that we've gotten *that* out of the way," he continues with a widening grin, "you ready to admit it?"

Frustrated for too many reasons to name, I roll my eyes. "Admit what, West?"

"That you want me," he answers quickly. "That you made a mistake turning me down a few weeks ago."

He's so focused on this conversation that he's turned to face me full-on now. I also notice he hasn't blinked even once since I peered up at him.

My heart does this weird thing I can't explain, but I give nothing away, keeping my expression even.

"Well, I suppose I'll admit all that around the same time *you* admit you're an ass and have secretly wanted *me,* since day one. So, I guess that would be, mmm … never?"

Laughing at the ridiculousness of it all, I take a step away, thinking this would be the perfect time to make my escape. Only, I feel a firm grip at the bend of my elbow, and it causes me to stumble back in place. My back slams firmly against West's chest and I feel his racing heart. When he leans down to speak into my ear, I stare out across the sea of headstones to Parker, our audience of one.

"How about I call your bluff," he says, loosening his grip as both his hands move to my waist.

I'm holding my breath, and the only thought in my head is a memory of his delicious mouth. Even now, I remember its heat, imagining it moving over my skin.

"I'm an ass," he admits with an air of honesty I don't miss. "And I've wanted you since day one." He's challenging me, throwing my dare right back in my face.

"West, I..."

"Don't feed me that bull about all the shit I've done," he groans against my ear, "because the things I've done would only hurt someone *normal*. And own it, Southside. We're both pretty fucking far from normal."

I have serious concerns that my heart might actually beat out of my chest. The music seems louder, echoing inside my bones as he holds me against him.

"Sticks and stones can't break us. Because, you and me ... we're already broken."

My eyes fall shut when he summarizes the entire script of my life with that one statement. It leaves me feeling bare, like he and I are one in the same. Only, we can't be.

I mean ... *right*?

He's insane and I'm ...

Damn, maybe I'm insane, too. I *must* be to let him get inside my head like this. To let him *touch* me like this.

At this very moment, something clicks. I get what it is about him, why I get revved up whenever he steps foot in my direction. He draws out the numbness, the mental Novocain that's helped me get through all the pain and bullshit. He makes me face it all. Makes me *feel* it all. He doesn't let me hide behind the crumbling wall made up of the half-cocked *'everything will be okay'* and *'it'll get better'* rhetoric the rest of the world feeds me. West forces me to see the truth, that life really is a shitshow, and he's the one person not afraid to admit that. Not afraid to *live* that.

If he weren't so sick in the head, I might consider this an honorable trait. But instead, I see him becoming my crutch. The thing I lean on to feel real.

Even if all he makes me feel is his darkness.

His touch has become familiar. My skin knows it well. His palm splays flat across my stomach and I'm melting into him as it rises higher, until his thumb brushes the wire under my bra. I'm certain I'll disappear if I give in to what I want.

"Come with me, Southside. This is my second and final offer. There won't be a third," he warns

I stumble before catching my balance when he backs away, leaving me to stand on my own. My eyes chase after him, following as he disappears in the shadows of a mausoleum that looks to be as old as this cemetery.

I glance at Lexi and consider shooting her a text, but my focus is on the dark space where West just disappeared, and … I can't fight it.

I follow the devil right into the unknown.

Chapter 31

WEST

Her silhouette darkens the doorway and I'm actually shocked she came. If she were any other girl, I could've staked my life on her accepting that invitation, but not Southside.

This girl ... I can't pin her down.

Smiling, I call out to her when she hesitates. "Get your ass over here."

She doesn't move, but folds both arms across her chest instead. "Say please," she teases, but I've had about all I can stand and take large strides forward, drawing her right into a kiss.

She leans to the side when I push my hand along the smooth skin of her neck. The throb of her pulse hammering against my fingertips causes mine to race, too.

What is it about her? I've never met anyone who makes me break my own rules, makes me forget all the things I should hate about her. Even if only temporarily.

I'm pulled from thought when her soft hands push up my back, then latch onto my shoulder blades. I hate clingy chicks, but for some reason, this isn't so bad. Not even with her holding me so tight that I can feel she needs someone. I guess, for tonight, I'm that someone.

There's this frustrating sense of being too close and not being close enough, but I know which of those conflicting sentiments is controlling me, taking over my soul more with every second.

A sharp breath surges into her nostrils when I lift her onto a raised, cement slab. I'll tell her later it's some dead bastard's tomb, but for now, I settle between the softness of her thighs and drag the straps of her dress and bra down her arm. Goosebumps texture her skin where I kiss a trail down her neck to her shoulder. I want her so bad I can fucking taste it. No way she doesn't feel that.

I draw her to the edge by her waist and she snatches off the headpiece to my costume. Throwing it aside, her fingers push through my hair, gripping it tight.

Tugging the dress a little lower, I kiss the soft flesh of her tits until the material falls away and exposes more. First, my lips softly graze over her nipple, but when I tease it with my tongue, the bud of flesh tightens and I draw it into my mouth.

"Shit, West."

Her breathy plea makes it even harder not to rush things forward. More so when that tight body of hers arches toward mine. I make myself release her, placing both hands on the edge of the slab instead. It's the only way I won't tear her apart in the next few seconds.

Only, the instant I regain control, she snatches it right from my grasp again. All it takes is her removing her hand from my back, to then wedge it between our bodies. We're both damn-near vibrating with the most intense energy I've ever felt.

I sense where she's going with this, and when my waistband is pulled away from where it rides low at the base of my stomach, an alarm sounds off inside my head. It's the reason I decide now's a good time to warn her who she's dealing with.

"Easy, Southside," I groan, lifting my head to speak the words against her neck. "You're dangerously close to crossing the point of no return."

She ignores the first warning and rests her full lips against my collarbone before sucking there, driving me absolutely insane.

"If you aren't fucking sure," I speak up again, "Stop while you still—"

She shuts me the hell up by pushing her soft hand down the front of my boxers, unapologetically gripping my cock like she owns the damn thing. My chest moves against hers as I breathe deep. Then, my eyes fall shut.

This damn girl has me right where she wants me.

At her mercy.

Her hand works up and down my length and all the back and forth between us has built up to this. I'm tired of tiptoeing around what we're both really after, so I make up my mind to propel us to the next level. I reach beneath her skirt to grab her hip, and with one rough motion the seam of her panties starts to rip. Only, I don't get very far, because out of nowhere, we're engulfed in bright light.

Southside gasps and is quick to cover herself, pushing her straps back in place in record time. I, on the other hand, am not thinking about any of that shit. All I want to know is who the fuck just interrupted?

"Thought you'd like to know it's time for the Monster Mix."

I recognize Parker's voice. Even if it *isn't* all chipper like usual.

She doesn't leave right away, instead keeping that light focused on me and Southside while we fix ourselves. If history is any indication, Parker's going to cry herself to sleep about what she just walked in on, and I can expect a phone call about 3 a.m., when she'll feel the need to tell me what a good catch she is and how I'll miss her long before she'll miss me.

Blah fucking blah …

All bullshit.

Southside hops down from the tomb, brushing dust off the back of her costume, and I can't wrap my head around her leaving.

"We aren't finished here. What're you doing?"

She glances down to where I've just taken her wrist, then she passes a look toward Parker.

Before she even answers, I realize she's about to use that as an excuse to bail. "Kind of *feels* like we're done," she reasons.

I don't get another chance to plead my case, because she rushes off after that. I'm right behind her, grabbing my headpiece before pushing past Parker. She doesn't miss the death-stare I shoot her. It's the next best thing to actually being able to punch her, which I would've done without question if she were a dude.

Southside is moving slowly, and I can't help but to wonder if it's because she's hoping I'll catch up. Parker's lingering somewhere behind us, probably sulking, but I find it all too easy to forget about her these days.

An uncertain glance flashes up at me before Southside speaks. "What's the ... Monster Mix, or whatever?" she asks.

We're walking in step now and it feels a lot like I want to touch her, hold her hand or some weak shit like that.

I kill the urge because I'm not that guy. Never have been. Might castrate myself if I ever *become* that guy.

"... Uh, it's sort of a Monster Bash tradition," I finally answer. "It's just a drink concoction Marcus makes up. He puts it in this big, gaudy chalice and we all take a sip, drinking to the occasion."

And we're probably drinking to cold sores and mono, too, which is why my brothers and I have a standing rule where we drink first.

She smooths her costume again and this is where it gets weird. All because we somehow fell into the first normal conversation we've ever held with one another. It's jarring because that's not us. We don't do coffee dates or walks in the park with our twin puppies. We're sharp points, rough edges, and nasty insults.

And, apparently, we're a little bit of her touching my dick and me kissing her tits, too, but ... I guess that fits.

Sort of.

Glancing her way, she looks at least as uncomfortable as I do, but it breaks up some of the tension when Parker shoves her way between us, charging toward the crowd.

"Move it, assholes," she hisses.

I hold in a laugh, because I know I shouldn't find humor in Parker's frustration, and I guess I've gotten used to hiding what a sick fuck I am. But when I peer over at Southside again, she doesn't even bother trying to pretend. She's smiling big, maybe because she knows getting caught with me has just destroyed Parker on the inside.

Southside's a little crazy, and I might be a little obsessed with that side of her.

The distance between us has grown as we draw closer to the others. I slow down and she speeds up, until it isn't even obvious we came from the same place. Only *we* know the truth.

I unashamedly scan every face for hers when she disappears among the others, but I find her quickly. She's laughing and chatting it up with Rodriguez and a small group near the beer pong table.

Watching her, I brush my thumb over my bottom lip and I'm aware of the missed opportunity. Aware I'm getting deeper in this by the second.

Pull back, Golden. You know who she really is.

"Where'd you disappear to?" Sterling asks, slamming his hand against my back.

"Probably putting Parker's mouth to good use," Dane adds. "Anything to shut her up for a few minutes."

Meanwhile, barely listening to my brothers' speak, my eyes are glued to Southside. She, on the other hand, is doing everything in her power to avoid looking this way.

"Nah, not this time," I answer. "Found something ... a little more interesting to keep me busy."

"She got a name?"

Dane laughs at Sterling's question before asking one of his own. "Better yet, do you *remember* her name?"

All I give them is a vague smile.

The music quiets and Marcus climbs up on a table, already drunk off his ass, but that's not unusual when he parties. He's got a crooked crown resting on his fro and he pushes his kingly robe behind him in dramatic fashion.

"Here ye, here ye," he says into his scepter, using it like a microphone. Everyone laughs. "It is a time-honored tradition that all guests drink from the Chalice of Doom every Halloween. Should someone fail to complete the tradition, the curse of our most notable Cypress

Pointe founding father—Sir Vladimir Bledsoe—will be upon thee," he adds. "And nobody wants that because, as history tells us, the old man's insides leaked out through his arse, on a dreadful night from thenceforth known as the darkest, shittiest night in Cypress Pointe."

Cheers erupt as he spouts this made up BS, and all I can do is laugh. Details of his story change a little every year. But what's most important is that, aside from Bledsoe's name, nothing else is true.

"Bar wench, hand forth my chalice," he barks out, and Parker reluctantly approaches the center with said chalice in hand.

He accepts it and leans in when Parker pulls him close, whispering something so quickly I don't know if anyone else catches it. She walks away and Marcus smiles, staring at the skimpy piece of fabric Parker is trying to pass off as a costume.

"Shall we begin?" Marcus announces, prompting Sterling to shove Dane and I closer. You know, to avoid the whole *'mouth herpes'* situation.

We make our way to the front quickly. Helps a little that people know not to try us and back off when they see we're coming through.

"This year, I'd like to bring a little order to our tradition," Marcus announces. "We have a few new faces here, and being the thoughtful host that I am, what do you say we invite *them* to partake first?"

My steps halt and I scan the crowd again. There Southside is, trying to blend into the crowd in that short, stark-white dress and long black wig. She's the hottest thing out here, which means no one's going to mistake her for one of our regulars.

"No, really. It's okay," she insists when Marcus goes into the crowd to get her himself.

Rodriguez, half drunk and tripping over her own feet, is egging the whole thing on. Southside politely declines several more times before the chanting starts.

Now, she's not protesting so much, and as she looks around, I see her getting ready to cave.

Peer pressure's a bitch *any* day of the week, but it's inescapable when you've got a couple hundred kids all calling you out at once.

Everyone goes silent when Marcus raises his hand to let Southside speak. She looks like a deer caught in headlights. Turning to Rodriguez, she gets zero support.

"...Fine, I guess," she concedes.

More cheering and howling. Then, bottoms up.

Her face scrunches up and she shakes her head wildly, trying to get the taste out of her mouth. Sorry to say it, but it'll be sometime tomorrow when she's finally free from it.

"Sip and pass," Marcus instructs, handing the cup over to Dane next.

He reacts pretty much the same as Southside before I take a swig and give it to Sterling.

The stuff's always awful, but this year ... something tastes even more off than usual. I watch as others go in on it, but no one else seems to notice, so I figure it must just be me.

A second later, the music kicks up again and the chalice is already making its second round. Marcus is keeping an eye out for when it'll need another refill, which won't be long.

Joss bobs over, perfectly sober tonight. From what Dane told us, she got in pretty big trouble after Homecoming. My brother, the hero, was fully prepared to take the heat—despite having nothing to do with how much she drank that night—but Joss wouldn't hear of it. Possibly because we all know how much her dad hates him already.

Which isn't an overstatement at all. Judge Francois would skin my brother alive if given the chance. In his eyes, Dane's nothing but a self-absorbed pretty boy with nothing going for him, and I'm guessing he sees how he stares at his daughter. Still, the judge is only half right.

Dane would definitely kiss his own ass if he could, but the kid's going places.

"I feel like dancing," Joss announces.

Recalling the stunt Dane pulled at Homecoming, it's the perfect opportunity to get him back. So, I take Joss's hand before he has the chance.

"Know what? Me, too," I announce, cock-blocking Dane about as thoroughly as Parker did to me a little while ago.

Joss doesn't think twice about getting out there with me, and I hope Dane feels the burn. The same burn I felt in the center of my chest when he thought it was a good idea to grind all over Southside's ass. Granted, I'd never touch Joss like that, but he could still sit this one out, wishing it was him instead of me.

Not so funny now is it, dickhead?

Joss is vibing out, getting into the song and I'm only halfway there, because I'm on the hunt again. Like always. Hoping to catch a glimpse of the one girl I should never want as badly as I do.

I spot her and it seems she's already feeling the effects of Marcus's Monster Mix. She lowers into a seat and I recall my first taste of that shit. It hit me pretty much the same way.

"Uh-oh," Joss says, nodding to my left where Parker's storming toward me. "That's my cue to move it along. I don't do crazy. Later."

I wish I could make a run for it, too, but Parker's like a heat-seeking missile when it comes to me. There's no place to hide.

Not even in a mausoleum, apparently.

"We need to talk," she demands, flipping her dark hair over her shoulder. I hadn't gotten a good look before now, but that little number she's wearing is thinner than I realized.

I only follow her to the tree line so she doesn't make a scene.

"What?" I ask flatly, already wanting more space between us.

She flashes an incredulous look my way. "Are you kidding me, West? What the hell was that I walked in on? One minute you're giving me and the girls carte blanche to terrorize this bitch, then I catch you with your dick in her hand? I mean, I know you'll screw anything that moves, but she is way, *way* beneath you," she insists. "You have to know that."

My brow twitches with curiosity.

"Wait ... you don't realize that ... *you're* beneath me?"

The question has her mouth gaping open for a moment, but in true Parker Holiday fashion, she rebounds quickly.

"Don't be an ass West." She scolds me, then, which only encourages me to be even *more* of a dick.

"Ah, I see what happened. You're confused because I fucked you,"

I say with a grin. "Guess this mistake is right up there with you thinking that opening your legs for me will eventually lead to me feeling something for you." As my smirk turns into laughter, I feel an adrenaline rush coming on. "You really *are* a fucking idiot, aren't you?"

Even with what little light there is, I see her face turning redder by the second.

"You are such a dick," she scoffs.

I shrug. "I'm a dick and you give *terrible* head," I shoot back. "Honestly, you should consider taking pointers from some of your friends. Especially Ariana. I taught her well. Girl listened to every pointer I've ever given her."

I see tears and my heart beats faster.

Cry for me, bitch. I love that shit.

She's wounded and can't hide it. My words cut her deep and there's nothing I want to take back. Not a single thing.

Shaking her head, Parker backs off and relief sweeps over me. For too long, I've let her cling to me because I enjoyed the added benefits. Problem is, now, I've lost every bit of interest I ever had in the girl.

And with this one conversation, she knows.

Her thin arms cross tightly over her chest and I see more tears glistening in the corners of her eyes. She walked in on me about to go balls-deep inside another girl, and it took this, me spelling out that I don't want her, for the message to get through.

Just as quickly as the emotion flashes in her eyes, it's gone again, and she nods.

"If that's the way you want this to end, fine. I'm good with that," she lies. I could call her out on it, but don't welcome the extra conversation that would result.

"It's for the best," I add, reciting bull I've heard in the movies. Maybe it'll help her get over it.

She's starting to walk away, but not without looking me in the eyes again.

"Before you sever ties, ask yourself if your secrets are really as secret as you think," she warns.

With how confidently she just spoke, it makes me wonder if she knows, but that's impossible. Still, the reminder that there's info out there that could ruin me makes my stomach clench in a knot.

"Cut me off and I won't protect you, West. And, who knows?" she adds with a grin. "I might just be the one who eventually sets your whole world on fire."

She's grasping at straws. Has to be. I've been more than careful and those who know would never expose me. She tried, but that cryptic shit falls short of working.

"It's over, Parker. You should go before you make yourself look even more pathetic," is my parting advice.

"If you say so," she replies with a smile.

As much as I hate to even consider that she might have found me out, I'll keep an eye on her. According to my grandfather, hell hath no fury like a woman scorned.

Chapter 32

WEST

For the past ten minutes now, I've watched her just sit there, doubled over with both arms folded across her stomach. With every second, I feel myself being drawn over there but hold back.

She's not my responsibility and I'm not about to let her *think* she's my responsibility.

Still, I notice something seems off.

It's when Dane elbows me to get my attention that I realize I'm not exactly being discreet.

"Dude, just go talk to the girl," he suggests, calling attention to what I've tried to keep to myself—that I'm aware of her. All the time.

"I don't want to talk to her," I clarify. "She just doesn't look right."

I feel my posture stiffen, feel the tension in my shoulders. And then, seconds before I give in and walk my stubborn ass over there, she starts to slip out of her seat.

Some kid notices and catches her head right before it hits the grass, but I'm already sprinting that way, hurdling headstones and shoving aside anyone who's in my way.

"Move!" I shout, causing the crowd to scatter.

The kid who caught her backs away, too, lifting his hands into the air. "I didn't do anything, man. I swear. She just started sliding out of the chair."

I don't have time to tell him I already know that, so I ignore him instead, because I don't understand what I'm seeing. I thought she was just wasted, but her lips are blue, and her face and neck are covered in small, red hives. Leaning in, I hear a faint hiss and I go straight in to panic mode, realizing the sound is her wheezing because she's hardly getting any air.

"Rodriguez!" I yell out, prompting someone to nudge her drunk ass back to consciousness, hoping she knows what's wrong, but it doesn't work. She can barely open her eyes, which makes her completely useless to me right now.

I push my arms beneath Southside and hoist her up from the grass, carrying her lifeless body against mine. Before I can even think of what to do next, I haul ass down the hill, headed toward my car.

"What happened?" Sterling asks, chasing after me.

"I don't know, but she's barely breathing. Looks like some kind of allergic reaction maybe?"

I hear the panic in my voice, and I know whoever else is trailing me hears it, too. But fuck it. I care about the girl. Even despite myself ... I care about her.

We leave the dim light of the party behind and rush into the pitch-black woods beyond it. I'm going completely off memory at this point, knowing I don't have any time to spare.

Something's terribly wrong with her, something more than that drink going to her head. At this point, a doctor is the only one who can help.

Moonlight glints off the roof of my car and I breathe a sigh of relief.

"Someone get the door," I yell, which sends Joss running ahead to open the back one.

Sterling helps me slide Southside in and he takes my keys when I pass them to him.

"You'll have to drive. I need to keep an eye on her, make sure she keeps breathing."

He nods and I turn to Dane next.

"Stay here with Joss. She shouldn't walk back up there by herself in the dark."

He responds the same as Sterling, nodding once. "Text as soon as you have an update."

I assure him I will, then the next thing I know, Sterling's driving like a bat out of hell.

I've got Southside in my arms and she's getting worse. I pat her down for pockets, hoping to find meds or one of those EpiPen things for situations like this, but all I find is her phone. Grabbing it, I tap the screen to light it up, but its password protected, which means I can't even get in touch with her family.

I'm screwed.

The one thing I can do while Sterling barrels toward the hospital is harass the one I know is responsible for this.

"What the fuck did you do?" My voice is way too calm, and when I hear the fear in hers, I know I'm not wrong.

"I—I didn't think she'd react like this," Parker stammers. "I—"

"Tell me what the fuck you did so I can at least tell the doctors what she had!" The words ricochet off the windows of the car, but still, Southside doesn't move an inch. She's out.

Completely.

"Heidi went through her file," Parker admits. "She helps out in the office during her free period, so ... I thought we'd get some info to use against her. You know, personal shit," she explains. "But when I saw the note about a peanut allergy, I thought I'd have a little fun with her. That's all," she adds, pleading her case.

"Have *fun* with her?" I growl.

Parker's sobbing on the other end of the line and I want to reach through the phone and strangle her.

"I ... slipped a little peanut sauce into the Monster Mix," she admits, causing me to squeeze my phone until it creaks in my hand. "My cousin's allergic, too. And when *she* has a reaction, it just makes her lips and eyes swell. I mean, she *looks* terrible, but nothing else happens," Parker explains. "I thought this would be the same. I didn't think…"

"You—" A frustrated growl leaves my mouth when nothing else will.

I hang up because I can't take another second of this bitch's rambling. The only thing that's come of this is that I now know what caused the reaction.

I'm also now aware of the measure of Parker Holiday's stupidity.

And that shit is off the charts.

I told Sterling to take off once Southside was stable. I plan to call for a ride when I'm ready to go, but I don't expect that to be anytime soon.

It shouldn't jumpstart my heart the way it does when she finally comes to, but I'm on my feet and at her side. At first, I reach to grab her hand, but catch myself just in time, shoving them both inside my pockets instead.

Southside blinks a few times and then reaches for her head with a groan.

"Are you okay?"

It takes her a second to get her bearings, and then she settles her confused gaze on me. "Where am I?"

That inkling to take her hand is back again. And I resist it again.

"You're at the hospital," I say. "You had an allergic reaction to something you ate."

I don't give a shit about protecting Parker, but can't shake the warning she gave at the cemetery. I know that, if it gets out what she's done, the girl would sing like a canary, giving up every detail of whatever she might know. Do I believe she actually has something on me? Not quite. But are the stakes too high if she does? Completely.

"My head," Southside moans, letting her eyes fall closed again.

"Are you up to speaking with the doctors? They have a few questions they wanted to ask once you woke up."

It's still taking some getting used to, speaking to one another without there being venom in our words.

She nods. "Sure. I can do that."

I leave her for only long enough to stop at the nurse's station, then I'm back in the room, standing at her bedside like a dutiful boyfriend.

Dude, what the fuck are you doing?

I check my behavior and go back to the chair in the corner instead.

"Ms. Riley?" Dr. Turner says when he enters the room.

Southside offers a faint smile and sits up a little. "Hi."

"You gave us quite a scare," he adds with a smile. "Any idea what you ate that did this to you?"

I glance toward Southside and she's clearly confused. "No. I'm usually pretty careful, but ... I must not have been tonight."

When she goes quiet, Dr. Turner nods. "Well, we got some epinephrine into your system as soon as *this* kind, young gentlemen rushed you into ER. His quick action likely saved your life tonight."

Southside turns toward me, offering a tight smile that doesn't quite reach her eyes. My guess is it's weird hearing someone use any of those words to describe me. I'd have to agree with her on that.

"No EpiPen?" the doctor asks.

"I keep one in my purse, but I left it in a friend's car. Guess I thought I knew what foods to avoid," she explains.

"Sometimes these things can sneak up on you, which is why you never want to assume, understood?" he asks in a stern, and yet caring, voice.

Southside nods. "Understood."

Dr. Turner flips through his chart again. "I'd like to get your parents' contact information, so I can give them a call and let them know what's going on with you."

He clicks his pen expectantly, but Southside doesn't say a word. There are a good five seconds that pass until she finally speaks.

"They're ... unavailable."

Dr. Turner's brow tenses. "Unavailable?"

Southside nods. "Well, my dad's home, but he's pretty sick. And my mom's out of town. On business," she rushes to add.

If by home '*sick*' she means drunk off his ass, then that statement about her dad is completely true. And based on what Sterling said about the call he overheard from her mom, I gather '*unavailable*' is the best word to describe things.

Dr. Turner closes his chart and keeps his eyes trained on Southside.

"Well, you're eighteen," he says flatly, breathing a heavy sigh. "I'm not obligated to reach out to a guardian, but I'd like to keep an eye on you tonight. Might want to at least give your loved ones a call so they aren't worried."

With those words, he leaves us.

We're plunged into awkward silence and I'm reminded again that this is out of our element. We haven't called each other cruel names or tried to ruin each other's lives in a few hours, so things definitely feel like they're shifting.

"I thought you might need me to see you home," I say, regretting my choice of words right away. It sounds like something a guy would say to a girl who belongs to him. Southside isn't mine.

Clearing my throat, I start again. "If they're keeping you, I can go," I offer.

For all I know, she'd prefer to be alone versus having me hang around. Besides, it isn't like I don't have other things I can be doing.

"No, stay." She responds a little too quickly for it to seem casual. When her gaze slips from mine, I imagine she realizes this, too. "It's just that hospitals have always given me the creeps."

She moves her braid behind her shoulder, and I smile thinking about her costume, topped off with a black wig now balled in a bag with the rest of the getup. Most girls live for this time of year, to get dolled up and show off their goods, but Southside could've shown up in a potato sack and would've been the hottest girl at the party tonight. I mean, I'm not complaining about the minidress or anything, but she doesn't need all that. Jeans and a t-shirt, no makeup. I'll take her as is.

'You'll take her as—'
What the fuck, man?
Cut that shit out!
You're doing it again. You know what she's about. You know what she did. Even if she claims there was only ever that Ricky guy. Even if you see her life's shitty and understand why she could have possibly attached herself to someone like Vin—a predator. Nothing's changed.

She settles against her pillow, glancing up at the clock on the wall. "Do you um ... do you know where my phone is? I need to check in on Scar. She's spending the night with Jules, but I was supposed to call an hour ago."

Searching the bag hooked to the side of her bed, I find her cell. It lights up the second I grab it. A text that reads: *'Yo, you good?'* from someone she saved as *The Mistake*. My guess is it's Ricky.

"I'll step out," I say after handing it over.

"It's fine."

When I glance back in her direction, I see something in her eyes I'm not sure I thought I'd *ever* see. Something I'm not sure she should give a guy like me.

Trust.

I lower back into my seat. Something else I've noticed about her is the weird bond between her and Scarlett. It isn't anything like mine with Dane and Sterling. I love those dickheads, sure, but I don't look after them. Not like she does with her sister. Not like a parent.

She taps her phone screen a few times, first returning the text, I assume, and then holds it to her ear to talk.

"Hey," she says, relief heavy in her voice. "You doing okay?"

I can't hear the response she gets, but whatever is said brings a smile to her face.

"Good. And you ate, right?" There's a pause. "And you thanked Jules for cooking?"

I was right. These are questions I would never ask my brothers. Ever.

"Ok, good. I'll walk over and get you in the morning." Another pause. "K, be good. Love you."

The call ends and I lower my gaze, pretending not to be fascinated by their interaction.

"Thank you," she says, placing her cell on the adjustable table beside the bed.

"You didn't tell her what happened," I point out.

Southside shakes her head. "Nah, kid's had enough to worry about for a lifetime. No sense in having her lose sleep over this, too." She thinks for a moment, then presses a hand to her forehead. "But, of course, she'll read Pandora's post. She'll worry. I should've—"

There it is again. That fierce protection.

"She'll be okay," I cut in, encouraging her to relax. "Just shoot her a text, letting her know everything's cool."

Southside's at war with herself for a moment, and I guess she wants to call, but eventually settles for taking my advice and types out a quick message instead.

Seeing how tightly wound she is, I nearly ask a question about her childhood but hold it. I'm not allowed to be interested in things like that.

"Ever stayed over in a hospital?" she pipes, smiling a little when she meets my gaze.

"Once," I share. "Had my tonsils removed when I was seven. You?"

She nods. "More times than I can count. Mostly allergy related. In case it's still a secret, my parents aren't the most responsible people in the world. So, until I learned how to monitor what I can and can't eat for myself, a *lot* of mistakes were made."

She laughs after speaking, but nothing's funny.

"That's pretty fucked up."

She nods, agreeing with me, but doesn't speak right away.

The picture is becoming even clearer. She not only raised herself, she raised Scarlett, too. Because her parents didn't care enough to do it.

"But you know what they say. What doesn't kill you only makes you stronger, right?" The joke is meant to remind me of my own words from a few weeks ago.

"Yeah. Guess so."

I'm quiet again, but not because I'm thinking about *her* childhood, but because I'm thinking about my own. The shimmer faded for me early, too, but not because I'd been abandoned like it seems Southside was. For me, it was learning that my father isn't the god he pretends to be, discovering he's a mere mortal with a weakness for blondes with big tits and nice asses.

Like Southside.

Usually, being reminded of her connection to my father would piss me off, but I don't feel that now. All I feel when I think about it is pity, imagining what he must have promised her—money, admission into CPA, and who knows what else.

Of course, she'd take that deal. Hell, my own mother fell victim to Vin's game. For her, it was never about money, but rather a means of getting out of the small town where she grew up and everyone knew her as Boone Landry's oldest daughter. She hadn't seen much of the world and fell for every slick lie that fell from the bastard's lips. My grandfather—being a man who doesn't hold back—told me the whole story. How my dad came in, played nice just long enough to swoop Mom off her feet, then brought her north, to a city where she knew no one, to the city he runs and she has no allies.

Like I said, he's a predator. He separates his prey from the herd, then conquers.

When I glance up, Southside's dozing. She looks so damn innocent, like the scared girl I believe she keeps hidden on the inside. I think back on what she said, about being creeped out by hospitals, and I stay in my seat despite having made up my mind to go. If I'm going to leave her, this is the time to do it. But instead, I settle in, sliding off my shoes and propping them on the edge of her bed. She stirs a little when I disturb the mattress, but doesn't wake.

Seems she's faced most things in life by herself. Guess I just don't see why spending the night here should be one of them.

'She okay?'

I smile when Dane texts out the blue, proving that despite my best efforts to bring my brothers to the dark side, they're better than that.

'*She's fine. Sleeping,*' I shoot back.

'*Cool. Need anything?*'

My eyes go to Southside again and I take a breath, realizing that my feelings are changing.

'*T-shirt and sweats,*' I answer. '*Looks like I'll be here all night.*'

Chapter 33

BLUE

"I know you said you're not mad, but I'm seriously sorry. Like, eternally," Lexi grovels, bringing a laugh out of me as I adjust the straps of my swimsuit.

"Dude, if I was mad, believe me, you'd know," I assure her.

She secures the towel around her waist and slumps on the bench facing our gym lockers.

"Yeah, but if I hadn't been sloshed, I would've been able to keep a better eye on you, and—"

Her sentence cuts off when the girls from the dance squad pass by, casting their dirty glances our way as usual.

Once they're out of earshot, Lexi sighs before continuing. "If I'd been sober, I could've told someone your purse was in my car, and they could've gotten your Epi. I just—"

"Seriously. Stop," I say with a laugh. "I'm alive. No harm, no foul."

She nods in agreement, but it's clear she still holds a ton of guilt. I get it, but it isn't warranted.

"Fine," I sigh. "If you want to make it up to me, meet me here after tryouts today. I need a little more swim practice before Mrs. C. evaluates us for the quarter."

Lexi's expression doesn't change, but she nods. "Deal."

"Come on. Let's get to the pool."

She follows when I yank her off the bench. Then, the smell of chlorine gets stronger the second we exit the locker room and pass through the double doors. We're two of the last to make it out, so, of course, every eye shifts toward us.

Mine, however, go straight across the pool, meeting West's emerald stare. My chest flutters when he smirks a little, then lowers his gaze to the water.

No wicked glare. No intimidating stare-down. Just that one, smoldering look that now has my heart racing.

And I may as well confess, I've been ... looking forward to seeing West this hour.

I know, I know. Feeling *anything* for that dick is a heinous crime, but it's my current reality.

Things with him are ... different. I think it really hit home *how* different when I awoke in the hospital yesterday morning to find that he'd stayed. Sure, he looked *super* uncomfortable in that tiny chair, and he was way too tall to fit his whole body under that hospital blanket, but ... he stayed.

All night.

It shouldn't have meant as much as it did but knowing neither of my parents would've even shown that type of dedication, I guess I took West's gesture to heart.

I force myself to look toward Mrs. C. as she explains that we're near the end of this unit. With West's help, I've gotten over my fear somewhat and graduated from treading water to actually swimming less than a week ago. Which means I stand a chance of passing this semester.

"Ok, hop to it!" Mrs. C. announces, and the next second, we're all in the pool.

I've gotten into the routine of getting in at the shallow end, and then waiting for West to swim over. Today is no different. As he pops up from beneath the surface, pushing water from his eyes and face, I'm aware of how much deeper I breathe as I watch it run down his chest and arms.

Usually, he just starts barking orders, but not today.

"Hey," he says first, leading with an actual greeting.

I try not to let on that I notice it's different.

"Hey," I say back.

It's weird. Like, I'm not sure how to act around him now. He feels it, too. The awkward tension. I see it in his eyes. I suppose you can't touch someone the way we've touched each other and not see things change. Guess it's a good thing we stopped when we did. Even if my body still hasn't quite accepted this fact. Every inch of me wanted him the other night. Had it not been for Parker barging in, there's no telling what would've happened.

"I uh ... I guess we should get started," he finally says. I nod, agreeing.

First taking a deep breath, I plunge beneath the water and get my entire body wet and acclimated to the temp. When I pop up and clear water from my eyes, he's staring. Not at my face, but at my boobs.

I can't help but to wonder if he's thinking about it, too—what could've happened at that party, the missed opportunity.

"Should I maybe try making it across?" I ask, pointing from the four-foot marker on this side to the one on the other side.

The question seems to draw West from whatever thoughts he's having, and he focuses again.

"Sure you're up for that?"

I'm confused by what he means.

"Um, should I ... *not* be up for that?" When I smile, he glances at my lips before his gaze flickers back to mine.

"You could've died Saturday," he reminds me.

I shrug awkwardly. "Yup. Could've, but I'm all good now. So—"

My smile tightens and he is clearly not amused. The stoic look he gives tells me he's not so convinced. It also tells me ... he's concerned, and I'm not really sure what to do with that.

"Don't you think you should take it easy?" he pushes. His voice is low and stern, which, surprisingly, draws a laugh out of me.

"Relax. I've been dealing with this my whole life. Once I get meds and the episode passes, I'm in the clear."

He's still not buying it.

"What are you gonna do? Hold my hand during basketball tryouts this afternoon, too?" I ask, still smiling.

He still *isn't* smiling.

"Skip it," he says all authoritative-like. "I'm sure you can talk to one of the coaches and get them to let you do a run through next week instead, considering."

"What?" I scoff. "No! I'm fine."

I'm sure, to him, it sounds like I simply *want* to go to tryouts, but the truth is that I *have* to go. According to Dr. Pryor, at least.

"I think you're pushing it," he states firmly.

"West—"

"I know your mom isn't around, and your dad probably doesn't even know you didn't come home Saturday night, but…"

He pauses and I hold my breath, seeing something I never expected.

It seems West has been … *affected*, traumatized by what happened over the weekend.

"You don't remember how sick you were," he adds, holding that same stern tone.

If I didn't know any better, I'd think he even cares a little.

I don't mean to, but I find his hand beneath the water and hold it. It feels wrong. It feels right, but still, I let go quickly.

"I've been taking care of myself for a long time," I fill him in. "Which means I know my limits. If I didn't feel one hundred percent, I'd speak up," I add. "In fact, I feel good enough to even meet Lexi here after tryouts, to make sure I'm ready for Mrs. C's evaluation."

His brow twitches, but he doesn't speak. I'm pretty sure he has plenty to say, but instead, that tense look remains in place. When he barks an order, things feel a little more like normal.

"Down and back," he commands. "One time."

He steps back and I eye him, fighting a grin. "You sure you don't wanna grab me some floaties?" I tease.

His jaw tightens.

"Seriously," I add. "I think I saw lifejackets in the—"

"Shut the fuck up and swim," he cuts in, clearly trying not to smile.

I take the lap from one side of the shallow end to the other, feeling super accomplished when I touch the tiled edge of the pool. Pushing my hair behind me, I glance up at West where he's standing beside me.

"Was that good?" I ask, already knowing I've improved tenfold from when we first began.

He nods once. "It was decent."

"Whatever," I laugh, rolling my eyes when he downplays my performance.

"I'll admit you're getting better, but your form still needs work," he scolds me.

"Which I already know. Hence the reason Lexi's meeting me here later," I remind him. "I just need a little more practice and—"

"Yeah, those plans are canceled," he interjects, drawing a frown out of me.

"Excuse me?"

His eyes darken when they land on me. "If you fail, guess who gets blamed," he reasons coldly, but I'm not buying his excuse. It feels like there's some other hidden agenda.

"Mrs. C. made you *my* responsibility," he continues. "So, I'm seeing this through myself. No way I'm putting my rep in Rodriguez's hands."

My chest rises and falls when his command frustrates me. He doesn't even blink and I know that, regardless of whether I cancel with Lexi or not, West will be here.

"Whatever," I say again, too infuriated by his arrogance to come up with something more intelligent than that.

"Down and back," he orders.

I glare at him and ready myself to go again.

"And keep your head down this time."

"And kiss my *ass* this time," I mumble to myself.

It isn't until I see him grin in my peripheral that I realize he heard that.

"Just name the place, Southside," he teases, responding to what was never meant to be an invitation. When I meet his gaze, he eyes me in that lust-ridden way of his.

And just like that, I'm thinking things I shouldn't be thinking, aware of the need to put space between us. So, I take off into the water, knowing his eyes are glued to me.

Keep it up, King Midas, and we're going to get ourselves into more trouble than either of us are ready for.

Trouble I'm starting to think might be worth whatever hell there will be to pay afterward.

Chapter 34

BLUE

"Good job, Riley. The official announcement won't be made for a few days, but in case you're wondering, Coach Ryan and I already have our eyes on you," Coach Dena assures me.

She pats me on the back, and it feels better than I remember being praised for my performance on the court. I've always loved the game, but I'd accepted there was no room for basketball this year. Guess being forced into it by Dr. Pryor is just what I needed.

I say a few words to the other girls who tried out, then grab my phone off the bench. I shoot Scar a quick text to make sure she's at the diner doing homework—seeing as how I need eyes on her at all times now—then make my way to the locker room.

I'm exhausted, but the pushy bastard I love to hate is meeting me soon. So, I shower quickly, then get into my bathing suit for the second time today.

Exhausted, I'm dragging a bit as I close my locker before making my way to the pool. The heavy door slams behind me and my steps hesitate a moment. All because I wasn't expecting West to beat me here, but he did. He's sitting on the edge in his dark trunks, staring down into the water where his legs hang over the tiled edge.

I swallow hard when he peers up, because it hits me that it's just us here this time. Historically speaking, things between us go awry when left to our own devices—the locker room, Homecoming, the Halloween party—but I'm convinced this will be different.

Maybe.

Hopefully.

I don't say a word as I walk over and step into the pool. It's odd being here without the chatter and splashing of the entire class. West, on the other hand, seems perfectly fine with it just being the two of us here now. Adding to the strange vibe, the tall windows along the upper half of the space have gone dark, seeing as how it's after five and the sun has practically set.

"You're early," I comment, pushing my hands through the water to get acclimated to the temp. West slips into the pool next, walking toward me. I try to keep my breaths steady, but of course it doesn't work. Never does around him.

"Just told Coach I had an appointment," he shares.

I'm sure he didn't mean for this to happen, but his answer makes me feel like, I don't know. Like I might be somewhat important if he lied to be here. Then again, it could also be what he said earlier. That his grade rests on me passing, too.

"Tryouts go okay?" he asks, which comes as a shock.

"Yes, actually," I say a little too enthusiastically. "Coach Dena hinted that I've already made the team, so…"

He smiles a bit. "You some kind of superstar or something?"

I feel my face getting warmer. "I wouldn't say that, but I hold my own on the court."

West is thoughtful for a moment and I wonder if that came out cocky. If it did, that wasn't my intention.

"Sounds like I need to check you out once the season starts."

My heart beats rapidly and I nod, trying not to freak out at the thought of him coming to see me play.

"Guess so."

Things get quiet and awkward after that, leaving me desperate to change the subject, so I speak up quickly.

"Where should I start tonight?"

It's not the smoothest segue in the world, but talking about me has gotten to be uncomfortable. While West stares, I take the elastic band from my wrist to pull my hair into a ponytail. It's still wet from the shower, and while I probably shouldn't care what it looks like, I do.

Because of him.

"The big evaluation is coming up," he starts, "And ... I think you should try going to the deep end this time," West suggests, and as soon as I realize what he's about to say, I start shaking my head.

"No way."

Frustrated, he rolls his eyes. "Just today, I watched you swim across the shallow end without stopping, without needing to touch the bottom. Nothing's different," he reasons.

"Nothing's different?" I scoff. "What about the fact that I can't reach the bottom?"

The look on his face tells me he thinks I'm ridiculous. "This is the next step, Southside. You've gotta build confidence."

I don't care what he says. "Not happening," I shoot back defiantly.

The stalemate we've reached is eventually clear to him. Sighing, he turns away from me.

"Just ... climb on," he says dryly.

Smooth skin and ink meet my eyes when they settle on his back. Then, when I don't immediately respond to his demand, he glances at me from over his shoulder.

"I'll take you across so you can see there's nothing to be afraid of," he explains.

"You mean, *aside* from putting my life in your hands?"

He smirks at that, and I breathe deep when he holds his hand out for me to take. "It'll be fine."

I hold his gaze for a moment. Then, despite every silent alarm within me sounding off a red alert, I give in, slipping my palm into his, letting him guide me closer. He pulls me onto his back and both my arms lock around his neck. Next, he reaches back to bring my legs around his waist, and I don't miss that one of his hands lingers on my thigh longer than necessary.

"I have you," he promises, glancing back again. "Just don't let go."

A nervous laugh slips out. "Trust me. No chance of that happening."

He chuckles quietly and then I'm at his mercy. He moves us through the water slowly. I feel every muscle in his body as it tenses and releases—his shoulders beneath my arms, his hips between my legs. I hardly notice I'm chin-deep in cool water until West reaches the other side, bracing the edge.

I feel vulnerable, aware that the darker turquoise on this end means the bottom of the pool is so much further down.

"I'm not gonna let you drown," West promises. Probably because my grip around his neck has tightened.

I don't speak, fighting memories of that night I nearly drowned in the lake. The night Hunter saved my life.

"Here," West speaks up. "Hold the ledge."

"What? No!" I protest.

"Stop freaking out," he scolds me, clearly amused. "I won't let you go."

With one quick maneuver, he takes matters into his own hands and slips from beneath my arms, guiding me toward the ledge. He moves behind me, where he braces his hands at either side, caging me in. I stare at his fingers gripping the edge of the tile as his arms frame mine, pinning me lightly in place

"Told you you wouldn't die," he teases, but his voice sounds different. It's raspy and too close, right near my ear.

"There's still time for that," I shoot back, trying to keep my head clear of him, but it doesn't work.

I feel him everywhere, his chest to my back, the slow movements of his legs as we tread water.

One of his hands disappears from the ledge and the next thing I feel is his touch on my waist. Then, a warm breath against my shoulder. I haven't yet decided if he's *trying* to get to me, or if our current circumstances are just working in his favor.

The solitude.

The lack of clothing.

Whatever the case, I'm suddenly not thinking so much about not being able to touch the bottom of the pool. Because I'm thinking about how badly I want to touch *him*.

"Want me to take you back across?" he offers.

"I'm not in a rush," is the unbelievable answer that falls from my mouth, which makes zero sense. I even surprise myself, considering how terrified I was just a few minutes ago.

But, then again, it *does* make sense. Because I've been craving the closeness, having West's undivided attention.

He seems caught off guard by the response, too, which is the reason I come up with for why he hasn't spoken yet. His grip tightens on my waist and my eyes fall closed. The rim of my ear warms when his lips press against it and ... I lean into him.

"You don't want to go back," he rasps, making me come undone. "So, tell me what you *do* want."

There are words on the tip of my tongue, words I don't have the courage to say out loud. But as if he hears that little voice inside my head, the one I'm trying to ignore and silence, his palm moves lower, resting at the base of my stomach.

My breaths are deeper now, louder as I let my head fall back against the firmness of his shoulder. Smooth fingertips trace the elastic at the apex of my thigh, like he's contemplating his next move, unsure how far he's willing to go. I know I should be the one to stop this, I know I should revoke the unspoken permission I've given him to touch me like this, but ... I don't.

Instead, as his hand slips inside my bathing suit, I say absolutely nothing at all. Well, nothing that discourages him, anyway.

Only a whimpered, "...Shit."

My voice is quivering as his exploration begins. Heat from his mouth moves over my skin and drives me insane. A kiss is placed just beneath my ear, sucking first, then tracing slow, silken circles with the tip of his tongue.

"Shit." The word falls from my mouth again, but this time it's strained as he teases me with the tip of one finger. Then, finally, he slips it inside.

And then another.

I've completely given in. Completely. And he knows it. I push my hips back, pressing against him, in awe of how aroused he is from touching me.

"You're making it very, *very* tough to hate you tonight," I admit.

I didn't mean to whisper this loud enough to be heard, but I'm out of my head and can't stop myself.

"Haven't you figured it out yet, Southside?" he asks gruffly, breathing the words into my ear while still touching me beneath the water. "If you had to choose between killing me and fucking me, you'd be on your back every time," he explains, then a short, deep laugh vibrates within his chest. "And that goes both ways."

A chill shoots down my spine when he admits that, knowing he's so, so right.

His hand moves faster, and he presses against me, pushing his fingers deeper. Then, my breaths are coming faster. I'm panting while I squirm in front of him, hungry for so much more than what's being given, but unwilling to admit that out loud.

We've added kindling to this wicked fire for months now, stoking it day in and day out with our warped fusion of cruel words and ceaseless lust. Now, I'm not so sure we can contain what we've created. It has a life all its own. A monster that thrives on our hatred and sexual frustration. And believe me, we have fed this beast well.

I can't help but to question whether it will linger forever, breathing heat down our backs, forcing us to give in to it, one way or another. Like now, as the pressure in my core swells, becoming impossible to ignore. And even more as my thighs clamp tight around West's hand. As I arch away from his chest and drop my head back against his shoulder.

He's breathing in my ear again, making sure all my senses are overwhelmed by only him when he speaks next.

"Come for me," he whispers, soft and deep, an invitation.

He gets his wish, almost on command. A soft cry leaves my mouth and I'm shuddering in his arms, proving how badly I craved this. And it had to be him. No one else.

His hand goes still when I finish, and then, eventually, he slips it out of my bathing suit. I'm kept close, though, which I don't hate. The arm not latching us to the edge wraps around me and becomes something like an embrace. Despite myself, I revel in the feel of it and, after several seconds, my breaths slow to normal.

Silence creeps in and so does reality. Only, it's not nearly as uncomfortable as I thought it would be.

I feel his heart racing against me and don't fight when he spins me to face him. The sated look in his eyes is unexpected but fitting. This spark between us is unpredictable, untamed. It feeds into this obsession we have with one another. The one that causes us to make these erratic, split-second decisions. It's also the reason I'm suddenly triggered all over again, wanting him like I didn't just climax.

He grips the edge of the pool with both hands now, and I cling to him. Locking my ankles behind his hips, I bring him as close as I can, feeling the solid bulge in his trunks pressing into me. There's urgency in our kiss when his lips find mine. In the moment, I want nothing more than to taste him like this forever.

But I'm not sure I can keep this up, going to extremes with him. One second, he's hot, the next he's ice cold.

The sound of a door opening barely registers, but when it slams shut again it's slightly harder to ignore.

Reluctantly, West and I separate ourselves, but when I peer up, I don't spot anyone. We're still alone. I face West again and feel what he's about to say before he even says it.

"I should go," he announces with a sigh. "Practice probably ended by now, which is why I'm willing to bet that was one of my brothers coming to rush me."

Not wanting to seem desperate, I nod instead of asking him to stay a while like my heart is begging me to do.

"Okay," I say softly, reaching for the edge.

I'm trying to pull myself out, but West puts a stop to that, holding me in place. Just when I think he's finished with me, I'm brought close again. This time when his mouth covers mine, I'm aware of how different it feels. This kiss is heavy, it's emotional, it's not steeped in frustration or some hidden agenda.

It's ... just a kiss. Like the kind you give someone who means something to you. The kind you need to tide you over until you see them again.

When West pulls away, my head spins a little.

"You're coming with the team to regionals when we make it?" he asks, still breathing a bit raggedly.

First, I answer with a nod, and then volley a look between his eyes and lips. "How'd you know?"

He flashes a crafty smirk that makes my gut twist in knots.

"Not much gets past me," is his answer, which I already figured.

"Stalker," I tease.

His smile dims a bit and his intense focus feeds my ego more than I want to admit. "Only one I stalk these days is you, Southside."

He makes my heart do such wild things and, for the first time, the nickname he's given me doesn't sound like an insult.

Curious, I tear my attention away from his lips and meet his gaze. "Why'd you ask if I'd be there?" I question him.

He doesn't blink and I hold my breath.

"Because I'm tired of pretending this isn't headed where it's headed," he says boldly.

I taste him on my tongue, despite the distance between us.

"So, what do we do about that?" The question comes out softly and heat blooms in the pit of my stomach while I await his answer.

He glances down at my mouth again, but this time his eyes stay trained there.

"We fuck," he growls.

There's no apology embedded in that statement whatsoever, because West always means every word he utters and takes nothing back. Ever.

And, this time ... I don't want him to.

He's in my ear again and I feel every inch of my body screaming to be touched by him.

"Think about it," is all he says, and then he climbs out onto the tile. He offers his hand to help me, but once I'm on my feet he walks off like nothing happened, leaving me to ponder the proposition.

I don't think I've ever been faced with a more tempting offer, but I'm against the idea for obvious reasons. Still, with what I know about how things escalate when West and I are on our own, I'm not sure resisting him while we're away—*alone*—is something I'm even capable of doing.

There's only one person I trust to help me put this insane idea into perspective, and that's Jules.

Until now, I've left out so many details about West and me when I talk to her. Although that discretion has been for good reason, I think it's time I let her in. On everything. While I have no idea how to keep my distance from the one who's declared himself my enemy, Jules is certain to talk some sense into me. She almost always has the right answer.

Hopefully, this will be one of those times.

Chapter 35

BLUE

The last thing I needed was for my sister to see pics of me and West plastered all over social media, but it is what it is. I can't take anything back.

Thanks, Pandora.

Guess this is the price of living in Cypress Pointe. The cost of somehow being dragged into the fishbowl in which the north side's elite dwell.

After a lengthy conversation with Scar about how West and I were *not* screwing in the pool tonight, I finally got around to doing homework. Now that *that's* done, I've worked up the nerve to call Jules.

The line trills and she picks up on the second ring. That feeling of dread comes back almost instantly

"Dude," she answers. "If this isn't about you and West banging it out in the pool, I have nothing to say to you. What took you so long to call?"

I laugh a little. It's nothing short of a miracle she didn't call me first.

"We weren't having sex," I explain, sounding more and more like a politician, working to clear my name after a smear campaign.

"Well, it certainly looked that way to me," is her sassy response. "And ... it also looked that way to Ricky."

For some reason, hearing that makes my stomach drop suddenly.

"He called you?" I ask as casually as I can.

"Well, it started with him sending a series of texts, but I called *him* when I got sick of typing," she shares. "But ... yeah. Shit like that's just hard for him to see, you know?"

I *do* know this, which is another reason I hate that Pandora and her spies plaster things like this online for all to see. And with zero context at that. Not that context would've helped in this situation, but still.

"If it makes you feel any better, I covered for you despite being pretty sure the pic said it all," she adds. "I told him it probably isn't what it seems. Not sure he bought it, but I tried."

A frustrated sigh leaves me, and it isn't hard to imagine how upset Ricky must be right now.

"Thanks anyway. I'll give him a call tomorrow," I decide.

"Mmm ... maybe give it some time," Jules advises sweetly, likely to spare my feelings. "He's still processing the idea of you actually being with someone else. In his head, I think you're probably always gonna be *his* girl. It'll just take some time to accept that you're with West now."

I'm quiet, because I'm *not* with West, which brings me to the reason I've called her tonight. Drawing both feet onto my bed, I get comfortable before diving headfirst into an *uncomfortable* conversation. Falling back, I slink beneath a blanket and stare at the twinkling lights I've strung haphazardly across my ceiling with pushpins.

"Jules, I need advice," I admit, because it's the simple truth. "But first ... I need to tell you something I should've told you a long time ago."

"I'm listening," she says sweetly.

I force out a sharp breath and just go for it. "There *is* something going on between me and West, but it's not nearly as clean cut as that."

"Sounds juicy. Do continue," she teases, which makes me smile a little.

"The truth is that West and I have been in this really weird space," I start. "And it gets weirder and more intense by the day, but ... I'm not really sure how to handle it."

"Well, *that's* an easy one to help with," she chimes in. "You slingshot your panties at the guy and say to hell with all the rest of it. I mean, you have *seen* him, right?"

I'd forgotten how biased she is when it comes to the triplets, but that comment quickly reminds me.

"It's not that simple, Jules."

"Okay, okay. Then tell me why it's complicated and I'll do my best to help you figure things out," she offers. "That's what besties are for."

I swear I love this girl. She never misses a beat.

"First, I need to put a disclaimer out there," I begin. "You need to know that I withheld information from you, but only because I know you love me. I knew that, if I shared what I was dealing with, you'd feel compelled to advocate for me and things would get *really* messed up if that happened."

I pause, letting her digest that first.

"I know how things work at schools like mine," I explain. "The kind of pull and influence the parents of these kids have is off the charts, and I was—*am*—cautious about rocking the boat too much. Stepping on the wrong toes could mean putting a target on my back, and you know as well as anyone, I can't afford to screw things up anymore."

My heart feels heavy, knowing that everything I've worked so hard for has all been because of Scar. I *have* to make something of myself, so I can *be* something for her—a role model, a provider. I might not have it all together by the time she heads off for college, but I'll be close. I can pick up the cost of her schooling, put a roof over her head if she stays local, give her some type of stability for once in her life. I know what it feels like to fly without a net and I want so much more for my sister.

Because of this, I'll *always* do whatever it takes to make it.

Whatever it takes for her.

"Still waiting to hear what this has to do with that hot photo. The one you say *didn't* capture West doing a little deep-sea drilling," she teases.

"For the last time, Jules—"

"I know, I know," she sighs. "But you cannot tell me that was all innocent."

When I don't immediately answer, she reaches her own conclusion.

"I knew it!" she screeches.

"There was only ... hand stuff, so settle down," I clarify.

"You totally slutted out for him!"

"Jules! Shut up before your parents hear!" I shout back.

"Sorry, but I knew that wasn't innocent." It's a little too late to whisper, but she tries anyway.

"We were only kissing in the pic. Luckily, whoever was spying got there late and missed the rest, which I couldn't possibly be more grateful for," I add.

"Well, he might not have defiled you tonight, but from what I see, you two are *definitely* headed that way."

"You mean from what you *saw?*" I ask, but when she fails to answer, I know what that means. "You're looking at it again, aren't you, perv?"

"I mean ... I'm not NOT looking at it," she admits.

"You're disgusting."

"And you're fucking lucky," she counters, making me laugh again.

"Would you focus, please?" I ask playfully. "Still trying to bear my soul here."

"Okay, okay. Sorry. Continue."

Shaking my head, I move on. "Anyway, this all pertains to West because, well, before things went *way* sideways with us ... he did some pretty shitty things to me."

That part is difficult to admit. Mostly because I know what it makes me look like—weak, desperate, like a fool.

At least those are the things *I* would think of someone in this situation.

"You mean, like, removing the tires from your car?" she asks, reminding me she hadn't missed that little update from Pandora.

"Well, that's one of *many* things he's done, but ... yeah. Stuff like that," I admit.

"Okay, so, I guess the important thing to understand is why," she interjects. "I mean, you don't have to give details if you don't want to, but if he was targeting you, there has to be a reason. Unless it's just that he sucks."

The comment brings back the deep frustration that's never out of reach. "Believe me, Jules, I've tried to figure it out."

She's quiet again and, like always, I hear her wheels turning loudly inside her head.

"Just ask me," I sigh. "Whatever it is, lay it out there and I'll tell you the truth."

Seeing as how I've held this info for far too long already, I won't hold back anymore. Not with her.

She takes a deep breath and then speaks her mind. "Okay, so, how did you two get from point A to point B? From this dark place you're telling me about, to ... where you two are in that pic from tonight?"

It's a valid question, but I'm not sure I can answer it the way she'd like me to. For starters, West and I are *still* in a dark place—present tense. I'm actually beginning to think that's kind of our default setting.

Dark.

Cruel.

Realizing she sees it too—the contrast between what makes sense and the weird place West and I have settled into—I feel like an idiot.

"Honestly, I don't know what to say to that, Jules," I openly admit. "It's like, a switch got flipped and I just ... I don't hate him like I did at first. And he's not as toxic as he was either. Don't get me wrong, though; he's still no Prince Charming," I clarify.

"Is it strictly sexual?" she asks. "Like, is that the only thing pulling you two together?"

I think about that for a moment, and then remember that last kiss we shared. The one that made it seem like he knew he'd walk away feeling just a little emptier once we went our separate ways tonight. The one that makes me wonder if he's thinking about me right now, too.

I mean, is that so crazy?

"I thought that at first," I reply, "but I'm not so sure anymore. It feels deeper at times."

She goes quiet to think again.

"What's your gut saying?" is her next question.

Again, I don't answer right away, because I want to really search deep before I do.

"I'd like to say I know the answer to that, Jules, but I don't exactly trust my gut anymore." And there it is. The truth. The reason I've called her tonight.

"Do you think he's starting to care about you?"

Flashes of the brief moments of clarity I've had over the months come to me. Like, when West stepped between me and Mike. When he jumped into the pool to save me. Or when he grilled me about the bruises on my shoulder. The night he spent in the hospital with me.

When he touched me tonight.

"As crazy as it sounds ... I think he might. Does that make me delusional?"

She laughs at that. "You're the smartest person I know, Blue. So, no, that's not even an option."

"Then what is all this?" I ask, unashamed by how uncertain I feel. With her, there's never any judgment.

"Well," she says thoughtfully, "I think that, despite how things were in the beginning, you're both feeling something powerful for each other. And most importantly, I don't think you're crazy. You're not imagining any of this."

She has no idea how big a relief it is to hear her say this. Because, honestly, I wondered if I was misreading his signs, seeing what I want to see.

"My only advice is to proceed with caution," she gently warns. "As far as I'm concerned, *all* guys are to be fed with long-handled spoons until proven innocent. Not just West. So, while I'm all for keeping your heart open, never forget to keep your eyes open, too, you know?"

The tension leaves me and I'm so glad I opened up to her.

"Thanks, Jules. You always know what to say."

"No problem, kid," she teases. "Just remember this when I call *you* with boy trouble."

I laugh, because we both know she'll never take a guy seriously enough to let him give her trouble.

"Anytime," I promise.

She's quiet and it makes me suspicious.

"You're looking at that pic again, aren't you?" I accuse with a laugh.

Caught, she stutters a bit, then doesn't bother lying to me. Instead, the line goes dead when she hangs up, and I can only shake my head at her.

She's crazy, but she's also my best friend. The one who always knows how to make me feel better. Her advice is sound, suggesting that I keep my guard up within reason.

And I can do that.

As I begin to think about regionals in a couple weeks, my immediate plan is to keep West at arm's length. Still harboring some pretty deep-seated trust issues, I don't think we're ready for whatever aftermath we would face if sex were added to the equation. However, if I find him harder to resist than I expect, I'm also committed to not beating myself up if I give in.

As for the future, who knows where West and I will end up, but wherever we're headed, we'll get there at *my* pace.

Which, for now, is set to super slow.

Well, mostly.

... Kind of.

Why don't we just say I'm a work in progress.

Chapter 36

WEST

"You and Parker back at it again?"

I peer up from my duffle toward Dane when he asks. I'm confused at first, until he points at the strip of condoms I just dropped into the bag.

Smiling, I zip it closed. "Nope."

Curious, he shoots me a look. "Who then?"

I shrug, pretending not to have anyone specific in mind, but there is definitely someone specific in mind. My brothers just don't need to know that. Not right now, anyway. Eventually.

I've spent two weeks thinking about this weekend, and not because our team dominated in the district finals last week, clawing our way to regionals. What I look forward to has perfect C-cups and an ass I want to sink my teeth into.

Now that we're done with the swimming unit, I haven't had an excuse to be around her. No excuse to touch her. Sucks that I even need one. I've given her plenty of reasons to keep her distance from me over the past couple months, though. Now, she naturally avoids me.

She's at every game, snapping pictures for the paper, but as far as interaction goes, there isn't much of it between us. Not unless you count how we can hardly keep our eyes off one another during the one class we do share, when we pass one another in the halls and during lunch. I'm always aware of her.

Always.

I've even gone as far as telling the girls to pull back. Most couldn't care less either way, but for Parker, everything concerning Southside is personal. Probably because being told that her sole target since the beginning of the school year is now off limits serves as a glaring statement. It speaks to my growing respect for the girl I once vowed to destroy.

I haven't gone soft by any means, but I'm not so stubborn I can't see the need to reevaluate. Starting with a decision I made about two nights ago, when I couldn't sleep because I couldn't stop thinking about …

It actually doesn't matter who or what I was thinking about. The point is I was restless.

It was during this restlessness that I accepted something. Southside and I are long overdue for a conversation. One she's been asking to have since the beginning. One in which I plan to lay everything out on the table, including what I believe about her involvement with my father. Having had that man's heel pressed to my neck my whole life, it hasn't been hard to see how she could get roped into whatever happened between them.

If it's happened between them.

It's the reason I'm past the anger and looking forward to putting this shit behind us. Honestly, I just want the air between us cleared.

Finally.

So, while the team and dancers are all partying in Trip's room tonight, I'll be with Southside, laying my full truth bare. After that, neither of us will have any need to fight whatever happens next. All questions will be answered, all our secrets will be out in the open. A clean slate.

"All right, we gotta go. Bus leaves in forty-five." Sterling announces, hiking a bag up his shoulder.

Dane grabs his jacket and I shrug into a hoodie, since winter is officially on our heels.

A text has my phone vibrating and I glance down to read the message.

'We need to talk,' Parker insists. 'And don't blow me off, West. There's a chance I can help you. Whether you like it or not, you need me right now.'

That knot in my stomach is back and the text has me on edge, wondering what in the hell she's talking about. As much as I'd like to think none of those privy to the only secret I have would've told Parker, it's feeling less and less like she's bluffing.

"Everything okay?" Sterling glances back to ask when he sees I'm suddenly feeling anxious.

"Yeah, just a stupid text from Parker," I say, but I'm making light of things. Truth is, if this girl opens her big mouth, I can kiss my football career beyond high school goodbye.

We get to the elevator just as the doors are parting and the message I just received is shoved to the back of my head. Because, unfortunately, our escape route is now being blocked by our father, the oppressor himself. He's standing inside the brass box, brooding for reasons he has yet to share. But judging by the tie hanging loosely around his shoulders, and the vein throbbing on the side of his neck, it's safe to say he's worked up about something.

His eyes lock with mine, and what he says next is the last thing I want to hear.

"I need West for a few. You boys wait downstairs."

Dane and Sterling both shoot me curious glances.

"We'll wait in the car," Sterling says, stepping inside the elevator to head down to the lobby. But his eyes are set on Dad as the doors close again.

Now, it's just us, the man who rushed down here looking every bit as insane as I know him to be.

"What?" My tone is hard and unfeeling, which makes perfect sense, seeing as how I feel nothing for him whatsoever.

There's something in his eyes I don't expect to see, though.

Concern.

I'm admittedly curious now, wondering what this is about.

He leads with a gravely spoken, "Son ... we need to talk," that has my heart racing because he sounds just like Parker. No conversation in history has ever gone well after beginning this way, and as I stare into my father's eyes, I don't believe this will end any differently.

For the fraction of a second, I'm worried he's found me out, knows the huge mistake I made, but I force myself to relax and remember who I'm dealing with here. If he'd rushed down here because of a *'me'* problem, he'd be much more relaxed. He doesn't care about anyone that much. Which means this is a *'Vin'* problem.

What the hell has he done now?

Vin

"Care to explain this?"

West leans in and his expression never changes as he glances at the two-week-old picture. One that damn-near gave me a heart attack a few minutes ago.

Pam rushed into my study, hysterical, squawking about how she thinks our boys might be sexually active. After crushing her fragile heart with news that I'm positive they've had the pleasure of defiling at least a dozen girls each, she shoved her phone into my hand before storming off.

And when I glanced down at the screen, what the fuck did I lay eyes on? Like I don't already have enough shit to deal with? My son—the star of Cypress Prep's football team, and future quarterback for the best D-1 college in the state—dicking down a pretty blonde I know all too well.

"You fucking her?" There's no need to sugarcoat anything with my boys. They're cut from the same tough cloth as me. Not that flimsy shit they bypassed from Pam's side of the family.

He doesn't answer, but his stare is furious, and I can tell by the look in his eyes he feels something for this girl.

"This what you're doing now?" My teeth grit together upon

asking. "You ran out of *good* girls to screw, and had to start digging in the trash? Because that's exactly what this one is. Trash. Straight out of the gutter."

Again, he just stands there, clenching his fists.

"Do you care even a little about what this can do to your reputation?" is my next question. "Getting yourself caught up with one of the school's charity cases? Playing with south side filth isn't a good look for you."

Boy's head's as hard as a brick. Hence the reason I fight to keep him and his brothers in line. They need me. Whether they realize it or not. Even if they hate my methods.

"How could you possibly know that?"

His question catches me off guard and I don't miss the growing suspicion in his eyes.

"How could I know what?" I ask with a frustrated sigh.

"That she's not from North Cypress?" he clarifies. "That she's from the other side of town?"

Shit.

I'm usually very careful with my words, only saying things I mean to say. It's an art I've mastered, but West is usually the one to catch my slipups. Little shit is always in the wrong place at the wrong time, and usually asking the wrong questions. Like now. In my anger, I screwed up again.

Royally.

I don't immediately have an answer, which only makes me look guiltier, I'm sure. His expression shifts and it's hard to read. The uncertainty that creeps in has me on edge, though.

"You don't even have to say it," he suddenly interjects. "I've known for months."

I feel the tension in my brow, and right away, my thoughts are on the phone in the safe. The one I've secretly suspected West had already snooped through. Now, I'm more certain than ever.

"Son, you don't understand what you saw. It—"

"How long?" he cuts in. "How long were you screwing her? What'd you hold over her head to get her to sleep with your old ass?"

It's at this moment that I see where his mind has taken him. Only a boy would assume the obvious, but in this situation, it suits me that my son is a bit naïve. That he believes I only have one flaw—my weakness for young, pretty blondes.

Straightening my suit jacket, I hold in the triumphant smile that almost gives me away. Kid doesn't even know he's just given me the upper hand again. So, I play the part, pretend to feel shame for having been found out.

"West, I—I always intended to end it," I grovel. "Things between Blue and I are ... complicated. They have been for a while now."

"She's fucking eighteen," he shouts, showing more of his cards than I think he means to. Showing that he does, in fact, have one hell of a soft spot for this girl. All this proves is that I've taught him nothing.

"I know," I add with an air of regret, "Which is why we stopped for a while. She was seventeen at that time and I didn't feel right about things."

His face twists with anger and I welcome the idea of him being disgusted by me. Having him think I stuck my dick in some underage slut is better than having him know the truth.

I place my hand on his shoulder, knowing he doesn't want me near him, and he shoves it off like I expect.

"Don't fucking touch me," he warns. For a second, I think the kid might actually have the balls to swing, but he seems to think better of it and settles down.

"Son, you must know I didn't plan any of this. I love your mother," I remind him. "But—"

"Men will be men, right?" he cuts in, quoting a conversation we had a few weeks earlier.

Feigning remorse, I nod. "I'm not perfect."

"Truest shit you've ever said," he scoffs.

"I didn't intend to tell you all of this." When I lower my head, I impress *myself* with how genuine this is coming across.

He can't even look at me, and I'm okay with that. The boy's

resilient, bounces back from these sorts of things like they never happened. Just like his old man.

I peer up at him again, keeping my expression solemn. "I only came down here ... to warn you," I add, which I realize has piqued his interest when he meets my gaze. "That girl, she's playing you. Probably has been since day one."

Even in his silence, I see how I've broken him, see how I've started a fire and then doused it in gasoline. The rage I see growing inside him is exactly what I want to see, because it's what it'll take to keep them apart.

While I know the risk I've just taken, it was one-hundred percent necessary.

"She's using you to hurt me," I add. "She threatened to do it, but I didn't believe she had it in her. I should've known better."

This lie is the hardest to tell, because I'd die before I let someone manipulate me like that. In fact, I have people on the books strictly to prevent this very thing from ever happening. Sure, it isn't cheap, but it's proven more than once to be a worthwhile cost.

To clean up my messes.

Even to clean up West's.

"What's her plan?" West seethes, now filled with searing anger and pain.

"She seems to think that sleeping with you will punish me for not leaving your mother. If she didn't know I'd rake her ass over the coals, she'd probably try to sell the story to the first news outlet who'd listen, but she's no idiot."

When West doesn't have a snappy comeback, I can only guess he's bought what I just sold.

Damn, I'm good.

"You *never* leave your tracks uncovered. Ever. So, why this time?" A cold look flashes in my direction and there's one last hint of suspicion burning in my son's gaze.

One last doubt I need to stamp out of his head.

I make a false attempt at touching his shoulder again, but pretend to change my mind at the last second. Then, I lower my gaze in 'shame'.

"You're not gonna want to hear this," I begin, taking a deep breath, "but ... it wasn't just sex with her. It was ... *more* than that."

I pause, letting that sink in with him, humanizing myself in his eyes in a way I've never done before.

"I can admit that I fucked up," I add. "I let the feelings I developed give me a false sense of trust. Eventually, I told her things about me that I shouldn't have, told her things about our *family* that I shouldn't have, but that's how clever she is," I warn him. "She knows how to get inside your head, which is why I'm willing to bet you're having a hard time believing all this. But, as much as I wish it was all made up, as much as I wish I could turn back time and redo what I've done ... I can't," I conclude. "The only thing I can do from here is make sure she doesn't continue to use you, manipulate your feelings, just to get under my skin. Because, trust me, once that happens, it's hard as hell to get that one out of your system."

He's quiet. *Very* quiet.

"Have you told her about this? That you planned to tell me everything?" he asks.

My brow tenses, wondering why he's asking.

"No, West. My loyalty isn't to her," I assure him. "It's to you, this family."

Hearing that, his jaw ticks and he grits his teeth. "Fuck your loyalty," he growls.

I nod, agreeing like some sympathetic fiend, desperate for his approval. "Just tell me what I can do to make this right, son. I'm willing to do anything."

His gaze is cold and unfeeling when it lands on me. "The only thing I want from you, now or ever, is your word that you'll keep your fucking mouth shut. Don't tell her you came to me with this."

Again, I nod, but can't help but to ask one last thing. "Why? What's your plan?"

A normal kid would be scarred from the things West has seen and heard, but he's made of steel, unbreakable. Which is why I know hearing this has only given my boy a newfound sense of vigilance. Whatever he *thought* he felt for this girl, it should be dying a slow death inside him now.

West storms off without answering the question, but even seeing how this talk has wounded him, I regret nothing. As far as I'm concerned, I've just successfully avoided a catastrophic disaster. If sacrificing my son's perception of me keeps the Golden name from getting dragged down into the mud, keeps everything I've worked so hard to conceal from blowing up in my face, then … so be it.

Others might argue that the price might not be worth the outcome, but I would have to disagree.

Some secrets are never meant to be unearthed.

Blue

Not a word while we waited to load.

Not a word since getting on the bus.

I mean, I didn't expect to sit together or anything, but this feels … extreme.

It's not even so much that he hasn't spoken—because that isn't so far out of the ordinary for us—but he hasn't even looked my way. He's got his headphones on under a dark hoodie that hides most of his face, and it's like I don't even exist to him.

Well, I guess it's better to know where we stand than to be left in the dark. Right? Apparently, the request he made in the pool a couple weeks ago no longer appeals to him. With how I've seen girls shamelessly proposition him, I shouldn't be surprised he's lost interest.

Just wish I'd known sooner. For one, I wouldn't have wasted my time shaving this morning. You know, on the off chance that things *did* go further than planned this weekend.

But no chance of that happening now, and I can't afford to care. West is nothing to me and I'm nothing to him.

Obviously.

Lucky for me, when we loaded the bus, I didn't get stuck sitting by anyone I hate, but rather someone I don't know very well.

So far, Joss hasn't said one word to me, and I need something to distract me from glancing back at West every three seconds. So, I decide it's on me to break the ice between her and me.

"Excited about the game?" I ask when nothing else comes to mind. Guess I could've mentioned the weather, but it's cold and cloudy. Not much else to say about it.

She lowers the book she holds, smiling a little, which makes me feel less guilty about interrupting her.

"I am," she answers. "You?"

I shrug, realizing that I *was* excited, before seeing that West has flipped the switch on me once again.

"Sort of. It's kind of nice to be getting away from home."

Not only is the school paying for my room, but Scar is safe, too. She'll be with Jules the first night, and with Uncle Dusty the next.

"You play basketball, don't you?"

I wasn't expecting Joss to ask anything about me, because I didn't realize she *knew* anything about me.

"Yeah," I say with a smile. "They just made the final cut this past Monday."

She nods. "That's pretty cool. I've never been super athletic."

"Dance requires quite a bit of athleticism, doesn't it?"

Joss shrugs and actually closes her book.

"Sort of?" she answers with a laugh. "But I guess I'm referring to the whole hand/eye coordination thing. Dance is all about flexibility, strength, and good balance, but I couldn't make a basket to save my life."

I laugh a bit. This feels easy.

"I watch the guys out there on the field every week in awe," she shares. "Dane goes into beast mode and it's like watching art in motion. *All* the Goldens are like that, actually."

She cleaned that up nicely, but I don't miss that she mentioned Dane first. Nor did I miss the way she forced her expression to straighten after talking about him. It's the sort of thing Jules would've called me out on, but Joss and I don't know each other like that. So, I keep what I suspect to myself.

"Yeah, they're really good," is all I say back.

She eyes me with a smirk and I'm unsure what she's thinking.

"So, it's a little weird to have all those pics of you and West floating around on the net and yet, here you are, sitting with *me* instead of him."

Apparently, she's not as adverse to prying as I was a moment ago. I feel my face warm, which likely means it's red, too.

"Well, I—"

There's no real answer for that, so I pause. I showed up at the school today, expecting West to be at least a *little* warmer than usual, considering, but instead I got the cold shoulder.

"He's just a bit hard to figure out," I share with her, not feeling like I've said too much.

My statement draws a laugh from her. "Giving you whiplash, huh?" she asks, sounding like she knows a thing or two about that.

"That's one way of putting it."

She nods. "I will say this, though. Whatever the beef was between you two when you first got to Cypress Prep, West definitely seems far less hostile about it. Like, maybe he's starting to soften up a bit."

I suppose that would've come as a relief if I considered myself one of West's groupies, but I'm not. What has me feeling weird is how he's seemingly gone cold toward me again. No, he hasn't been cruel, but having seen that there's another side to him recently, I can admit to not being ready to let that go.

I enjoy that side of him.

I *want* that side of him.

It felt like things were changing between us—I mean, *really* changing—and now this.

"You two should just talk," Joss suggests. I'm not even sure she realizes how complicated something as simple as a conversation can be for West and me.

"Easier said than done," I admit.

"Tell you what. Trip and Austin are having everyone over to their room tonight. You should drop in and just, you know, pull West aside," she suggests. "Despite what he has you thinking, he's not a *total* d-bag. Actually, he's a closeted sweetheart," she says with a laugh. "You just have to get to know him."

I nearly laugh out loud. No way West Golden is a sweetheart. Not even on his best day.

"I'll think about it," is all I say, but I've already made up my mind.

I'm staying as far away from him as possible. I've already given him too much slack, too much access to my thoughts, my body, and my heart. I'm sick of being made to feel like a fool, but that's *exactly* how I feel every time I fall for West's games. If this cycle we keep repeating is ever going to end, it's up to me to end it.

So, that's what I'll do. Right here. Right now.

Whatever West and I were on the verge of becoming, it's officially dead.

Completely.

Chapter 37

BLUE

"This is so stupid."

I'm talking to myself, because I'm alone in my hotel room, being lame. A sharp sigh of frustration puffs from my lips as I stare at the ceiling.

It's eight P.M. and I'm the only person on the planet—under the age of seventy—poised to go to bed this early. But I have nothing better to do, and sleep is the only guarantee I won't do something I'll regret.

Like, taking Joss's advice and heading to Trip's room to deal with my West problem. Joss had even stopped by my room on her way to the party, and when I told her I was passing, she gave me her number in case I wanted to talk about everything later.

Of all the members of the dance squad, she's by far the most tolerable.

As a last-ditch effort to do the right thing, I check in with Scar.

"Are you in bed?" she asks after saying 'hello'.

"How could you possibly know that?"

"I can hear the lameness in your voice," she teases. "Isn't your boyfriend there? Why on earth aren't you out doing something fun right now?"

I sigh and, apparently, don't answer quickly enough for her, because she's on my case again.

"Get up, Blue!" she yells into the phone.

I don't even bother telling her West isn't my boyfriend. People seem to believe what they want to about that situation.

"Give me the phone," I hear Jules say in the background. "Did I just hear right?" she asks. "You're seriously in bed right now? While there's an entire football team on the same floor? And I'm guessing very little supervision?"

"You don't understand," I whine.

"What I *do* understand is that you're making the south side look really bad right now. Please, for the love of all that is holy, get up and do *something*," she pleads.

I glance at the clock. "There's a party, but—"

"No buts," Jules snaps. "Get up, shower, put on something cute, and go!"

I'm smiling, although I don't really believe heading to Trips room is the smartest thing right now.

"We could always watch something together on Netflix," I suggest next.

"I'm hanging up," Jules barks. "And when I check in later, you better have your ass out of that bed. Understood?"

It's impossible *not* to roll my eyes, knowing I'm about to actually go through with this.

"Fine," I give in.

The next second, the line goes dead and I slither out of bed, making my way toward the shower.

Here goes nothing.

As soon as I knock, I regret it.

On the other side of the door, I hear chill music and laughter. Surprisingly, despite knowing there are a ton of people inside, they aren't super loud.

"Sup, Southside," Dane answers with a grin. He's leaning on the door and I can't help but to peer over his shoulder, in search of the one I shouldn't even be thinking about.

"Hi," I say flatly, because I'm always leery of him and both his brothers.

"Come in," he says a little too sweetly for me. So, naturally, I'm eying him as I enter the room. "Grab a beer, get comfortable, and if you spot anything questionable or illegal," he adds, "just ... *unsee* it."

I offer an uneasy smile, feeling the vibration as the door closes behind me. Several girls from the dance squad are focused on me, and they're practically snarling as I pass by them. They don't even have to worry about me. I'll be avoiding them at all costs tonight.

Bunch of snobs.

There's another room connected to Trip and Austin's. From the looks of it, that one's packed, too, and I assume it's where another pair of players are staying this weekend.

A bucket of ice sits on the dresser. Beside it, a stack of red, plastic cups and a cluster of empty beer bottles. How they smuggled this stuff in here without getting caught, I'll never know, but I would imagine this group has plenty of experience with such things.

But anyway, I'm not here for any of this.

While I showered, I decided Joss is right. If I'm going to move on, if I'll ever have any measure of peace where West and I are concerned, a conversation is one-hundred percent necessary. No more of this BS with him not stating clearly what I've done to warrant his hatred. I'm not expecting it to go well, but I'm sick of this. *All* of it. Either we fix things and move forward—whatever that means for two people like us, the broken. Or, we burn the bridge that connects us.

And when I say burn it, I mean we burn that bitch down to the studs.

"You came!"

Joss is clearly a little tipsy, which accounts for the overly enthusiastic greeting. I'll take it, though. At least *someone's* happy to see me. She hops off the chair she's seated in and squeezes me around my neck like we're old friends.

"Yeah, guess I had a change of heart."

I leave out the part about how Scar and Jules pretty much threatened me.

Joss backs off a bit, but apparently notices how my eyes dart around. Doesn't take her long to figure out who I'm searching for.

"Last time I saw him he was headed back to his room," she whispers with a smile.

"Alone?" I ask, feeling my heart race with the question.

"Far as I know," she adds with a shrug. "Room 271."

I appreciate the fact that, even drunk, she's still discreet.

I offer the best smile I can give. "Thank you."

She nods and staggers back into her seat, picking up whatever conversation she was having before spotting me a moment ago.

Seeing as how I didn't want to come here in the first place, I'm beyond eager to leave. And, no, not because I'm in a rush to confront King Midas. Actually, it's the opposite. My ego is still wounded from being ignored before and during the bus ride and, again, since settling into the hotel. We've been here for hours and he hasn't stopped by my room to say a single word.

If his goal has been to make me feel iced out, mission accomplished.

Was it ever even real, though? What I thought he'd begun to feel? Or is he just like all the other guys—horny and heartless?

I'm a little embarrassed I'm even asking myself these questions. Of course, he's like the rest. Actually, he's worse.

The walk to his door is a relatively short one. Just a trip down the hall and around the corner from Trip's room. But the spaces between these are notably bigger. Doesn't take long to realize the difference is that the rooms down *this* hallway are suites. Already frustrated, this discovery only adds to my disgust with this guy.

Couldn't even slum it in a regular room like the rest of us for one weekend?

My hand lingers in the air, and then I just do it. I knock. Then, I fix my clothes, because despite every ugly thing he's done, and every terrible thing he's said, I still care what he thinks of me.

Damn him.

I hear his heavy steps padding toward the door, and then there's a pause. I imagine that he's looking through the peephole, realizing it's me. For a moment, he seems to hesitate to turn the lock, but then he does, and despite thinking I was ready for this, it's a completely different story as we stand face-to-face.

Chapter 38

BLUE

The room behind him is dark and he squints to adjust to the light from the hallway. He's shirtless, his hair's disheveled, and a pair of black sweats ride low on his hips. And, based on the unobstructed outline of his dick through the fabric, he's not wearing anything underneath them.

Focus, stupid.

"I didn't mean to wake you, but—"

"I wasn't asleep." His tone is deep and cold, confirming what I already believed.

The switch has flipped.

Again.

Heat spreads up my neck and face and I'm doing everything I can to control my temper. Because I want to slap that cocky look right off his face. That one that makes me wonder if he knew I'd show up at his door.

But I can't worry about that right now. I need to get everything off my chest. Once and for all.

"Do you have a few minutes to talk?" I ask.

He gives a nonchalant shrug. "I'm listening."

How did I ever feel anything for this asshole?

At any rate, I'm here now. So, here goes.

"I have no idea what's changed between us overnight, nor do I think it's even worth discussing at this point, but for some stupid reason I need to say it," I admit.

There's fire blazing in his eyes when he stares and I'm so confused. It's like I've slept through some offense I've committed against him. Because his hatred is so real, so raw.

Tangible.

He works his jaw and I swallow hard. He leans away from the doorframe and glances behind him, into his room.

"You can go now," he says to someone I can't yet see.

"What?" a feminine voice asks. "We're nowhere near fin—"

"Go!" West yells, cutting the girl off midsentence. "Get the fuck out!"

My heart sinks, hearing that some other chick was here with him, but it shouldn't even affect me. Still, I feel like running off, hiding in my room to keep him from seeing how ashamed I am for coming here, but I fear that'll make me look even more pathetic. Like some lovesick weakling who can't stand the thought of some guy who isn't even hers being with some other girl.

I need West to think I don't care. Need him to think this doesn't hurt.

While, on the inside, I'm gutted.

Of all the girls it could've been, Parker comes into view, and before moving to the dresser to gather her things, she shoots me a dirty look. I imagine she's equally wounded for having been dismissed when I showed up, but it's not like that. I have no priority where West's heart is concerned.

As far as I can tell, no one does.

She slips a t-shirt over her bra and refastens the button on her jeans. She has several items to gather, which leads me to believe the plan was for her to spend the night.

I have to look away, choosing to stare at my feet instead.

Another dagger to my chest. Another wound that'll take forever to heal. As if I didn't already have enough of those.

The corners of my eyes burn, and I hold my breath when Parker comes closer. She stops beside West and hatred flares across her face.

"You're an idiot," she hisses at him. "When shit blows up in your face, don't say I didn't warn you."

With that, she storms her way between us, slamming her shoulder against mine on her way out. She mumbles something scathing under her breath, but I don't catch it. Then, West stands aside, silently inviting me into his space.

The space where he'd just been doing God-knows-what with Parker a moment ago.

Her perfume lingers in the air, making me secretly grateful when West opens the sliding door that leads to the balcony, letting in fresh air. Light from the city filters in, too, and my gaze shifts to the bed. It's still made, but two distinct imprints show where West and Parker did ... whatever they were doing before I showed up. Again, I force myself to look away, slowly dropping down into the chair where West's black and gold jersey hangs over the back of it.

"You wanted to talk, so talk," he sighs, resting against the edge of the round table in the corner.

First, I take a deep breath, and then just ... unload on him. Because I'm full to the brim and if I can make him feel even a *fraction* of what I'm feeling, I'll be satisfied.

"You are, by *far,* one of the shittiest human beings I've ever met. If I can even call you that," I start. "You use people, and you hurt people, and you don't even give a damn!"

My chest tightens with emotion and I know I should probably just abort mission and leave, but I can't.

"I fell for it," I admit. "Two weeks ago, in the pool, I let myself think I might actually feel something for you, then you completely ghosted me today. And for what? Parker-fucking-Holiday?"

Slow down, Blue. Don't let him see too much.

"I keep asking myself what I could've done to deserve being treated the way you've treated me, and it took me until tonight to accept that the answer to that question is *'nothing'*. I've done nothing.

You're just mean, and twisted, and there's no one to blame for you being such an evil bastard but you."

"Maybe," he cuts in. "Or ... maybe my father's to blame."

I'm already rolling my eyes. "Fuck your father. Whoever the hell he is," I snap. "He might be awful—and believe me, I get that—but you don't get to use that excuse. Not here. Not with me," I hiss. "Yeah, having sucky parents makes life harder, and it gives us a fucked up view of the world, but that's not a crutch, West. It doesn't give us an excuse to become awful people."

And now, there's a tear. I feel it rolling down my cheek and I'm sure there's enough light coming into the room that he sees it, but I'm too pissed to care.

"I'm an idiot," I admit. "Because you showed me exactly who you are from day one, and I let myself fall right into your trap anyway."

I pause when a realization hits home. I'm becoming my mother despite every effort to be nothing like her. I'd spent most of my life judging her, thinking how weak she was for getting into the situations she's landed in over the years, and here I am. Crying in front of the one person in this world who doesn't deserve to see me cry.

"Don't mistake me being emotional for more than it is," I warn him. "I don't fucking love you, West. I don't even *like* you. I just stupidly let myself get attached."

I regret even admitting that, but it's out there now.

He pushes off from the table and I'm instantly on guard. When he stands before me, I can't even look up at him. I'm not sure what I'll feel if I do and I can't afford to hate myself more than I already do.

"What do you want from me?" The rawness of his deep timbre works its way to my bones.

"I want you to be real with me," I answer. "For once, just ... give me *something*."

That sounds dangerously close to pleading, but I don't feel like myself, and it just comes out.

"You're not here to hear about my problems," he deflects, leaving me weary. "You say you want to know why I am the way I am, but you don't. Not really."

He pauses and I almost tilt my head back to meet his gaze, but I fight it.

"You don't really want to hear me say it," he concludes.

Instantly, I'm infuriated by these walls he casts up, frustrated by the riddles and double-talk.

"You think I came here to have this conversation with myself?" I shout. "That's no different from the usual, West. I want you to man up and talk to me! Be honest for a change. Say something! Anything!"

I'm aware he could interpret this as desperation, but so what. It can't be taken back. One thing I *can* control, however, is this obvious power play with him standing over me like I'm one of his damn subjects. So, when I can't take it anymore, I stand from the chair. I expected him to back off and give me space, but he doesn't even budge.

Immediately, I'm aware that I've made a mistake.

We're face-to-face, and as much as I hate him right now, I feel it. That thing that's always there, festering between us like an open wound that never heals. We're raw, we're damaged, making it so easy to grieve over our unspoken hurt together.

"I hate you." My voice quivers with the admission as I peer up at him, but he takes it.

"You try, but you don't," he bites back, calling my bluff.

"No. I mean it. I hate you with everything in me. You're cruel and thoughtless and—"

I lose my words when he steps closer, overwhelming me. "And ... what else?" he presses.

My chest vibrates when my heart speeds up. "You're getting off on this?" I barely speak the words higher than a whisper.

He doesn't respond, but I know the answer to this question is 'yes'. I shouldn't be surprised, but I am.

"You've told me a million times I'm sick," he reminds me. "Name one time I denied that."

We have a standoff where neither of us speaks or moves, but then he cranes his neck down to whisper in my ear—soft, deep.

"No one handles me like you do, Southside," he croons. "And as much as I hate to admit it, that shit's like a fucking drug to me."

His voice has my entire body quaking with need, but I manage to stay focused.

"Well, as flattering as that is, I'm not here to amuse you," I snap. "I only came to you for the truth. That's the only thing I want from you at this point."

"Then take off your clothes." I'm shaken by the authority in his tone. "If we're ever going to learn one another's truth, that's where we'll find it."

A quivering breath passes between my lips, but I'm determined to resist.

"In bed? That's where you think normal people learn one another's true colors?" I question him sternly, wanting him to know I'm not going to break for him. Even if my body is already fighting the decision.

"Not normal people. Just us," he answers.

My chest rises when I draw in a powerful surge of air, holding his gaze when I speak again.

"Do you think I've forgotten Parker was just in your bed, asshole?"

The bastard actually seems surprised that's a factor. "Is that what has you so upset?" he has the balls to ask, like him having her here is nothing.

The space between us disappears even more and he reaches to rest a hand on the small of my back, drawing me toward him.

"I didn't touch her," he claims, sounding annoyed that he even has to say it.

When I scoff and slip from his grasp, his eyes follow me toward the balcony where I stand just inside the threshold.

"She was in your bed, half-naked, West. And you and I both know there's not much that bitch won't do for you."

He brushes his thumb over his lips, hiding a slick grin.

"She came here to talk, and also thinking I'd let her spend the night, but only because she's delusional," he adds with a sigh. "The conversation got heated and she said some shit that pissed me off, and in Parker World, you make things up to people with sex. But I swear to you, I never touched the girl."

I stare at him, glaring because this feels weird, having him explain *anything* to me so emphatically. Like ... he actually cares. Meanwhile, I can't tell if he's just a really good liar, or if this is all true.

"Doesn't it count for something that I put her ass out the second you showed up at my door?" he asks with a throaty laugh. "Or ... have you forgotten that little detail?"

He's baiting me. I'm convinced of it when he comes toward me again.

My eyes drop to his waist, where the muscles there are unbelievably cut, giving a preview of what's just below the band of his sweats.

Don't let him get inside your head, Blue. Just ... don't.

He's in my face now, closer than he ought to be, breathing down on me when he speaks again.

"I couldn't even get hard for her. Not like I do for you."

He's lying.

He has to be.

Before I can even finish the thought, he takes my hand and lowers it between us, forming my fingers against his dick, making me feel that the opposite is true right now. He's solid against my palm and his size never ceases to impress me.

I stop breathing altogether when he takes my chin, forcing my gaze to meet his. I know he intends to kiss me, because he always preys on the weak, but I snap out of his spell just in time, remembering how I'd been given the cold shoulder.

"I've been an afterthought for you all day. And you think you're just going to talk your way into my pants now?"

He has zero response and it burns me up.

"You are *such* a damn fuck-boy," I hiss. "You think you can do and say whatever the hell you want and just—"

I go silent when his mouth covers mine. He swells in my hand and I grip his length tighter, knowing some bruised part of his soul just enjoyed that insult, enjoys being verbally destroyed.

"Tell me what else," he insists, pushing his tongue inside my mouth right after.

I can't remember the last time I've been this angry with someone, but for some reason, I can't put distance between us.

"You're a walking tragedy," I continue, speaking my mind in a trance as his lips move down to my neck.

"What else?" His breath is warm against my skin when he asks, making me lose my foothold in reality a little more.

"You're stubborn and I hate it," I say next. "Sometimes, I get so frustrated I think I could actually kill you."

A soft laugh leaves his mouth after I speak this time, the reaction vibrating against my neck, but he doesn't stop kissing me there. Instead, he sucks the hollow of my throat and I'm officially losing this battle. He pushes the top of his sweats down a few inches and I feel more of him, skin-on-skin, but he hasn't exposed himself completely. Not yet.

"I need a second," I manage to choke out before pulling away.

He's quiet, panting, but there aren't words.

Those godlike features of his are highlighted in faint light and I don't miss the desperation that's overtaken his expression.

"I'm not leaving," I rush to tell him, although I know I should. "I just ... I need a second."

The rims of his nostrils flare as his need becomes even more apparent, but he gathers himself and nods. He steps aside and I rush to the bathroom, close the door behind me, and turn on the light.

Staring at myself in the mirror I'm not even sure who I'm looking at. The Blue I knew a few months ago wouldn't be here tonight. Not with someone like West. Someone who definitely doesn't deserve her company.

And yet, not a single part of me wants to leave his room tonight.

I rinse cool water over my flushed cheeks and feel drawn to the other side of the door, where temptation on two muscular legs is waiting for me to return. It dawns on me that West and I have accomplished nothing here tonight. We haven't worked out any of our issues, and I wonder if this is the only possible way to have him.

Broken.

Twisted.

But maybe I'm willing to settle for that.

His words ring inside my head, his declaration that the only path to unearthing our truth being between the sheets. I also can't deny the part of that statement concerning the two of us being far from normal. On that point, he's right. Possibly about *all* of it.

Maybe intimacy *is* the only way to tell if any of what we suspect the other feels is real. The only way to tell if what we, ourselves, feel is real.

My gaze shifts to the door again and I ask whether I'm willing to be denied something I want so badly, but I don't have to wait long for an answer. Knowing my fate is sealed, I turn off the light when I'm done, and easily see my way to the bed.

West is seated on the edge. When I step between his knees, he slowly peers up and I see more of him than before. The tender parts of his soul he keeps hidden beneath everything else. I'm reminded of what Joss said, about him being a sweetheart underneath it all. For now, I'll have to just take her word for it, but by some miracle, maybe I'll see that for myself one of these days.

He grips the back of both my thighs and draws me close. I watch as he undoes the button of my jeans and slides them down my legs, along with my underwear. I step out of them and lift my hands when he takes off my shirt next. Reaching back, I undo my bra as he stands, towering over me, too beautiful to really be human.

He holds my gaze, daring me to look away when he pushes his sweats down toned hips, baring himself to me completely. I only have a moment to steady my breath before the soft flesh of his lips meets mine. He kisses me deep, gripping the back of my hair. My head spins every time his tongue moves over mine.

A crinkling sound catches my attention and he backs away, only long enough to roll a condom into place with one hand. Then, I'm pulled down onto his lap when he sits. Heat moves through my back where he holds me tight. His hips flex between my thighs as I straddle him, feeling him all but begging to be let in. I show no sign of intending to make him wait, so he reaches between our bodies, aligns himself, and then guides me down onto him by my hips.

A whimper leaves my mouth and it's steeped in relief, finally feeling him completely, in ways I've longed for since the first time I laid eyes on him. My lids fall closed and I ride him slow, drawing a deep moan from his lips.

"Your eyes," he rasps. "Open them and fucking look at me."

I meet his gaze, taking in the sex-drunk look set on his face. He's barely coherent as our bodies move together, him wanting my full attention. He has it all, just like he wants. And, suddenly, I understand why I'm not allowed to turn away.

There's an intensity he exudes, and he needs the same in return. I willingly give it, grinding on him faster, harder as my arms lock around his neck. I give him everything. Every ounce of hate, every ounce of anger I have inside me, and he happily receives it, absorbing it all.

His fingertips dig deep into my hips and tension builds in my core. My breaths are quiet moans now and West swallows them down when he captures my mouth with a kiss. Leaning back, he brings me down on top of him. Then, my every move is guided by his hands, the churning of my hips in rough, grinding circles as he thrusts hard underneath me. The combination has me on the verge of a scream. His head pushes back toward the mattress, and he can hardly catch his breath. My fingertips tighten on his chest and I'm so close.

"Don't ... come yet," he says with erratic pauses between the words, still controlling me.

"I'm not sure I can wait," I warn. My body has a mind of its own and he's so, so deep.

In an attempt to slow my mounting climax, he eases up a bit, slipping one hand upward to grip me just under my ribs. It feels like my heart is on the verge of beating out of my chest, but then a menacing smirk curves West's lips.

Out of nowhere, he begins the assault once again, catching me completely by surprise. This time, I can't hold out like he's requested, but I'm guessing that's the point.

"Don't stop," I mutter incoherently, squeezing my thighs tightly against him.

He continues to work my hips, grinding my body against his until I begin to quake all over. The powerful swell of tension between my legs mounts, peaking with a euphoric explosion I feel from the inside out. I revel in the moment only seconds before West's body writhes beneath me. He thrusts his hips a few final times, gripping me so tightly it hurts, and then I have the unmatched pleasure of watching King Midas get his release.

It plays out through a series of high-inducing expressions. First, it's unbelievably tense, followed by pure bliss, and finally it floods with calming relief. Right after, he lets out a breathy grunt and goes completely motionless beneath me.

I find myself staring down into his vibrant eyes, but neither of us speak. It's that lack of words that leaves me a bit unnerved, overwhelmingly aware of what we've just done. From there, it doesn't take long for the full scope of things to hit me. Then, in an instant, I'm an insecure mess on the inside, hoping West doesn't notice.

That insecurity grows and I move to climb off him, thinking a bit of space might help clear my head, but just as I do, his arm holds me in place. Locked against him, there's tenderness in the touch I'm not sure he means for me to notice, but I do. Maybe because I'm so desperate for that, some sort of sign that I'm not the only one who just felt that—the blinding energy that just exploded between us.

His lips part and he has my full attention, thinking he'll speak. Thinking he'll say something that will further drive away this heavy sense of dread. Despite life having taught me that putting any measure of hope into a guy like West is a risk.

His chest moves when his breathing picks up again, and his gaze lowers to my mouth. Being held like this, I feel so much. Things I've already sworn I'll deny feeling until the day I die. But I notice something. It's slight but doesn't get past me.

As West scans my face with a quick, sweeping look, his grip on me loosens and, just like that, he's suddenly someone else. The shift leaves me breathless and I feel like the rug has been snatched out from underneath me.

Whatever false reality being intimate had just erased for him, it comes flooding right back to him like a storm surge. I can't help but to hear his words again. That our truth would be revealed through this single act.

Maybe that's what this is. Our revelation.

I move aside when West slips from underneath me without any kind of comfort, and then storms toward the bathroom. There's anger in his stride, in those rolling hills of his shoulders and back and, watching him, my chest tightens with grief.

There's not a question in my mind of whether I've made a mistake. Only of the magnitude and lasting impact it will have.

He pauses at the bathroom door but doesn't turn. For the fraction of a second, that inkling of hope returns, but then it's snatched away with three little words.

"You should go."

Then, he disappears around the corner, slamming the door behind him. The sound has me shaken, and I'm frozen in disbelief for a moment.

He wouldn't just do that. I know we're screwed up, but ... just dismissing me?

But then it registers, and I realize what this was. Just sex. Nothing more than that, and now he wants me gone. Just like he'd demand with any other girl.

It's pride that draws me to my feet on autopilot, stifling the many emotions beginning to swirl inside me. Through tear-blurred vision, I'm in search of my clothes, knowing that, for my own sanity, I cannot still be here when he gets back.

If I'm going to hold it together, I have to get as far away from him as possible and go right into emotional-damage-control-mode. But before I can even get that far, I'm beating myself up. It starts the second I flee from his suite with my shoes in hand, trying not to hyperventilate as I rush to my own room in an epic walk of shame, fumbling with the key at the door.

How could you be so stupid?

Did you really not see this coming?

You're so screwed. You're so broken. You're officially a slut. At least with Ricky, it meant something. To you. To him.

Damn.

I make it inside and don't bother with the light. If I have to look at myself in the mirror, I might not be able to pull it together. This is the worst thing I've ever done, and there's no taking it back.

As far as regrets go, it doesn't get any worse than this.

Chapter 39

BLUE

I'm on autopilot, just moving through this day so I can put it behind me. The only thing I want is for this weekend to be over. Never in a million years did I think I'd miss home, but I do.

I miss it and I've spent the entire morning and afternoon so far trying not to cry and even now, I'm sure I look a mess. My eyes sting every time my thoughts slip back to last night, to the contrast of extreme highs and lows. To say that I'm devastated would be a huge understatement. My heart feels broken, but that can't be right. That would have to mean I'd given it to West at some point and that's a lie.

Our team pulls out another touchdown and I'm relieved when I look at the time on the scoreboard winding down. We're up by several points and it's nearly over. And as for West, this will be his second win in twenty-four hours. The first being tricking me into sleeping with him. All so he could shut down and humiliate me afterward.

I'm an idiot.

So stupid.

I shove the thoughts aside and just keep taking pics. Several carloads of CPA students drove up for the big game, so this small section of the stadium is filled with familiar-ish faces. I'm posted a couple rows behind the dance squad, doing my best to forget everyone exists.

As soon as the game ends, I'll go to my room to pack, and then the last storm I'll have to weather will be the bus ride home in the morning. If I can avoid West completely, it'll be fine.

At least that's what I keep telling myself.

Dane scores big, narrowly avoiding a nasty tackle from two of the biggest seniors I've seen in my life, but he's too quick and makes it into the endzone. The entire crowd goes wild, but no one's as ecstatic as Joss. I think back on the few times I've noticed how she and Dane are together and I fight the jealousy that creeps in. There's an ease to what they have—even if it is only friendship—but I'm almost certain it's something I'll never experience.

With anyone.

Two girls from the dance squad turn and zero in on me just as my gaze slips from Joss. Their eyes are wide, and one has her hand clamped over her mouth, but she quickly averts her attention upon realizing she hasn't been as discreet as she first thought.

A loud cackle from the other end of the bleachers gets ignored because I'm focused on getting a shot of the ball in midair after West snaps it, but then, all of a sudden, the air is abuzz with a symphony of phone notifications. Even my own is vibrating in my pocket.

"Is that her?"

"Oh my God!"

The chatter around me picks up volume, but I'm still mostly numb to it, still focusing on getting this job done so I can curl up in the hotel room bed and pretend I'm invisible.

Right now, that sounds like heaven.

I snap another photo—intentionally avoiding West's face—and glance at the scoreboard. Only a couple minutes left in the quarter and it's a guaranteed win. Not that I care at all about that.

"Well *somebody* just got famous for all the wrong reasons," a girl to my right says loud enough to catch my attention. And now that she has it, I realize she's looking right at me.

In fact, *several* people are looking right at me.

And those who aren't, are glued to their phones.

There's a sinking feeling in the pit of my stomach, although I don't yet know why I feel it, but it has my hands shaking as I reach into the pocket of my hoodie to pull out my phone.

And the second I do ... bile rises in my throat.

"Guess we all know where *you* spent last night."

I don't know who said it, nor do I know who's laughing now, but it sounds like everyone.

Everyone is laughing at me.

I glance at my phone again, unable to believe what I'm seeing, but there it is, plain as day.

Me and West. In his bed last night. Naked.

And it isn't just a picture ... it's a video.

My head is spinning and I'm on my feet and pushing my way through the crowd to dart up the stairs of the massive stadium. I'm willing to bowl over anyone who dares to stand between me and the exit, because I have to get out of here.

Have to.

How is it possible that one mistake has humiliated me *twice*?

I can hardly see through the tears that come, as I search desperately for the way out of this place. My phone is to my ear and I feel it shaking in my hand. I need someone to get me as far away from here as possible, and there's only one person I can think to dial.

My call is answered on the first ring. "Hello?"

"Can you please come get me? I can't stay here," I say, sobbing so hard it's a miracle I can even be heard. My stomach is in knots and my chest burns with rage and humiliation.

"Text me the address. I'm on my way."

I lower the phone and run faster than I've ever run before, all to get away from the one I no longer trust myself around. Not because I fear I'll let my guard down with him, but rather because I couldn't say for sure I wouldn't kill him.

Of all the things I believed West to be capable of doing, I never saw this coming. Not ever. But one thing he should have learned about me is that I'm no pushover.

If it's a war you want, West Golden, then that's precisely what the fuck you're gonna get.

The Golden Boys

Thank you so much for reading!
Hopefully, you enjoyed the wild ride with West and Blue

NEXT IN SERIES
1-Click your copy of Kings of Cypress Prep book 2 today!
Exclusively on Amazon, FREE on KU!
https://books2read.com/u/3nW6GK

I'd also love for you to pop into the
KINGS OF CYPRESS PREP Spoiler Room,
https://www.facebook.com/groups/334449267794145/
where you'll get exclusive bonus content, including
Chapter 1 of book 2!
Just check out the group's pinned announcement post. Can't wait to chat. See you there!

A NOTE FROM THE AUTHOR

Thank you so much for reading **the Golden Boys,** *Book 1 in the Kings of Cypress Prep series.* If you have enjoyed entering Cypress Prep, show other readers by leaving a review!
Just visit: *The Golden Boys*
https://amzn.to/34cKgAO
The series continues with book2 coming this December, so stay tuned!
Join my readers' group for more news: *The Shifter Lounge*
https://www.facebook.com/groups/141633853243521
and my *Newsletter*
http://eepurl.com/chIkpH

Love ARCs, random giveaways, and fun bookish conversation? Come hang out in my Facebook group for readers,
THE SHIFTER LOUNGE!
https://www.facebook.com/groups/141633853243521
Can't wait to chat with you :)

For all feedback and inquiries email me to author.racheljonas@gmail.com

SOUNDTRACK
(Listed in no particular order)

Music is a very integral part of my writing process, and I carefully choose songs that fuel each scene. The lyrics may not always be spot on, but sometimes it's more about the emotion evoked. While writing *The Vampire's Mark*, I selected music that brought out the intense emotions Cori felt during various scenes throughout her journey. I hope this list enhances the reading experience for you, like it did for me while writing.

Note: Piracy is unlawful, and using sites where music can be downloaded for free is equivalent to stealing from the musician. Buying the song or album directly from the artist will always be the best way to show support and appreciation for the artist's work.

"Gambling Hearts"—Harrison Brome
"Shelter"—Harrison Brome
"Come Together"—Gary Clark Jr.
"Gold"—Kiiara

Soundtrack

"It was a Good Day"—Ice Cube
"There's No Way"—Lauv
"Ruin"—Shawn Mendes
"Slow Dancing in the Dark"—Joji
"Falling For You"—The 1975
"Often"—The Weeknd
"She Wants"—Metronomy
"Crave You"—Clairo
"Time of the Season"—The Zombies
"Bad Things"—Cults
"I Found"—Amber Run
"Teeth"—5 Seconds of Summer
"Novacane"—Frank Ocean
"We Can Make Love"—SoMo
"Losin Control"—Russ
"Who Needs Love"—Trippie Redd
"Body"—Sinead Harnett
"Abandoned"—Trippie Redd
"Run"—Joji
"Candy Castle"—Glass Candy
"Yeah Right"—Joji
"I think I'm Okay"—Machine Gun Kelly
"Bad Things"—Machine Gun Kelly
"Tearing Me Up (Remix)"—Bob Moses
"Stuck in the Middle"—Tai Verdes
"Sweater Weather"—The Neighbourhood
"Broken"—lovelytheband

About the Author

~Rachel Jonas also writes as Nikki Thorne.~

Hey, I'm Rachel! Consider this your formal invitation to hang out in my private Facebook group, THE SHIFTER LOUNGE. You'll get fun book convo, exclusive giveaways, and other random acts of nerdiness!

Don't usually talk to strangers? No worries! Allow me to introduce myself. I'm a Michigan native, wife, and mother of three who made a career of indulging the voices inside my head :) With several completed series, and stories in both the paranormal and contemporary YA/NA romance categories, there's something for everyone!

Happy Reading!

Twitter: @author_R_Jonas
IG: @author.racheljonas
Rachel's Facebook: https://www.facebook.com/authorracheljonas/
Reader Group:
https://www.facebook.com/groups/141633853243521/
Amazon: amzn.to/2BHiLlS
Goodreads:
https://www.goodreads.com/author/show/16788419.Rachel_Jonas
BookBub: https://www.bookbub.com/profile/rachel-jonas
Nikki's Facebook: https://www.facebook.com/nikkithorneauthor/